NOT HER FIRST MURDER

A

Cassie Windom
Mystery

Also By Danith McPherson

<u>Cassie Windom Mysteries</u>
Averted Vision
Not Her First Murder

Monarch of Lightning
fantasy novel on a volatile planet

Blade of Mad Vision
young adult fantasy novel (with swords)

Roar at the Universe
speculative fiction collection

NOT HER FIRST MURDER
Copyright © 2025 by Danith McPherson, Matthew Clausen, and Aaron Clausen

First edition, August 2025
ISBN 978-1-950506-16-3 (print paperback)
ISBN 978-1-950506-17-0 (ebook)
Library of Congress Control Number: 2025916006

Cover design by D. L. Clausen

Published by Wayward Serpent, Farwell MN
Up to no good but means well

Not Her First Murder

A Cassie Windom Mystery

Danith McPherson

Wayward Serpent

*For my McPherson grandfather, aunts, uncles and cousins
who made growing up an adventure*

Chapter One

Cassie Windom leaned into the wind that raked back her short, dark hair. She could see the island now, its birch, oak and fir separating from similar vegetation that lined the lakeshore behind it. A few acres of land isolated from the rest of the world, the mound seemed to rise like an awakening beast as the motorboat sliced through the water, aimed toward its rocky edge.

The handsome, mysterious, stranger at the wheel nudged the throttle, adding speed. Thrilled, Cassie gripped the co-captain's chair feeling slick vinyl. With the rushing air fueling her anticipation, she spotted a tan patch that marked the sandy landing point.

"Are we there yet?" Mrs. Something screeched over the engine's roar from a rear seat.

The eternal question deflated Cassie's euphoria. She turned sideways, planning to point toward their destination. Her sandal brushed the bag at her feet, spilling her sketch pad and art supplies across the tilted deck. Her precious pencils rolled to the stern. A woman seated by the motor scooped them up and stored them safely in a pocket of her smock. A scarf swooping across her forehead held back her long gray braid. A second wrap tied under her chin kept the first one from being torn away. Cassie tucked the spiral binder of thick paper and her other items back into her bag and nodded a thank-you. She'd seen the short, plump woman several times in the produce section of the Falls Market where Mrs. Finster, a wizard of verbal clickbait, her metal-blue hair curled into claws, regularly delivered exaggerated versions of local events to her cult followers.

The woman smiled and nodded at Cassie in return. Since her hair was always bordered by a colorful band, Cassie had unimaginatively dubbed her Scarf Lady, as if an accessory could describe an entire person. Which it couldn't, and it certainly didn't in this case. Instead of having a cloth wrapped around her head, Cassie thought she should be wearing it like a superhero cape for being the only one brave enough to challenge the grocery store gossip.

Seated beside Mrs. Something, Mr. Something gestured to the left. He was off target, but Cassie didn't correct him. She turned forward, swiping at strands of hair stuck to her face. As she had for the past few months, she lamented having been talked into the bob cut with the dreaded bangs that wouldn't grow out fast enough.

Late August weather hung on to summer warmth as if it would never let go. Cassie tugged at the ill-fitting orange life vest she'd been forced to wear. The straps seemed adjusted for a sumo wrestler. If the boat suddenly swerved, flipping her into the frothy water, she'd slip out of the jacket on impact. She judged the distance to the shorelines on each side, and the span to the island ahead of them. Her swimming skills were rusty, but she was sure she could make it to land no matter which way she went. She suspected Trevor Rothman, in the captain's chair beside her, had a casual relationship with responsibility, so she wanted to be prepared.

She glanced at him, reconsidering her previous musings about "handsome," "mysterious," and "stranger."

He wasn't exactly handsome. More like handsome-adjacent. Midthirties, maybe? Longish light brown hair scrunched into a rubber band at the nape of his neck. Cassie guessed he was going for a trendy, creative look. His faded t-shirt, surfer shorts, and sandals crafted from recycled material gave off more of a retro-hippie vibe.

And he wasn't really mysterious. Just an unknown at the moment. Unattached, Cassie decided with no evidence whatsoever. Relaxed. Used to things going his way.

He definitely was a stranger. His unexpected phone call had been friendly and to the point.

"We haven't met yet," Trevor had said. "I'm one of the teachers with the summer art program. I know you're a judge this year. Thanks for doing that. But that's not what I'm calling about. My art club goes sketching at local places. We'll be out your direction this morning. We wondered if you wanted to join us."

Cassie had mentally prepared a polite refusal. People didn't understand that working at home still meant, you know, *working*. Sure, she could toss in a load of laundry at an odd moment, but as the sole employee of her own graphic arts business, she had to produce. No taking a brain holiday while an underling struggled to turn her pencil slashes on a Post-it note into a full-page magazine spread.

Plus, she'd already gotten herself into a time crunch by agreeing to select winners in the student competition he'd mentioned. Megabytes of images sat on her tablet waiting for her review before the meeting tomorrow.

"It's nice of you to ask," Cassie had said, ready to claim that Wednesday was always her busiest day.

Trevor had interrupted. "We're going to Wolf Haunt."

Wolf Haunt. The refusal had caught in Cassie's throat. Before she could stop it, "That sounds great" had popped out of her mouth. Then the justifications had started rolling through her mind. A little fresh air and inspiration couldn't hurt. And it was in a group, just in case he was a serial killer.

"You're on Beauty Lake at the Schroeder place, right?" Trevor had said, not really asking. "I'll pick you up at your dock."

Of course he knew where she lived. She'd moved in three months ago. By now everyone in Glacier Falls, in Granite County and in most of Minnesota, could recognize her car, name her favorite color, and recite her Social Security number.

"Ah, no dock." No boat either. Cassie considered getting a kayak, *if* she stayed on Lake Beauty, but she only had a one-year rental agreement with Aunt Renee for the cabin. Some days she was content in her self-imposed limbo and didn't think about going anywhere else. Other days, she was deeply aware that her situation was temporary, a chance to catch her breath before plunging back into her derailed life.

"Your neighbors must have one," he'd said.

The Johnsons were weekenders who lived in a Minneapolis suburb. From her deck, Cassie could see their white roll-a-dock sticking out into the water. If she'd still lived in Los Angeles and some guy had called and quizzed her about her property and her neighbors, she would have broken the connection immediately. But this wasn't LA. "Yes."

"They won't mind if we use it. I'll meet you there in a half hour."

Are you picking me up in your yacht? Cassie had been about to ask.

"Wear shorts," he'd said. "And be prepared to get your feet wet."

He'd clicked off without clarifying.

The craft Trevor had arrived in was more beer with the bros than champagne on the sundeck. He'd tossed out introductions to the other three people. Cassie's fear of embarrassing herself by tripping into the lake as she awkwardly stepped from the Johnson family's dock into the rocking boat affected her hearing, so she hadn't caught a single name. The rumbling engine, sounding like a very loud cat with asthma, had made conversation impossible as they'd motored through a wide outlet off the southern end of Beauty Lake into a lobe of Lake Blanchet.

Now as they neared the island, a bald eagle perched at the top of a bare branch watched them with little interest. They weren't food, and they weren't a threat, just an annoyance.

Mrs. Something shouted again. "Are you sure that's where we're going?"

This time Cassie ignored her and stared ahead.

Wolf Haunt. That might be its official name, or might not. It didn't matter. That was what the locals called it. The land had been a peninsula jutting into the lake until a spring flood had carved a channel, slicing it from the mainland.

Trevor swung the boat along the high shore to where the sandy patch sloped to the water. He cut the power and raised the engine, letting momentum carry them in. Still eight feet from dry ground, he dropped the anchor and hung a short ladder over the side. "Sorry, you'll have to wade. I can't get any closer or the prop will clip the rocks."

Cassie shed the orange vest and eagerly grabbed her bag, slipping the strap over her head in a cross-carry so both hands were free.

"We should have a good two hours before rain sets in," Trevor said. "Up the path and to the right."

Cassie knew the way, but she wasn't going to tell him that. From the gray sky, she thought he was overly optimistic about the weather. She refused his offer of help getting onto the ladder. This wasn't her first wet landing.

In her standard summer wardrobe of shorts and rubbery sandals that could go anywhere, Cassie hadn't needed to change for the outing. As her foot eased into cool liquid, she reevaluated Trevor's ability to handle a boat. He'd found the perfect spot where the stern remained in deep enough water for the motor while the front half snuggled onto a shallow shelf. She guessed he was a frequent visitor. The art class must come here a lot.

This was one of those times she was glad to be a long-legged five feet ten. She sloshed to shore, picking her way across mossy stones without doing a face-plant into the lake, arriving safely at the sandy area that wasn't big enough to be a beach. She climbed the slight incline and stopped at a sign stuck in the ground. The weathered wooden placard looked as if it had been there forever, the lettering repainted (not always with the same color paint) many times.

PRIVATE PROPERTY
NO TRESPASSING

Cassie took out her phone, moved to get just the right angle, and snapped a photo.

She texted the image to her sisters.

> Guess where I am.

This wasn't Cassie's first time on Wolf Haunt. She dashed along the tree-lined path into the clearing, barely glancing at the large protruding stone. Her goal was beyond it, behind a dense screen of fir and sumac.

To her surprise, over the years a break had formed in the vegetation. She kept her gaze on the gap, shifting until it framed the small building she knew was there. She paused to absorb the view.

The shed stood as she remembered, yet not as it had been. Speckled shingles flaked from the slanted roof, leaving ragged tar paper and bare wood. A corner sagged on a broken post, as if the structure hunched like a troll under the evergreens. A shadowed hollow showed where a door once hung. Twisted rivulets of green paint clung to the boards between streaks of sun-bleached ecru and damp charcoal. A border of wild rye swayed, lightly brushing against it, the golden seed heads ruffled like feathers.

Cassie almost drooled over the glorious lines. The overcast sky bathed the battered shanty in moody light, just as it had on that other day when she'd been here. She pulled out her phone and clicked. Even at a distance, the building oozed character. But this was not the perspective she wanted. She must find The Spot, the place where she had perched on a tree stump and sketched when she was thirteen.

Eyes on the shack and not the terrain, she stubbed her foot against a log. Jolted out of her memory haze, she looked down. Her sandal had not bumped a fallen pine.

The body lay face down, arms stretched forward, as if worshiping an angry god. The fingertips almost touched the painted rock that dominated the clearing like a tilted monument to death.

Chapter Two

Dale Steinhaus shuffled down the beige hallway following the students in front of him, trying not to get stepped on by the students behind him. He hadn't been on a field trip to the Granite County Historical Society Museum since the Minnesota history unit in sixth grade. It hadn't changed much. He noticed efforts to include newer events, such as a World War II display in the Lake Mille Lacs gallery. But mostly the museum still concentrated on the years before the territory had gained statehood in 1858, a fact he still remembered.

Rows of grainy gray-scale photographs lined the walls. "They all look like their pets died," Richie said. He waved a finger at a stoic young man, hair parted down the middle and slicked back on each side, who seemed strangled by his high, round collar. "This guy, his Chihuahua got squashed"—he pointed to the scene next to it, where a pair of oxen in a wooden yoke stood hitched to a plow—"by these ED bruisers."

ED, Expletive Deleted, the substitute they'd come up with so they wouldn't get reprimanded in school for saying the forbidden words they'd freely used all summer.

In the next rectangle a woman in a print dress soberly faced the camera. Behind her a sod house about the size of Dale's room crouched on an open prairie.

"This babe," Richie said, "her yoga goat got trampled"—he gestured to a double row of men in suits and hats who'd stopped their parade long enough to get their picture taken —"by these guys." He read the banner held by the two leaders. "Son-ner of Norg-ee. Is that like son of a bitch? I'd march with them."

"More like Sons of Norway." At six foot three, Dale easily looked over the stream of high school students. Most of them were in the junior class with him and Richie. A few seniors. Some sophomores.

Ahead, Jennifer and Heather Petrosky tilted their heads in almost identical moves, their matching ponytails swaying. Did Jennifer glance back at him with a little smile? No. Just his imagination.

"They're like Vikings," Richie said. "And freakin' Thor." A t-shirt and jeans hugged his skinny frame that refused to bulk up, despite a diet of fast-food burgers and fries. Nine inches shorter than Dale, he swung his shoulders in a swagger and spoke in a deep bass. "Don't mess with me, dude. I'm a Son-ner of Norg-ee."

"They don't look that tough."

"We should do it again," Richie said. "You know."

Used to his friend's quick change of topics, yeah, Dale knew. He stifled a groan. "It was too much work for nothing."

Richie grinned. "Not for nothing. You'll see."

Oh, great, Dale thought. *One of Richie's surprises.*

Flashing a smile at the girls and ignoring the boys, a museum guide who looked barely out of high school himself funneled them into the exhibit hall. The students spread out to roam through the displays. Richie charged off. Vanishing was his superpower.

Dale took out his worksheet, planing to get the assignment

done quickly so he could find a corner to sit in—okay, hide in —until it was time to get back on the bus. The optional field trip to see the student art competition was not his idea of a fun morning, but he and Richie agreed you couldn't just blow off a chance to build up easy bonus points before school even started. Dale's dad had groused about farm chores going undone while his son looked at junk, but it was a school thing, so his mom supported the outing.

Dale smoothed the paper across the cardboard back of a spiral notebook and read the instructions.

> Joy of Discovery! You are the judge. Evaluate at least
> five works of art in the high school category, using the
> Big Seven criteria below. Then choose your winner!

Under that and spilling onto the back of the page were ten identical blocks listing the elements Ms. Whitman forced all of her students to memorize: line, shape, form, color, value, texture, space. Each word was followed by the numbers 5 to 1. Five being Rembrandt and 1 being your four-year-old cousin's pudding smears on the living room wall. Simple. Circle the numbers, then add them up. Dale considered doing a couple of extra items for bonus points.

He didn't want to start with the first space on the worksheet, because that might look suspicious, like he was scoring something before he even saw it, which he was.

He jumped down to the third. Each entry was identified by a number, not a name, so you wouldn't be influenced by your feelings for the kid who made it. Anyway, that's how it was supposed to work.

Dale put in HS12, the code for Richie's project. He circled five for each element, as he'd promised he would. A perfect score. He hadn't looked at a single piece, and he already had his winner.

But he did want to see what his best friend had come up

with. Richie had been secretive about it, which was strange. He usually couldn't stop himself from telling Dale everything.

Jennifer Petrosky elbowed Dale and pointed to a drooping yellow vase that looked as if it had been sculpted from butter and placed on a warm stove. "That's Sean's. He calls it *Urn in Sunlight*. As if he knows what an urn is. Code 16, like his IQ. He thinks it's a masterpiece."

Dale knew she meant Sean Fluge and not Shawn Miller. He thought the senior spent his summers at a series of football camps. His stepmom must have forced him into the art program.

Dale gave Jennifer a nod. "Got it." He added the entry to his worksheet, marking two's and three's. "Have you seen Richie's? HS12."

"Is it the dinosaur made out of bottle caps?" Jennifer asked.

Her shoulder was only two inches lower than his. Dale felt as if they shared the same stratosphere. "That's a good guess, but no. It's metal pieces glued together."

"Shouldn't metal be welded?"

"If you were the teacher, would you let Richie light an acetylene torch in a room full of kids?"

"I wouldn't let him use glue either," Jennifer said. "He'd smear the stuff on a can of body spray and hand it to some unsuspecting guy, who'd have trust issues for the rest of his life."

"Yeah, he should be restricted to reusable tape."

Heather, Jennifer's equally tall twin, squeezed next to them breaking the illusion of aerial privacy. "Paige says Kaitlyn had a fight with a girl from Sunset over a necklace that the girl entered in this contest. Kait says it belongs to her."

Dale thought the story sounded weird. You had to sign up for the summer program, go to class and be supervised by a teacher in order to get your thingy in the competition. Paige must have it wrong.

"Yeah, but you know Kait," Heather said. "Anyway, it's code HS24."

Dale wrote the number on his worksheet. "The girl from Sunset has my support. I'm giving it all fours and fives."

Jennifer made circles on her paper. "It's totally getting fives from me. Evaluating art is easier than I thought."

"Kait will be all drama-drag when she finds out," Heather said.

"I'd like to vid that and post it on Falls Chit Chat," Jennifer said. "Too bad she isn't here."

"More joy of discovery for us," Dale said, using their teacher's favorite term.

A shout boomed through the room. "Who took my dick?"

Dale cringed, recognizing the voice. His instinct was to flee in the opposite direction, but he pushed between the museum guide and Missy Meirer, who seemed creepily close together, to reach the source.

Richie stood before a three-foot-high structure mounted on a pedestal. Metal rods, tubing and wires caged a small skull. A spiderweb of cracks radiated from a chipped left eye socket. A handle from an old pail formed a horizontal oval under the framing, the ends fastened together by a long bolt in the front that supported a buckle. The lid from a chewing tobacco tin swung below it.

Dale got it right away. An industrial representation of a human torso encasing a real skull. Art from found parts. And he knew exactly where those parts had been found.

Shit, Richie, he wanted to shout. *Shit, shit, shit.*

Richie flicked a finger against the metal disk, ringing it like a gong. "The dick's been swiped. My guy's been catted."

"Castrated," Dale said in a daze.

"Yeah, I've been sensed."

"Censored," Dale said.

"Yeah. ED, man."

Chapter Three

It's always Sunny at SunnieChat!

> Guess where I am.

HOLLY

About to get arrested.

ASHLEY

In a horror movie.

KAYLA

Rocky Horror Picture Show! Take the risk!

ASHLEY

K, did you ever tell mom and dad we took you to that show on Halloween?

KAYLA

If I had, you'd still be grounded.

> Did you ever tell mom and dad we took you to Wolf Haunt?

KAYLA

If I had, you'd still be grounded.

Thirteen-year-old Cassie watched her older sister Ashley stalk around the clearing, avoiding the circle of charred sticks where many fires must have burned over the years. "This place doesn't look haunted to me." At fifteen she carried a pudginess that would soon fuel a growth spurt. "And I don't see any wolves."

Cassie was disappointed in Wolf Haunt too. But she didn't want to say it out loud to Rob and Cliff, who'd planned the trip. The notorious party island was a totally inappropriate place for them to take their innocent younger sister Laurel and their visiting cousins. The boys had come up with the cover story of going to see lady slippers that grew wild on park land adjacent to a public beach. They'd convinced their parents to let them use the two fishing boats equipped with small motors.

Holly doubted the story would hold up, but Cliff assured her the same flowers grew on the island. They could snap a few photos as proof. The adults they answered to wouldn't be able to tell the difference.

The illicit outing to a forbidden locale had seemed so delicious in Cassie's mind. The overcast sky had promised a chilling gloom. She'd shivered on the ride here, as if getting ready to watch a scary-but-not-too-scary movie filled with skeletal trees in an ocean of perpetual fog. Instead, flat gray light covered leafy birch and oak like a dreary blanket.

"Wolf is the guy's name." At eighteen, Cliff had shed his boyish looks and taken on sharper, more adult features, but he was in no hurry to grow up. "He was a French trapper who slaughtered a whole pack of wolves. That pissed them off, so every night they hunt him across the island."

"Ghost wolves run around chasing a ghost guy in a coonskin cap," Ashley said.

"Wolf-pelt cap," Rob said.

"Maybe he should switch to a wool hat, instead of

reminding them of his bad behavior," Ashley said. Laurel snickered. The same age as Ashley, she'd latched on to the bolder girl, maybe as a defense against her brothers.

"It doesn't look like a rave site," Holly said, as if she'd had experience with such places. Cassie knew she hadn't. At seventeen, Cassie's oldest sister preferred reading historical romances (and complaining about the inaccuracies) to boat rides, trees, and the threat of mosquitoes.

Kayla danced from fir tree to fir tree, sticking her head into the prickly branches. "Lala, be careful," Holly shouted, calling her youngest sister by her nickname.

"I'm looking for snakes," Kayla answered, as if serpents in trees were perfectly safe.

Aunt Renee wouldn't give permission for the outing unless they took along the eleven-year-old, who shouldn't be deprived of seeing Minnesota's state flower in its natural habitat just because she hadn't reached puberty (although Aunt Renee hadn't stated it that way). Extending that adult logic, Aunt Renee had insisted Holly go along to make sure Kayla didn't drown or get attacked by woodchucks. (Again, not the actual way she'd phrased it.)

"The Brighton family owns the island." Rob gestured in the general direction of the mainland. "You can see the top floor of the house from here. They judge party activity by the amount of trash. If we keep it clean, they don't check it as often."

Cassie thought Rob's "we" was semi-accurate. He and Cliff had probably been here plenty of times, but hard-core barley pop bashing wasn't their style. Her cousins had too much fun being tricksters to dull their senses with alcohol. Holly had opposed the trip from the beginning due to trust issues with her male cousins. She'd made it clear she would spill everything to Aunt Renee and Uncle Steve if one of the boat motors suddenly sputtered and "ran out of gas."

Ashley slapped a large slab slathered in rusty-red paint.

About a foot thick, three feet of stone jutted out of the ground. More probably remained hidden below the surface. "What's this?"

"Don't touch it," Cliff said.

Ashley ran a hand across the flatter side as if looking for a smooth spot. "Cassie, give me one of your pens."

"I don't have pens," Cassie said. "I have pencils, and they're for sketching, not graffiti."

"No one messes with the rock," Cliff solemnly told Ashley.

"Afraid the Brights will put barbed wire around the place?" Ashley challenged.

"It belongs to Trapper Wolf," Rob said. "You don't want to make his spirit angry."

Ashley flipped her dark brown hair behind an ear. "What happens if I do?"

"He won't let us come here," Cliff said.

And he'd have to repaint the rock, again, Cassie thought. At the soil line she could see strips of old layers that hadn't gotten covered by newer coats. Scarlet, cardinal, wine, ruby. Different shades of red. Always red. It looked like Wolfy was stuck on that part of the color wheel. But even the current rusty-orangey tint seemed old, as if the fur trapper's ghost had lost interest.

"I don't know why this Wolf guy lets anyone come here anyway," Ashley said. "If I had an island, I'd want it all to myself. I'd terrorize whoever came near it, especially if I was a spirit. I'd sink their boats and give them embarrassing rashes."

"I couldn't live on an island," Holly said.

"England is an island, and you want to live there," Cassie said.

"Okay," Holly said, "I couldn't live on an island unless it had humungous libraries."

Kayla twirled to another tree. "I love islands. I want to visit every island in the world."

"Remember—" Holly said.

"I know," Kayla said. "We didn't go to an island. We went to a beach then walked to a park and saw lady slippers."

"And?" Holly prompted.

"And," Kayla recited, "I sat down in the boat like I was told and didn't squirm around or anything."

The last part was as much a lie as the rest. Kayla, who swam as if she'd been born a dolphin, had no fear of the water. Cassie had tried to get her to sit still during the voyage, but the girl had excitedly traversed from bow to stern and back again several times.

Cassie hugged her bag. Ashley wasn't going to get so much as a charcoal stub from her precious art supplies. Cliff had promised there would be something more interesting than sumac bushes to sketch. Hoping that part of his island hype was true, she headed off in a random direction away from the clearing.

Swaying spruce and birch thickened and closed around her, filtering the leaden light as if it were the layers of paint on the stone. She felt it now, the possibility that ghosts roamed here.

A clapboard shed painted dull green stood encased in foliage of brighter hues, as if its construction had happened first and the trees had clustered around it, advancing from saplings to towering maturity while the simple structure remained a constant. Cassie perched on a cracked tree stump patterned with concentric rings. She took what she needed from her bag and started sketching.

"The proportions could be better."

Cassie froze at the unfamiliar voice at her back. She stared at the rough-sided shed that had flowed from her pencil onto the thick paper. How much time had passed?

Snapped back to the real world, she realized that an isolated, foliage-choked island was likely to spawn a crazed, hockey-masked killer swinging a machete.

Cassie jumped up, a helpless summer camper about to be slaughtered.

Or at the least, a trespasser who'd been caught.

She turned to face her fate.

"Sorry I startled you," the woman said. "I couldn't resist peeking over your shoulder. I apologize for the unsolicited critique. Perhaps you're going for a skewed perspective. Then it's perfect."

Although barely a teen, Cassie already topped five feet seven. The woman was at least five inches shorter. A loose t-shirt and baggy shorts hung on her gaunt frame, as if she'd dressed in a rush and grabbed a larger person's clothes. Fatigue dwelled in the earthy eyes. Skin sagged into hollows below the cheekbone ridges. The thin nose led to slender lips over a narrow chin. She seemed worn out, yet not old enough for the silvery wisps of hair that escaped from under her brimmed hat.

Cassie imagined that once the face had glowed with a blushing fullness, until a harsh life had drained away the joy, leaving a melancholy that carried its own kind of beauty.

"I know I'm not supposed to be here," Cassie stammered. She cringed at her own panicked stupidity. She should have bluffed. Pretended she thought she was on public land, or that the island was owned by a friend.

"Me neither. Funny how that happens." But she looked as if everything was very serious.

"We just came to see lady slippers." Cassie realized she'd said "we," pulling her sisters and cousins into the crime.

"You're with the noisy group by the stone," the woman said.

Cassie tried to conjure up a statement that fit the wildflower scenario. Something about being biology students doing a summer project.

She let her shoulders sag, unable to spin a convincing lie to those experienced eyes. "Family."

The woman nodded, as if that one word explained the world. "You're too late to find them in bloom, but the leaves have interesting shapes." She pointed toward where Cliff and Rob had anchored the boats. "Take the path to the beach. You'll find them off the trail to the right. Jack-in-the-pulpits grow a little beyond that. Their berry clusters are developing about now."

"Is that why you're here? For the plants?" Cassie didn't care. She just wanted to study the shadow cast by the hat brim, the head tilt, the expression that was neither a smile nor a frown.

"I'm looking for my necklace. The pieces, anyway. It broke. I didn't notice at the time and only realized later." The woman paused to take a long breath. "It isn't worth anything, but I helped make it."

"Is that what you do?" Cassie asked. "You make jewelry?"

"I used to. Mostly now I paint."

An artist. A real artist. Cassie wanted to dance circles around the woman. "I can help you look for your necklace."

"Thanks, but that's okay. It's silly, really. I lost it a while ago. But lately I can't stop thinking about it." She paused, needing to take another big breath.

Or was she changing her mind about what she was going to say?

"It's always been important to me."

Cassie understood the feeling with every atom of her being. "I want to be an artist," she blurted out, her voice booming too loud, too eager, too thirteen.

The woman's lips twitched into the barest beginning of pleasure. "An artist isn't something you *want* to be, is it? It's something you know you already are."

Unable to speak, Cassie nodded. Yes. She was an artist, even if no one else thought so. Her whole life she might do no more than the equivalent of waxy scrawls while holding down a nine-to-five job to pay for the crayons. But she'd explore color and shape like Henri Matisse, try shading techniques like Artemisia Gentileschi, play with perspective like the guy who uses chalk to make it look like there's a hole in the sidewalk.

She'd study and learn and experiment, and she'd live the joy of creating. And maybe someday her painting or sculpture or crayon scrawl would be displayed in a gallery. And someone would buy it because they felt something the moment they saw it and they couldn't live without it.

"Have you been to the Granite County Historical Society Museum in Sunset?" the woman asked.

Cassie shook her head.

"You might like it. It's not the Louvre—and ignore the beaver—but it's close by. It has pottery, weavings, and photographs. I used them for inspiration when I was your age."

Cassie silently repeated the museum's name to herself so she wouldn't forget. Not that it was hard to remember. She was already standing in Granite County. That made her think about where she was and how she'd gotten there. "I didn't see your boat at the landing."

"I came another route."

That made no sense to Cassie. What other way was there? Her clothes were dry, so no swimming. Had she skydived onto the island? "We can give you a ride somewhere."

"I'm fine, thanks. Sorry I disturbed your sketching." The woman turned away.

Cassie watched her stroll toward a bank of scrub oaks. White specks from the birch trees beyond peeked through the twisted branches. She wanted to call after her, say something that would make her stay. Ask for advice on how to fix the misaligned drawing of the shed. Ask how to embolden the timid artist that dwelled inside her.

"Cassie!"

She turned in the direction of Holly's shout. "Be right there!" She looked back toward the oaks, wanting to say goodbye to the woman. Wanting to say, "I hope I see you again. Thanks for being nice to me and not treating me like a stupid kid with stupid dreams."

The words caught in her throat. The woman had vanished.

The encounter seemed unfinished, as if Cassie had walked across a bridge, gotten turned around in the middle of the river, and found herself back where she'd started.

"Cassie!" her sister called again.

She wove through the tangle of fir and sumac to the clearing. Kayla hung over the Wolf Stone, her hands stretching to touch the ground. "No lady slippers," she complained in a deep, monstery voice.

"How come she gets to touch the stone?" Cassie asked.

"Because I am wolf," Kayla said gruffly, "who eats lady slippers."

"They're just off the path that goes back to the boat," Cassie said.

"How do you know?" Rob challenged.

"I met this woman."

"When?" Cliff interrupted.

"Where?" Rob asked.

"By the shed I was sketching," Cassie said. "Just now." But it already seemed like forever ago.

"Was she alone?" Rob wanted to know. "Did she order you to leave? Is she going to call the sheriff?"

"She was nice." Cassie said, feeling the need to defend her almost-mentor. "And she was trespassing too. She must have her own boat."

Rob seemed to relax.

"What is tress pass singing?" Kayla asked in her monster voice.

Cliff gave a crooked grin. "I didn't see any boat."

Cassie's defenses always went up when her cousin smirked

like that. "Well, she didn't dog paddle here. Maybe a friend dropped her off and is picking her up."

"There is no boat, no friend, and she's not going to swim away," Cliff said. "She can't leave the island. It's her home."

"No one's living here," Ashley said.

"No one *living* lives here," Cliff said.

Holly folded her arms in disgust. "A ghost? That isn't funny, Cliff. Don't go scaring Lala. She'll have nightmares."

"You can *try* to scare me," Ashley said.

"Yeah," Laurel said, "but *we* don't get scared."

"It's your fault," Rob told Ashley. "You smeared your fingerprints all over Wolf's sacred stone. He sent one of his indentured spirits as a warning."

"'Indentured spirits.' You got that out of a comic book," Ashley said. "Lala's been climbing all over the thing. Maybe it's her fault."

"Not Lala," Kayla said in a rumbling voice. "Al-yak the Terrible."

"She's just a kid," Rob said. "She doesn't count."

"Not kid. Al-yak," Kayla said. "Al-yak count. One. Two. Three . . ."

"Where are those lady slippers?" Laurel asked with the same enthusiasm she might have said *Let's go get that skunk out of the wood pile.* She pulled a small Canon out of her bag, ready to snap proof of a visit to a public park to show her mother.

Cassie pointed, then trudged after her cousin in the direction of Minnesota's state flower. Behind her she heard Ashley.

"Guys, you need to work on that story. It would be more fun if Cassie's ghost was a time traveler."

Cassie's Ghost.

Her cousins and sisters were sure to tease her, turning the unexpected meeting with the nameless woman into a joke when it was serious and important to Cassie.

That night, unable to sleep, she sat up and rustled the quilt over her head. The fabric smelled of cedar from the chest where Aunt Renee stored it. She pulled up her knees to make a cave, her own quiet space after a day spent with too many people. She clipped a reading light to the calico square near her head.

She opened her sketchpad and examined the lines of the shed in relation to the greenery around it. The woman was right about the scale. And the composition was awkward and uninteresting. She resolved to do better. To practice. To learn the craft.

She flipped to a fresh, creamy page. Holding her pencil lightly, she closed her eyes and formed a memory in her mind. Then she drew the angular face, lips parted in the almost smile, weary eyes shadowed by the brimmed hat. Each stroke added life to the portrait.

It was her first ghost but not her last.

Chapter Four

Cassie's stomach clenched at the hand that seemed to reach in desperation for the painted stone. A mass of congealed blood obscured the ragged wound in the back of the head. She thought of Vicky first. Then Glenna, her young friend with a tendency to make high-risk choices, who had left without a word. The last time Cassie had seen the girl, Glenna's mop had been stark white. Her hair could be any color now. It could be raven black like the tousled locks covering the ashen face.

Cassie squatted and took a deep breath. She pressed two fingers against the girl's exposed neck below the swept-up curls, hoping she'd be surprised by a flutter of life but knowing that was unlikely.

Cold. No pulse.

Cassie pulled in another deep breath. And another. She wanted to brush dark strands from the face turned toward her in profile as it must have been when the blow came. Wipe dark clots from the cheekbone. Dab streaks from the pale lips tinted with scarlet gloss brighter than the blood.

Young, but not Glenna.

Trevor's shout came from the boat landing. "Careful on the path."

Cassie rose and sprinted to intercept the others. Scarf Lady puffed up the incline, carrying a bag, easel, and a folded camp chair. Seeing Cassie, she set down her burdens and pulled a bundle from a pocket. "Here are your wayward pencils. I think I got them all. It's going to take the Sams an hour to get down the ladder. By then it will be raining."

Cassie shoved the pencils in her bag. "Please go back. There's been an accident." She'd let someone else, someone with "responsible for identifying foul play" in their job description, declare it a murder. From the body's appearance that seemed the obvious conclusion. And as the girl had fallen, her last thought wouldn't have been "OMG, I have to fluff out my 'do." Someone had disturbed her hair, exposing her neck, after she was on the ground.

Scarf blanched and pressed a hand to her forehead. Cassie feared the woman would burst into hysterical screams. Instead she repeated flatly, "An accident."

"Keep everyone at the boat. I'll call 9-1-1."

Scarf collected her belongings and trudged back in the direction of the landing site.

Cassie punched the emergency digits into her phone as she returned to the clearing. The even-toned man who answered told her to stay on the line until someone official showed up at the island. She guessed if a herd of elephants stampeded through the call center, his heart rate would remain below eighty.

Thunder rumbled in the distance. "I'll try, but I only have one bar that comes and goes," Cassie lied. Large drops plopped down from the gray sky, as if nature mocked her for being agile enough not to slip and become soaked while wading from the boat to the shore. The crime scene would be drenched by the time someone showed up to investigate.

"Tell them to bring a giant umbrella." She faked bad

reception and broke the connection. She retraced her steps, careful not to disturb the site any more than she already had. She attempted to aim her phone's camera at the gruesome subject, but her hands hung heavy.

A familiar darkness rose up to swallow her. The blackouts had become more frequent. She might as well sink to the ground now, before her mind blanked and her body collapsed.

Vicky stood beside her. Cassie held still, calm, not turning her head to look at her best friend. Vicky was often with her in dreams but had never before visited when she was awake. At least, Cassie thought she was awake, and conscious, and aware. She felt Vicky's hand brush hers, a comfort as much as an encouragement. She heard the familiar voice in her head. *"Girl, you can do this."*

"Optimist," Cassie countered. *"Is there a ghost here?"*

"Well, duh," Vicky communicated to her.

"Not you. I brought you with me." Fat drops plopped into Cassie's cropped hair and dotted her shirt. She took a wide stance for stability and gulped wet air. Then she lifted the weighty phone, centering the girl on the screen.

This wasn't like Vicky's blood-soaked murder, she told herself. This prone figure wasn't Vicky. This girl wasn't anyone she knew. That changed things. But it didn't.

"You got this," Vicky whispered. *"It's not your first dead body."*

Cassie captured the image. *"And you're not my first ghost."*

Chapter Five

Dale's backpack shivered as he walked out of the art room at Glacier Falls High School doing his chill-guy saunter. Sharp pings chirped around him as if the hall had suddenly become infested with electronic insects. It seemed he was the only one who knew how to silence his cell phone.

He ignored the texting frenzy. He didn't need to see the latest video of another truck getting stuck under a bridge, or a selfie of a guy bragging about committing a crime. Which was more brainless: stealing a plastic pink flamingo from your neighbor's yard or confessing to it on social media? He and Richie had always been smart enough not to broadcast their adventures.

Until now.

He'd delivered his worksheet to Ms. Whitman, slipping Richie's into the pile along with it, even though part of the assignment was to hand it over in person. On the bus ride back to school Richie had complained about his sculpture being vandalized. Dale had wanted to talk about the really important aspect of his friend's artwork. He hadn't dared for fear of being overheard.

Over the past few days girls had been putting up

inspirational posters and decorating their lockers. Only a few minutes ago they'd been squealing with delight, showing off their creations to one another. Now a creepy vibe seeped through the hall. Ahead of Dale, a bunch of girls formed that huggy-huddle thing females seemed to know how to do from birth, where they draped themselves on one another in a mutual-support kind of way. The formation shook with loud sobs. Dale guessed someone had broken up with her boyfriend. He planned to swerve around the emotional knot.

"Ella's at home," Missy said. "It isn't her. Honest. I called her right away. She's okay."

"You don't think it's Crystal, do you?" Paige mock whispered.

Dale froze.

Crystal Swenson. Dale's ex-almost-girlfriend. If he and Cassie Windom hadn't solved two murders, she'd be here right now, entwined with teary-eyed Missy, Jessica and Paige.

Dale moved out of the flow of traffic, a little closer to the girls. He poked at a pocket in his backpack, as if he wasn't sure he'd put something important in it.

He glanced up and down the hall. Shit. Something bad had happened. Kids studied their phones, faces aghast. No viral video could be that gruesome.

Jessica spoke with the authority of a BFF, Best Friend Forever. "Crystal's living with her grandparents while her mom's at a spa having a trauma drama."

Yeah, Dale thought, *a nervous breakdown on a beach at an expensive resort, paid for by her parents since her husband's assets are tied up with defense lawyers.*

"Maybe she snuck back," Missy said. "You know, to see—"

Me, Dale wanted to shout. *Maybe she raced back in her criminal father's cherry-red Mustang convertible to meet me.*

"—Todd," Missy said.

Todd Ashland. Crystal's real ex-boyfriend. Her friends

could never imagine that Dale and Crystal had almost happened.

But they had. Almost.

Dale pulled out his phone and checked his texts as he headed toward the exit. One from his dad asked if everything was okay, if his friends were okay. That was strange. But not. His dad was a Spark, a volunteer firefighter, called in when tragedy hit. So were the fathers of most of the students in the hall.

He wondered how many of his classmates had read similar messages. Kids wouldn't let that go without asking probing questions. Dale guessed it hadn't taken long before the adults had cracked like cheap plastic. The horrible news, whatever it was, had already spread faster than the vid of the guy being slammed in the balls by a seagull.

Dale opened a text from Richie.

> Dead Girl 🐺 wolf f*ucking island

An explosion rocked Dale's brain. He headed for the door, trying to hide his inner panic behind a wall of chill. And pretty sure he failed.

Heather intercepted him. "Hey."

Most people couldn't tell the twins apart and tended to lump them together as if they were the same person. Dale instinctively recognized the differences, even way back when they were little and their mom had dressed them in matching outfits.

"Yeah, I heard." He swallowed the tremor in his voice. "I gotta meet Richie." He pushed out the door, wishing he could make his mind numb. But his thoughts swirled with speculation. What if. What if. What if. And all the threads ended in "then we're screwed."

Chapter Six

"You've already contaminated the place, you might as well be useful," Sheriff Justin "Justice" Wells told Cassie as he escorted her past a corral of yellow tape to where a blue tarp covered the body.

Cassie resisted pointing out that, in addition to his officers, the site was crowded with Sparks, members of the Glacier Falls Fire Department. Although she'd only lived here for a short time, she could name a few of them. The rest she could identify if given a multiple-choice test. The fire department was one of her clients. She didn't have to stretch to find activities to publicize. The group seemed involved in everything. In addition to financing band uniforms and the food bank from their bingo proceeds, they organized the annual Tornado Daze festival (which seemed a strange thing to celebrate), and probably rescued kittens in their spare time.

Cassie buried her hands in the pockets of the oversized windbreaker that smelled of fish and seaweed. When she'd gone to give the art club an update, she'd found the group snuggly under a canopy that had been opened up to cover most of the boat. Trevor had pulled the jacket from one of the storage bins and presented it to her as if she hadn't already been splashed by the intermittent rain. Still, she appreciated the extra layer and wished he'd had real shoes in her size to lend her too. Her sandals threatened to slide off with the weight of the mud clinging to them.

"I'm making you a volunteer member of the Sheriff's Posse," Wells said.

"Is that a real thing?" Cassie didn't point out that, unlike the Sparks, she hadn't volunteered.

"Very real," Wells said solemnly, as if trying to impress her with the gravity of the honor.

"Do I get a badge?"

"You get the community's heartfelt appreciation and a certificate." Wells stopped at the large stone that stood like a graveyard marker in front of the body. "We've already processed this area."

From a distance, Cassie had watched Officer Quigley take photographs before the Sparks showed up. She always thought of him as Robocop because of his obsession with order and procedure. The rain had formed puddles and rivulets by then. Cassie thought the images she'd taken earlier would be more valuable. She decided not to tell Wells about them. Not right now, anyway. The sheriff might decide to confiscate her phone. Later, after she had a chance to review them herself, she'd send them to Officer Rhonda Olson. The woman was a friend and would forgive Cassie's "forgetting" to hand them over to law enforcement.

The sheriff gestured to the stone. Crudely painted lines and figures spotted a cayenne-red background glossy with rain. "Rhonda thinks it's a good idea for you to draw this."

Which meant he thought it was a waste of time, but Cassie was already on-site and he liked to keep Rhonda happy.

"Don't worry about the rock," Wells said in his slow way, never directing his molasses-brown eyes straight at Cassie. "Get the cartoons. Be accurate. Don't fancy them up."

"So, make it a drawing that looks like a photo," Cassie said. The sheriff didn't so much as flinch.

Raindrops made dull plops against the heavy fabric protecting the body. Cassie studied a thin curve of dark hair snaking from under the covering. The twisted strands framed indentations in the clay. She pointed to the hollows.

Wells cut her off before she could speak. "Don't worry about anything else. We've got the whole scene on film. If you have to move around, look before you step."

Cassie decided not to tell the sheriff that Robocop's Pentax was digital and didn't use film.

"Look before you step, people," Wells bellowed at the Sparks hauling parts of a pavilion-sized tent from the boat landing. "Don't you go trampling my crime scene." He looked them over and picked out one. "Boomer, I've got a job for you."

Chapter Seven

Puddles from the storm that had shot through eager to get somewhere else dotted the school parking lot. Dale spotted Richie, arms folded, leaning against his patchwork car, a.k.a. The Fart Bomb. In heavy conversation with Bridget, he seemed unaware of the traffic buzzing around him.

Dale considered pulling a quick pivot back into the school building, but he and Richie had things to work out *now*.

A sophomore, Richie's unsteady (in more ways than one) girlfriend barely reached five feet tall. Dressed to show off her curves in shorts and a knit top, she picked at a curl in her currently bright red hair. Which was more fire hydrant than Irish heritage.

Richie shook back the dark blond hair that fell to his chin in disagreement with something she said. He focused his light brown eyes at a point in the distance, listening to her next rant in his "whatever" attitude.

Well, probably not really listening. Bridget often used a lot of words that didn't convey much information. She backed away, then sort of trotted over to a group of senior guys. If Richie's life had been normal, he might have been with those upperclassmen, doing the pal thing. But he'd been held back in kindergarten, making him a junior like Dale.

All slouchy and superior, the seniors awkwardly flirt-chatted with a cluster of younger girls. Dale had known most of them since kindergarten. Todd Ashland, not looking at all as if he missed his ex-girlfriend Crystal, said something to Whitney, Bridget's best friend. She laughed, tilting her head so the blond streaks in her currently dark hair caught the light. Not a strand slipped from her moussed and sprayed hairdo. Dale wanted to puke. You'd think Todd and the other guys would be better at the cooler-than-cool bit by now with all their practice. Bridget joined them. The group divided up and climbed into three cars.

Yeah, Dale knew how that would turn out. He slow-rolled to the Bomb, letting the domestic strife settle before he reached his friend. "Hey."

"Hey," Richie said back.

They got into the green and rust (real rust) car that might have started out as a Toyota. It had been rebuilt so many times by Richie and his uncles that it was hard to tell its origin.

"She dump you?" *Again*, Dale stopped himself from adding. Like the car, the Richie-and-Bridget show got torn down and rebuilt a lot.

"She doesn't want Whitney going off with those guys by herself."

"Sure." Whitney wasn't exactly by herself. Other girls got into the cars too. But Dale couldn't say that. He had to be in supportive-pal mode. Plus, this rift was sort of his fault. Bridget wanted Whitney and Dale to be a couple. It made sense to her that her best friend and her boyfriend's best friend should be crazy in love. Dale was sure Bridget had created a future in her head with the four of them bonded for life. Double dates. Richie and Dale presenting engagement rings at a cozy dinner. A double wedding. Side-by-side, open-concept houses. Carpooling to their kids' volleyball games. Shared pudding at the senior Living Memorial Forever Home. Adjoining cemetery plots.

Dale had tried. Whitney was even shorter than Bridget. He felt like a giant next to her. She was pretty in a way, but she wore the same vampire-clown makeup as Bridget. If she read anything longer than 280 characters, it was celebrity gossip blogs. Dale didn't know how to build a conversation around that.

Richie pressed his head against the zebra-striped headrest. "You think they're okay?"

What did it mean to be okay? Dale relied on the word a lot. When Richie flipped a "You okay?" at him because he thought Dale was being especially moody, he'd say, "Yeah, I'm okay." When his mom quizzed him because her parental radar picked up the red blip of his worry about a chemistry test, he'd say, "I'm okay." The response popped out automatically. It didn't mean anything. And it was usually a lie.

Dale thought that most of the time Bridget and Whitney were a long dirt road away from okay. But right this minute were they on that bumpy lane in a car with rapist/serial-killer/senior guys? "No way to know, man."

"Yeah, no way to know."

Richie put the key in the ignition and coaxed the engine past the coughing stage.

"You should have talked to me about your sculpture," Dale said.

"I'm way past pissed. We need to call that guy who runs the museum a bunch of times, like we're different people. We can use Uncle Wyatt's burner phone, so they can't trace us. I'll do my Aussie accent." Richie tried it out. "Crikey, you ruined that guy's art. Ya gotta put back the dick, mate."

"That's limp. Don't do that. But what I mean is, you should have talked to me about it before you made it."

Richie blasted the Bomb forward, cutting off the driver education car that crept toward the exit.

Dale winced at the screeching brakes. At least he was sure both the startled student behind the wheel and Mr. Dahl, the instructor, were wearing seat belts.

Richie ignored the stop sign and swung the car out of the parking lot. "I'll start a post. 'Put Back the Penis.'"

Dale thought of the tobacco tin and the empty place in front of it where something had dangled. "Richie, what did you use for the dick?"

"That thingy." Richie gestured with both hands, leaving the steering wheel on its own. "See, the buckle is on the bolt holding the handle together in a circle, like a guy's hips. And the thingy hangs down from the buckle. It looked so max." He grabbed the wheel and swung the Bomb around a corner.

Dale pressed his fingers into the upholstery. "You used the skull. And the wire handle, and the thingy, and the buckle."

"Bolts and can too."

"We dug up that stuff on Wolf Haunt, where they just found a dead girl."

"Sooooo penultimate, right? I bet old Trapper Wolf scared her to death."

"Wells and the state crime guys will be all over the island."

"Nothing to do with us. No one knows we were there."

"Someone knows."

Dale had gone over their movements a hundred times since that night at the island. They'd heard noises. Maybe. On an adrenaline high and suddenly worried they'd get caught, they'd rushed to where they'd beached their ride. Which one of them had carried the shovel? He couldn't recall, but he could picture the tool wedged between rocks to keep it from clattering down the incline into the lake. They'd stashed their treasures in the boat and hefted the craft back into the water. Dale had been ready to climb in when he'd realized neither one of them had retrieved the shovel. He'd scrambled back up the slope to where he was sure they'd placed it.

No shovel. Not anywhere. Gone. Disappeared. As if Trapper Wolf had snatched it up.

Chapter Eight

Cassie cradled her sketchpad in the crook of her left arm, and manipulated the pencil in her right hand. Her drawing was a cross between the photograph-ish rendering Wells wanted, and the smoothing out and filling in of crude figures on rough stone that she guessed Rhonda expected. This would have been easier if the original artist had more skill, had been working on a flat canvas, and hadn't used colored felt-tipped pens.

Cassie wondered exactly when she was going to get the promised heartfelt appreciation and the certificate. She'd rather have a badge. And a magical weather wand to make the drizzle stop. The source of the precipitation seemed centered directly above the island.

Boomer Danowski held a striped golf umbrella over her head. At least five inches shorter than she was, he extended his arm in what must have been an uncomfortable angle to accommodate her height. The gaunt, wrinkled man stood outside the awning's protection, insisting Cassie needed the entire space to herself, since her elbow was flapping about.

"This wasn't always an island, you know," Boomer said. Any of the other Sparks would have stood silently. To them

Cassie was an outsider. Well, a semi-outsider. She got a slight status upgrade since her aunt and uncle had lived in the town for years. Even with that boost, she was at least a decade away from being considered a local.

No such barrier existed with Boomer. He chatted at her as if they'd been next-door neighbors in the primordial ooze. "Fur trappers camped here and pretty soon there was a trading post." Streams ran off the brim of the baseball cap protruding from the hood of his dark olive poncho. Cassie's supply bag was looped over the arm he kept under the loose wrap that advertised the Danowski Family Polka Band in neon green lettering across the back.

"That's why the lake's got a French name. One of the trappers, Pierre somebody, he was called Wolf because he said the wolves he killed and skinned followed him as ghosts. Personally, if that happened to me, I'd switch to rabbits. Then we had this heavy winter. You're probably too young to remember. Covered most of the state. Kids got a bunch of days off school. You could hardly plow your driveway 'cause there's no place to throw all that snow. The melt came quick that spring. Flood waters ran real fast. Sliced through right over there." He poked out the poncho with the hand hidden under the plasticky fabric. "Cut the Haunt clean away, and suddenly Blanchet's got a big old island."

A huge lemon appeared exactly where Boomer pointed. Officer Rhonda Olson trudged out of the trees in her yellow slicker and boots. A matching floppy hat covered her scarlet hair. Holding a department radio in one hand, she pressed a cell phone to her ear with the other.

"Rhonda must a been checking the channel," Boomer said. "I heard she's working on getting an airboat, like they use in the winter to rescue anglers when the chunk of ice they're fishing on cracks away and floats off on its own. It can handle a stretcher. You know, for this poor girl. Granite County doesn't have one, but we stay friendly with those that do."

"It sounds like something Sparks bingo could finance," Cassie said. The firefighters raked in big bucks from the locally popular game.

"That's a good idea," Boomer said. "I'll bring it up at the next meeting."

A woman in shorts, a rain-repellant hat, and a poncho far more designer posh than Boomer's stomped into view and spoke to Rhonda. A Spark offered her an umbrella. She refused, as if insulted by the implication that she couldn't handle a little sprinkle.

"Whoa, Ms. Brighton herself," Boomer said. "Bet Tammara's got her undies in a bunch that this poor girl had the nerve to die on her precious property."

"I haven't met her." Finished with the stone, Cassie flipped to a fresh page in her sketchbook while Boomer was distracted. He didn't have to know she was done with her assigned task and that technically his umbrella duty was over. She studied indentations in the clay near the fallen girl. Hoping Boomer wouldn't notice, she placed a sandaled foot close enough to provide scale. Partially sheltered by the stone, the tarp, and Cassie's presence, the depressions hadn't yet filled with water.

"Oh, she's too Kardashian to mix with us," Boomer said. "Although she might like you, since you're an artist and you've lived farther away than Fargo."

"She can't think it's so bad. She still lives here." Cassie drew the ruts and ridges left by objects that were no longer there. About the size of marbles, the missing spheres had patterned the dense soil as if leaving a message.

"Only because she came back to manage things when her mom died and her dad went into care for Alzheimer's. She sure wasn't going to let her brother do it. She and Marty get along but don't, if you know what I mean."

Cassie wasn't sure she did.

"Money and illness put a strain on a family," Boomer

continued. "Shame. They were close when they were kids, before Tam went away to a East Coast boarding school, then one of those Harvard colleges. Always the smartest cookie in the family jar, which is saying something since her dad, and probably her mom too, was a genius before old age crippled his mind. She put together a tech company. Sold it for a football field full of cash."

"I don't know how much money a stadium can hold, but I'm guessing it's a lot."

"A lot and then some," Boomer said. "That would have been enough for me and most others, but I guess she got bored, so she started another business. Runs it out of the family mansion. Can't imagine how you can do that, but if it can be done, she'd be the one to do it. And she is."

Deputy Adam Berger assisted the Sparks who buzzed around Cassie and Boomer, struggling with metal posts and yards of canvas to erect the tent that St. Mary's Catholic Church used for the annual pancake feed. Cassie feared important evidence had already been washed away in the rivulets snaking into Lake Blanchet. Little would be left by the time the state crime lab investigators arrived from St. Paul.

Tammara Brighton dashed up to Adam. "Make sure they are careful with the spikes," she shouted louder than necessary over the drone of steady rain. "Don't go tearing up the ground."

In her muddy sandals, Cassie envied the way the woman's running shoes shed moisture. A high-end brand, they looked suitable for jogging all the way to the Boundary Waters. Cassie suspected most people who owned such footwear never traversed a trail more challenging than the Mall of America parking lot.

"So glad you're here, Ms. Brighton," Adam said. "We could really use a statement from you." He directed her to Rhonda, who spoke into the two-way radio in one hand while thumbing a message into the cell phone in her other hand.

Tammara humphed and clomped away toward Sheriff Wells instead.

Boomer chuckled. "She'd got a lot of her dad in her. Her brother does too, although he hides it better. Wouldn't want to be in the middle of any of their family rows."

A rumble rolled through the slate clouds overhead. It occurred to Cassie that they were doing everything they shouldn't when there was a threat of lightning. Standing under trees. Handling metal poles. Holding umbrellas! If the Greek god Zeus aimed a bolt at Boomer, she'd be fried too. It seemed Tammara had proved her smarts by going umbrella-less.

"You know how they used natural borders before satellites and GPS," Boomer said. "Well, the Brighton deed stated the lake was the legal boundary to their land. You wouldn't think a narrow little channel would be a big deal, but some developer from the Cities thought it qualified as a property line. I bet his eyes lit up with dollar signs when he saw this great big hunk of prime lakefront he thought he could snatch up from the county cheap." Boomer chuckled. "He didn't know the Brightons have money, and Tammara's dad read law books like other guys watched baseball. Course, they hired Harry to do the actual lawyering. You know Harry. He's sort of retired now . . ."

Cassie tuned out the town history, glad that Boomer didn't require her to participate in the conversation. She put her concentration into her sketch of the depressions at her feet, so close to the lock of hair that curved from beneath the blue covering. She let her eyes find the peaks and craters, as if she observed the textured surface of the moon through her telescope, then she translated them into space and shading with her pencil.

"Rhonda recognized her right away," Boomer said softly.

Cassie paused, struck by the change in her guardian's tone. "Who? The girl? This girl?"

"Kaitlyn Hanson."

Cassie's eyes went to the tarp. The canvas no longer spread over an anonymous landscape. The rises and dips shaped a specific human being who had family and friends worried about her, wondering why she hadn't come home. It made the scene less lonely in a way. But somehow more tragic.

"She'd be a senior this year," Boomer said. "She went to the station a day or so ago and talked to Rhonda about something. That family's had more than their share. At least this time they can say a proper goodbye. Small grace." Boomer twitched, shedding droplets from his poncho. "Gotta wonder though. Wolf Haunt and all."

A shiver ran through Cassie that had nothing to do with a sudden blast rippling her borrowed jacket. She looked around. Everyone was too busy with their own tasks to notice her. And Boomer watched everyone else while he rambled along another historical path. She squatted. Using her pencil as a ruler, she measured the depth and circumference of the impressions in the clay, then noted them on the edge of her drawing.

She stood, surprised she wasn't shaking. Since she'd gone that far and gotten away with it, she took out her phone and clicked more photos of the stone, the divots, and the tarp.

Cassie thanked her umbrella-wielding protector and released him from duty. She retrieved her bag from him and tucked away her sketchbook before anyone could see her work. Adam lifted the yellow tape for her as she stepped out of the cordoned off area.

"I've done what I can. I need to finish in a dry environment," she told him.

"As soon as possible would be good," he said.

Rhonda joined them. "The crime lab folks are going to chew my ass over this one. They hate it when you disturb so much as a leaf." She flipped back the brim of her floppy hat.

"These aren't the worst conditions we've dealt with, but I wish there was a double-wide bridge to this place."

"Boomer told me about the airboat," Cassie said.

"It's the best I can do for her," Rhonda said. "I'll need a tall scotch, neat, tonight."

Cassie knew about her friend's preference for single malt, but she doubted Rhonda would be having any soon. It seemed the more stress the woman was under, the more she stayed cold sober.

Rhonda's phone chimed before Cassie could ask her why Kaitlyn Hanson had recently visited the sheriff's department. Now was not the time for that discussion anyway. Rain pelted down with serious intent. Cassie clutched the windbreaker's hood around her face and watched the yellow-clad deputy jog away toward Sheriff Wells.

"That jacket's not really your style," Adam said. "And it's sort of big in the shoulders."

"It belongs to the guy who brought me here. He let me borrow it."

"Your date didn't hang around to take you home?"

Cassie was startled by the comment. Adam usually did cartwheels trying not say anything personal when he was on duty. "Don't pull that crap with me. You know it was an art club outing. You probably took Trevor's statement and told him he could leave."

Adam shrugged. "The Sams were shivering."

"The Sams?" Cassie remembered Scarf had referred to the couple that way.

"Mr. and Mrs. Olson. Samuel and Samantha. I don't want the sheriff's department to be responsible for their getting pneumonia. I told Mr. Rothman to take them and Ms. Moreau home, and we'd make sure you got back to your place safely."

Cassie noticed he used the plural "we," instead of saying he'd personally escort her to her door. Should she tell him she only met Trevor a few hours ago? Absolutely not. She'd been expecting an invitation to dinner and a movie from Adam. If seeing her wearing another man's coat, out of necessity in a downpour, made him back off, then the hell with him. They weren't in high school. The captain of the football team hadn't staked a claim by draping her in his letterman's jacket.

"Ms. Moreau is the woman in the scarf? And can I get that ride soon?" Cassie asked.

"Yes, Mel Moreau." He'd toggled back into his role as Officer Berger now. "Boomer might be the only one available to take you home. Sorry you ended up in the middle of a murder."

In the middle of a murder *again*, Cassie thought. She was becoming a magnet for dead bodies. Every time a corpse showed up, would Adam think of her?

"I'd appreciate it if you'd keep what you drew and what you saw confidential," Adam said.

Who would she tell? Cassie had met a lot of people in Glacier Falls, but Rhonda was the only one she would confide in. And murder seemed an inappropriate topic for casual conversation. "I think I'm legally bound to silence. Wells made me a member of the Sheriff's Posse."

Adam looked impressed. "Not just anyone gets that honor."

Cassie thought that, actually, just about anyone did. Wells had probably bestowed certificates on the workers at the Dairy Queen who served him Dilly Bars. "Are Mr. and Mrs. Olson related to Officer Rhonda Olson?"

"You'll have to ask Boomer."

Chapter Nine

Dale watched familiar scenery whiz past, as his friend urged the Bomb to defy the speed limit. "Richie, I don't remember if I wore gloves all the time. What about you?"

"Get over the shovel, man. No one took it. It just fell into the lake."

"Sure." But Dale hadn't heard metal scrape across the stones. He hadn't heard a splash.

"It's not a big deal, anyway," Richie said. "So what if our fingerprints and skin cells and stuff are on the island? Wells and the state CSI dudes are going to find piss from lots of guys. If they look. But they probably won't, because it must have been a heart attack. And if someone did take the shovel, that doesn't mean they saw us."

Except Dale was convinced that the shovel thief must have seen them. Not when Richie was scanning with the metal detector, and not when they were digging. Hypervigilant, Dale was certain he would have felt a presence if someone had crouched in the sumac spying on them. But the last part, when they were at the stone, he'd been so pumped he wouldn't have noticed if a spaceship landed beside him and a crew of gray blobs built a campfire and roasted marshmallows.

And there was the noise. Each time he replayed the scene in his head, he was more convince that they'd really heard something that wasn't the wind or a random critter.

And they'd only left the shovel wedged in the rocks for a few minutes before they'd gone back for it. And it wasn't there.

Yeah. The thief saw them for sure.

"Maybe the Brightons' maid or footman found it," Richie said. "That was two whole months ago. I bet it's been cleaned a bunch of times by now. Like on those Brit shows where they're always dusting paintings of the queen and polishing the silver."

The shovel wasn't the only thing that worried Dale. "Someone might recognize the stuff in your sculpture."

"I turned them into art," Richie said, as if that made the items unidentifiable.

Dale thought through each piece of Richie's creation. The bolts were indistinguishable from any others of that size. The pail handle could be from anywhere. The buckle wasn't special.

The animal skull, the trauma of its death apparent from the damaged eye socket, had the potential to trigger someone's memory. Still, it could be explained. Dale wasn't good at fabricating stories, but Richie could pull a lint-covered cough drop out of his pocket and describe how that actor from that movie had given him a bunch of them so he wouldn't hack his germs all over the limo.

Okay, Dale thought, they could get through this. It wasn't like a million people visited the fake barn every day. "We're lucky the thingy got removed before a bunch of people saw it."

"KOK," Richie said, pronouncing it "cock." "K-O-K. Keychain of Keychains. Maybe a Bible camp went on a field trip to the museum and the adults were really shocked and took it so the kiddies wouldn't be led into sin."

"Brighton probably has it. When the display closes, he'll

have to give it back to you. We'll strip down your sculpture and toss the pieces in a lake."

Richie spread a palm across his chest. "That's my creation, man. It's my soul."

"Okay, then we'll hide it for a while." Dale wasn't worried about crushing his best friend's spirit. Although Richie's statement was true today, his soul would be somewhere else in a week or so.

Richie swung the Bomb off the tar road onto the Steinhaus driveway and crunched to a stop in front of the farmhouse. Dale grabbed the handle to open the door. "But we have to dump the rest of the junk we dug up, like right away."

"About that—" Richie's phone chimed. He slid it from his pocket. "Wait a sec. Bridget probably ditched those guys and needs a ride."

Dale pulled out his own cell, which had buzzed with messages during the drive here. He read the oldest message, then quickly scrolled through the rest.

It had to be a mistake. One of those viral things that you learn later was a hoax. "Shit. Shit."

"Max, ultra shit," Richie said, reading his own screen. "Penultimate ED."

The dead girl on the Haunt had been identified. Kaitlyn Hanson, who hadn't been on the field trip this morning. Kait, who'd ordered everyone to ignore entry HS24.

"We should say a prayer," Richie said.

"Which one? Yours or mine?" Not that it mattered. They'd had long discussions comparing their Catholic and Lutheran Sunday school experiences, not really seeing a difference. "We don't believe in that stuff anyway."

"Maybe she believed. It might mean something to her."

Maybe, Dale thought. But being dead probably put you beyond caring about religion.

"So who was the guy?" Richie asked quietly.

"What guy?" Dale accepted that a new thought now careened around his friend's brain like a kid in an inflated castle.

"She's too young for a heart attack, so she was totally murdered, so there was a guy. We know her, so we know him too. He might be a serial killer. Like that Hannibal dude."

Dale couldn't breathe through the tightness in his chest. "It takes three bodies over a bunch of months for that."

"So, two more."

"Probably just the one." Dale felt a pang, wishing he could take back his words. No one was a "just."

"I bet a baller did it."

Dale could tell this was no longer about Kaitlyn. The guys who'd driven away with Bridget, Whitney and the other girls were all involved in sports where you kicked, dribbled, tossed, and/or punched a ball. They'd given themselves the unclever, stud-implying nickname of ballers.

"I want to watch that arrest." Richie burst into big gestures. "A letter-jacket guy locked up in handcuffs right in school. All the cheerleaders crying in the hall 'cause there's one less team hero to ask them to homecoming. A thousand videos streaming the perp-walk in real time out the front door to the sheriff's cruiser. And bonus: great pics for the yearbook. Epic, man."

Dale would like to see that, too. Especially if it was Todd Ashland being escorted out of GFHS by officers. He didn't bother pointing out that even if the entire population of the high school crowded the hallway, there would only be about three hundred witnesses to the event.

Richie fiddled with the radio. "I want to be called Rich from now on."

Another ricochet in the bouncy house. "Why?" Dale felt he had to ask because he knew Richie wanted him to. Sometimes, like now, he wished his best friend came with an off switch.

"It sounds like I'm rich."

"You're not, so far."

"Neither are any of the clowns we know." Richie tried out a new catchphrase. "You can get richer, but you can't get Rich."

Richie's quest for treasure had plunged them into this situation. Dale didn't blame him, exactly. Well, maybe a little. He needed Richie to understand that they were on the edge of serious trouble. "With it being Kaitlyn—"

"I know. DEFCON 3, man. Yellow alert."

"We can't talk to anyone about having been to the Haunt."

"Got it." Richie stayed quiet for a nanosecond. "About tossing the junk we dug up into a lake. What if I don't have all of it anymore? What if I gave some away?"

Chapter Ten

Exhausted, Cassie shivered in Trevor's damp jacket as she shuffled across the Johnsons' dock to shore. Patches of blue showed through gaps in the clouds.

Sure, *now* the rain had stopped. Or maybe it had stormed over the island and nowhere else. She could barely lift her hand in a goodbye gesture to Boomer as he revved the outboard and sped away.

On the trip back from Wolf Haunt, over roars and pops from the sputtering engine, he'd shouted the genealogy of the Samuel Olson family. Not to be confused with the Paul Olson family or the Lloyd Olson family, although Paul and Lloyd were cousins, but not first cousins. None of them was related to Deputy Sheriff Rhonda Olson unless you went *way* back. You needed to look at the church records for both St. Mary's Catholic Church and Faith and Hope Lutheran, since there were Olson brothers some generations back who didn't get along and refused to be in the same building with one another while they celebrated the peace of Jesus.

Cassie trudged up the hill to the cabin, carrying her bag and a complimentary Danowski Family Polka Band poncho. Jupiter scooted out the cabin door the moment she opened it.

He leaped down the deck stairs and charged across the lawn to his favorite place to mark his territory.

She kicked off her muddy sandals on the deck. All she wanted was a steaming shower, but the app for a courier service had chimed at her all morning. Notifications told her how excited they were that her package had been loaded onto the truck.

It was out for delivery and would arrive any moment now.

The driver could see her house and was waving if she cared to wave back.

Success! The package has been delivered to the location she'd indicated.

The driver sent a personal thank-you for keeping her dog inside.

Would she please take a moment to fill out a brief survey?

Cassie wasn't expecting a package. During Boomer's recitation of the Olson family entanglements, she'd followed its progress through the texts and let her mind speculate about the wonder that awaited her. Perhaps a diamond-encrusted watch from some adoring fan who'd fallen in love with her drawing of a wild mustang posed nobly on a mesa at sunrise, tossing its head so the wind lifted its luxurious golden mane. She couldn't remember what product the ad was selling. Something that had nothing to do with horses or an Arizona landscape.

More likely the packet placed in the weatherproof box beside the door by the cheerful delivery person was from her former boss/occasional client Prentice Royer at Fontana Media. The last one had contained a bottle of ketchup buried in packing peanuts, sent as inspiration for an ad he expected her to whip off by the next day.

She scooped the bundle out of the For Deliveries container. An adrenaline boost surged through her as she read the return address: AweMazing Chocolates, New York, NY

A job that had started out energizing the company's drab

website had expanded into other projects. All of them proved challenging in a good way and satisfying financially. She rushed into the kitchen, hoping for something more inspiring than a condiment. She tore through the cardboard and slid out a carton adorned with the new company logo. Eagerly, she lifted the cover. Inside, creamy tissue paper glowed with her design of lavender calla lilies and blush-pink peonies tipped with gold.

Gazing at the beauty in her own work, Cassie forgot about her dirty, bare feet and damp clothes. Only one thing could make the experience better. She reverently folded back filmy layers to reveal—

Chocolates!

The assortment sparkled: dark brown mounds drizzled with soft pink icing, nougats encased in gold foil, pale molded shells, milk chocolate hearts.

Cassie plucked out a note card that still carried the old, boring, unimaginative, drab logo, so unworthy of being near her fresh floral masterpiece.

Cassie,

Thank you for your AweMazing designs! I hope you're ready for our next adventure. Details to come soon.

It was signed by the company president, who was now Cassie's favorite chocolatier in the entire world. She popped a raspberry truffle into her mouth, savoring sweet and tangy flavors and the comfort of continued employment. The sensation was beyond delicious.

Her euphoria quickly dissolved as she read the line scrawled below the signature.

Did you like the chocolate-covered strawberries?

What chocolate-covered strawberries?

She checked the delivery company's app, scrolling back to the journey her favorite coffee pods had made from the warehouse to her door. She'd barely glanced at the texts at the time. Now she saw notifications for the missing package mixed in with them.

Cassie felt totally cheated. What she'd lost suddenly eclipsed the (almost) full box of chocolates right in front of her. She looked out the window and watched Jupiter sniff the grass, trying to track Kevin. Could the stubby-tailed, thrill-seeking squirrel have dragged away the treats and left the coffee? The pest was definitely a villain. He tormented Jupiter and raided the bird feeder.

No. She eliminated him as a suspect. Although he tried again and again, he hadn't been able to open the latched bin. Not yet.

She imagined the delivery driver being seduced by the company's name to peek inside, then spending a long lunch break devouring the luscious delights.

That was unfair. The woman who drove this route operated by bar codes and was unlikely to glance at the sender's address.

Charlie patrolled the road several times a day. Maybe he'd noticed a suspicious character in a sugar coma. She'd dubbed him the Sentinel of Beauty Lake and knew he wasn't the thief. He took his neighborhood-watch duties seriously. Besides, health problems kept him on his ATV, and he couldn't reach the bin with his mechanical grabber.

Cassie came to a logical conclusion.

A porch pirate had plundered her deck and sailed off with her chocolate-covered strawberries.

There's always a friend at SunnieChat!

Porch pirate stole my chocolate. Gift from a client.

ASHLEY

Cruelty beyond words.

HOLLY

Did you report it to Deputy Adam?

No, but I documented in case it turns into harassment. If something happens to me, you know how to bait the trap to catch this guy.

ASHLEY

Love your client. I need a gig like that.

I'm tempted to tell him to pay me in sea salt caramels.

HOLLY

And I thought having a parking spot less than a mile from my office was the best perk ever.

KAYLA

Can't remember the last time I tasted chocolate. No such luxuries on the good ship Austere. But honestly instead I'd settle for a shower that lasts longer than three minutes.

HOLLY

Water water everywhere and all the boards did shrink, water water everywhere nor any drop to shower. It doesn't scan as well as drink, but I don't think the Ancient Mariner was concerned with showers.

KAYLA

We read that poem in Ms. Osland's class. I felt sorry for the albatross.

ASHLEY

One of the great literary "don't ever get on a ship" tales.

HOLLY

Right up there with Moby Dick and Billy Budd.

KAYLA

Hey I'm on a ship!

Twenty Thousand Leagues Under the Sea

ASHLEY

Kidnapped

HOLLY

The Count of Monte Cristo. But he does end up rich.

KAYLA

Does Pirates of the Caribbean count?

No

ASHLEY

No

HOLLY

Neither does Titanic.

KAYLA

Sorry. When it comes to the ocean, I read about the organisms that live there. Not so interested in people dramas.

HOLLY

K, how is YOUR people drama going? Have you decided about the New Zealand job?

KAYLA

Complication. Funding might be extended here but decreased. I'd rather stay on this project. Love the Galapagos! But one of us five would get dropped. Liam's turned into a shark. Finding ways to show the boss how valuable he is.

HOLLY

Showing off, you mean.

ASHLEY

Kissing ass, you mean.

KAYLA

Both of those. He's good at self promotion. I'm not.

K, your romance on the rocks?

KAYLA

More like in a maelstrom.

HOLLY

So your choices are Liam, New Zealand job, Galapagos job.

KAYLA

The way Liam is acting, he's currently in third place.

Chapter Eleven

Dale let his hand slip from the door handle on the passenger side of the Bomb. "What do you mean, you don't have it all anymore? What exactly did you give away?"

Richie tapped the steering wheel to the beat of the pop song on the radio. "You know. Stuff."

Dale wanted to puke. He'd tried to shut down the scheme the moment Richie had shoved the *Falls Press* article in his face. He really had.

He should have flat out refused to go along with it. But he hadn't.

Richie was his usual enthusiastic self the day he came up with the plan. He stabbed at the photo of a deformed bottomless container. "Two hundred and fifty bucks! For a beat up old thing you can't even use."

Dale read the headline.

Treasure Found Near Turtle Lake

Like a good friend, he dutifully skimmed the print. The brass kettle, which to Dale looked more like a cone you put on a dog so it can't scratch its ears, was from around 1800. A girl had found it on her grandparents' farm. The family had donated it to the Swedish Immigrant Collection at the Granite County museum.

The paper's editor was probably grateful for a summer story that didn't involve water safety, mosquitoes and the guy who restores vintage manure spreaders

As usual, Richie overflowed with excitement about his own idea. "We can find shit like this. Easy money, man."

"This says the estimated value is two hundred and fifty. No one actually paid anything for it."

"That's 'cause they gave it away. Which was dumbass stupid. We'll sell our stuff on eBay and make a fortune."

"We've never done that," Dale protested.

"A guy Uncle Wyatt knows does it all the time. It can't be that hard. We're smart guys. We can figure it out."

Dale understood that meant *he'd* be the one at the computer. "I'm not going all the way to Turtle Lake. It's barely in the county. I don't think we'll find anything anyway."

"Sixth-grade Minnesota history, dude." Richie had loved that unit. When he graduated (if he graduated), Dale thought trading posts and fur pelts might be all his friend remembered from fourteen years of education. "The voyageurs canoed all over here. I bet they left behind lots of kettles and spatulas and things. And we've got the best place ever to look, right close by."

Dale folded up the paper. He could guess where Richie had mentally put a gigantic treasure-mark X. Wolf Haunt. "It gets as much traffic as the Dairy Queen." Okay, that was an exaggeration, but it made the point.

"Not so much anymore. Not like it used to."

"It's summer," Dale countered. "Parties happen."

"No prob-lem-o." Richie tapped his head. "The Rich-o-matic has it all worked out."

Dale gave in, knowing it was too late to redirect his friend's energy. He felt the same resignation as when Richie had talked him into hauling bowling balls up Red Hawk Hill. They'd sent the polished boulders rolling down the slope, expecting them to travel in straight lines and mow down the bricks they'd stacked at the bottom. One had smashed into Dale's ATV. The other had bounced into a hole only a few feet from the launch point and was still there.

Dale thought about those bowling balls on the June evening they executed the plan. He watched Richie sweep the metal detector under a bush. The device was b-wop, borrowed without permission, from Richie's uncle Wyatt, along with a shovel and a small fishing boat.

Dale was uneasy about the wop part, but Richie assured him they'd get everything returned before it was missed. "Anyway, if Uncle Wy can't find something he always figures I've got it."

A breeze off Lake Blanchet brushed a chill through the early summer warmth. Richie circled the coil around a spot, getting no reaction from the machine. "I don't know why we didn't think of this before. Guys have been getting drunk out here since pioneer days, since Trapper Wolf himself. This place is like a bank. And this isn't even stealing."

Of course it was stealing. Wolf Haunt was private property, no matter how often it was invaded by raving teens. Which really wasn't as frequent as you might think from its reputation. The complications of getting to an island when sober and leaving while under the influence dampened party activity. Mostly, you went so you could say you'd been there, so you could post photos on social media, then go somewhere else to indulge in the toxin of your choice.

But Richie was semi-right. This wasn't the same as relocating a Snicker's bar from the gas station. It was more like walking off with a hoodie at a garage sale and hoping to discover a grungy twenty crumpled up in a secret pocket. Not that anything like that had ever happened to Dale. Not that he'd ever heard of a hoodie with a secret pocket. But that would be a cool thing.

Dale leaned uncomfortably on the shovel. Designed to be tossed into a wheelbarrow for a day of gardening, the short-shafted tool, impractical for someone of his height, forced him to hunch over.

So far they'd found two dollars and twenty cents in coins; bent nails, which they ignored; a handful of ten-inch-long hex bolts; and a scratched-up chewing tobacco tin barely older than they were. Richie had latched onto a pail handle. He was sure the curved wire indicated that an antique kettle, like the semi-valuable one in the newspaper article, hid nearby.

Richie zigzagged the metal detector into the clearing dominated by the spirit stone, swinging it closer and closer to the rock. "Come on, Wolfy, give us a sign."

The device beeped.

Richie whooped. "ED hot, Wolfman!"

Dale tugged his gloves tight and thrust the shovel into the turf, sure they were *not* about to find a pot they could turn into gold, and wondering how he had ended up with the manual labor part. He sliced a circular perimeter and pried up chunks of grass and dirt, releasing the pungent smell of decay.

Pebbles dropped from a clump, bouncing back into the hole. Richie dumped the machine in the grass, squatted, and plucked out several spheres. He rolled them in his palm, spitting on them to clean off the clay. "Marbles maybe. How'd they get so deep?" He stretched out a hand to grab more.

Dale blocked his arm with the shovel. "Stop."

Richie saw it, pulled back and landed on his butt. "Fucking shit."

Dale lowered the blade into the crater, lifted out a small skull, and gently placed it in the grass. Shadows from the low afternoon sun accentuated an elongated snout. Richie peeled off grayish lumps and brushed away loose dirt, revealing spiderweb cracks from an eye socket to the back of the cranium.

"Baby raccoon?" Richie speculated.

"Buried on purpose?" Dale scooped out small bones tangled in scraps of tattered canvas. More spheres protruded like bubbles from thick clots. A dolphin figurine poked out of a mass of trinkets on a carabiner clip attached to a buckle. The heavy fabric and hardware reminded him of the old-style bag in the attic of his grandfather's house.

He tossed aside the shovel and knelt beside Richie. A shiny spot in one of the clumps caught his eye. He crumbled soil from a flat oval linked to a ratty leather strip.

A dog tag. Dale showed Richie the engraved letters etched into the plate.

"Gizmo," Richie read. "Like from that flick with those things. I bet a wolf snatched Gizmo and ate him right up."

"And put him in a sack, and buried him with this other stuff?"

Richie absorbed that for a moment. "So it's like a grave, like in a pyramid with things to take into the next world. And we're grave robbers. What's that black-and-white movie with those guys who get cursed by that mummy?"

"*The Mummy's Curse.*"

"Best ever."

Richie stuffed their new discoveries into a plastic shopping bag from the Falls Market that held their other finds. He placed the skull in last.

"We can't take that," Dale said.

Richie protested. "Uncle Wyatt collects them."

"That's why he lives alone."

"It'll make up for our b-wopping his gear. He'll clean it up and be respectful and everything."

"You're not worried about a curse?"

Richie picked up the shovel and held it out to Dale. "Fill up the hole. Then there's a thing we have to do. To protect our territory."

"If that means pissing all over this island, you're on your own."

Dale leaned into the Bomb's odorous upholstery. "The stuff we dug up that day on Wolf Haunt, the stuff you gave away. We have to get it back."

The song on the radio ended. A new one began, sounding a lot like the previous tune except out of synch with Richie's taps on the steering wheel.

"Tough one." Richie stopped drumming. "Those round things buried with Gizmo weren't marbles. They're beads, like they fell off jewelry. I gave them to this girl in my art class, and now they're jewelry again. Totally circle of life."

Chapter Twelve

Cassie ruffled her hair, damp from a morning shower. No amount of water could wash away her weariness caused by yesterday's tragedy. She wanted to spend the day sitting on the deck immersed in one of the many books from her "to read" pile. Unfortunately, she had pressing obligations.

She'd expected to come back from the island with a new drawing of the shed she'd sketched when she was thirteen. Instead she had death-adjacent scenes that needed her attention.

They would have to wait while she tried to decipher the JPEG of a clay blob on her tablet's screen. The elementary-aged creator had made a dog? Mouse? Snot monster?

Cassie squirmed in the squishy living room chair. Who'd suggested she'd make a good judge for the student art show? She suspected it was Rhonda. The woman seemed determined to yank her into community activities. Caught off guard by the pleading tone of the volunteer coordinator who'd called her, Cassie had agreed. After all, how hard could it be?

She flicked to a fish with a gaping mouth and spiked fins,

then to a bottom-heavy bird that could never fly. She'd been naive to think there would only be a few entries. Dozens of creations awaited her scrutiny. She was determined to review every piece before she met with the other judges in a few hours. She tried not to think of the task as suffering before the great altar of Art. *View fresh perspectives,* she told herself. *Encourage young talent.*

Martin Brighton, director of the Granite County Historical Society, had sent her a link to the web site where she had downloaded the photos. She realized he was Tammara's brother, the one Boomer had called Marty.

If the Windom family property became a murder scene, Cassie would drop everything else for at least three days, but the director hadn't canceled the judges' meeting. Did that mean he couldn't because there was no one else to manage the task? Or that he didn't care about the family estate? Or something else?

She tried not to let the time crunch tense her shoulders as she slogged through pinched pots, coil pots, wheel-thrown pots. Fluted. Squat. Glazed blue. Glazed green. Etched with flowers. Etched with skulls. One sprouted handles that looked like ears.

It seemed the summer mentorship program had overflowed with students. Cassie suddenly understood the desperation of the person who'd contacted her. The majority of local artists would have been recruited as teachers, leaving a short supply of others with artistic credentials to select the award winners.

The pottery mentor must have had a kiln fired up all summer so every child in the county could let loose their inner Rodin. Although none of the baked items came close to *The Thinker,* parents would hang on to these treasures for years. They'd arrange them beside graduation cakes. Then, after the crumbs got brushed away, they'd shove them back into storage under the stairs, where they would dwell until Mom and Dad sold the house and moved to Arizona.

Determined to perform her due diligence, Cassie flicked through middle school students' depictions of anime characters, flowers, superheroes. A parade of painted cats, cats in charcoal, cats in yarn, and quilted cats drained away her concentration. Did the other judges struggle as she did? She wondered who they were, and if they had real studios with space for paints and canvases. Did they have showings at posh galleries? Would they view her as a pretender because she paid the bills by creating images of frothy bars of soap nestled among brightly colored fruit?

Was their art better than hers?

She peered at a watercolor that might depict a bear asleep beside a giant artichoke. Or might not. The painting was identified as HS2. High school level, entry number 2. No name was attached. The blind submission process kept the focus on the piece and not the artist. Cassie thought the approach was wise in an area where the judges couldn't help knowing most of the students.

She wished each age group had been subdivided according to medium. She was stuck evaluating the merits of the confusing painting against a sculpture of metal scraps.

The skeletal framework of HS12 encased a small skull that looked real. The design intrigued her, although it felt unfinished. She moved the photo into a Favorites folder.

She halted at HS24, recognizing it from an article on the competition in the *Falls Press*. Subconsciously she'd been looking for this necklace.

On the left, five vertical rows of fat beads molded with an intricate pattern cascaded like tears. On the right, a metal oval hung horizontally. Cassie was attracted to the asymmetry. She couldn't wait to see the real thing. In the newspaper photo, ornate letters engraved on the disk had been difficult to read.

Now she enlarged the image on her tablet, wondering what elegant word hid in the loops and flourishes.

G-i-z-m-o.

Gizmo.

Chapter Thirteen

Cassie parked her sunflower-yellow Mini Cooper away from a blue bus with "Camp Wildstone" stenciled on the side. It wasn't her first time at the Granite County Historical Society Museum. She snapped a picture of the genuine woodcut sign at the entrance. She approved of the rustic placard she remembered from when she was thirteen, although her advertising mind labeled it boring.

The two-building complex should have been located in Glacier Falls, the county seat. But the Anderson family—that is, one of the many Anderson families in the area, some of them related and some of them not—had donated five acres here in the town of Sunset. "Free land" had sliced and diced through blustery political opposition and community rivalry.

Cassie thought her memory might have romanticized the farmhouse built a century and a half ago, but the place really did have gingerbread trim curling along the eaves, and newel posts supporting a fat railing across the broad porch. This was far from the sod hut of a prairie buster. A forward-thinking Swedish settler had starting a sawmill, turning trees into lumber. He'd constructed the two-story home as mate bait, to convince the widow with forested land bordering his to marry him.

Cassie grabbed her tote bag and unfolded herself from the ultra-compact Cooper. The air, humid from yesterday's storm, dampened her skin. She clicked a photo of the house and sent it to her sisters.

> Guess where I am.

She headed to the modern building next to the preserved home. Unsuccessfully disguised as a barn, the structure held the formal displays. A greeting in Ojibwe should share space with *Valkommen* on the welcome sign at the main door, but it didn't.

A woman stood near the large red Dala horse statue stationed beside the entrance. Sunlight flared from the jewelry on her wrist as she massage her forehead, shielding her face from the day's glare. Cassie pegged her as a Camp Wildstone counselor in need of fresh air and a sedative. As she got closer, she realized she was wrong.

Tammara Brighton had shed the drenched poncho, shorts and running shoes from yesterday. The thin face framed by a sleek haircut was now free of the rain-repellant hat. Her knit shirt, cargo pants, and slip-on footwear blended together in shades of taupe. How could she spend so much on designer labels and still look dull?

Cassie wondered if the owner of Wolf Haunt would recognize *her*. Her instinct was to duck her head and pretend to dig in her bag for something important so she could avoid eye contact. If only she had a floppy hat to hide her face. She did not want to deal with the woman's frustration at having her property violated, especially since she'd been one of the violators.

She snuck a quick glance and wished she hadn't. On the

island Tammara had been rigid with fury. Now she seemed wilted.

Had she and her brother been discussing the portion of the family estate that was now a crime scene? Since the siblings' relationship was an arctic one, that would have been a difficult conversation. Cassie imagined the exchange as formal and reserved—with posh British accents.

> Tammara: I say, Martin, remember the charming little picnic spot on the estate where we used to romp as tots?
> Martin: Where I smashed your dolly, and you put deer scat in my tea?
> Tammara: That very one.
> Martin: Fond memories. Was there an annoyance? I so hope it hasn't collapsed into the sea.
> Tammara: Unfortunately, a person perished there.
> Martin: Recently?
> Tammara: According to the authorities, an evening ago whilst I sipped my gin and tonic.
> Martin: Such a tragedy.
> Tammara: Yes. We might as well construct a folly on the site.

"Do I know you?" Tammara Brighton Meyer challenged.

Cassie was disappointed by the normal Minnesota accent. She realized her glance had turned into a rude stare. "We haven't met, but I"—Cassie didn't want to say she'd found the body, didn't want to mention anything connected to death—"was with the sheriff's department. On the island. It must have been very upsetting. I'm sorry you had to go through that."

"You tracked me down to tell me that?"

"No, I—" A detailed explanation almost burst from her mouth, but she held it back. The dab of sympathy she'd felt for the woman evaporated. She was sure they would never share tea and cakes together. "I'm here on business."

"It's a nonprofit museum," Tammara scoffed. "What business could you possibly have?"

Cassie gave a corporate smile. "*My* business."

She pushed through the double sets of doors that formed an airlock into a climate-controlled chill. A stuffed beaver greeted her. The creature sat up on its haunches, supported by a broad tail. One claw grasped the gnawed stub of a birch tree. The other held a welcome sign (as beavers are known to do in the wild). It hadn't blinked or budged an inch since she'd been here as a teen. She wrinkled her nose. It hadn't been cleaned either.

An optimistically large donation box sat at the animal's feet. Giant pine cones rested around it, suggesting all offerings should match their size.

Above the beady-eyed guardian of the museum, a monochrome photograph showed a row of fur trappers in caps made from the beaver's relatives. Fox and sable pelts spread across the foreground. The men leaned on rifles before the rough exterior of a trading post. Their grainy, bearded faces seemed grim. The canoe commute must have been a bitch that day.

Cassie introduced herself to the man at the faux antique information counter who slammed brochures into a multitiered stand as if it were therapy.

"I'm Martin Brighton, the museum director," he said as if he'd rather be the stuffed beaver.

Cassie was beyond disappointed, and not just by another flat Midwestern tone. She'd expected a professor-ish tweed jacket with leather patches on the sleeves covering a starched shirt. And she'd hoped for a bow tie. Instead, a sports coat hung over Martin's polo shirt. Shaved head tinted by sunburn, he looked as if he fixed the furnace, washed the windows, and dug up the artifacts himself after free climbing at Gooseberry

Falls. Round glasses on a round face, he could have been the inspiration for the clay fish, which had not made it into her Favorites folder.

Was he upset by his sister's visit, or did he always arrange inanimate objects as if he could force order on an unruly universe? He couldn't be expressing personal grief. According to Boomer, the deceased girl had no connection to the Brighton family. Maybe Tammara blamed her brother for the desecration of the family property, berating him for not installing a barbed wire barrier around the island.

Cassie scribbled her name onto a blue line in the visitor book, remembering how carefully she'd penned her signature the previous time.

Martin stored extra brochures behind the counter and heaved his shoulders as if shrugging off whatever had happened between him and his sister and shifting into director role. "Thank you so much for agreeing to judge our contest, Ms. Windom. It seems you're famous."

Cassie stiffened. Exactly which "famous" did he mean? She swallowed down sour fear that he was going to quiz her about Vicky's death and Jordan's murder trial. Her best friend's shadow wavered behind him. She tried to recall the deflective, noncommittal responses she'd developed for use with the media and the real-crime fanboys. The curt phrases refused to form.

Looking down at the bald man from her five-inch height advantage, she reminded herself she stood in a temple to the local past. The high priest, protector of black-and-white photographs and taxidermied beavers, was not the type to be entranced by anything since the end of World War II. She hoped his limited vision could protect him now that his ancestral home was about to be associated with a murder.

"A real-life illustrator for a major Los Angeles agency," Martin said. "When a board member told me about you, I got inspired to curate a special show. 'Advertising trends through history.' I'd like to get your perspective on the topic, once several other matters are settled."

So the tweed-jacket academic she'd imagined dwelled at the center of the handyman Tootsie Pop.

"That sounds really interesting," Cassie lied, relieved the project fell into the "when I get time" category. With luck that meant never. Her career was totally twenty-first century. She'd been trained to think ahead to the next trend, not historically, unless the newest thing was retro. Even then, her knowledge barely went backward past disco dancers in white boots that she'd researched for a perfume ad.

And apparently she wasn't *really* famous, since someone needed to tell Martin who she was. Cassie had to revise her assumption that Rhonda had put her on the museum's radar. The deputy was more gun club than museum board. Cassie didn't think her friend had time for both while also maintaining an active social life, which she definitely did.

Cassie pointed to a colorful poster directing visitors to the Summer Student Extravaganza in the Lake Superior Room. Square inserts pictured the instructors. Most were candid shots. Trevor Rothman's was professionally posed. His slick smile made Cassie think, *Don't let your daughter near this guy.* "I was hoping to do a quick review of the exhibit before the meeting," she told Martin. That was true, although she hadn't expected to be this early. She still calculated travel time according to her old LA habits, factoring in a margin for heavy traffic and accident congestion. The roads had been free of both on the two-lane route between Glacier Falls and Sunset.

"Very prudent of you." Martin led her through a maze of hallways. The architecture seemed to encourage getting lost. He stopped at the double doors to the Lake Itasca Room and pulled a jingly key ring from a pocket. He sorted through the notched keys, selected one, and seemed surprised that it released the lock.

Cassie took a slow step over the threshold. The items she'd seen in the photos seemed hastily squashed against one another in display cases, and crowded onto panels and counters.

"Please forgive the chaotic presentation," Martin said. "We had to change the location."

Cassie sensed he was more irritated by the disarray than she was. And that the "we" was really just him.

"We, uh," Martin stammered, "experienced water damage and had to move the entire collection. Still, despite the difficulties, it's our best competition ever. Except for some unfortunate pieces." He scowled at the parade of lumpy creatures Cassie recognized.

"Forgive me," he said. "I shouldn't have expressed a personal comment, especially not to a judge. I hope you don't think I'm trying to influence you in any way."

Cassie's gaze shot straight to the gapping-mouthed, bulging-eyed fish that reminded her of the director. "Of course not."

Martin motioned for her to follow him through a zigzag path to a glass-paneled door in a side wall. He sorted through the keys again.

"You said someone on the museum board recommended me." Cassie waited as Martin examined then released each key. He reached the last one, then started around the loop again, mumbling to himself.

"Who was it?" Cassie blurted out.

"Oh," Martin said as if he'd forgotten she was there. "One of our volunteers, I think, who told a board member who told me."

"And that was?"

"I don't recall. She heard about you from someone, possibly a person in her landscape club. They go around and sketch, ah—" He flipped through each bit of toothed metal a third time and finally separated one from the others.

"Landscapes?" Cassie suggested.

"Exactly." Martin jammed the key into the lock and gave a twist. "You'll be using this conference room to discuss your selections. I hope it won't be too noisy. The Wildstone group is almost finished in the farmhouse and will be in this building soon. I apologize for the inconvenience."

He reached through the doorway and flipped on a light, showing a tiny space with an overly large table and mismatched, almost throne-like wooden chairs. "The museum survives on field trips, and the art competition is a big draw. We can't close down every time something unforeseen happens."

Cassie suspected he'd told his sister the same thing.

SunnieChat makes your day glow!

> Guess where I am.

HOLLY

Laura Ingalls Wilder invited you to a quilting bee.

ASHLEY

You finally cracked time travel.

> The guy built this house to attract a mate.

KAYLA

Like a frigatebird. The male builds a nest and puffs out his red chest to get a female's attention. She inspects the nest. If she approves, she stays. If she doesn't like it, she checks out another male and his building skills. She keeps doing that until she finds the right nest.

ASHLEY

So if it has good closet space, a view of the ocean, and the kitchen cabinets are white, she moves in with the guy. If not, she goes on to the next open house. Not a bad plan.

HOLLY

C, first the island, now this place. Did your ghost appear again?

I'll tell you about the island later. I'm judging a student art contest at the museum.

ASHLEY

Dad told me he always made ashtrays in art class.

Deformed animals are the new ashtrays.

KAYLA

Is the beaver still there? Send me a pic.

Chapter Fourteen

The curvy vase, celadon green with an ecru frosted rim, looked better in person than in the JPEG on Cassie's tablet. On her Favorites list, she moved it ahead of the acrylic painting showing a coconut tree on an undisturbed stretch of sand bordered by gentle blue waves titled "My Goal." Cassie thought it should be called "A Long Way From Minnesota" and wished the artist luck finding an ocean-front beach that wasn't packed with people.

Against a wall on a waist-high stand painted matte black, she found HS12, the wire framework that implied a human torso. The skull mounted inside appeared to be that of a small animal that had met a tragic death. Up close, her original impression still held. The composition seemed off-balance. Was that on purpose, an artistic statement? Or had the artist run out of creativity? Whatever the reason, it remained one of her top picks.

She reached the end of the disorganized exhibit without finding the intriguing asymmetrical necklace of sliced metal and patterned beads. She doubted the material would have been damaged by the water leak that had forced the displays to be moved to the Itasca Room.

Martin hadn't said when the catastrophe occurred. If it had been during the storm yesterday, the necklace could have been left behind in the rush to relocate the items.

Cassie stepped out into the empty hall, wondering if the director hovered nearby. "Hello?" Thick with photographs, and arrowheads mounted in shadowboxes, the beige walls absorbed her call.

She walked back the way she'd been led in, past weathered wood signs burned with the names of the rooms. Lake Mille Lacs. Lake of the Woods. Open doors gave her views of glass cases, a wild rice exhibit, and a birch bark canoe hanging from the ceiling.

Feeling like an early explorer, she went straight at Mississippi River instead of turning toward the reception area. She took a left at Sauk River and discovered Lake Superior. A poster on the closed double doors still indicated it held the student competition.

Cassie knew she shouldn't go in. She really shouldn't. The room was probably locked anyway.

The fake barn stood two stories tall. Rain driven into the building through a faulty roof would have flooded the room above before dripping into Superior. A leaky pipe between the floors must be the real culprit. The necklace was probably buried under a collapsed ceiling.

Yes, that's what had happened. The precious item would be swept out with the debris unless she, Cassie Windom, rescuer of art and defender of culture, rushed in right now and saved it.

Okay, that seemed unlikely. Still, she could use the possibility as an excuse.

Cassie put gentle pressure on one of the doors. To her surprise, it gave way. The lights were on but no one occupied the room. She swung the panel open, so it wouldn't look like she was sneaking around. Which she was, but she'd pretend that she wasn't.

Movable cabinets rested at odd angles. Empty hooks hung from display boards jumbled against the back wall beside the fire exit. Her footsteps echoed hollowly on a bare floor, clear of any rubble that might hide a lost item. The wooden slates under her feet weren't exactly level, but they hadn't buckled from moisture. Cheap acoustic tiles formed the ceiling. Yellowed with age, they were unmarred by scalloped water stains. The walls, painted the same mushroom shade as the Itasca Room and everything else, showed scrapes and scratches, but no damage.

Cassie saw no reason to move an entire exhibit. She went back out into the hallway, knowing she was about to stir up trouble.

Well, it wouldn't be the first time.

Chapter Fifteen

"Hey!" A young man in a polo shirt approached Cassie. A smear below the museum logo might be pizza. A name tag identified him as Mitch. "If you're looking for the art competition, it's in the Itasca Room."

"Why was it moved?" Cassie asked.

"Uh, you know, water leak."

Cassie guessed his chin-length brownish hair was slicked behind his ears as a mandate from Martin and not his usual style. "That's awful," she said, as if she hadn't already heard that explanation. "I hope no artwork was damaged."

He pressed his lips together and crinkled his eyes as if preparing to break the tragic news that her pet iguana had been squashed by a scooter. "A few pieces were, ah, lost."

Cassie felt a chuckle buried under his deadpan tone. Was he happy the museum had suffered a setback? "Do you like being a guide here?"

"Love it," Mitch said with the same skewed sincerity, confirming this was a summer job and not a career choice. He flashed a grin. "Itasca is"—he pointed his index fingers at the ceiling and spun his hands in circles, as if selecting from a dozen possible routes, then aimed down the hall Cassie had come from while shifting his shoulders the opposite direction in an exaggerated dance pose—"that a way."

Cassie forced herself to return his smile. The move was not as cute and charming as he probably thought it was. "You're the professional." She retraced her steps, glad the guide wasn't dedicated enough to escort her.

Martin stood beside the Itasca sign, checking his watch. "We've been looking for you." She guessed "we" meant that he'd sent the guide to find her while he stood in one spot tapping his foot. "The other judges arrived some time ago."

She'd only been gone a few minutes, so that couldn't be true. It seemed the director didn't like her wandering around on her own, and he was no longer grateful for the presence of a famous person, who could be off somewhere else, doing something more famous than volunteering her famously valuable time at a tiny county museum. "I have questions for you, and the other judges will want to hear the answers too." She wove through boisterous Wildstone visitors, thinking Martin better be following her.

"Hey, this one's mine," a boy yelled. "Come look!" He motioned for his camping mates to gather around a spot at one of the display cases.

Cassie caught the gesture in her peripheral vision. She looked down, so she wouldn't accidentally see the item and connect it to the young man. The glass door to the conference room stood open. Had the other judges glanced into the exhibit hall at the shout, tainting their decision-making? Cassie squeezed into the overly furnished room, shuffling sideways around the table.

Martin entered behind her and shut the door.

Scarf, the woman from the boat and the grocery store, thrust out a hand. "Mel Moreau. Just call me Mel." This time a single band of silky cloth swimming with orange koi held back her long gray braid. "I'm sorry we didn't have a chance to meet properly yesterday."

"Cassie Windom. Cassie."

The woman turned to the other judges. "We went sketching with Trevor's group."

Cassie sucked in a breath, fearing her new acquaintance would describe the tragedy on the island. She didn't dare look at Martin.

Mel shrugged. "But it rained."

Cassie exhaled, but didn't relax. Until the tale of their trip to Wolf Haunt became public, Mel had her locked into a secret. As much as she admired the woman's spunk when standing up to the town's Gossip Queen. Cassie wasn't sure she wanted that bond. She quickly shifted the conversation. "I've seen you at the Falls Market."

"In the produce section, I suppose," Mel said, "where Aileen Finster calls out the sinners. But don't lump me in with her poodle-permed, blue-haired disciples. I hang around the edges so I can throw darts at their balloons and let out the hot air."

Martin introduced the other two judges. A reddish tint to his curly beard, Graham Anderson looked as if he could cosplay one of the fur trappers in the photo at the museum's entrance. He might or might not be a member of the family that donated land for the museum. Cassie guessed he was mid-fifties and that he probably came up to her shoulder.

Sutton Graywind didn't match her stature either. She hated that she noticed a man's height right away. She blamed the hyperawareness on too many short-guys who'd asked her out then dumped cold water on the flame of romance by telling her to wear flats.

The trim of Graywind's thick, dark hair balanced bold features worthy of being chiseled into the side of a mountain. His tailored linen jacket emphasized the results of a regular exercise routine. Was the suit a knockoff, or were the man's initials embroidered on the inside label along with the name of an Italian designer?

"Please call me Sutton," he said, shaking her hand.

Cassie was glad to do that. Thirtyish, with manners, good looks, and a keen fashion sense, he was a surprise. He seemed more like a banker than an artist. Maybe money was his day job and art was his side gig.

But then, what did an artist look like? Mel didn't have paintbrushes tangled in her braid, but she seemed very creatively chic in her flowing scarf and peasant blouse. Graham wore splotches of periwinkle blue on his black t-shirt. Cassie wondered if the smears were there on purpose to advertise his craft.

Did the others think *she* fit the role? She plopped into a high-back chair and addressed Martin. "Why was the exhibit moved to a room with inadequate space and poor lighting?" She resisted adding a comment about the ugly flooring she'd noticed.

"As I previously explained," Martin said, "we experienced water damage. It seemed prudent to move the exhibit. This was the best we could manage on short notice."

Cassie held out her tablet. A photo of the necklace she'd searched for filled the screen. "Why is this item missing from the exhibit?"

"Oh." Martin inhaled as if he couldn't gulp in enough air, looking very much like the gaping fish figurine. "Well, that is, my apologies, I realize that I should have told you. We may have had a small robbery."

Chapter Sixteen

"So there's nothing wrong with the building," Graham said.

"Only the usual things," Martin said. "Most of the rooms need paint. The security system hasn't been upgraded since— well, I don't know when."

"Before 2003?" Cassie suggested.

"Most definitely," Martin said. "The inventory system is just as antiquated. And there's a gigantic elusive spider that thinks it owns the basement."

"You lied about why the exhibit was moved," Mel said.

Martin winced. "I wouldn't put it so harshly."

"What do you mean, you *may* have had a robbery?" Sutton asked.

"We'd appreciate your not sharing that information." Martin glanced out the glass door at the children wandering through the displays. "We have a full slate of field trips scheduled. We don't want to alarm anyone."

"This necklace is missing." Cassie showed the photo to the other judges, then she shoved the tablet at Martin.

The director pulled back from the screen's glare. "Unfortunately, that appears to be the case. We're doing a full review. So far, it's the only piece we can't locate. The thief must have grabbed whatever was convenient before being scared off."

Maybe spider-zilla jumped out at him, Cassie thought. She could make a sign.

Warning: Protected by Attack Arachnid

"Or the robber broke in to steal that particular item," Graham said. "It's my top pick in the high school category."

"The thief didn't break in exactly," Cassie said to the director. She'd seen the concentration on his face as he'd unlocked the Itasca Room and this conference room. "The thief has the master key, leaving you with a ring of individual ones you don't usually use."

Martin mouthed a few noncommittal syllables, then finally found a sentence. "It does seem to be missing."

"You should have informed the board immediately," Sutton said. "Does Tammara know about this? We need to have a meeting as soon as possible."

Now the banker vibe made sense to Cassie. Sutton Graywind served on the board of directors along with Martin's sister. Cassie bet he made sure the accounts balanced to the penny. He could also be an artist. Photographer? She imagined him slogging through cattails to get the perfect shot of a pair of nesting loons.

Frustration crumbled Martin's professional persona. "This shouldn't have happened. Thieves are supposed to target the Louvre and the Metropolitan. They should be stealing Rembrandts and Vermeers. We serve history. We provide context for the past so people can understand the present. The items we display are significant for their time period. Few of them have monetary worth. Someone put that in jeopardy so they could steal a bauble in a childish summer competition. Probably so an acrylic painting of an action hero or a tasteless, age-inappropriate sculpture would win."

Cassie hoped the curator wouldn't cry. Well, part of her wanted to see him weep for not telling the truth from the beginning. And for not taking responsibility for his own carelessness, which had allowed the theft to happen. And mostly for thinking the creations she could see through the glass door had little significance because the artists hadn't died a century ago.

"It's more than a bauble to the artist who made it." Cassie watched the children from Camp Wildstone dribble out of the exhibit hall, herded by their adult chaperones. Sad that Martin only agreed to showcase student art because it brought bodies past the beaver. She should look away from the boy who lingered behind, but she didn't. He stood with his back to her, blocking her view of the cabinet that cradled his work. Paper clip sculpture or oil painting, it didn't matter. It was his, and the most wonderful thing in the world.

"You believe the necklace was the intended target?" Sutton asked Martin.

"That is the sheriff's assessment," Martin said.

"The artist must be very upset," Mel said.

"Since the student is a minor," Martin said, "we notified the mother."

Coward, Cassie thought. *Forcing the parent to break the crushing news to the teen.*

"The competition is still on, isn't it?" Graham asked.

"Of course." Martin opened the door, preparing to escape.

"Let's do the high school level first," Graham said, "so we can deal with the necklace right away."

Martin paused. "As I informed the student's mother, the rules require the physical presence of the artwork. Therefore, the necklace is no longer an entry."

"I need to see those rules." Cassie wondered if they existed.

Martin left, closing the door behind him without responding. Cassie, wedged between the massive table and the heavy chair unable to move either piece of furniture, felt helpless watching him rush off. She pulled her long legs under her and stood on the wooden seat. Grateful for the room's high ceiling, she stepped onto the table. Two strides took her to the door. If she'd been a superhero, she would have smashed through the glass. Since she was an ordinary person with an aversion to getting sliced to ribbons by pointy shards, and with sympathy for whoever would have to sweep up (superheroes never think about the mess), she scrambled down and swung open the door like a civilized person who'd always had to clean up after herself.

"It isn't fair!"

Cassie heard her own thoughts shouted from the hallway. She dodged around displays and into the corridor.

"Look!" A girl of high school age shoved a phone in Martin's face, her brown curls bobbing around her oval face. "Here it is. It's not my fault your security system is as old as you are."

"You're the artist who made the beautiful necklace?" Cassie asked. A little flattery never hurt. She'd often used the strategy to deescalate a tense situation. In this case it was the truth.

"Are you with this bullshit place?" The girl clutched her phone to her chest.

"I'm one of the judges for the art competition." Cassie used the calm, reassuring tone she'd developed for dealing with irate clients. The one that conveyed to Mr. VP in Charge of Marketing for a multimillion-dollar corporation that everything was going according to plan, and the new advertising campaign would come in on time and under budget. Which, of course, it wasn't and it wouldn't.

"You can't disqualify me because my entry was stolen," the girl said. "I shouldn't be punished for what someone else did." She thrust her phone at Cassie. "Look! The thief is wearing it! Right out in public."

A video jerked across the screen showing a dark-hair girl ducking away from the camera, her hand raised to block the aggressive photographer. "It belongs to me!" she shouted. Cassie caught a glimpse of dark eyes, bright lipstick, and a necklace dangling with bronze beads. "Give it back!" screeched the angry voice of the person doing the recording each time the scene played in a loop.

The girl standing in front of Cassie paused the video. "I took this three whole days ago and gave a copy to Sheriff Wells right away. She's probably being arrested right now. As soon as I get my necklace back, I'll bring it straight here."

Cassie didn't want to tell the girl that it wasn't as simple as tossing fairy dust in the air and wishing really hard. From experience, she knew that law enforcement and the legal system rarely worked quickly or ran smoothly. But since the museum was at fault for not keeping the necklace safe, the girl deserved special consideration. "The judges will need to discuss it." Cassie hoped to give the impression that they were a large group with many opinions. "I'm sure Mr. Brighton can guide us through."

Martin tugged at his jacket and blinked as if emerging from cold water. "This has never happened before. It's supposed to be a blind judging, but now the two of you have interacted. It's completely unprecedented."

"I'm sure we can work it out," Cassie said.

"Perhaps." Martin might be calculating the difficulty of getting a replacement judge. If he axed Cassie, he'd have to lure a stranger off the street with the promise of bad coffee and stale donuts (only so far there hadn't been so much as a half cup of brownish water and a paper plate of day-old crumbs).

"I'll have to consult the rules." Martin scurried off.

Cassie still wanted to see those. She smiled at his retreating back, glad he'd found an excuse to flee so she could talk to the girl.

"I'm Cassie Windom." If she got deposed from her lofty position as judge for introducing herself to an almost-contestant, she might be able to convince the rest of the committee (all three of them) to refer to the notes she'd made before she knew about the theft.

"Mariah Lund."

"I'm sorry your necklace was stolen. Why does that other girl say it belongs to her?"

"Because she's glue-huffing crazy. *I* designed it, and *I* made it. Just ask Trevor."

"Trevor Rothman?" The guy who woke up this morning, tracked down Cassie's phone number, and suddenly asked her to join his group's trip to an island with a dead body?

"Yeah, he was my teacher. I only took the class so I could enter the contest. My necklace turned out so totally great. Trevor has all these jewelry-making tools. I don't have any of my own. I told him about this girl and asked him to help me, but he said the police had to handle it."

"What medium do you usually work in?" Cassie asked.

"Pencil, mostly, because I can sketch anywhere. I don't have much space at home. I do paintings when I can. But I definitely want to concentrate on wearable art." Mariah sagged. "Look, I know this isn't an important competition, like at a big institute. It's just a little county thing—no offense, you being a judge—but it's important to me. The *Falls Press* loves stuff like this. They do a huge spread on the winners that I could show people. You know, that I'm an artist. Then people couldn't say that I'm not."

Cassie wondered who those people were. Her peers? Parents? Admission directors at art schools?

"I *can't* be disqualified," Mariah said. "This is the best

piece I've ever done. And it's way better than any of that other stuff." She flung a hand in the direction of the exhibit hall. "I know I'm not supposed to say that, but it's true. I've worked at my art since I was a kid. Really worked at it. People don't see that. They pat me on the head and tell me I have a nice hobby."

Cassie knew what that felt like. Even though she'd been employed at a prestigious advertising agency, some relatives kept expecting her to get a real profession instead of doodling all day. Which meant they didn't understand advertising. And they definitely didn't understand the value of doodling. She'd gotten some of her best ideas letting her pencil roam freely.

"I was trying to get Mr. Brighton to let me talk to you," Mariah said. "All of the judges, I mean. So I can tell you what happened, and that it isn't fair, and that all you have to do is wait until the sheriff gets the necklace back."

Cassie wasn't so sure that would be enough to sway the other judges. Still, the girl should be given a chance to plead her case.

"I have a suggestion." Looking at the earnest young face, Cassie had to admit she felt far from impartial. "The blind judging part is important, so it's best if you don't meet any of the others. Instead, write a letter to the committee explaining the circumstances. Ask them to delay making a decision about the high school category until your necklace is recovered. We're meeting right now, so you have to do it immediately. Do you have paper?"

Mariah patted the backpack hanging from a shoulder. "I have a notebook."

"Keep it short and to the point," Cassie said. "Don't sign it with your name. Use 'Artist of HS24.' As soon as you get it done, give it to Mr. Brighton and tell him the judges are expecting it."

Mariah nodded. "Okay." She sat on the hallway floor, leaned up against the wall, and dug into her pack.

Cassie checked her watch and went back to the conference room.

"What was the excitement?" Graham asked. The man could have seen it for himself, but he'd stayed safely tucked away from the action.

"It was nothing," Cassie said.

Graham grabbed the scoring sheets, apparently thinking he was in charge. "This shouldn't take very long. We can start by narrowing down our selections from the photographs. Now, for the high school entries—"

"Starting with the elementary group will be much more fun," Cassie said. She gave Mel an amiable smile, hoping to make use of their secret, decoder-ring bond.

Mel seemed to get the message. "I agree. There's a fanciful beanbaggy frog I'd like us to consider. Entry E44. I find it whimsical and absolutely charming." She placed her phone on the table. The screen showed a squatting green amphibian with a lopsided head and protruding tongue.

Sutton winced. "I hope we can agree quickly. This has already taken longer than I expected. I have to get back to the Star soon."

That would be the Blazing Star, Cassie realized, the casino on the edge of Sunset. She was right about his connection to money and sorry she planned to keep him from his job for some time. She put her tablet beside the phone. "I'd like to add this lizard as a top contender. E37." An elongated tube painted black and blotched with yellow filled the rectangle. Two toothpicks stuck out of each side.

"Are you sure it's a lizard?" Graham asked. "I thought it was a garter snake with stabilizers."

Cassie put her hand over her watch, wondering how long she'd have to stall.

Chapter Seventeen

Cassie pushed open the museum door to a blast of summer heat, disappointed by the results of the art competition. The other judges had failed to appreciate the rebellious disregard for line and structure in the lizard/snake she'd advocated for. Instead, the frog had won at the elementary level, its anatomically incorrect tongue jutting out as if to comment on the honor.

In the middle school group, a tween-angst painting of an empty boat floating on a bleak river edged out a giraffe composed of yarn and seeds, and a pencil drawing of either a very round cat or a jack-o-lantern with ears, depending on how you looked at it.

For the high school category—

Mariah slumped on a bench beside a bed of native cone flowers. Cassie walked over, feeling obligated to give her an update. The girl jumped to her feet. "Please say I'm in. Please, please."

"You wrote a very persuasive letter," Cassie said. "The committee voted to consult with the sheriff's office before deciding."

The girl clenched her face in frustration. "So they didn't

totally agree to wait until I get my necklace back. You told them how important this is, right?"

"Mariah, when Mr. Brighton brought in your letter, I explained to the other judges that I'd suggested you write it. Since I know who you are, I had to let them deal with it." She'd wanted to speak on the girl's behalf, but that might have put the validity of the entire event in jeopardy. It would be a shame if the frog's creator lost out on a ribbon because Cassie had inappropriately advocated for Mariah.

Staying out of the discussion had been hard. Cassie had plenty of practice keeping her opinions to herself, but that didn't mean she was good at it. Martin had added his own biased commentary as he'd relayed a summary of the girl's handwritten plea. Cassie had wrenched the sheet from his grasp and given it to Graham to read out loud.

She was proud of Mariah for keeping her message on a single page. In contrast, the rules governing the competition spread across multiple sheets in tiny print. Cassie had a copy tucked in her bag. She suspected she would be the only judge to actually study the regulations.

"Fair and impartial sucks," Mariah said.

In this case Cassie silently agreed. "I know it isn't the complete victory you'd hoped for, but the necklace wasn't disqualified. It's still technically in the competition."

"I guess. Thanks anyway." Mariah hefted her backpack from the bench and hoisted it onto a shoulder. "I didn't even know she existed before this. And she doesn't know me or anything about me, but she threatened to expose me on some podcast, like *I'm* the criminal. She's destroying my whole life. And she isn't even from here. She goes to Glacier High."

Cassie had thought of the thief as a classmate of Mariah's, someone from Sunset. Her mind flashed to the dark-haired girl in the video, face partially obscured, lips like bright red flares. Cassie braced herself. "What's her name?"

"Kaitlyn Hanson," Mariah said as if swearing.

The air thickened, too heavy to breathe. Cassie swiped at her clammy forehead. She heard the plop, plop of fat drops against a tarp. Could see black locks shimmer in the mud.

Boomer's voice whispered, *Kaitlyn Hanson.*

"Please don't faint, please don't faint, please don't faint." It wasn't Boomer's voice begging her. Cassie took a few wobbly steps.

"Sit! Please, please, please."

Cassie felt a shove, and landed on a slated seat.

"Drink this."

A papery box pressed against her palm. She found the straw, and followed orders. The liquid glided down her throat, sharply sour with a sweet aftertaste.

"Cran-grape." It was Mariah who spoke to her. Her co-conspirator in the fight for justice. "Sorry, I already drank out of it, but I don't have any germs."

Cassie took a few ragged breaths. "It's okay. I'm just—"

"OMG, you're pregnant," Mariah shouted. "I'll call an ambulance."

"No." Cassie put a hand on the lit rectangle that already showed a nine. "Don't call anyone. I am *not* pregnant. I'm not. Just shocked."

"Shit shit shit," Mariah said. "You know her. She's your cousin or neighbor or something. I shouldn't have blurted it out like that."

"I don't know her, but I know who she is," Cassie choked out. "I can't explain right now." She'd promised, as a newly deputized member of the Sheriff's Posse, that she'd stay quiet about the gruesome scene on Wolf Haunt.

As if her thought had conjured it, a county cruiser pulled up to the curb. Sheriff Wells eased his considerable bulk out the door and sauntered over to them as if out for a Sunday stroll.

"Ms. Windom, you seem to show up everywhere. It's like you've got a bunch of twins."

Afraid of what was to come, Cassie gripped the juice box, on the verge of crushing the flimsy container.

Wells raised his thin eyebrows at the girl. "Are you Mariah Lund?"

"You know who I am, Sheriff. I talked to you and Officer Olson at the station." Mariah's face glowed as if anticipating good news. "You arrested Kaitlyn Hanson, right? You got my necklace back!"

"There's been a complication in the case," Wells said. "I'm hoping you can help us out. I need you to come in and provide more information."

Mariah's shoulders drooped with disappointment. She crammed her phone into her backpack. "Sure, but I don't know what else I can tell you. Okay if I stop by in about an hour?"

"Thing is," Wells said, "I need you to come with me right now."

"I can't," Mariah said. "That's way over in Glacier. I'll have to drive my mom to work so I can use the car."

"I'll be providing your transportation," Wells said.

"She has a right to know why she's being arrested," Cassie blurted out.

"Arrested!" Mariah shouted.

"Not arrested," Wells said slowly. "We just have to get some things straightened out. That's all."

Cassie shot up from the bench and pushed close to the sheriff. Two inches taller, even with the lifts the man wore in his shoes, she pulled herself up straight and looked down her nose at him. "Tell her."

"Ms. Windom, are you trying to intimidate an officer of the law? Because if you are, then you and Ms. Lund are both getting a ride at the taxpayers' expense in my cruiser."

Cassie gave him a smile. "Of course not, Sheriff." Without giving up her invasion of the man's personal space, she turned to Mariah. "Kaitlyn Hanson is dead, and you need a lawyer."

Mariah clutched her backpack. Her eyes darted to the Granite County Historical Society sign, then to the building's framed entrance. "Sanctuary!" she shouted, dashing toward the glass door. "Sanctuary!"

"Mariah!" Cassie reached out in a useless gesture, juice box in her hand, just as Wells lurched after the girl. The two collided. A geyser of cran-grape shot skyward. Gravity caught the liquid, wrenching it back to earth. Burgundy blooms pelted the sheriff's thinning hair. Droplets speckled his military-creased khaki shirt.

Undeterred by the sticky trickle heading for his nose, Wells plowed Cassie aside in pursuit of the fleeing suspect.

Cassie tossed the empty box into a nearby bin. She shook ruby drops from her hand and rubbed her stinging wrist, wondering if she was about to be arrested for assaulting an officer of the law. The Mini, bright as a sunflower, sat a short sprint away, but she couldn't abandon Mariah. She sat down on the bench and waited.

Later, as the cruiser rolled toward the Granite County Sheriff's Office, never exceeding the posted speed limit, Cassie calmly explain to Mariah that churches could provide protection to suspected criminals, but county museums could not. Although deeply worried about the girl, she wasn't bothered by the handcuffs, metal grill, and sporadic radio chatter.

It wasn't her first time in the back of a patrol car.

Chapter Eighteen

Celebrate your day with SunnieChat!

I got arrested.

ASHLEY

Really arrested or Officer Adam with handcuffs arrested?

Really. By Wells. Obstruction of justice.

HOLLY

Do you have a lawyer? Are you out on bail?

ASHLEY

Not the first family member to be a guest at the Glacier County jail. Did you find Rob and Cliff's initials carved in the wall?

Charges were dropped. It was a mishap involving a juice box and the sheriff's uniform.

KAYLA

Adding to my list of what I miss while being on a boat. Strawberry banana juice box.

Danith McPherson

ASHLEY

No jury will convict you. We've all been drenched by the dreaded juice box. Not that I'm blaming my lovely nieces and nephew.

HOLLY

I've given up trying to get out the stains. I just soak the entire garment in juice and pretend that was the original color. In our next Christmas card photo we'll be wearing matching grapeberry shirts.

Chapter Nineteen

Cassie leaned back into the seat of the Ford Expedition, massaging her left arm. "It's his own fault. The sheriff crashed into *me*. My wrist still aches. I don't think I can hold a pencil. I may have to sue for lost income."

"You're right-handed." Adam pulled onto the two-lane state highway, aiming the vehicle toward Sunset. The town, not the daily event.

Cassie hated that he acted all stoic. She'd endured a traumatic day that had left her stranded at the sheriff's department in Glacier Falls while her beloved Mini Cooper sat sad and alone in the museum parking lot. She didn't want the man next to her to be Deputy Berger. She wanted almost-boyfriend Adam beside her so she could rant and shake her fist at the sky (that would be her right fist).

She would not apologize for blurting out that Kaitlyn was dead, and for telling Mariah to get a lawyer. Or for confronting Wells. "I suppose this means I'm kicked off the Sheriff's Posse."

"No certificate for you." Adam kept his eyes on the road as if the lone car coming from the other direction deserved his full attention.

"Is this really Rhonda's car? It's huge."

"Mostly she uses it off-road. Hunting and hauling. She needed my cruiser for official business." Adam gave a little smile. "If you like, we can stow the Mini in the back, and I can drive you both home."

A chink had just popped out of Adam's defensive armor. Cassie felt a dab of frustration waft away. Well, maybe two dabs. But definitely not as much as a swatch. "Don't go making fun of the Cooper."

"Wouldn't think of it."

"I hope Mariah will be okay." The girl's mother had arrived at the station. Cassie wished she could have talked to her, cautioned her, repeated the need for legal counsel.

"Mariah has a motive," Adam said. "In her own video she behaved aggressively toward the victim."

"So she gave an incriminating video to the police, then ran out and committed the murder?"

"I'm not saying it's logical. I'm just suggesting you keep a healthy distance."

"My sugar addiction and sudden cravings for red licorice are well documented. Healthy is not built into my lifestyle."

Adam smoothly parked the SUV an empty space away from the Mini Cooper. "Answer me honestly. Do you think Mariah killed Kaitlyn?"

"Honestly," Cassie said, "I just met her today. She talked about expecting Kaitlyn to be arrested and hoping to get her necklace back. When I told her Kaitlyn was dead, she seemed genuinely horrified. Although, if I were the killer in the same situation—" Cassie halted, on the verge of confessing *I would gasp in astonishment and you'd never know I was faking*. She changed course. It was better if Adam stayed clueless about her acting talent, especially in relation to gasping and faking. "Well, I suppose I would try to look surprised."

One arm draped over the steering wheel, Adam shifted in the wide bucket seat to face her. "It's good that you haven't made up your mind. You have to stay in that place of not knowing."

Place of not knowing? Cassie lived in a damn *palace* of it. She'd thought it was over when the verdict was read at Jordan's trial.

Guilty.

She'd imagined the word scratched onto an iron ball he'd wear chained to his ankle for eternity. But Jordan's attorney had immediately filed an appeal.

Each thick white envelope that arrived in the mail from the man who killed her best friend seemed heavier than the last as she carried it from the mailbox and placed it— unopened, unread—into the plastic bin in the basement.

Jordan might stay in a prison cell forever, or he might be released without her knowing it. He could be walking along the beach this moment, enjoying the California sun; or he could be stalking her, stealing chocolate from her deck.

Jordan: convicted but maybe not, a variation of Schrodinger's cat.

Cassie didn't know how to express any of that to Adam. Instead she said, "I don't like unsolved puzzles."

"You can't be the one who does the solving," Adam said. "Not this time. The drawing you made of that painted rock is evidence. When the case goes to trial—whoever is charged, Mariah or a serial killer or someone else—there can't be any question about its accuracy. If you insert yourself into this girl's life, anything you touch will be worthless for prosecution or for defense. You have to stay away from her and any other suspects."

"Got it."

"You're going to leave investigating to law enforcement."

"Absolutely."

"For real."

"Promise." In her head Cassie adjusted that to "promise to

publicly stay neutral." No one could blame her for privately speculating and maybe poking around a bit.

She wished Adam hadn't said serial killer. Now the image of an axe-wielding maniac was in her head. She'd be sleeping with the windows closed and locked, when she'd rather have fresh air sweeping through the cabin.

Actually, since the missing chocolate, she'd done a lot more closing and locking, treating her home more like a vault.

"Can we get the finished drawing from you soon?" Adam asked, as if it moved them into less tense territory, which it didn't.

"It's drying, and I need to clean it up. Sorry, but I've been busy judging what's left of an art competition that was burgled. And trying to help a young artist-slash-murder-suspect, which I've now been warned not to. Oh, and getting arrested took up a chunk of time."

"A typical day, then."

"Pretty much." She doubted the rock contained a coded confession from the killer, but that was for the experts to determine. "I'll do a digital version and send you the file."

"We'll also need the original. The sheriff is a paper kind of guy."

Should she confess she'd stealthily sketched impressions in the ground beside the body? That drawing might prove valuable. Or not. Either way, Adam didn't have to know about it right now. Maybe never.

He leaned toward her, supporting himself with a hand on the console between them. "You'll keep this quiet, right?"

"I'm sworn to secrecy as a member of the posse."

Adam barely smiled. "I'm worried about how Father Anderson and Reverend Gunther might react to the markings on the stone. Nothing raises Sunday attendance like Satanic Panic. They'll be giving sermons on the evils of beheading chickens and chanting prayers backwards."

Cassie leaned toward Adam. "Then there'll be a letter to the editor saying the town's under a coven's spell."

Adam grinned. "Mrs. Finster will swear she saw a hooded figure walking down the street at midnight swinging a burning sword."

"Mayor Bob will want to do an exorcism at the county courthouse."

Adam moved closer, tilting his head. Cassie closed her eyes as his lips press against hers, welcoming the soft kiss.

Adam jerked back.

"Seriously?" Cassie said. "You're leaving me hanging mid-pucker?"

"Sorry, I shouldn't have done that. The kiss, I mean. It was unprofessional."

"It's not like we're in a county car with your badge number on the hood. This is Rhonda's private property. And no one can see us." Cassie wasn't sure that was true. How much protection did the smoky tint on the large windows provide? Rhonda wouldn't object. In fact, Cassie was certain their friend would be pleased in an annoyingly smug way. The roomy vehicle had probably been the site of a lot more action than a single smooch.

"I'm in uniform," Adam said.

"That's not a permanent condition. It does come off, right? Metaphorically speaking," she added, not wanting him to think she was suggesting he strip out of his khakis to his well-toned body right here in the Expedition. Although she wasn't opposed to it.

"Not tonight. I have to interview a grieving father." He studied the Ducks Unlimited decal stuck to the dashboard. "About hysteria over the figures on the stone, that wasn't just speculation. It could happen."

"I hope they don't get around to witch-burning." Cassie opened the door and got out. "I better go home and hide my black candles."

Chapter Twenty

A package leaned against the critter-proof bin. Someone wanted to make sure Cassie saw it as soon as she got home. She was lucky to rescue it before tennis-ball-stealing Kevin the Squirrel got his paws on it.

Or was she?

The creepy symbols adorning the Wolf Haunt stone had danced through her head on the drive back from the museum, filling her with an eerie chill.

She unlocked the cabin door and let Jupiter out. The puppy celebrated her return by charging across the lawn to attack a squeaky toy shaped like a pig.

Cassie folded her arms against her chest and crouched down to examine the box. The familiar return address indicated it came from AweMazing Chocolates, her favorite client. The label plastered across the plain cardboard assured Cassie the package had been sent via the usual delivery service. But she hadn't gotten any recent messages marking its path to her door. No greetings from the driver or thank-you for keeping Jupiter inside.

Was this the shipment of chocolate-covered strawberries she should have received days ago?

She should be elated.

She should rush into the kitchen with the treasure, tear off the wrappings, and shove her face into the delights the chocolatier had sent her as a reward for her fabulous artwork that was sure to make his company famous!

But she wasn't elated.

And she didn't rush.

Crunched corners showed the trek to her deck had included rough handling. She cautiously ran her finger over wrinkles in tan strips holding the top flaps closed. The sticky substance seemed wrong, different from standard packaging. She tugged at an edge, curling back the masking tape to reveal a clear layer below it. The wider, stiffer sealant was split where the two flaps met.

The package had been opened, then resealed. Possibly by a sadistic chainsaw murderer with a sweet tooth.

Or a pseudo-Satanists who roamed the county painting rocks and delivering decapitated Kevins to select residents. If so, she hoped Mrs. Finster got one.

On second thought, no, she didn't. That would be too good a story for the woman to spread. One true event with a carcass to back it up would give power to the string of innuendoes, misinformation and outright lies the gossipy woman usually spewed.

Jupiter bounded onto the deck, dropped his toy, and sank onto the boards, waiting for her to take up the squeaky-pig challenge.

She tapped the cardboard. "Jupiter, earn your bacon treat."

The puppy gave a sniff from his prone position. With one finger, Cassie slid it closer to his fuzzy face. Jupiter sniffed again. Finding nothing interesting in this game, he got up and gave a shake, sending tufts of fur flying like dandelion fluff. He snatched the pig, giving it a noisy chomp as if he'd won, and ran down the stairs into the yard.

No dead critter.

Maybe the porch pirate had a chocolate allergy and a guilty conscience.

Or maybe a neighbor with a grudge had a bomb-building podcast.

Feeling both foolish and brave, Cassie carefully carried the brown carton and its unknown cargo down the stairs. She set it in the grass, turned on the outside faucet, and unrolled a length of garden hose. From a distance she sent a frigid shower of well water sputtering onto the container. The cardboard darkened as the liquid soaked in. The flaps sagged and pulled free from the masking tape.

Almost sure it was too drowned to explode, Cassie changed the sprayer head setting to "jet." Feeling like a powerful warrior, she blasted the container, caving in the sides.

She turned off the hose and stalked to the dripping mess. She peeled back the soggy wrappings to reveal an inner rectangle smeared with what was left of her beautiful logo design.

The cover fell to bits as she lifted it. She picked away matted lavender and pink tissue paper that should be concealing a tray of cocoa mounds.

A single brown lump sat desolate and mushy in the crumpled pastel nest.

A shredded whitish blob curled beside the lone swelling, like a gas station receipt that had gone through the washing machine in the pocket of her favorite black pants. Cassie poked, exposing smeared ink. A note. Probably from the chocolatier, praising her work. The present should have been a celebration, a reward, appreciation for her talent.

The sadistic porch pirate had taken that from her, then made sure she knew what she'd lost by leaving one inedible morsel.

Cassie took the dripping package to the garage. She shoved it into a trash bag, securing the plastic with a zip tie. If the next delivery blew up her kitchen or held a Kevin carcass, she wanted evidence of a pattern of harassment.

Document, document, document. Keep a record of every event. That's what she'd helped Vicky do. Every threatening text, every screaming phone call, every twisted "gift."

Cassie's legs suddenly wouldn't hold her. Jordan's face flashed through her mind, not the confident mask from before the murder, but the raw, sharp features she'd seen when she'd visited him in prison as he'd railed at her that Vicky's death was her fault.

She leaned on the workbench and forced slow breaths. He was halfway across the continent, locked behind high walls. He couldn't have tampered with the package. He couldn't touch her here.

But he did. Through his appeal that kept the case active. Through the media that wouldn't let go of a juicy story. Through those damn letters he sent her.

And where was Vicky when she needed her?

Cassie regained her balance. She shoved the bag onto a shelf next to a set of jumper cables.

Don't leave me alone, she silently told her friend. *Not yet.*

Sunny SunnieChat Day!

Schrodinger. I hate that paradox.

KAYLA

The theory wouldn't work with a dog in the box. A dog would bark so you'd know it was alive.

HOLLY

If it sounded like a Rottweiler, I'd never open the box.

ASHLEY

Which is worse? Lifting the lid and discovering a cat corpse, or finding an angry living cat who'd pooped all over the interior without the benefit of litter?

Cat corpse

KAYLA

Angry poop cat

HOLLY

Either way, someone has to clean up the mess.

KAYLA

That would be Schrodinger's mom.

HOLLY

Promise me you'll never mention this theory to my kids.

Chapter Twenty-One

T**ime for a SunnieChat!**

ASHLEY

Here's a picture of your new niece or nephew. Please don't say it's cute or adorable. It looks like a staticky transmission of an alien blob floating in a snowstorm.

HOLLY

How are you feeling?

ASHLEY

Barfing every morning. Zach treats me like I'm made of glass. He's talking about getting married.

HOLLY

To you?

ASHLEY

Is there a smartass emoji? Insert here.

Do you want to marry Zach again?

ASHLEY

I don't want to divorce him again.

> That's different from not wanting to get married.

ASHLEY

I want everything to be okay. It doesn't have to be perfect. Just okay.

HOLLY

I appreciate calm and dull.

> I'll make greeting cards. Wishing you a boring day. No exclamation marks.

KAYLA

You can't stop me from using !!!!! and being excited about my new niece/nephew who is definitely cute!

> And adorable! Despite the static and snow.

KAYLA

Baby presents for my alien niece/nephew in the womb: upgraded wifi, stocking cap, parka.

Cassie printed the ultrasound image Ashley had sent her. Did it look okay? Did it seem different from the first images of Holly's pregnancies? Was there more fuzz, less shape?

It reminded her of gazing through her telescope at Jupiter (the planet, not the puppy) and seeing the swirling Great Red Spot, which she'd only managed to catch once. She'd tried to sort out the currents, which looked so clear on the glossy photograph in the astronomy magazine she subscribed to. But through the eyepiece the details she craved eluded her, as they did on the ultrasound.

She worried every minute. Her sister had suffered through a series of miscarriages. Several times Ashley would have died if she hadn't gotten the medical care she'd needed.

Cassie propped the portrait of her niece/nephew against her Scooby Doo plushy. She read the text from Adam, reminding her to bring the sketch to the VFW/sheriff's office ASAP. Or should he send a patrol car to pick it up? And she needed to make a formal statement.

If he'd volunteered to collect the drawing himself and interview her at her kitchen table, she would have answered right away, but he hadn't. So she didn't.

She understood the pressure the department was getting to solve the murder, but it was only Friday. The vellum had air dried nicely. She sharpening the lines of the images drawn on the stone, only slightly defying Wells's order not to embellish.

Unsatisfied, she set the paper aside and went to her tablet. She opened the photo of the rock she'd taken while Boomer was distracted by his own monologue. The muted light of the stormy day had challenged her older phone's camera, but the pic provided color, which her pencil sketch did not.

Spots of cardinal showed through the current coat of cayenne paint. The artist had mistakenly thought the rough surface would make a good canvas for felt-tipped pens. The black, or maybe dark blue, forms were easier to pick out against the pepper-red background than the shapes that might have started out as leaf green and lemon yellow.

Using her favorite software, Cassie added a new layer to the photograph so she could draw on the image with her stylus without impacting the original.

She let raw impressions guide her, outlining each figure in black as if it were a cartoon.

A telephone pole. Dripping tears. A head sprouting triangular horns. An oval blob supported by four sticks with a scythe protruding from one end. Maybe a bird perched on a stack of progressively smaller tires or soft-serve ice cream. A kidney bean wearing a hat. Smudges under the tires and the bean could be runes or letters.

Rudimentary drawings, crude composition, questionable

color choices, no establishment of scale. Had it been drawn by a committee? Maybe Trevor had brought his summer students to the island on a field trip and they'd created it as a bonding exercise.

Cassie sat back and stared at the result, expecting a revelation. She should get it now. The message should be clear, if there was a message, which maybe there wasn't. But maybe there was and deciphering it could reveal the killer. Who definitely was not Mariah.

Jupiter bounded into her office. Ears perky, eyes wide in the dark mask that covered his face, he gave her an excited woof, then scampered away. Cassie looked out the window. Dale sauntered around the side of the garage.

Cassie followed the puppy to the kitchen, carrying her tablet and saving the file as she went. On a whim she sent the altered image to her sisters, sure they would provide an abundance of ideas, while not sure any would be useful.

Chapter Twenty-Two

Dale parked the ATV in Cassie's driveway and walked up to the cabin, surveying the yard for the best place to put a kennel for Jupiter. Cassie had texted asking if he wanted the job. He thought it was a good idea. The puppy was getting older, bolder, and more independent. Which meant he only listened to humans when he wanted to. An outdoor space of his own would keep him from running after cars and trying to make friends with a coyote.

"Hey," Dale said to Cassie when she opened the door. Jupiter ran out, did a spin around him, then bounded back in. Dale followed him into the kitchen, bent down, and ruffled the puppy's thick fur. "So, you're going to get your very own kingdom."

"He already thinks he owns the county."

"I hope you're not planning on fencing in the whole yard. I really don't want to dig that many post holes," Dale said, joking but not joking.

"He'll have to settle for something smaller for now." Cassie gestured for him to sit at the table. "Before we map out his domain, I need your thoughts on something else." She sat down and propped her tablet in front of him.

Dale's stomach lurched. He stared at the digital illustration, struggling to keep his face blank as he pulled out a creaky wooden chair that didn't match any of the others and sat opposite her.

Could he bluff his way through? He wasn't very good at keeping things from Cassie. Maybe because she treated him like he was an okay guy. Like he was smart and had opinions. He felt he could lower his deflector shield when it was just the two of them.

But not right now. *Stay chill,* he told himself. *Icy. Arctic.*

"What do you see?" Cassie asked.

He didn't want to see anything, didn't want to recognize anything. But there was the stone, blotched with colored figures.

He'd stick to the basics, to exactly what she asked. That usually worked when his parents quizzed him about where he'd been and what he'd been doing. "It's this rock. On this island. Wolf Haunt."

"You've been there?"

Dale shrugged, trying to be casual. "Yeah. Sometimes there are parties."

"Forget that you've been there."

Dale was glad to do that.

Cassie pulled the tablet away, tilted it so he couldn't see, and tapped on the glass. Then she turned the screen back toward him. "Tell me what you see now."

Dale pretended to examine the lit rectangle. The colors were gone. Black outlines showed only the figures, stark against a white background.

Dale tried to think of a response that would show he wasn't stupid while avoiding the truth. Prehistoric cave paintings. Egyptian hieroglyphics. A child's scrawls. Everything he thought of was more sophisticated than what they really were. "Emojis."

Cassie sat back as if he'd broken a secret code. Then she

tilted her head, studying him. "You knew that before I showed you."

"Well, yeah," Dale stammered.

"Do you know who drew these?"

Shit. Caught in a direct question. Dale could tell the truth, or he could lie. Third option: lateral dodge. It worked in video games when the boss monster attacked. The same move wasn't so easy in conversation. "Does it matter?"

"It would help relieve tension around a—a situation if people knew these were just simple drawings and not signs of a bloodthirsty cult."

Oh, great. An appeal to his civic duty. The *situation* was all over the news. From what Cassie had put in front of him, Dale guessed she had a connection to the investigation that went beyond a deputy sheriff—who was more terrified of dating than Dale was—being wild-crazy for her. "Was Kaitlyn murdered?"

Cassie gave him a level look. "Wells is calling it a suspicious death."

"What are you calling it?"

"A tragedy." Cassie nudged the tablet a little closer to him. "Please tell me this was a hoax and not the work of a cult."

Crap. Cassie was almost as good at this as his mom.

Dale had been horrified that day on the island when Richie pulled a bundle of felt-tips from a pocket in his cargo shorts, picked out the dark blue one, and put a circle in the center of the Wolf Stone.

"You brought markers?" Dale asked. They'd already desecrated the place by digging up poor dead Gizmo. Now they compounded their offense against the Haunt with graffiti.

Richie added pointy ears. "We'll make it scary, so everyone will stay away."

"I don't know about this." Dale couldn't do it. He wouldn't.

Richie added a dagger. "Fuck you to all the ballers who think they own this place. They make up stuff about the Wolf and the stone so they can push around the rest of us. This is *for* the Wolf, dude."

Dale had doubts about the purity of Richie's motivation. And he knew for sure that a stick figure of a cat head wasn't going to protect the island from trespassers. Still—

At his first party on the Haunt he'd stumbled into that stupid boulder and had been forced by jeering jocks to calm the Wolf Spirit by chugging a beer he hadn't wanted. Tradition, he'd been told. All in good fun. Be one of the guys and play along. But Dale had recognized it for what it really was.

Richie shoved a tube of brown ink into Dale's hand. Feeling as if he flipped his middle finger at the bullies, Dale squiggled a poop emoji onto the rock. Giddy, he added more figures to the rough surface and finished it off with his initials.

Then there was the noise he and Richie weren't sure they heard.

And after that, the disappearing shovel.

Now in Cassie's kitchen, Dale considered ways to confess that he'd trespassed on private property, vandalized a famous landmark, and possibly contaminated the environment with toxic ink. "You know how you expect something to go one way and instead it does a one-eighty?"

"Been there," Cassie said.

"We did it a few months ago. It was supposed to be like a warning that the stone's spirit was angry and would make creepy stuff happen unless everyone stayed away."

"I thought kids didn't go there anymore."

"Not so much for parties. Too much stuff to haul and no place to recharge your phone. The island's become more of a photo-op destination." Dale pulled out his cell and opened an app. "At least one guy went there a couple of days after we did the stone. He posted a pic. In less than an hour it was shared over two thousand times. Then things got crazy." He punched at the screen. "I'll show you one of the Haunt's media pages."

"How many does it have?"

"I don't know. Most of them are quack, you know, fake." Dale found a posting on Satan Rocks the Haunt from twenty-three minutes ago. He tilted his phone so Cassie could view the image of skeletal trees bleached white and veiled in mist, their roots sunk into swampy water. He read the caption: "Slammin fog at the isle. Full moon ritual tonight. Be there. Virgins beware."

"Total fraud," Cassie said with mock seriousness. "The King of Hell would know the full moon was days ago."

"And no one says 'slammin' anymore."

"Any real posts from Tuesday night?"

Dale flipped to Faceless at the Haunt, a reliable source for island activity. The most recent additions were dated a week ago. "Nothing."

He showed Cassie an overexposed photo taken in the dark of a hand spread across a red surface. Pointy ears of what was supposed to be a cat's decapitated head that Richie had drawn peeked through a gap in the splayed fingers.

Cassie took the rectangle from him and scrolled the site. "I thought it made the spirit angry if you touched the stone."

Dale wondered how she knew that since she hadn't grown up here. He didn't ask. "It's okay to take a hand shot as long as you don't make contact. And you can't show your face. If you do, you're cursed." He wondered how many curses a guy could collect at one time.

"Cursed how?"

"Usual stuff. Falling off a cliff. Eyeball gouged out. No

evidence outside of Photoshop and a claim that it had happened to a close personal friend." Dale's favorite was the unnamed video gamer who supposedly licked the stone. The next day, bam! His thumb got sliced off and he'll never play *Call of Duty* again. "I figure the no-faces legend got started to keep jocks from taking selfies while holding a beer. Footballers don't understand that underage drinking gets you kicked off the team." He decided not to add that other recreational substances often showed up, sometimes resulting in Jesus cosplay, attempts to walk across the waves back to the mainland.

"I see a watch in this one," Cassie said. "A class ring. Distinctive nail polish. It would be easy to identify most of these kids."

Dale knew the shiny black nails belonged to Bridget. That meant Whiney had been on the island then too. They went everywhere together, like support parakeets.

Cassie gave him back his phone. "Why did you want to scare people away?"

Dale fidgeted. They were at the "digging for treasure and stealing" part. That was a step he didn't want to take, especially since it involved another guy and that guy was Richie. "I just did." Had he said "we" before? He couldn't remember.

Cassie nodded, as if accepting his nonanswer. "Is it okay if I ask you about Kaitlyn?"

"I guess. I've known her since we were kids. I suppose we were friends, the way you are with everyone at school, but she was a senior. We didn't hang in the same tribe." He didn't say that she was a mean-girl bitch most of the time who considered Dale a gum wrapper under her shoe.

Cassie tapped at her tablet. She swiveled the device toward him. "Did you ever see Kaitlyn wearing this?"

Ignoring the beads, Dale's eyes were pulled to the oval as if by a tractor beam. The dirt had been polished away, the leather collar had been removed, but he immediately recognized the tag.

Gizmo

The dog's name jumped at him from the screen, as if the animal itself attacked. HS24 was stamped on the photo. Dale remembered scoring it on his worksheet at the museum, giving it high marks because Kaitlyn wanted it trashed.

Okay, he'd answer Cassie's question with a plain statement. *I never saw Kaitlyn wearing it*, which was the truth. Then he'd shut up.

"I dug up Gizmo," Dale blurted out. "On the Haunt. I didn't mean to. I reburied him right away."

Cassie flipped to another photo. "Did you miss a bone?"

The cracked skull, caged by metal ribs, seemed to sneer at Dale. "Yeah. That was a mistake." Not the only one he'd made. And they were all getting harder to correct.

"You should tell the sheriff," Cassie said.

"That I found a dog that died under suspicious circumstances? Killing a pet is against the cosmic code, right up there with stealing a Bible. But it's still a dog." Dale glanced down at Jupiter, who tugged at a lace on his work boot. "No offense, Jupe." He tried to gauge how serious she was about his confessing his crimes. "You're already worried people will think there's a crazy cult running around. If it gets out a dog was buried there, the zip will be that Gizmo was sacrificed to open a portal to hell, or to make a pact with the devil so the Icebergs win her state football championship."

"From what I've read in the *Falls Press*, that last one *would* require demonic intervention."

"The Gizmo tag has nothing to do with Kaitlyn," Dale said.

Suddenly pale, Cassie closed her eyes and clutched the

table's edge. Dale pulled his legs under him, causing Jupiter to scurry away. He was ready to spring up and catch her if she fainted. She'd collapsed before. When she got triggered, she dropped like a skyscraper in a disaster flick.

A creepy itch crawled up Dale's neck. "Where is Gizmo's tag now?"

Cassie opened her eyes. "I don't know."

"You don't know because you don't know? Or you're saying you don't know because you don't want to tell me?"

"I don't know and I couldn't tell you if I did."

Dale folded his arms and leaned back in his chair. Let her faint.

Cassie put her tablet onto the home screen, which showed three kids making silly faces. She smiled at the photo. As if by magic, the color returned to her cheeks. "Thank you for telling me about the drawings. Now let's find a place for Jupiter's new empire." She stood and walked toward the door.

Dale grabbed his phone and followed her. What? No demand that he call the sheriff and spill his guts? No plea to his better nature, moral responsibility and all that?

He rubbed the itch at the nape of his neck, feeling as if he and Richie stood at ground zero of a giant nuke while the spirits of Trapper Wolf and Dead Dog Gizmo snickered.

Chapter Twenty-Three

Cassie froze at the slow notes of a funeral dirge. She'd programmed the somber ringtone for a specific set of in-coming numbers hoping never to hear it. Confirmation of what she already knew from the dreary music glowed on the screen. The call came from the California district attorney who'd prosecuted Jordan. Well, from the guy's office.

Let it go to voicemail.

But she might have questions.

And it could be good news: Jordan decided incarceration suited him and has dropped all appeals; Jordan confessed in a puddle of contrition and self-pity and will be locked up forever; Jordan fell in the prison kitchen while helping to prepare last night's gourmet meal and died from twenty-seven accidental knife wounds. She wished for the second scenario. Although she'd be just fine with the first or the third.

Resigned that none of those seemed likely, she pressed the circle, just to get it over with. "This is Cassie Windom."

The voice that responded seemed young, an underling, the lowest-wrung clerk who could be bossed around. Maybe a mail room sorter or a parking garage attendant. "District Attorney Hastings asked me to inform you that Mr. Jordan

McCray's lawyers have filed paperwork claiming the discovery of new evidence that proves their client was wrongfully convicted. You'll be receiving an official notification from the DA's office when more details are available."

"What else?" Cassie asked. An actual voice contact meant there must be more.

"Uhh." He seemed surprised by her prompt. "A witness has come forward, providing Mr. McCray with an alibi."

In her mind, Cassie heard Vicky's voice: *Prepare yourself, girl.*

"Could the guilty verdict be overturned?"

"That is one possible outcome," the intern said slowly. "The defense is strengthening their case by proposing an alternate perpetrator."

"And?"

He lowered his voice almost to a whisper. "That would be you, Ms. Windom."

"Again?" The intern didn't know the case very well. This wasn't the first time she'd been accused of Vicky's murder. "Any chance he'll be released during the appeal?"

"That's unlikely in a murder conviction."

Cassie would have preferred a hard "no chance in hell." She closed her eyes and saw Jordan's twisted face as he ranted at her from behind the visitor room plexiglass. "You'll let me know if I need an armed bodyguard?"

"Our office will keep you informed."

Chapter Twenty-Four

S**un Sun SunnieChat!**

KAYLA

Obvious to me. Dagger, drops of blood, cat head, cat body, poop, eggplant. You'd recognize them if you let me use emojis.

HOLLY

I get plenty of cartoons from my kids. With grownups I want words.

ASHLEY

We all know you have a doctorate in adulting.

HOLLY

You sure that's a cat and not a devil?

A devil would be scarier.

KAYLA

Devil has curved horns, not pointy ears. I know this from extensive texting with my numerous occult friends.

Your friends are all scientists. Not the occult type.

Danith McPherson

KAYLA

Jessica has skeleton earrings.

ASHLEY

Dinosaur skeletons. I've seen them in photos.
They don't count.

HOLLY

A Satanic cult that uses emojis. Very techie.

They consult their spell book on e-readers.

HOLLY

They probably have a blog. Everyone does.

KAYLA

And a podcast with tips on how to diy your
own hexes.

ASHLEY

They video their spells then play them back
whenever they need them. That way they
don't have to go out at midnight naked under
a full moon all the time.

HOLLY

Very practical. Great for January when it's
twenty below.

KAYLA

I bet they have their own youtube channel.

So all put together what do the emojis mean?

HOLLY

No idea.

KAYLA

Dagger cut off the cat's head, cat body
pooped. Don't know how the eggplant fits in.

ASHLEY

One of the cultists couldn't help bragging
about having sex.

KAYLA

Cassie didn't select the main number for the sheriff's office. Instead she chose to infringe on her friendship with Officer Rhonda Olson by punching up the woman's private number.

"Tough couple of days," Rhonda said. "Good thing you called my cell. The office phones are jammed. We've got everything from the media wanting every tiny detail, which they know we can't give out, to a confession from a guy sitting in a Waffle House in Tampa, Florida. Seriously. I heard him order a pecan plate and black coffee. I radioed law enforcement in that area. Two officers were already on-site. I guess it's a popular place. They could see him sitting in a booth talking to me. He's in custody, still insisting he killed our girl but unable to explain how he traveled the seventeen hundred miles without being caught on any gas station cameras."

"I'm guessing there's no record of him on a Delta flight."

"None. Hillsborough County is checking on a private plane, but that seems unlikely."

"He might have killed someone else."

"Could be. Glad it's Florida's problem and not mine. I've got plenty to deal with, and it'll get worse. Wells is doing a press conference as soon as the tip line is in place. The hardest calls are from grieving parents trying to find their missing kids. You can tell them we've got a solid ID on the victim, but they still ask if she's a certain height and if her hair's the color of caramel."

Or shiny ebony. The image of tangled raven hair burst

into Cassie's mind. Her vision blurred. She panted, unable to pull enough air into her lungs. Vicky stood behind her. Cassie reached back a hand, afraid if she turned around, her friend, her best friend, would vanish. She stretched her fingers, feeling a brush of warmth.

On Cassie's first day back at work after the funeral, she entered the conference room, dreading the meeting that Vicky should be at but wasn't. Roger, an account manager, swooped toward her about to invade her personal space. From any of the other people in the room, the hug would have been a gesture of caring. Experience told Cassie that Roger viewed her grief as an opportunity for contact with female breasts without fear of sexual assault charges or a reprimand from human resources.

If this had been a normal day, she would have used one of her ninja moves to avoid him. If this had been a normal day, he wouldn't have dared try the assault in front of witnesses. But today Cassie was raw and vulnerable.

She clutched her tablet to her chest, wishing it was armor. Although perfect for taking notes and projecting her work onto the room's giant monitor, the slight rectangle wasn't large enough to protect her upper-body's personal parts.

"Sorry, I forgot something." Cassie pulled a quick U-turn, rushed back to her office and closed the door. She grabbed the large, sturdy leather portfolio she sometimes used to transport physical drawings. Slowly, she counted to ten, willing her heart to stop racing.

She forced herself to returned to the conference room. Prentice, her boss, had everyone seated at the table. He might have noticed the completely useless portfolio she held too tightly, but he said nothing. She plopped into a chair beside him. A safe chair that he'd saved for her, with Anna, who'd taken Vicky's place for this project, on the other side.

Roger sat across from her, sipping his coffee, acting clueless. But he wasn't.

Cassie felt like a coward for fleeing, for not planting her feet and standing her ground. She should have put out a stiff arm to stop the predator's advance and shouting "Back off." She should have, but she'd been raised Minnesota nice, so she hadn't.

Maybe that was why, later in the elevator, she'd done what she did.

***

"Cassie," came Rhonda's concerned voice over the phone. "Honey, you sit down right now."

Following the gentle words, Cassie lowered herself to the floor. The rug over the hardwood planks was soft and nubby under her palm and knees. She let her forehead drop onto the cushion in a yoga pose.

"Deep breath."

Cassie obeyed.

"That's good. Let it out."

Cassie exhaled in a whoosh.

"Deep breath."

Cassie felt air rush in.

"Let it go."

But she couldn't. She wouldn't betray her friend like that. Letting go meant Vicky had never laughed and danced and cried and said wonderful things and silly things and ordinary things.

It meant Vicky had never been Cleopatra, ruler of Egypt, for Halloween, while Cassie had dressed as Andy Warhol, which most people thought was Albert Einstein.

"Sorry," Cassie said into the phone. "I hiccuped."

"No, you didn't," Rhonda said. "I'm sending someone to check on you."

"Please don't do that. I'm fine. Really."

"Two days ago you discovered a murder victim. That takes a while to process."

Process? Death isn't a theory or an idea, Cassie wanted to say. *You can't think your way through the end of a person's existence. A life that's gone is a page torn from a favorite book. Even if you hold the paper in your hand, the story has changed.*

"It's okay." Cassie rose from the floor and eased into her desk chair. Curling into a fetal position wasn't going to help Mariah. "Have you ever been on Wolf Haunt? Before. You know."

"A couple of times. I took an art class. We painted trees. That might excite you, but I was more interested in the gorgeous instructor than in how the light fell on the branches of an iron wood. I quickly found out his preference ran to eyelash-fluttering, scrawny girls rather than to a curvy woman with a gun. Of course, he might have been put off by my lack of talent. And that my only experience with brushwork was watching Bob Ross videos."

"Did you notice the rock?"

"It was more brownish than it is now. I remember thinking it looked like dried blood. No markings on it then. You did a nice job drawing those, by the way. Justin was impressed. He even put on his glasses."

Cassie put the phone on speaker, set it on her desk beside her computer and tapped on the keyboard.

"I experimented with a bit of embellishment and speculation, which is what your boss told me not to do. I just emailed you a JPEG." She could hear Rhonda's keyboard clacking.

"I'm looking at your doodles. So they're just emojis."

"No sacrifice to the devil. No cult. Just a prank unrelated to—to what happened."

"Is that part of the speculation, or do you have additional information you'd like to share with the sheriff's office?"

Darn. Cassie should have known Rhonda would quiz her. She couldn't explain the origin of the devil-cat and its accompanying poop without involving Dale, which she was determined not to do. He had to make that decision for himself. "I found social media posts, showing the marks were on the stone weeks ago."

"Whether it's related to the murder or not, it has to be investigated."

"Sending you the link to the site." Cassie shamelessly directed Rhonda to the anonymous hands not touching the stone. "You must have a lot of leads you're looking into: Kaitlyn's frenemies, boyfriends, ex-boyfriends, online romance with a Nigerian prince, hobbies."

"Like model trains?"

"Something like that." This was where Cassie could casually mention that she'd made an unauthorized sketch from an unsanctioned photo. Her tablet sat propped beside the computer, showing depressions where spheres molded with ridges and ravines had pressed into soft earth.

Cassie had checked the scale and pattern of the negative space against the picture of Mariah's art competition entry. She was convinced the divots had been made by the beads strung beside Gizmo's tag.

Kaitlyn had been wearing Mariah's necklace when she'd been murdered.

"I think Kaitlyn would be more into media influencers than trains," Rhonda said. "We've interviewed witnesses to the confrontation between her and Mariah. Kaitlyn claimed the necklace belonged to her aunt Robin. Except Robin Snyder disappeared in 1983 when she was sixteen."

"Mariah just made it this summer," Cassie said. Technically the necklace was new, although the unearthed dog tag was old. Where had the beads come from? Dale would have told her if he'd found them on the island too. Wouldn't he?

"It could still be the reason she was killed. Seems we should have found it on the body. Since we didn't, the killer must have taken it. That doesn't point to a boyfriend, a satanic cult, or a model train enthusiast. It seems more like an angry jewelry maker."

"Allegedly." Cassie bit her lip. Officer Rhonda had followed a logical route and reached Mariah. Cassie couldn't stop herself from thinking of the similar path she'd followed straight to Jordan when Vicky had been killed. But the two situations were galaxies apart. Jordan was guilty. Mariah was innocent. She looked at her drawing of the place where beads had been. She should tell Rhonda. She really should.

But she wouldn't be providing any new information. The sheriff's department had examined the area before she'd been allowed within the yellow-tape perimeter. The official photographs, taken by Officer Robo, must be far better than the ones she'd snapped with her ancient cell phone. Her enhanced drawing of the indentations was just speculation.

"Speculation isn't evidence," Cassie said.

"No, but it can lead to evidence," Rhonda said.

Chapter Twenty-Five

Cassie remembered sitting at the meeting between Prentice and Anna, who tried their best to keep her engaged. Unable to maintain enough energy to be angry with herself for avoiding boob-crushing Roger instead of dealing with him, she drifted through the meeting. When it ended, out of habit she escaped to the lobby of the LA skyscraper that housed Fontana Media. At the smoothie kiosk she ordered a kiwi-acai.

"Only one today?" the juice barista asked.

Yes, only one from now on.

Cassie stepped into the empty elevator, gripping the paper container, the cold numbing her fingers. Two men got on, turned their backs to her and faced the sliding door.

"She flirted with me all the time," Tan Sports Coat Over Brown Slacks said.

"I never saw her in our department," Pinstripe Suit said.

"I'd see her in the coffee shop. She'd give me that smile. You know."

Pinstripe made a noncommittal sound.

Cassie had opted not to take a plastic cover. She swirled

the biodegradable straw through the thick slush. She swirled and swirled.

"I heard she liked it rough," Tan Sports Coat said.

"Where would you possibly have heard that?"

Cassie eased the straw from the cup, trying not to disturb globs that clung to it.

Tan Sports Coat shrugged. "You know. 'Man talk.' After work. She was into macho types. Cavemen who made her beg for it."

"Hmm."

"I guess the foreplay got too hot and heavy."

Cassie gave the dripping tube a quick flick forward. Greenish goop splattered across the pale linen in front of her. It soaked into the dry-clean-only fibers and slithered down the fabric like the first strokes of a Jackson Pollock, or the results of projectile vomiting.

The elevator jolted to a stop. Cassie plopped the straw back into the tall cup. The men got out. The doors closed.

Vicky's voice came to her, *Girl, I do love your artistic flare.*

Cassie took a long, cool sip, amazed at how satisfying passive aggressive behavior could be. She rode up the additional two floors to her office, feeling more relaxed than she had in days.

Chapter Twenty-Six

"I think my dad's been swapped with a pod dude," Richie said, "like in that flick."

"*Invasion of the Body Snatchers.*" Dale sat in the passenger seat of the Fart Bomb, watching the parking lot at the football field fill up around them, even though the event wasn't scheduled to start for another hour.

"Yeah, that one. The original, not the other one."

The stark black-and-white version of the horror film always gave Dale a chill. Its shadowy tones seemed like a warning that the world was doomed. The color remake couldn't match that.

"Pod-dad gave me the 'future' talk," Richie said.

"He always does that when school starts." Dale knew it word for word. He'd heard Richie recite it every fall, using a bad imitation of his father's voice.

"Yeah, but it's only Saturday and classes don't start 'til Tuesday, and this time it got penultimate weird. Not just 'work hard and take things serious.' My dad asked me questions. Hard ones. Worse than in social class when we have current-event quizzes. As if I'm supposed to memorize the news."

"Asked you what?" Dale thought Richie's dad was an okay

guy who tried to be a good parent, but he expected his son to be a clone of himself. A baseball and apple pie buddy. A straight-line thinker. A kid who followed a normal path. Richie's mind didn't work that way.

Richie mimicked his dad's tone. "Richard, what do you want to study?" He slapped the steering wheel, and went back to his own voice. "*Want* to study! Like I have a choice. I was, you know, trapped. I could have pulled something out of my ass. Zebras or clouds or that history stuff we saw at the museum. But then he'd expect me to *do* it, in real life. I gave him the 'I haven't decided yet' line. Then he wanted to know what's my plan for after graduation. Graduation! That's a whole century from now."

"Well, two years," Dale said. It probably seemed like a hundred to Richie.

"He was in counselor mode. But more scary because he's my dad."

"Pod-dad counselor."

"Yeah, like that. Too much family time, man. The guy needs a hobby. Something with power tools and a blog."

Dale noticed how slowly people climbed out of their cars and ambled toward the entrance to the bleachers. No one wanted to be here on the Saturday of Labor Day weekend. Members of the student council handed out candles. The stadium would be a giant fire hazard tonight. His dad would love it.

"Kaitlyn," Richie said. "She didn't have a chance to do anything. She'll always be a high school kid. Forever. Like Peter Pan."

Dale was pretty sure Peter Pan had never gone to high school. "I don't like that story as much as I used to. Limp ending."

"My dad should have been talking to you. You're the one who needs a plan. He says Minnesota has this PTSD program. It sounds more like your thing than mine."

"PSEO," Dale said. Postsecondary Enrollment Options. High school juniors and seniors could take courses at state colleges and technical schools, earning credits without having to pay tuition. A free head start on a degree, it was a good deal. A brightly colored poster outside the counselor's office gave a website for more details. Richie probably never noticed it. Dale saw it every time he walked that hall. The nearest university was an hour away. "That's for guys with a car. And money for gas. And books. And food."

"Duh, that's why you need a plan."

"I don't know."

"Yeah, you do." Richie patted the steering wheel. "You can use the Bomb. That's a start, right? Course, you'd have to fill out all kinds of paperwork and everyone would know your first name is really Sherman."

The entire county already knew that. His parents were finally making an effort to call him Dale, even though he'd been objecting to Sherman since he'd turned thirteen.

A girl walked past carrying tagboard lettered with marker and adorned with pink hearts.

LOVE YOU KATE LYNN

Shit, Dale thought. *Some people can't even get your name right when you're dead.*

Richie stared out the windshield. "We have to do this?"

"If you don't want to, you can pick me up later."

"Naw, I already got dressed up."

For Richie, that meant an almost clean t-shirt. A tuft of black fur clung to the AC/DC logo on his chest. The Danowski's cat had made the F-Bomb its clubhouse and somehow found the car no matter where it was parked.

"You don't have to worry about me," Richie said, "I mean, if you do the PS thing. I know you're not going to stay in this town forever."

"I'm not going anywhere today." Dale wondered if he would ever be able to leave. He'd never say it out loud, but he *did* worry about his best friend. And Crystal, who should have been his girlfriend but who was somewhere else now and not likely to come back. And he worried about Bridget and Whitney and the kids he nodded to in the school hallways and joked with at lunch.

A zombie-ghost face suddenly materialized at Richie's window. Dale jumped. As if he'd summed her with his thoughts, Bridget peered in at them, her mascara and eyeliner already smeared with tears. She was sure to cry through the entire memorial and probably faint from dehydration before the service was over.

As Dale climbed out of the car, he saw Principal Westlund escort Kaitlyn's dad through the stadium gate. Mr. Hanson, bent with grief, moved like a shadow that might blow away if the other man's hand wasn't there to guide him.

We owe him our presence, Dale thought. *It doesn't matter if we only saw Kaitlyn from across the street every now and then or if we talked to her every day. It doesn't even matter if we liked her or not. Or if she liked us.*

Damn. Dale felt on the edge of bawling. He walked behind Richie and Bridget, who had a way of linking together as if they were one entity.

Ahead, a guy stood facing the parking lot. He ran his fingers through walnut-brown hair, then settled a baseball cap on his head. Dale caught the guy's profile as he turned to join the line to get into the stadium. The sloped nose and muscular build seemed familiar.

Dale took a few long strides to Richie's non-Bridget side. "Who's that guy?"

"Which one?"

"Black baseball cap, dark shirt."

Richie scanned the crowd. "That's half the guys here."

Dale tried to catch up to the stranger he almost

remembered. He was outmaneuvered by a gaggle of young girls, who looked more prepared for a party than a wake.

A senior he knew shoved a candle at him.

"No thanks, I've got an app." He thought the candles were pointless anyway, since the service would be over before it got dark. Tiny flames, even a couple hundred of them, didn't make much of an impact in daylight.

"Me too," the girl said. "But people like fire."

"Do you know the guy who came through before the girls with the balloons? Black baseball cap, dark shirt."

"That's every male except for the Sparks," she said. "But if you mean the babe with the mournful-puppy face who obviously works out, sorry, don't recognize him. Maybe he's one of Kait's relatives."

"Sure," Dale said without believing it. He scanned the bobbing heads as he passed through the stadium gate and climbed the stairs to an upper row. If only he could get a better look at the guy. It wasn't just that Black Hat was a stranger. Something else caused his spidey-sense to tingle.

Maybe it was the prickly thought that Kaitlyn's killer could be here. Watching. Getting off on all the tears and sorrow.

Red Sparks caps stuck out like bright polka dots. He easily spotted his dad, who towered over his shorter buddies, radio in hand, ready to assist with crowd control.

"Hey." Richie called to him from where he and Bridget had settling in beside Whitney.

Damn. Whitney. Dale wished he'd let Richie talk him into blowing off the memorial service. Now he was stuck.

Chapter Twenty-Seven

SunnieChat is here for you!

KAYLA

> Truth. How is Ashley? C and H, you have to
> tell me if something goes wrong, even if Ash
> makes you promise not to.

> You want me to break a promise to my sister?
> You realize then I could break a promise
> to you.

HOLLY

> That's like Queen Elizabeth's dilemma over
> executing Mary Queen of Scots. If you say it's
> okay to kill one queen, then it's okay to kill
> another queen, which might be you.
> Eventually she chopped off Mary's head
> anyway. Still managed to keep her own, but
> it's a risky practice.

> K, I'll tell you if there's something you need to
> know. Right now, Ash alternates between
> hungry and nauseous, normal according to
> her doctor.

Not Her First Murder

HOLLY

Crackers and popsicles got me through
morning sickness, which seemed to last
all day.

KAYLA

Ginger and peppermint work.

You've never been pregnant, right, little sis?
Please confirm.

KAYLA

Relax, never preg. I've been researching. Liam
was nervous until I explained.

HOLLY

Any revelations?

KAYLA

Some biggies. Like you can't apply results
from animal models to humans.

HOLLY

Translation?

KAYLA

Don't compare rat pregnancies to people
pregnancies.

Wouldn't want to do that anyway.

KAYLA

But that's what medical researchers have
done for a long time.

What else?

KAYLA

Human pregnancy lasts longer than it should,
compared to other complex species.

HOLLY

It sure seemed that way to me, especially the
third time.

KAYLA

Human labor and delivery last longer than they should too.

HOLLY

That got faster with each kid. Andi popped out on her own. She's still like that. Everything is a sprint.

KAYLA

Seahorses do it the right way. The female passes fertilized eggs to the male. He carries them around until they hatch.

Men should have to do that.

HOLLY

We'd be extinct if men had to go through labor.

KAYLA

The guy would need a pouch.

Would a fanny pack work?

HOLLY

A man bag?

KAYLA

Liam has a sporran. Not on the boat but I've seen pics. It's like a man bag. He wears it with his kilt. Not appropriate for incubating eggs though.

HOLLY

Share those pics of Liam. Any pics. Please. Your sisters live vicariously through you.

The seahorse method wouldn't work. Ashley is a wreck but Zach is worse.

KAYLA

How do we help?

Not Her First Murder

HOLLY

Like always. Tell her it's okay to be scared. Let
her know we're with her no matter what.
Listen to her cry if that's what she needs.

KAYLA

Someone send her ginger and peppermint
from me.

HOLLY

I'll put together a morning sickness basket
from all of us. I can take it over this weekend.
It will be a treat to get out of the house.
Should I feel guilty wanting a few hours away
from my kids when my sister might never have
one of her own? I'd say I wish I could give her
one of mine, but once you've got them,
they're yours. Although maybe I could put
Colin in the basket and smuggle him into her
house. He's on a Superman kick. Auntie
Cassie, if a box shows up at your place with
air holes punched in it, open it right away.
Your favorite nephew is inside.

Each one of your kids is my favorite.

That doesn't mean you can send me three
boxes.

KAYLA

You could send Colin to me, but it would take
a month for him to get here. And there's barely
enough room in my cabin for one.

You seem to have room for Liam.

KAYLA

Sometimes.

Cassie thought about her oldest sister's threat to send her nephew to her as she set the cardboard box on the living room floor and knelt beside it. She'd made a quick trip to her parents' place. She'd grown up in the house, but she'd stopped thinking of it as home when her father had repainted the bedroom she'd shared with one or more of her three sisters in various combinations over the years. Now her mother's craft projects flooded the beds. Ring binders stuffed with research on zoning regulations, petitions, and the voting records of elected officials had turned the carpet into a maze.

Patrick and Constance Windom were preparing to rush off when Cassie arrived. "Sorry," her mom had said, "but we have to stake out a good spot for watching the Band Festival Parade. Then we're going to a potluck picnic at Lion's Park. You should meet us there. Pork chops and corn on the cob. Your dad made a walnut salad. Everyone would love to see you."

A tremor had gone through Cassie at the thought of a field of people staring at her, whispering old rumors about Vicky's death. Never let the facts ruin a good story. "Just grabbing some of my stuff so you have more space."

"You'll just encourage her to join another committee," her dad had said as he'd put a round loaf of whole wheat bread from his latest community education class into a bag for her.

Cassie had only taken one carton from the closet, which probably disappointed her mother. Jupiter sneezed at the dusty smell, then trotted across the cabin floor to the patio door, perhaps hoping to find Kevin the Squirrel trespassing on the deck.

Cassie lifted out a bundle of sketchpads. A variety of sizes and brands, most had been purchased at a discount chain that no longer existed. She'd spent a good portion of her youth with one of the spiral-bound books tucked under an arm or hidden in a tote. She wished she'd put dates on them.

Someday she'd figure out the chronological order. But not today.

She'd doodled on most of the covers. One of them was bound to shout Made by a Thirteen-Year-Old. None of these did, so she set them aside.

She grabbed five volumes held together by a wide rubber band that had grown brittle, turning from ecru to the yellow of fall leaves. At her touch the strip shattered into crumbs. One book fell free.

Cassandra.

She'd inscribed her name across the thick cardboard in bold script. Sunflowers and cartoon stars danced around heavily inked letters declaring "Private" and "Personal Property." The warnings were meant to keep her sisters from snooping. They'd had the opposite effect.

She flipped back the cover and riffled through the textured pages. Drawings crafted in pencil, charcoal, pen, and marker flashed past. Flowers. Dogs. Trees. Cats. Imagined goddesses with flawless skin and tiny noses whose coiled hair never suffered split ends and gossamer gowns never wrinkled. She cringed at multiple depictions of an Adonis she'd had a crush on.

Then she found it; the shed on Wolf Haunt!

Cassie quickly turned the page to the drawing she'd made in her little quilt cave.

Face framed by a wide-brimmed hat, the woman gazed slightly to the left, as if contemplating that very instant of that very day. Skin clung to her cheekbones and caved into hollows below. Dark crescents sank under weary, peaceful eyes. She carried her own beauty, her own understanding that kind things happened and harsh things happened, with no way of knowing which would be next. This woman was true and honest, untainted by false perfection.

This portrait marked a change. Thirteen-year-old Cassie stopped choosing media idols and fantasy princesses as her subjects. The Adonis was just a boy with an uninteresting face. Her sisters' twisting mouths and crinkling eyes became puzzles to transfer to paper. She vowed to conquer her art nemesis: water! Spraying fountains and dripping faucets. Running streams and still lakes, even if it meant drawing a thousand fish.

Cassie opened her tablet and navigated to the *Falls Press* web site. On the home page Kaitlyn Hanson hugged a guitar and grinned at her.

GFHS Student Found Dead on Island

She clicked on a sidebar.

Local Family Has Tragic History

A small school photo framed a girl caught in an uncomfortable smile. The assembly line head shot showed sunken cheeks, and dark half-moons under the eyes. The column of text next to it chronicled how sixteen-year-old Robin Snyder hadn't arrived home one night. She'd disappeared. Vanished. Never seen again.

Except—

Cassie held her sketch next to the screen. A cry caught in her throat. The thin girl had become an even thinner woman. The years that had passed between the photo and the pencil portrait could not account for such a pronounced transformation.

Cassie wondered what illness had plagued the Robin she'd met. Had the woman survived much beyond that day at Wolf Haunt, or had the unknown disease drained away her life?

Cassie hoped with all her heart that Robin Snyder had beaten the nastiness that ravaged her body. She tried to image a healthy Robin playing pickleball in Sun City West, but she couldn't get beyond the gaunt features in her own drawing.

She flipped more pages, hoping to find a date beside the sketch of Cliff's scruffy shoe, Aunt Renee's roses, a wooden rowboat. Nothing. Her teenaged mind hadn't viewed chronology important enough to scrawl a few numbers in the corner of each work.

She remembered taking her sketch pad with the new portrait in it to the museum, wishing the woman would be there. Silly to think the artist hung around the place all the time just because she'd recommended it. Cassie had longed to watch the woman's expression as she examined her own image captured in graphite lines. Cassie had imagined her nodding with pleasure, again confirming that the insecure girl could be —that she was—a real artist.

Make your day bright with SunnieChat!

> H, what's the statute of limitations on keeping your kids artwork?

HOLLY

I'll have to consult my guide to perfect parenting. You know, the volume that magically appears with the birth of your first child.

> Mom and dad still have our handprints enshrined in plaster from kindergarten.

KAYLA

Not mine. When I learned about time capsules, I buried it in the backyard.

ASHLEY

Dad put our stuff in labeled boxes. When mom helped me move, she snuck one into the kitchen stuff without my knowing it.

At least she didn't toss it out.

ASHLEY

No but I did.

KAYLA

I bet they have all of Cassie's artwork.

HOLLY

When C is famous, they can sell them.

I hope they aren't expecting my finger paintings to fund their retirement.

ASHLEY

I hope your finger paintings won't be my inheritance.

Chapter Twenty-Eight

Heather Petrosky plopped a chocolatey Blizzard in front of Dale and shimmied into the booth beside him, blocking his escape route. Her sisters Jennifer and Brianna slid across the red plastic bench on the other side to face him. They'd ambushed him after the memorial, inviting him to the Dairy Queen, their treat. It felt strange, like the beginning of a horror flick. Weird, but not so weird that you'd suspect a monster lurked in the shadows. He'd agreed because it got him out of an awkward situation with Whitney. And because they were the Petrosky girls, half of them anyway. They probably just wanted a favor of some sort. What could go wrong?

Yeah, that's what the first victim thinks when he steps into the spooky house, just before a demon slices out his heart for a midnight snack.

"So, what's this about?" Dale asked. "You want me to beat up some guy who trash-talked the girls' basketball team?" That seemed unlikely. All three of the sports-obsessed, fitness-focused athletes stood over six feet. They'd have to be attacked by a car load of machete-wielding psycho-ninjas to need his help.

"You're not dating anyone, are you?" Brianna asked.

"We agreed I was going to do this," Heather said to her younger sister.

Brianna rolled her eyes. "Just establishing a baseline." She looked at Dale. "Whitney sort of thinks you're going with her." The two girls didn't hang out together and were a year apart in school. Dale suspected that information had come through Heather or Jennifer. Or not. Whitney was likely to tell anyone anything. And post it on the numerous social media sites she prowled.

"I see her sometimes." Dale had always been comfortable with the Petrosky girls, and with the entire family, until now.

Jennifer stretched her long legs into the aisle. Heather and Brianna kept theirs tucked under the red plastic table. Dale couldn't move without bumping against bare knees.

"Are you"—Brianna made exaggerated air quotes—"in a relationship?"

Dale tried not to squirm under the pressure. If he said yes, it would sound like he and Whitey were a solid item, which they weren't. Whitney wasn't a solid anything. If he said no, it made him look like a loser who couldn't get a girlfriend. "Can't we talk about movies and sci-fi books? Or you guys can talk about basketball and I'll nod as if I'm following along. You know, like I usually do."

"So that's a hard no on the Whitney scene," Brianna said. "Pass to you, Heather. Take the shot."

"We have a request," Heather said.

Dale turned a little and scrunched into the corner so he could semi-face her.

He'd known Heather since they'd scampered around together in the Otter group in kindergarten. As a Muskrat, Jennifer had been a room away.

From those early days, Dale always knew which one was Happy (Heather Anne Petrosky) and which was Jappy (Jennifer Anne Petrosky). He'd never call them by those nicknames now, just as they'd never call him Sherman.

Streaks of summer sun lightened Heather's brownish hair scraped into a ponytail. She gazed at him with the same calm assurance as when she approached the free-throw line. "Dale, will you be our date to the homecoming dance?"

Dale pushed back hard into the booth. He must have heard wrong. "What? I think my brain glitched."

Brianna looked at him as if his brain was on an eco-vacation saving llamas in Peru. "We—want you—to go to—the homecoming dance—with us. Got that?"

Dale looked around, wondering who was seeing him here, in public, with three girls asking him for a date. He suddenly worried that a hidden camera recorded him being punked. At another table a family argued over french fries. A pair of seniors he knew were too fascinated with one another to notice the rest of the world. Large windows gave anyone cruising up to the drive-through a clear view of Dale practically imprisoned by the girls. He hoped Richie wouldn't get a craving for a Buster Bar.

"The three of you?" Dale asked.

"At least he can count," Brianna said. She pulled out her phone and read the screen, as if a cat video was more interesting than the teenage boy across from her.

Dale asked Heather, "What about Roger?" The two had been an item since the winter SnoBall last year.

"He's dirt and I hope he dies," Heather said, settling that issue.

"We've got it all worked out." Jennifer took a piece of paper out of her backpack and placed it in front of Dale. A check-off box sat before each item on the long list. "Our dad will pick you up and bring you to our house, so we can do photos in front of the fireplace—"

"Wait," Dale protested. "Jen, Mark Gavin asked you to the dance. I know he did." Dale immediately wished he hadn't said it like that. What if she quizzed him about how he knew? He didn't want to admit that the guys' soap opera network was just as active as the girls'. But, like Brianna, he had to establish a baseline. Mark was shorter than Dale (like almost everyone else in the world) but a weight lifter with an entire football team behind him. Dale didn't want to piss him off, and end up stuffed in a locker with a sweaty gym sock in his mouth.

Jennifer scowled. "It wasn't an *ask*. It was a *command* with a 'terms and conditions apply' clause. He would grant me the great honor of his royal football-ness escorting me across the stage, as long as I wore flat shoes and hunched over. He's got this Neanderthal idea that the guy has to be taller than the girl to show his superiority."

"That is so quack," Brianna said. "Petrosky girls do not hunch."

Dale started to make a suggestion.

Heather interrupted him before he got out a single word. "Don't even."

Dale tried to defend himself. "You don't know what I was going to say."

Heather spoke to her sisters as if she were Dale. "Why don't you march with one another?"

Jennifer put her hands to her cheeks in mock horror. Brianna dropped her phone in her lap, grasped her throat in a stranglehold, and gagged.

Dale tried to defend himself. "I wasn't going to say that." It was exactly what he was going to say.

Heather pinned him in a stare. "We each deserve our own personal turn in the spotlight. Understand? First you'll escort Brianna in the freshman group under Petrosky. Then you and I will march with the sophomores under Petrosky. Then you and Jen will march with the juniors under Steinhaus."

"Jen lost the coin toss," Brianna said.

"Dale," Jennifer said, "Heather and I are almost as tall as you are, and we're going to be wearing heels. If the height thing is an issue, you better say so right now."

Dale felt a fist slammed into his ego. He wasn't being asked on a date by three semi-gorgeous (in a natural, sporty kind of way), popular girls because he had a heart-melting grin or was on the A-list himself. They'd selected him for his Steinhaus DNA. "So this is because I'm the second-tallest guy in school. Did Luke turn you down?" Luke Johnson topped Dale by an inch. An okay basketball player, he lacked the coordination needed to pull the boys' team out of its mostly losing tradition. (Go Icebergs!)

Brianna picked up her phone and flipped a finger across the screen. "He's strictly an NPC."

Non-Playable Character. The side guy in a video game who does nothing but repeat the same three lines of dialog over and over.

Dale stifled a laugh, thinking that was an accurate description of Luke on and off the basketball court.

"You're tied for second tallest," Brianna said. "I did the research. Jimmy Burke is six-three, same as you."

"He's a freshman," Heather said. "Too young for Jen and me."

"And he's named Jimmy, and he's a creep," Brianna said. "You're the Goldilocks dude. You know, like a planet."

Dale nodded. "Yeah, I get it. Not too cold, not too hot. Just the right distance from the sun so no one freezes to death or bursts into flames."

"And you're a nice guy," Heather said, slapping another scoop of insult onto the pile.

Dale kept his expression blank while he groaned inside. He wanted to slide under the table, but with all the long legs there wasn't any room.

He knew what Heather was really saying. It would probably be chiseled onto his tombstone.

RIP Dale Steinhaus
A guy you could trust with your sister

Jennifer pushed the paper at him. "Here's a hard copy of the itinerary and the address for the tux place. I'll also text it to you. We'll pay for the rental. We expect you to have a responsible adult along when you pick out the suit."

"That means not Richie," Brianna said. "I'll go with you."

"No, you won't," Heather said. "You'd talk him into a powder-blue reject from the opening of a car dealership." She turned to Dale. "Jen and I will take you."

Dale shoved away the paper and the container of melting ice milk the girls had gotten for him. "This is too ultra-weird for me."

"Says the guy who put live chickens in Principal Westlund's car."

"That was years ago," Dale said. "And it was just one bird. Maybe two."

"Five. I counted. And it was last year." Brianna giggled. "It went viral. I watched the whole thing a bunch of times. It was extrav'."

"No chickens were harmed in the making of that video," Dale said soberly.

Jennifer nudged the cup and paper back toward him. "I know it's a big favor, but we'd really appreciate it."

Traffic at the drive-through stretched out behind a dad-van crammed with kids in matching jerseys. Dale watched the driver lean out the window and shout at the microphone while squinting at a notepad that must be scrawled with a large order. The man cringed as if in pain from the squealing of future soccer stars who bounced in the confines of their seat belts.

Dale empathized with the haggard coach. The man had probably been guilted into volunteering by a whiny kid and a wife who wanted them both out of the house so she could sit with a glass of wine and listen to the quiet.

He refused to wipe away the sweat forming on his upper lip. Show no weakness. "I can't be bribed with a Choco

Brownie Extreme. Besides, dancing gives me hives." That wasn't an exaggeration. He'd broken out in angry red welts at the sixth-grade mixer.

"You don't have to dance," Heather said. "Just escort each of us through the march. It's all in Jennifer's schedule."

Dale took a sip and looked out the window, searching for an inspired way to get out of the multi-date plan without turning the Petrosky girls into enemies. A blue Chevy slid into view two cars behind the dad-van. The guy at the steering wheel gave his baseball cap a tug. A nut-brown tuft stuck out over his ear.

The guy from the memorial ceremony.

Dale almost choked on the smooth drink. A memory flashed through his mind. He and Richie had sat in the F Bomb at a stop sign, waiting for Chewbacca to amble across the intersection.

If another car or a human pedestrian had been in the way, Richie would have careened around the obstruction, but he always gave Mr. Ziegler's blind, deaf dog with a bad heart the right-of-way.

The blue Chevy had rolled up next to them, almost paused, then swerved around the corner, running the stop sign. Dale had gotten a quick glance at the driver in the black baseball cap, and he'd recognized the girl beside him

Kaitlyn Hanson.

"Earth calling Dale," Brianna said.

"Who's that guy?" Dale pointed out the window.

The twins swiveled their heads, like coordinated cranes. Brianna didn't move except for her thumbs tapping on the phone's screen.

The guy revved his engine, swung out of the line like a frustrated NASCAR driver and zoomed away.

The twins shared a look. Dale wished he could eavesdrop on the private conversation they seemed to be having via invisible lasers beaming from their eyes.

"We know who he is." Heather put an elbow on the table and cradled her chin in her hand. She gave Dale a sly smile, as if she were about to break a tie score with an awesome slam dunk. "I'm wearing a killer dress and sparkly four-inch stilettos to the homecoming dance. Are you going to walk across that stage with me or not?"

Between a rock of his own making and three teenage girls, Dale weighed how badly he wanted intel on Black Hat. The guy maybe wasn't Kaitlyn's killer, but maybe he was. And if he was, Dale couldn't just forget that he'd seen the two of them together. And if he wasn't, it still might be important that the guy had been with her.

Dale looked from Heather to Jennifer to Brianna, then back to Jennifer.

Well, it wasn't exactly a deal with the devil. No slapping a bloody thumbprint on a contract he wasn't allowed to read. No burying a beating goat heart at the crossroads at midnight.

"I'm in," Dale said. "Who is he?"

Jennifer nodded, as if she never doubted he'd agree to the scheme. "You saw him four days ago."

Dale wanted to interrupt but didn't. His glimpse of Kaitlyn with the guy had been more like a week ago.

"He's the guide at the museum," Jennifer said. "The one who took us to the Itasca Room to see the art display."

"Really? That guy?" Dale remembered squeezing between the older boy and Missy. If the guide had been wearing the black baseball cap, it might have triggered the scene at the stop sign. But he'd been capless with his hair slicked behind his ears.

"He hit on most of the girls, including Jen," Heather said. "You know the thing, boy or bear?"

Dale nodded. He'd heard girls talking about the question going around. Which would you rather meet in the middle of the night, a strange boy or a bear?

"He's why we choose the bear," Jennifer said. "He started

off with 'I bet you need a sunroof in your car.' As if I'd never heard that one before. Then he made a crude remark about the part of my anatomy he could reach without a ladder. Like I would think that was a clever line. I told him I only date guys who can shoot a three-pointer from midcourt. Humiliation works so much better than 'fuck off.' Although I said that too."

Dale was relieved not to feel his cheeks flush. He must have been close by when it happened. Sexual harassment, practically right in front of him, and he'd been clueless. He glanced at Brianna, thinking she was too young to hear this.

Jennifer noticed. "Don't worry about Bri. We didn't raise our sister to be a fairy-tale princess."

"Boys have the frontal lobes of fungus gnats," Brianna said without looking up from her phone.

"So you probably didn't get his name and exchange friendship bracelets," Dale said.

"We like to know who the pond scums are so we can do our civic duty and alert others." Heather scrunched up her face as if she'd smelled a corpse flower. "Mitch Hendrick. Lives in Sunset."

"Serious tox-creepazoid," Brianna said.

"How did he know Kait?"

"Maybe he didn't." Heather raised her eyebrows at him, like he should be able to figure it out himself. "The place was packed with weepy girls."

"You think he went to a memorial service to hook up?" The thought made Dale's stomach churn. Hendrick made bad "tall" jokes, thought a lewd comment was a great pickup line, and couldn't wait five minutes behind a kiddy soccer team in order to get his DQ fix. He was capable of any depravity.

"He knew her," Dale said. "I saw them together."

"Probably just 'catch and release,'" Heather said. "Kait didn't do commitment." She slid out of the booth. "I'll get the car and pick you up at the door."

"You have your license?" Dale asked. Most kids turned

sixteen during tenth grade. That made it a big year for driving.

"Almost." Heather headed for the door.

Dale turned to Jennifer. "What does that mean?"

Jennifer got out of the booth and gathered up the empty cups. "She's taking the driver's test tomorrow. I'm not taking it for a couple of weeks yet so I can practice parallel parking some more."

Brianna scooted off the bench. "Don't worry. She'll pass." She followed her sister to the trash bin.

Dale stretched his cramped legs, climbed out of the plastic trap, and trailed behind them like a puppy. Customers crowded around the service counter, waiting for their orders. A guy in a black baseball cap wove through them, carrying a sundae thick with red goop.

Dale froze. Mitch Hendrick must have thought he could get faster service at the counter than at the drive-through.

Jennifer shoved empty cups into the bin, then did a one-eighty toward the exit. Hendrick stepped to block her. "Hey, Amazon, we meet again. It must be fate."

Dale forced himself to move. To get to her. Not to ride in on a white horse wearing shining armor, of course, because that would be insulting, like implying she couldn't take care of herself. But, yeah, to rescue her. Or at least to provide backup. His long strides couldn't close the gap fast enough.

Jennifer extended her middle finger and flicked an imaginary strand of hair from her temple. Hendrick stood at least four inches shorter. She slowly lowered her hand until the gesture was level with his face. "Get out of my way, Dopey."

Hendrick jerked back, trying to cover his shock with a sneer. "Not very sociable."

Jennifer strolled away. Brianna giggled as she brushed by the guy. At fourteen she was at least two inches taller. "More like Grumpy."

As Dale went past, he pointed to a blotch of strawberry

goo that had sloshed out of the sundae onto Hendrick's Arctic Monkey tee. "Nasty stain, man. Looks like you got stabbed." He pushed out the door into the heat, wondering if the guy was the vindictive type.

The Petrosky family van idled outside, unlicensed Heather at the wheel.

Jennifer slid open the wide door in the back so Dale could climb in. "Thanks for doing the homecoming thing."

Brianna yanked open the passenger door and climbed into the front to ride shotgun. "Don't screw it up."

Chapter Twenty-Nine

When Rhonda answered, Cassie apologized for calling her private number for official business—again. She promised to use the sheriff's office number from now on, but she didn't mean it. Her last call to Rhonda had triggered an anxiety attack. Everything coming through the switchboard was recorded. She couldn't take the chance that an episode would become part of the public record. "You know I spent time here during the summer when I was growing up."

"You make it sound like a prison sentence," Rhonda said.

"I loved it most of the time. When my cousins weren't being brats."

"I've heard stories about Cliff and Rob. Where did they get all those buttons?"

"Not a clue."

"Since they don't live here anymore, I'm guessing this isn't to make a formal complaint against them."

"I'd love to," Cassie said, "but it's long past the statute of limitations. And this is something else. They were involved. But not *involved* involved."

"Nachos on the side, not the taco."

"Something like that." Cassie tapped the letters spelling

out her name on the thick cardboard cover protecting her sketches. "I know this is going to sound unlikely."

"I'm listening, hon."

"Kaitlyn's aunt. Robin Snyder. I saw her."

"When was this?"

"July or August of 2003, when I was thirteen. I recognized her from the photo that was just in the *Press*."

Rhonda was silent for a moment. "You saw her twenty years after that picture was taken. Twenty years after she disappeared."

"Yes."

"How sure are you it was her? Give me a rating on a scale of 'I saw her on the Jumbotron at a Twins game' to 'I noticed her working at a furniture store wearing a Hello, My Name Is Robin badge,' to 'she bought me ice cream and showed me her driver's license.'"

"No ice cream was involved, but I talked to her. I'm certain it was Robin Snyder."

"Even after thirty plus years, it's an open case. Officer Quigley is assigned to it. You'll have to talk to him."

Officer Robocop Quigley. Cassie could already feel her frustration building. "Can't I just chat with you about it?"

"Sorry. We have to follow protocol. And I'm not it."

Cassie told herself it could be worse. At least she wouldn't be questioned by Deputy Adam Berger. She hadn't seen him since the semi-kiss in Rhonda's Expedition, which had barely quivered the needle on the date-o-meter.

Father Anderson at St. Mary's Catholic Church and Reverend Gunther at Faith and Hope Lutheran were wasting their time covertly competing for the honor of officiating at the hypothetical wedding.

"What about the nachos?" Rhonda asked.

Cassie was confused for a moment. *Oh yeah, Cliff and Rob. And Laurel, Holly, Ashley, and Kayla.* "They can verify where I was when I talked to her." She hoped none of them would be interviewed. The moment they referred to the mystery woman as Cassie's Ghost her credibility would dissolve.

She suddenly worried about the family fallout. Aunt Renee might not be surprised that her sons had transported their sister and cousins to party central, notorious producer of empty beer cans and used condoms. But Cassie dreaded explaining to her parents that their sensible daughters had allowed themselves be led astray by the unruly duo.

"I'm not doubting you," Rhonda said, "but I hope you have something solid to support your story. Any chance you got her autograph? A movie ticket with her fingerprint on it? A selfie of the two of you together?"

"Sort of. I'll bring it with me."

"This could be big."

"Rhonda, there's an odd part." Cassie hated that her voice wavered.

"Odd is permanently on my bingo card."

"Robin Snyder. I saw her on Wolf Haunt. She told me she was searching for a necklace. Now, fifteen years later, her niece has a dispute over a necklace and is killed on that same island."

"Okay, I've got that square marked off for the day."

Chapter Thirty

Cassie flipped her phone into silent mode when the calls started and prepared herself for what she would find on her news feed.

> Convicted killer Jordan McCray, in his appeal to have his case overturned, stated that the real killer of Victoria Danner was the victim's close friend Casandra Windom. Through his lawyers, McCray contends that Windom was jealous of his growing romance with Danner and that several times she flew into violent rages over the relationship. McCray had previously dated Windom but was forced to severe contact because of her obsessive behavior toward him.
>
> The district attorney in charge of the case issued a statement affirming there was no evidence to support McCray's accusations, or to link Windom to the murder.

Cassie wondered if any readers would scan all the way down to the "no evidence" part. She and Jordan hadn't been on a single date. Their only relationship was that she hated his guts.

A clickbait blog was more creative.

Will Cassandra Windom confess, "I killed her!"

The accompanying image showed a woman with ash-blond hair cascading to the waist of her tight, sparkly jumpsuit. Her raised hand, adorned with shiny fuchsia nails, failed to block her rouged face, which definitely was not Cassie's. She turned from the camera but still managed to flash a shocked expression worthy of a silent movie star.

Cassie laughed, not at the hair she would never have, or the manicure she would never spend money on, or the makeup and ski jump eyelashes she would never allow on her face, or the outfit she would never wear. She hooted until she was weak at the sight of enormous breasts spilling from the low, sequined neckline.

No danger of anyone recognizing her from that photo. It would take expensive implants and suspension of gravity for her to achieve such voluptuous cleavage.

She immediately sent the link to her sisters.

Happy SunnieChat Day!

KAYLA

C, Are you sure that's not you?

HOLLY

Wasn't that Ashley's Halloween costume one year?

ASHLEY

No it was mom's.

For the chamber of commerce gala?

ASHLEY

Book club party.

HOLLY

C, are you still getting letters from Jordan?

Still getting letters. Still not reading them. Still storing them in the basement with the broken fan and two decades of Aunt Renee's gardening magazines. You know where they are in case anything happens to me.

KAYLA

He's locked up. He can't get to you.

ASHLEY

He might encourage his cult groupies to do something.

HOLLY

Like steal a delivery of chocolate from her deck?

What cult groupies?

ASHLEY

On social media. Free Jordan.

HOLLY

Checking it out right now.

ASHLEY

Mostly they claim to be married to him and having his child.

HOLLY

Found it. Wedding photos! Jordan's face plastered on balloons as stand-in grooms.

ASHLEY

I follow it for the knitting circle who all married
him in one ceremony. Recent posts show
them with baby bumps working on booties.

KAYLA

It sounds harmless.

HOLLY

Until you read the comments.

ASHLEY

Lots of flame wars over who knows what's
truly in his heart, what he had for breakfast
and the date he plans to escape. Death to all
false brides.

HOLLY

C, Your law enforcement boyfriend needs to
move in with you.

Dinner and a movie first.

Chapter Thirty-One

Dale thought Heather drove like an accountant doing taxes—slow, precise, and quoting the appropriate statutes. He waited until the van crunched around the circular path of the gravel driveway and headed back toward the county tar before he went into the house. Clattering came from the kitchen, the mom kind that said "I'm efficiently getting out the exact things I need because I know where everything is." Not the cupboard slamming, "where the hell is it" dad kind.

Home from her shift clerking at the drugstore, his mom poured shell pasta into boiling water. "Hot dish for supper."

He hoped she hadn't noticed he'd arrived in a smooth-running family van instead of the F Bomb, which had a questionable muffler.

How to tell her that he and the entire family were headed toward an end-of-the-world disaster? The doomed homecoming dance was sure to cleave a rift between the Petrosky clan and the Steinhaus clan that would stretch into infinity. He'd sold the family cow for a handful of non-magic beans just because he was curious about a random dude.

Except the dude wasn't a rando. And what Dale had

learned about Mitch Hendrick made the off-balance sensation tugging at his gut even worse.

"Anything interesting happen today?" his mom asked, as if making casual conversation.

Dale's parent-radar buzzed like a hornet's nest. "Did you and Mrs. Petrosky come up with this homecoming dance plan?"

For a moment his mother looked as if she would play innocent. Dale was relieved when she didn't.

"Sherman, it was completely the girls' idea. Anne asked me if I thought it would be okay, and I said any young man would love to go to a dance with her daughters. And she said that wasn't true because they're so tall. And I said even if my son wasn't over six feet, that wouldn't bother him because he's not insecure like other boys his age."

Dale wished he was that guy, the one his mom thought he was. But he wasn't. If he'd gotten his height through her genes instead of his dad's, if he stood under five feet six in thick-soled boots like the men on his mother's side, he would have stayed away from the Petrosky girls.

Yeah, he was as pathetic as any dude. He imagined cans of male-teen body spray. *Insecurity, the perfect scent to go with your zits.*

Dale was kind of glad he'd already agreed to the Petrosky Scheme. Well, not glad about having three dates (who weren't really dates) to one dance, and not glad about having to go to a dance at all, but glad that he wouldn't have an argument about it with his mom. He'd decided himself, with his own free will (sort of), before she had a chance to guilt him into doing it anyway.

And now he knew that Black Hat was a minimum-wage museum guide. He hated the guy for the slimy way he talked to girls, to Jennifer. For his being on the prowl in the Itasca Room while his maybe-girlfriend was being taken to the morgue.

Okay, that last part was unfair. The Petroskys hadn't heard of any relationship between the two on the local rom-com network. When Dale saw Mitch with Kaitlyn in the car, the guy might have been giving a friend a ride home. The two weren't snuggled together like a couple. But then, seat belts complicated physical contact.

Romance or no romance, when Mitch was playing predator at the museum, he couldn't know Kaitlyn was dead.

Unless he was the one who'd killed her.

Dale wanted to puke.

Chapter Thirty-Two

"Ms. Windom, I apologize for having you come in for an interview on a Sunday."

This wasn't Cassie's first experience with Officer Robert "Robocop" Quigley. She sat across the vinyl-covered card table from him in a room off the bar area at the Veterans of Foreign War post. Plans to rebuild the sheriff's office and jail that had been damaged by a recent tornado proceeded at a crawl, causing speculation that the VFW would never be rid of its tenants.

Officer Robo seemed so young, and Cassie felt so old for thinking that. A buzz cut accentuated his square face and prominent jaw. The bristly scalp suited him, because who could bother with hair when there were criminals to apprehend. His light brown eyes registered no interest as she showed him the article on the *Falls Press* website and explained that she'd met Robin Snyder on Wolf Haunt.

"The date of this encounter?" he asked.

"Summer 2003." Cassie could almost hear the whir of flywheels as he processed the information. She took a sip of coffee from a mug stamped with the logo of a tattoo salon in Minneapolis, probably the place Rhonda went to. The steaming liquid, strong enough to give an elephant caffeine shakes, countered the tepid breeze from the squeaky free-standing air conditioner. Her chair, an upgrade from the garage sale relic Robo sat in, wobbled a beer coaster off plumb.

Pause. Whir. "Could you be more precise?"

"July." Cassie wasn't sure. "July-ish. Or August."

"A precise date would be more helpful."

"I don't remember." She wondered if the artificial intelligence running him had been trained with William Gibson novels or Excel spreadsheet manuals. Probably the latter.

"Are you sure it was 2003?"

"Absolutely."

"How can you be certain?"

She pointed to the portrait she'd placed on his desk. "I drew this that evening on that same day. I was thirteen." *You'll understand when you become a teenager*, she wanted to add but didn't.

Robo examined the sketch as if he were the stoic art teacher she'd had in college and never liked. "I see it is a reproduction, not the actual drawing."

This wasn't Cassie's first time dealing with evidence. She was not going to release her precious portrait and notebook of teen-angst scribblings to anyone, especially him. "The original is at my parents'." It was a small lie. If she'd said it yesterday, it would have been the truth.

"This is your only proof that you met the missing woman."

"She has a name. Robin Snyder."

"Were you alone?"

"My three sisters and three cousins were with me."

Robo shoved a yellow legal pad at her. "Write down their names and addresses, so I can get their versions of the event."

Despite the heat, Cassie felt a shiver as she printed Kayla

Windom across a line. "They'll remember the trip to the island, but they didn't see Ms. Snyder."

"Have you shown them or anyone this drawing?"

Sisters, no. Cousins, no. She'd been shy about her art back then, and the portrait had felt too personal to share. So the answer would be zero. She wasn't going to tell auto-cop that. "I don't recall." She realized she sounded like a gangster who'd been arrested on RICO charges.

"Is there anyone who can corroborate your supposed sighting of Ms. Snyder?"

"How about you locate Ms. Snyder and ask her about it?"

"Sarcasm is unproductive."

Cassie flicked her bangs off her damp forehead. "I find it satisfying."

"Don't expect special consideration because of your personal connection to the sheriff's department."

Oh, he was one of those. Disappointed that Adam hadn't asked him to be best man at the wedding. "I wouldn't think of invoking my privileges as a member of the Wells's Posse."

"I need to take custody of the copy of the drawing," Robo said, as if the lines and shading showed a bowl of fruit instead of a person, "since it's the only thing tangible you can supply." He paused. A trip hammer clicked in his head. "You'll get a receipt."

Cassie imagined the mechanical brain printing the details and a strip of paper spewing from the officer's mouth. She shoved the legal pad at him.

Robo looked over the six names and addresses. "You did these from memory."

"I send birthday cards. Never late. I'm famous for it."

He pointed to the first entry. "Is this supposed to be humorous? Kayla Windom. Galapagos Islands. On a boat."

"That's her permanent address. No post office. I send her e-cards."

He shoved the notepad back at her. "Email address for her, and phone numbers for the others. Please."

Cassie had hoped he wouldn't notice the omission so she'd have a chance to warn her relatives. She took out her phone, looked up the information and added it to the sheet. "Kayla is on a research vessel. Internet service is spotty." The ship had solid access to satellite communication, but Robo didn't have to know that. "You can try to contact her, if you really need her insight from when she was eleven years old."

The officer made marks on his interrogation checklist. "I'm required to add a notation that you did not immediately notify the sheriff's office."

"What do you mean by 'immediately?'"

"Directly after you saw the missing person."

"Rob-in Sny-der." Cassie over enunciated each syllable.

"Yes. Ms. Snyder."

"I'm not psychic. At the time I didn't know her name, and that she was considered missing. There was no mystic vision that fifteen years later she'd be connected to a murder."

Pause. Processing. Gears spinning. "It seems you would need to have the subject in front of you in order to get an accurate likeness."

"Give me a pencil and paper right now and I'll draw Sheriff Wells."

"Do you keep all your sketches?"

"No."

"You kept this one."

"Apparently I did."

"I'm finding your attitude hostile."

Robo thought *she* was hostile. He better put on his riot gear before he interviewed the rest of her family. She gave him her calm, corporate look, the one she'd used on clients when they needed redirecting. "Don't you want to know why Ms. Snyder was on the island?"

He scanned down his list of prepared questions. "I was getting to that. You told Officer Olson the woman searched for a lost necklace." He pulled a photo from a folder and placed it before her. "Did it look like this?"

Cassie folded her arms and leaned against the chair's slatted back without glancing at the image. "To clarify, lost means gone. Not there. She didn't have it, so I didn't see it." She let her gaze slide to the photo. "Why, Officer Quigley, are you trying to trick me? That's Mariah Lund's project for the art competition, which she just made this summer."

Robo returned the glossy to the folder. He took out a larger copy of the tiny school portrait that had been in the newspaper and placed it on the vinyl card table beside Cassie's drawing.

On the right, mature Robin seemed peacefully anchored in the moment.

On the left, young Robin forced a smile. A dark line circled the girl's neck. Cassie tilted forward to catch the detail. A string of beads. A necklace. The one her Robin had searched for on Wolf Haunt. She was certain of it.

"Ms. Windom?"

Cassie pulled back, startled. The repurposed storage room smelled of stale beer, and floral-scented soap. She gripped the seat of her chair and blinked, wondering if Robo lathered his bald head with lavender suds.

Had she frozen? Gone to the in-between place again? She hadn't fainted; that would have been embarrassing.

"Do you want to amend your statement?" he asked.

Cassie rubbed the goose bumps on her arms. It wasn't the first time she'd been asked that question. The detectives who'd interrogated her after she'd discovered Vicky's body had also given her a chance to confess.

The officer tapped the portrait of adult Robin with his pen. "Did you draw this when you were thirteen? Or"—he tapped young Robin's face—"did you see this in the paper and draw an extrapolation?"

Cassie stood, rattling the uneven chair. "We're done. And there better not be so much as a speck of ink from your cheap ballpoint on my artwork when you return it to me."

"Please sit down, Ms. Windom. I have more questions. I would prefer not to arrest you in order to get them answered."

"Arrest me."

Officer Robo didn't stand or make a move to stop her. He seemed permanently attached to the chair. Cassie guessed he wasn't programmed for this scenario.

"To summarize," he said, "you went to an island but can't provide the date. Once there, you met an unidentified woman searching for a necklace. Although you were with six other people, you are the only one who saw the woman." He made checkmarks on his written notes. "No date. No witnesses. No confirmed identification." He put down his pen and folded his hands on the notepad. "Ms. Windom, I find no verification for your supposition that Robin Snyder was alive in 2003. Or that the event you described ever occurred."

Putting her back to the officer, Cassie walked to the door and grabbed the handle. Damn. She hadn't gotten a receipt, which she wanted if only to irritate Officer Robo. And she really, really needed to examine young Robin's photo more closely.

It was Robo's case. Asking Rhonda or Adam to go behind the anal-retentive officer's back to get her a copy would be abusing her "special connection" to the department. Ordinarily the abusing part wouldn't bother her. But she didn't want to get her friend and her potential boyfriend in trouble with a colleague.

She halted her semi-dramatic exit, on the verge of deciding to take the hit to her pride, turn around, and beg Quigley for her very own laser-printed copy of high school Robin. And a receipt.

"I caution you not to consult with anyone on the list." Officer Quigley's annoyingly even tone might have been ordering more pens and legal pads. Or reminding the laundry to put extra starch in his boxers.

Cassie stalked out, mentally composing the texts she'd send to everyone on the yellow paper. She'd take on the toughest ones first, her cousins Cliff and Rob.

Chapter Thirty-Three

Celebrate your day with SunnieChat!

CLIFF

Cassie's ghost rises again

No ghost, a real missing person.

ROB

Wells doesnt believe you

Quigley interrogated me.

ROB

That guy can only follow one line at a time.
Show him a plaid and his head explodes

CLIFF

We'll swear we saw her too

I already said you didn't. Don't turn this into
one of your capers.

ROB

Ok we didnt see her but we saw the boat that
brought her

> No you didn't.

CLIFF

Did. Inboard new high end chriscraft. Did you think she swam to the island or took an uber

ROB

Been done. Not the uber the swimming. Drunk. More than once. Not me. A friend. Not really a friend. A guy I know

CLIFF

Yeah I know that guy too

> The only boats at the landing were ours.

ROB

Water was really high. He moored on mainland side. Good pilot. Bet your ghost barely got her feet wet

> He?

CLIFF

Guy waiting on the boat

> For real?

CLIFF

Real

ROB

Would we lie to you

> Most of the time. Did you recognize him?

CLIFF

Baseball cap sunglasses beer

> Oh that guy. Quigley can have you pick him out of a lineup.

Not Her First Murder

ROB

Didnt get a good look. Were trespassing.
Didn't want him to see us

CLIFF

I could pick the boat out of a lineup but its
probably docked at the great harbor in the sky
by now

I need a serious answer. Was there another
boat and a guy in it?

ROB

Yes. I swear on my radiohead collection

CLIFF

Yes. I swear on robs radiohead collection

Quigley is going to ask you what day we went
to the island.

CLIFF

Tuesday

ROB

I'll consult my diary. And I hate this chat app.
Its too cheerful

Were you ever going to admit I didn't see a
ghost?

ROB

Not me

CLIFF

Nope

Cassie signed off, imagining Rob and Cliff starting their own thread so they could LOL one another. Her cousins had grown older on the outside, but inside they were still the wild-haired boys who'd put a humungous snapping turtle in the bathtub for Aunt Renee to find.

A big disadvantage with texts was that she couldn't look into their eyes to see if they were telling the truth. Not that being face-to-face would help much. Knowing their techniques did not immunize her against their confident delivery of absolute nonsense.

After fifteen years, she'd finally discovered the mystery woman's name. Now, if her untrustworthy cousins were telling the truth, a different unidentified person had joined the party.

Jupiter lay prone on a small rug, one of the many soft, cuddly things he'd claimed as his own. He pressing his nose against the full-length glass door to the deck and growled. Outside, Kevin the Squirrel perched on an Adirondack chair and swiped a paw in the air as if flipping off the Akita. Kevin scampered down to the black walnuts dotting the boards. He scooped up one of the green spheres dropped by an overhanging tree and whisked it away to his lair.

Jupiter saw no difference between the fuzzy coating protecting the nut inside and a tennis ball. To him, each one snatched away by the little furry critter for winter storage was a theft of the highest order.

Cassie understood the puppy's frustration. She shouldn't let it bother her that Robocop wouldn't take her seriously. She shouldn't, but she did. His treating her like a Mrs. Finster, who had a way of putting herself at the center of every crime, itched in her mind like poison ivy. She couldn't allow him to snap his mechanical fingers and negate a significant event in her life. Especially now that the ethereal woman had solidified into a real person with a name and a history.

Cassie grabbed a sketchbook and a pencil, preparing to doodle her way to remembering the date of her trip to the island, and earning an apology from Quigley. While she tried to think of something concrete she could feed into the deputy's data-driven brain that would prove she was right, she sketched a Robo version of him with a helicopter propeller sprouting from his head.

The only thing the likeness showed was that—as she had told him at the interview—she could draw a face from memory.

She drew a robin, the bird this time. When Robin the girl disappeared, Wolf Haunt stuck out into the lake, a fat peninsula with a narrow gravel road connecting it to the rest of the world. Not an island. Not then.

When Robin, the grown woman, visited the island, did she know she was supposed to be dead and buried there? Maybe not if she'd been living in some other state. But the mystery man, who'd navigated Lake Blanchet without damaging his shiny speedboat, must have been local. Boat Guy would have known the story by heart. Had he told Robin or kept it from her?

Cassie could picture the figure strolling away from her that day, melting into the pine trees as if she belonged to the island.

Was the tale about Robin being murdered true, but the timing wrong? Had the mature woman been killed *after* her meeting with Cassie? By Boat Guy? That would give him a reason to perpetuate the story that Robin had died when she was sixteen.

If he existed.

If she could trust her cousins.

Which she couldn't.

Chapter Thirty-Four

It's always Sunny on SunnieChat!

HOLLY

She wasn't a ghost?

ASHLEY

Rob and Cliff lied. So shocked!

What do you remember about going to the island?

KAYLA

Rob wouldn't let me steer the boat. Lady slippers. Jack-in-the-pulpit. I checked the trees for snakes, didn't find any, disappointing.

Snakes in trees? Is that a thing in MN?

KAYLA

Garter snakes like to curl up on conifer branches.

HOLLY

Artificial Christmas tree from now on.

ASHLEY

It was the summer of sex texts. The football team had a burner phone.

Ash, how do you know that?

ASHLEY

Football players brag, especially when they are being stupid.

HOLLY

That's when I learned not to open texts from an unknown number. It stopped after a few days.

ASHLEY

Someone might have signed up that cell number for daily inspirational messages from Jesus.

ASHLEY

And today's horoscope with Madame Natasha. One minute meditation. A cat a day.

ASHLEY

Duct tape crafts you can do at home. A guy made his own tux.

HOLLY

On behalf of all teen females in Glacier at the time, a big thank you to Someone.

ASHLEY

You're welcome.

Back to my current drama, anyone remember the exact day we went to the island?

HOLLY

July

ASHLEY

Late July?

HOLLY

Rob didn't have a job because he, Cliff and Uncle Steve just got back from fishing in Montana.

Not helping.

KAYLA

Two days later Aunt Renee bought me the crassula ovata for being a good girl at the place with the beaver.

HOLLY

You mean the jade plant that's still alive, that owns our parents' living room and sucks up all the sunlight from the picture window.

ASHLEY

Little shop of horrors. Mom secretly feeds it dad's blood.

HOLLY

K, you didn't even deserve it. You were a terror at the museum.

K, we went to the museum two days after the island. You sure?

ASHLEY

Sounds right. Aunt R couldn't take more than a day of C begging to visit that place.

HOLLY

Aunt R didn't need C's whining. She was glad to have any excuse to go to Sunset, home of Sunrise Sunset Garden Center.

KAYLA

Two days. 100%.

Chapter Thirty-Five

The Fart Bomb growled like a sulking beast. Richie fed it more gas to improve its mood. Dale tried again to explain the penultimately horrendous situation he'd gotten himself into. He felt like he'd sold his soul to the devil—well, a sisterhood of devils—for unsatisfying scraps of information that made the strange sensation tugging at his gut even worse.

He couldn't get his best friend to understand the weight of it. To Richie, a date with three babes was a sure shot at a grope-fest. "I'd help you out, but Bridget's had a dress for months. She's having her hair done and everything. Girls think it's a big deal, getting all glammed and standing under a bunch of flowers or balloons or whatever it is this year." Richie suddenly got excited. "The theme should be something underwater. Then the arch could be a shark head, like on the poster for that movie. And we'll walk through this gigantic mouth all lined with teeth. That would be ultra-cool."

Dale hadn't thought about the theme. He hoped it wasn't a repeat of the year the committee had decided on "Back to Our Roots." They'd decorated the auditorium to look like a barn with the stage representing the loft. Couples in rented suits and sparkling gowns had marched under an arch of hay bales. Cameras captured their sneezes as shredded yellow stalks sifted down.

Dale had been too young to attend that one. He wondered why anyone would bother building fake animal stalls and hauling rusty milk cans into the school when you could just have the dance in a real barn.

Manure jokes had circulated for weeks.

"The shark thing would be awesome," Dale said. "We should suggest it for next year." Not that the alums running the show would listen to them. They leaned more toward "Night of a Thousand (fill in the blank)."

Richie roared the Bomb into Cassie's driveway and slammed to a stop. "Whitney was hoping you'd ask her to homecoming. But that's okay. She's got a backup."

They hauled lumber and a roll of wire fencing to the future site of Jupiter's kennel. Together they measured out the space and put down stakes at the corners.

Jupiter rushed to Dale as Cassie came out with cans of Coke. Richie pounced on the puppy and rolled across the grass, tumbling the dog with him.

"Okay if Richie helps?" Dale asked Cassie. "You don't have to pay him."

Cassie handed him a bright red can. "That doesn't seem fair."

"Richie's not really into employment, but he likes to do stuff." Dale didn't add that his friend's choice of stuff to do was often questionable. "He'll probably spend most of the time keeping Jupiter out of the way."

"It's Sunday afternoon of your last weekend before school starts," Cassie said. "You don't have to do this now."

"No problem," Dale said. He didn't add it was the excuse he'd given his parents for not being able to toss candy at the crowd from the fire truck during the Labor Day parade.

Richie scooped Jupiter into his skinny arms and walked over to them. "Hey, I was with Dale when we found the"—he dropped his voice to a whisper, as if afraid of upsetting the furry bundle he cradled—"dog bones. He didn't want to tell you I was there, because of the murder, but it's okay that you know."

Richie, obviously thrilled at having Cassie's attention, spewed out the details of the unauthorized visit to Wolf Haunt with a metal detector. "It was sad, you know. Gizmo got his head bashed in, then he's tossed in a hole like an empty beer can. We didn't find any old buckets, but I got stuff I used in my art project."

"You gave Mariah the Gizmo plate for her necklace?" Cassie asked.

Dale wished he knew how to move the topic to something else.

"Yeah, Trevor had us bring in junk for inspiration. I brought in the grave bag. Mariah wasn't feeling the muse, so I told her to check it out."

"What else did she take?" Cassie asked.

"Some beads." Richie tucked Jupiter under an arm. The puppy hung there, content. "I thought they were marbles or ball bearings until I cleaned them up. I didn't spill where I got them or what happened to Gizmo. Didn't want her to think they had bad energy. Trevor was always talking about putting energy in our art. I put max-tons into my masterpiece." Richie swept a hand as if showing them a marquee. "*Penultimate Dude*. That's what I named it. Then some ED jerk messed with my artistic vision and sensed it."

"Censored," Dale said.

"Yeah, that," Richie said. "I got interviewed about it and everything. Some guy started a media site. Missing Dick. It's got all these followers."

"Richie." Dale wanted to melt into the ground. And he wanted Richie to shut up, but that wasn't likely to happen.

"What?" Richie said. "Cassie, I can say dick in front of you, right? It's a guy's name, and you date and everything."

"It's fine," Cassie said.

Jupiter squirmed. Richie set him down and took a pop can from Cassie. "The little guy's got some weight on him. He's going to be a monster."

The puppy ran to the Bomb, did a one-eighty back to Cassie, then dashed to the car again. A furry black blob hung out of the rolled-down window, aloof and unconcerned with the creature bouncing on the ground below.

"Muffin's in your car again." Dale hoped the distraction would get Richie to stop talking about their criminal activities. He hadn't noticed the cat on the ride here. The dirty clothes and assorted items in the backseat provided plenty of cover.

"You have a cat?" Cassie asked.

"Muffin just likes to ride around," Richie said. "I'll drop him off at his house on my way home. He belongs to the Danowski kids. It's like he's got a built-in app for finding the Bomb."

"Jupiter thinks Muffin is Kevin the Squirrel," Cassie said.

"You name your squirrels?" Richie asked with interest. "Cool. It's hard to tell them apart."

"I just call them all Kevin," Cassie said.

Richie popped open his Coke. "That works."

Dale took a gulp from his can and set it in the grass. Richie's talking to Cassie made him nervous. The guy had few filters and little understanding of social norms. It was best to keep him busy. "Okay, let's get this done."

Richie ignored him. "Did Dale tell you he has three hot dates for the homecoming dance?"

Here's your SunnieChat!

It's someone else's cat but it lives in his car.

Not Her First Murder

Not my cat. It's a thing. There are videos.

HOLLY

I think our cat has another home. We feed her healthy food to keep her fit but she's turning into a whale.

KAYLA

I read you should hide food around the house and make your cat search for it. Keeps their hunter instinct sharp.

HOLLY

Our cat would be a skeleton in a week.

ASHLEY

Cat-sharing sounds good. I'll do the feeding if someone else does the litter box.

HOLLY

Does Schrodinger know about this?

Chapter Thirty-Six

Standing at the museum's information desk, Cassie resisted pelting Martin Brighton with pine cones from beside the donation box. "It's important." The Labor Day patrons were mostly families cramming a summer's worth of education into an hour of touring the historical displays.

Martin fanned a stack of brochures across the counter with a precision sure to instill awe in a geisha. Managing glossy trifolds seemed to be his stress-relief task of choice. "You've mentioned that several times, but not explained the issue or how the museum's visitor log from the summer of 2003 is connected to your emergency."

Cassie caught the implication: *Her* emergency wasn't *his* emergency. She figured he wouldn't be moved by a heart-warming story about the lovely day she and her sisters had spent here admiring the diorama of a fox mother and her pups frolicking beside a stream—just before they were caught, slaughtered and skinned by French trappers. She wasn't going to confess she sought the date she'd visited the museum when she was thirteen to prove to Officer Quigley that she wasn't a deranged attention seeker who inserted herself into official investigations.

In fact, attention was the thing she'd come back to Minnesota to avoid. So far, that wasn't going well. "It's connected to the break-in here at the museum." That should be important enough for him. And it was true, sort of.

"That doesn't seem likely. Considering the time gap, I'd say it's impossible."

Cassie dodged. "It's background information on what might be a family connection to an individual related to the theft. That is, the individual is related to the theft and related to a visit to the museum." The stuffed beaver smirked at Cassie, as if entertained by her linguistic gymnastics.

It had been harder for Cassie to probe Aunt Renee's memory about the museum trip without revealing the whole story. When she'd called her aunt, she'd babbled about having done a drawing that summer. Searching for it in her disorganized collection of sketches would be simpler if she could narrow down the date.

Aunt Renee recalled having a lovely day, confiscating lip gloss from Kayla, and stopping at the plant nursery, but few other details.

Cassie tried a more direct approach with Martin. "The museum is a public institution. So the guest books are public records." She had no idea if that was a real thing, but it sounded good.

"Hmm." Martin didn't seem moved. "We've never had a request to examine one before."

"An officer must have looked at your visitor records after the break-in."

"Complying with law enforcement when the museum has been the victim of a crime is entirely different from handing over information to a common citizen."

Cassie bet he wasn't so dismissive of common citizens during the annual fund drive. "You do have the visitor log from the summer of 2003, right?"

"Of course. It's a historical document, but that was some time ago."

"That's what makes it historical," Cassie said.

Martin was not amused. "After so long, even if you had permission from our board of directors, I couldn't say where it might be stored."

Cassie gritted her teeth. He was a cataloger, an organization freak who probably sorted his socks by color. She guessed he could pluck the correct volume off a shelf as if he were God in an Indiana Jones movie finally retrieving the Ark of the Covenant from a warehouse of identical crates.

"Oh, I'm sorry, Martin," Cassie said as if she spoke to a child who had skinned his knee. "I thought you had the authority to release it to me. I'll contact the board of directors. You manage the museum so well that, when they give their permission, I'm sure you'll be able to find it."

The director seemed caught off guard by the slam to his divine power followed by a compliment "I like things to run smoothly."

"I can tell." Cassie didn't remind him of the sham security that had made it easy for Mariah's necklace to be whisked away.

Martin straightened. Cassie slipped her smile into neutral, sorry she'd layered on the flattery. Males often adjusted their posture, trying to appear taller just before—

"I hope you've given some thought to the history of advertising project I mentioned to you earlier." Martin rocked forward, balancing on his tippy-toes. "We could discuss it over coffee."

"That would be great." Cassie wondered how old he was. Funny, men were self-conscious about a height difference but never considered age as an obstacle. "I've been wondering, when did Wolf Haunt become an island?"

Martin lowered himself back onto his heels. "I don't recall.

I was away at college for some time. I pursued several fields of study in addition to history. Art, architecture, psychology."

Cassie raised her eyebrows as if impressed. She wasn't. He'd been a young man with money and time. No student loans piling up. No need to rush into a job. No ambition.

Okay, that was too harsh. Cassie suspected his motivation was more basic. Martin had collected fields of study like baseball cards because higher education was his comfort zone, where he felt safe.

"It must have been a shock when you came home from school and saw the flood damage," Cassie prompted.

Martin averted his eyes. "That chunk of land is an albatross. But it's my sister's problem. She's the one who lives at the manor house."

Squish. Cassie had stepped in a sticky puddle of family conflict. She was never going to get the gunk off her shoe.

"Not to be rude," Martin said, sounding very much like that was exactly his intent, "but a busload of campers is due. Perhaps I'll find time to look for the guest book you want when schools go on Christmas break."

Or not, Cassie thought. She thanked him for his time and retreated to the Mini Cooper. She checked the glove box for a bag of pretzels she wished was there, knowing it wasn't. She craved salt and carbs to help her think.

No long vehicle appeared to belch out a crowd that would cover her sneaking back into the barn-shaped building, so she could slip downstairs to the storage room, battle spider-zilla and find the visitor log herself.

She found a chocolate square under her proof of insurance slip, tore off the foil wrapper, and popped it into her mouth The sugar rush cleared her thoughts.

Sutton Graywind was a board member. She didn't have a phone number for him, but she knew where he worked.

She examined the Blazing Star's website on her cell and

found an autodial link. Clicking on it imprisoned her in a frustrating circular game of menus that she lost. She should have expected that from a gambling establishment.

The place wasn't far from the museum. Cassie pulled out of the parking lot and headed for the casino.

Chapter Thirty-Seven

A big box store for gamblers, the Blazing Star sparkled on the edge of Sunset like a sequin on denim. The volume of cars and buses filling the parking lot confirmed that plenty of people were eager to toss away their cash on a holiday. Or maybe any day.

It wasn't Cassie's first casino. She stepped through the doors from a world rotating on its axis, driven by calendars and changing sunlight, into a cocoon that existed in a space of its own. Slot machines in tidy rows on the overly patterned carpet flashed neon. The cave-like interior, devoid of windows and clocks, marked time by the next spins of the machines. Days could go by unnoticed in the glitter and the illusion of opulence.

Cassie could almost smell the seductive promise of easy wealth that floated through the constant beeps and blips. Except for an occasional Powerball ticket, she wasn't a gambler. She couldn't think of money as a toy. Plunking down her hard-earned cash on one of these games would be like playing fetch with Jupiter. When you tossed the ball, it might be delivered back to you, but mostly it wouldn't.

Men in tailored charcoal suits dotted the floor, looking as

if the establishment got a group discount at Subtle Intimidation R Us. Cameras in smoky bubbles speckled the ceiling. Management wanted you to know you were being watched, but to quickly forget that you were.

Cassie walked up to the nearest suit. "You look like you can help me."

"Yes ma'am."

At least six feet tall with broad shoulders—although some of that was padding—he seemed more football jersey than formal wear. A bit of plastic in his ear made Cassie wonder what voice was in his head.

She put on her friendly, assured corporate face. "I need to speak with Sutton Graywind."

"Unfortunately, Mr. Graywind's schedule is full. And he doesn't do interviews." Football Jersey pulled a card from his breast pocket and handed it to her. "Call this number and you'll be directed to our public relations department."

"I'm not a reporter." The plain card with the Blazing Star logo showed the same digits that had entangled her in the maze of dead ends. "I'm here on business." That was a stretch, but he didn't know that. She took out one of her own cards and held it out to him, keeping eye contact until he finally accepted it.

"You're an artist. The gallery is to your right. They can help you." He used the polite, commanding tone of an assistant principal telling her to hurry on to class. "Please excuse me." He touched his earpiece, as if the voice directed him to something more important, when it probably told him to ditch the annoying woman who wasn't spending any money.

She knew she shouldn't let herself be so easily redirected, but she couldn't pass up a gallery. She hoped it would be more than a single still life stuck in a nook with bad lighting. To her great joy, an archway led to a quiet reception area and a room adorned with paintings, sculptures and fabric art. A plaque declared the space dedicated to MMIW, Missing and Murdered Indigenous Women. She examined a shiny brochure touting the exhibit of contemporary Ojibwe artists.

Serious art in a casino. This must be Sutton's influence.

She wondered what his position might be here. In addition to gambling, the Blazing Star had a bar, dining room, hotel, and swimming pool. How much of it did Sutton manage? Enough so that the staff played gatekeeper to protect his time.

He definitely ranked above the linebacker who'd brushed her off as if she were cat fur stuck to his worsted wool sleeve. She pretended to read bios of the artists while considering ways to get past the human equivalent of the automated phone menu.

A Sharpie sat on the receptionist's counter. Seriously. Right out in the open. Tempting a frustrated patron down to his last chip to grab it and slash a black streak across the waterfall rendered in chalk that enticed visitors into the exhibition.

Cassie snatched up the marker and spread the trifold across the counter.

In large letters, she printed a message. Then she walked out to the bay of slot machines and held the paper over her head like a banner, aiming it at the closest smoky bubble.

SUTTON, MUST MEET NOW CW

That should get his attention.

Chapter Thirty-Eight

The alcove in the large, dim casino dining room had been set up just for her, Cassie was sure of it. Well, arranged for Sutton Graywind's meeting with the psycho woman who had triggered a security alert. Linen tablecloth, china with the Blazing Star logo, fresh-brewed coffee, three-tiered platter of pastries from the casino bakery that Cassie found distracting, even after she'd—politely, delicately—devoured a scrumptious tea cake.

She'd been escorted here by Gerald. With a slim build and impeccable manners, he was far more *GQ* than the suited linebacker she'd dealt with before him. Definitely an upgrade.

In between nibbles, she'd apologized to Sutton for the spectacle and explained her quest for the museum guest book.

Sutton sat across from her sipping his coffee. "Are you sure you understood her correctly? That she'd lost a necklace on the island?"

The cut, fit, and fabric of the suit he wore today convinced Cassie his tailor resided in Italy. The elegant style was matched by the business card he'd placed on the linen for her. A sleek version of the Blazing Star logo rose from the rectangle's metallic finish. Sutton's name was printed below it, along with a phone number. Cassie noted it was not the one for the menu maze.

No job title. Which meant Mr. Graywind didn't need to advertise his rank in the corporate structure.

Wow. He must be king of the whole sandbox. Somewhere, on one of the floors above, sunlight flooded through gigantic windows into his private office, spilling across thick, pale carpeting. A message scribbled on a brochure wasn't going to open the door to that secure territory. You'd need to swear a pinky oath just to get on the elevator.

Still, a secluded conversation over coffee and goodies was more than Cassie had expected. She'd imagined trying to shout her pitch at Sutton while the linebacker slung her over his shoulder, hauled her out the double doors and deposited her in the parking lot like a cigarette stub.

"I'm positive that's what she said." Cassie put the last bit of a cherry tart in her mouth and gave her plate a little nudge to the side. A server, assigned exclusively to their table, whisked away the cream-and-gold china. With it went any chance of Cassie scoring another pastry.

"The guest book would only prove that you went to the museum," Sutton said. "Not that the person you met on the island was Robin Snyder."

Cassie felt a twinge of encouragement. He didn't sound as skeptical as Officer Robo. "I'm hoping it will establish the date. That should be enough to start a new investigation. The man on the boat will know if she was Robin or not."

"If the sheriff can figure out who he is."

"I'm guessing the boat is easier to trace than the person. Watercraft are registered. And around here, people remember anything with an engine."

Sutton's interest made Cassie wonder. "Do you know the Snyder family?" She really wanted to ask something else, but that seemed too bold. Oh, what the hell. "Maybe you met Kaitlyn Hanson?"

Sutton showed no sign that he was surprised by the question. "Mariah's mother works here, but I didn't know Mariah had entered the art competition, and I didn't learn about her conflict with the Hanson girl until the judges' meeting. I apologize if I was rude to you that day. You were very annoying. It seemed we'd reach a decision, then you'd spin us around, and we'd have to start over. I almost walked out. When Mariah's letter showed up, I realized you'd been stalling so she'd have time to write it. Later she told me the whole story, including that she got you arrested."

Cassie acted insulted. "I am perfectly capable of getting myself arrested, and that wasn't the first time I've proven it."

The edges of Sutton's mouth curved up slightly. "Thank you for helping her, and for being with her."

So Cassie wasn't the only judge who'd lost her impartial status. She hadn't seen him smile before. She liked the economy of movement. "Mariah's pretty good at standing up for herself. Is she doing okay?"

"She hasn't been charged. Having an argument over a necklace might be motive, but you need more to build a case. She has an excellent lawyer, who pressed that point with Sheriff Wells."

Excellent meant expensive. Cassie wondered if she was sharing coffee with the man paying the bill. The situation was not as simple as he made it sound. From what Mariah had told her and what she'd seen in the video, the argument on the street in front of witnesses had come close to causing bodily harm.

Sutton set his cup on the matching saucer. The watchful server glided over, refilled it and stepped back into anonymity. "Any murder is tragic, but my sympathy only goes so far. That Hanson girl was a thief. She spread lies about Mariah and goaded her into a public scene. Now she's being portrayed as a sweet, innocent saint. If Mariah had been killed—" He couldn't finish the thought. He paused and tried again. "No one cares when it happens to a Native girl. Forty-eight hours of news coverage. They show a photo twice. Then the media move on to something else. And so do the authorities." He spoke calmly, as if he'd grappled with that truth more than once.

Cassie wondered if he could recite the names of some of those lost girls. "I noticed the plaque in the gallery room."

"You found the exhibit brochure useful," he said, steering her away from a painful topic.

"The collection is wonderful. I want to camp out in it for a few days. Martin is lucky to have you on the museum board."

"I'm only one member. With the robbery, I hope the others will reconsider my plans for a new building."

"Please, one that doesn't look like a barn."

"Something with modern security and space for a culturally balanced view of state history. I don't expect to be successful. The museum's supporters cling to the idealized home of a wealthy Scandinavian because they view it as their own heritage."

Cassie thought it more likely that their ancestors had worked for the wealthy Scandinavian, who paid them crappy wages.

Sutton put an elbow on the table and bent closer to her. "What if the elusive Aunt Robin makes regular trips to Wolf Haunt? Maybe she's been doing it for years."

"Are you implying Kaitlyn knew about the visits and met her aunt there?"

"It's a possibility."

"Which provides another suspect." Too comfortable in the squishy chair, Cassie leaned forward. Huddled over gold-trimmed china on fine linen, she felt they'd become collaborators grappling with the same puzzle. But not exactly. She'd done her share of nudging, guiding, and suggesting. She recognized when the same tactics were being use on her.

Sutton nodded. "The Hanson girl claimed she owned the

necklace because the pieces used to make it belonged to her family. She and her aunt met on the island. Robin saw her niece wearing what had once been hers and she snapped."

Cassie wondered if Sutton had hired a private investigator along with an attorney. She didn't want to tell the handsome man, who smelled like fresh bread and strawberry jam (or was that the pastries?), that she thought his scenario was bonkers. But she did. "I think there are more feasible explanations to explore."

Sutton abruptly took his elbow off the table and pulled away. "You mean the sheriff's notion that Mariah killed the girl."

"No, of course not," Cassie said quickly.

Sutton stood. "Excuse me. I have a casino to run."

Cassie watched him saunter through the neon glow. Security guards filled in behind him as if she might grab the butter knife and fling it across the room into his back.

She took a sip of coffee that had cooled as suddenly as Sutton had. So, he was just another guy who paraded away in a huff when a woman didn't drool with delight over every stupid thing he said.

Gerald was at her elbow. "Thank you for being our guest, Ms. Windom."

Translation: Hit the road, babe. No logbook for you.

Cassie smiled at him and pointed to the arrangement of flakey crusts with sweet fruit fillings on the three-tiered serving stand. Were the gaps where she'd already raided the treats too obvious? "Can I get a box for these?"

Chapter Thirty-Nine

The cream-and-gold box fit neatly into the black-and-gold cloth tote splashed with the Blazing Star logo that was supposed to make Cassie feel special. It didn't. But the pastries inside the box inside the bag did.

The moment she rose to leave the intimate table she'd shared with Sutton, servers whisked it away, and replaced it with the larger one that had originally been there. It was time for the valuable space to start making money again.

Cassie smiled at one of the uniformed girls.

The girl smiled back. "I knew you'd find me."

"Glenna!" The young woman's hair, previously shocking white, shone a midnight blue-black. Cassie's stomach clenched as it had on the island when she'd first worried that the girl stretched out before the stone might be Glenna.

"I'm Rebecca now." She pointed to the employee badge on her vest. "I hated to give up Glenna, 'cause it's so cool, but Nate, he's my boyfriend—Nate Dalton, isn't that a dreamy name—he said if I took Rebecca's place, I could work here. She moved to another country. Canada or Mexico. So she doesn't need this job or her driver's license anymore. That's why I have dark hair, to match my license. I'm twenty-three, from New York. The state. And I've got a clean record."

"Judy and I have been worried about you. We've left messages."

Glenna rolled her eyes, thickly outlined in black. "It's soooo crazy. I lost my phone. I don't know how I did that. I was always real careful with it. Nate don't want me to use his 'cause it's for business. He's gonna buy me a new one, but he hasn't yet 'cause he's been so busy. Anyway, he said I shouldn't call you or Judy." She put a hand over her mouth and spoke through her muffling fingers. "I can't tell you why."

"Glenna, we need to talk," Cassie said.

"Oh, I so want to do that, but I really have to take my job serious. I have to get you a drink or something so it doesn't look like I'm goofing off. You can have anything you want for free since you're a special friend of Mr. Graywind."

"Water." Cassie needed to splash it on her face so she wouldn't get sucked into the alternate reality Glenna wrapped around herself. In the girl's mind having a license stating she was twenty-three-year-old Rebecca was the same as if her birth certificate verified it.

"Is club soda okay? With a twist so it looks like a drink?"

Cassie nodded and dropped into a chair at the nearest empty table. The fake ID and missing phone set off sirens in her head. Glenna was in an unhealthy, possibly dangerous, relationship. Again.

Cassie called Judy to let her know their friend was alive and not eating her meals out of a dumpster behind a truck stop.

Glenna returned with a glass expertly balanced on a tray. She placed it on the Formica table along with a paper napkin. "I'd be glad to answer any of your questions about the Blazing Star," she said in a rehearsed voice. "Nate helped me practice that. There's a whole script all the servers have to memorize.

It was hard, but it's like being an actress. So Mr. Graywind's your boyfriend now?"

Cassie shook her head. "I just met him today."

Glenna smiled wistfully. "See, you're real pretty even without makeup, not plain like me. And you've got this aura. I bet rich guys come up to you all the time and want to buy you a drink. But you don't have to do that, so you say coffee and they say sure."

"It wasn't like that."

"Is he taking you to dinner? I bet he asked and you said no 'cause you're engaged to Officer Berger."

"No dinner invitation." Cassie didn't have the energy to explain her non-romance with Adam.

"Mr. Graywind is Nate's boss. Well, he's Nate's boss's boss. Or maybe there are a few more people in between. Mr. Graywind runs almost everything. It would be great if you'd say something nice about Nate to him. You wouldn't have to give away that you know Nate is working for him—no one is supposed to know that. But you could say your friend, that's me, has a boyfriend who's a terrific guy and responsible and everything, and you don't know what he does, but he should get a promotion. And a raise. It would be great if you added the raise part."

"Didn't anyone notice you aren't Rebecca?" Cassie asked.

"I said I was a different Rebecca, just like Nate told me. He clued in my supervisor, and she's okay with it. This is just a little place, not like the casinos in Vegas, so everyone's relaxed."

Cassie very much doubted that was true. Where there was money, there were always people trying to stuff it into their own pockets. The entire machinery of a casino was designed to control the flow of currency, preferably to the house.

"You already know I'm okay, with your gift and everything. But I still love that you came to see me."

Cassie resisted interrupting her. Glenna saw no difference

between astronomy and astrology. Sometime ago, she'd decided that Cassie studied star charts to aid a psychic ability. Cassie's repeated denials had not been able to shake that belief.

Glenna went on, "I miss Judy and the kids so much, especially Jessie. I've got a job and a nice guy and an apartment. It's real small, but okay for now. Nate says we'll get something better soon."

Yeah, Cassie thought, *right after he gets you a new phone.* "What work does he do?"

Glenna picked up Cassie's unused napkin and replaced it with another tiny square, as if she were tending to a customer. "I'm not supposed to say. But you'd figure it out anyway, so it's not like I'm telling you anything. He does security for the casino, undercover, like a spy. He was probably in the slots room when you walked through, and I bet you never picked up any vibes. Nate watches how people move around and where they go. You know, in case they're doing something wrong. I help him out by talking to guests and the other workers and finding out stuff about them. It's super interesting. Nate says I've gotten real good with people. Much better than I was before."

"Glenna," Cassie said. "You trust me, don't you?"

"Sure. Otherwise I wouldn't have told you about Nate's secret job."

"This is not a good situation for you."

Glenna put a hand to her throat, as if she'd swallowed a mosquito. "You did my star chart. That's why you're here. Something bad's going to happen." Tears threatened to spill over her eyeliner. "Just when I'm happy and everything's about perfect."

"Let's go to Judy's," Cassie said. "She'd love to have you stay for a few days. That will give us a chance to sort this out." Glenna had lived with Judy and her kids in the past. With Judy's abusive husband in jail, the farmhouse was a safe place.

As she made the offer, Cassie had no idea what sorting out Glenna's situation would look like. She only knew she had to get the girl away from the boyfriend and whatever scam he'd dragged her into.

Shamelessly, Cassie grabbed at the most heart-twisting ammunition she could think of. "Jessie can read that bunny book to you." Using Judy's youngest child and a talking rabbit to manipulate Glenna wasn't the worst thing she'd ever done.

Glenna almost melted into a puddle. "Oh, I adore that story, and Jessie learned to read it just for me. But I can't leave. I'm helping Nate."

Cassie looked around at the cameras and the sentries in their dark suits. She didn't need special powers to know that Nate would soon get caught doing whatever it was he was doing. When that happened, he'd throw Glenna under the bus in a second.

Cassie could almost hear him whining to the sheriff. Glenna got cozy with him because he knew his way around the Blazing Star. She convinced him to steal an ID for her so she could get a job close to all that money. She came up with the scheme that was supposed to make them both rich. He'd been seduced, lured in by sex with a beautiful woman to commit a crime.

It was her fault, all her fault. In Cassie's head, the voice was Jordan's, blaming Cassie for Vicky's death.

Cassie hated exploiting the girl's belief in psychic nonsense. She did it anyway. "Glenna, this is important. You're on the wrong path. There are warning signs."

Glenna blinked away tears. "You're just seeing that Nate's job is dangerous. And I'm helping him, so I'm in danger too. But not like getting attacked danger. He explained it to me. And he'll protect me. He's smart and he's strong and he cares about me."

She grabbed Cassie's hand. "You can feel it, right? That nothing terrible is going to happen. And if it does, well, bad things have happened to me before and I'm still okay. Better than okay. I don't want to know what your spirits told you unless it's a car accident or our place is going to burn up."

Glenna let go of Cassie. "I have to get back to work, and we can't meet later 'cause Nate wants me at the apartment straight after my shift. He won't be there, 'cause he'll still be on duty, but he likes to know I'm at home. This is really wonderful, seeing you and everything. And I'm sorry you were worried. I'll call you and Judy when Nate gets me a new phone, promise. Hug Jupiter and Jessie for me." She dashed off like a frightened fawn.

As she often did after talking to Glenna, Cassie felt drained. She pulled out her phone and the metallic business card with the sleek logo.

Sutton answered. No automatic roll into voicemail. No gatekeeper. "I know this is a big imposition," Cassie said, "but could you meet me again, right now? I have something to discuss that involves the casino. And, so you know up front, I have a big favor to ask."

A beat went by. Cassie prepared herself for a polite version of "give me back my card and delete this number from your contacts."

"Gerald will escort you to where we can talk privately," Sutton said.

"Okay. I'm by the—"

"I know where you are."

Gerald was suddenly at her elbow. "Ms. Windom, a pleasure to see you again so soon. If you would please follow me."

Chapter Forty

The huge expanse of the casino looked the same as it had when Cassie first arrived. The lights hadn't brightened or dimmed. No shadows had moved to show the passage of time. Slot machines continued to beep and chime as if discussing the silly humans who paid to poke at them and watch their graphics roll by as if they told a story. And maybe they did have their own narrative.

Yeah, Cassie thought: *Sucker.*

She walked down the row of machines and plopped onto a red vinyl stool in front of a screen. Rainbow colors gushed at her in a nightmare of overstimulation. She'd planned on being home by now, but that was an emotional shock and a club soda ago. She'd sent Dale a text asking him to check on Jupiter.

Acting as if she did this all the time and enjoyed it, which she didn't, she fed a ten-dollar bill into the machine in front of her and selected her bid.

The young man next to her played slowly with his body turned toward the middle-aged woman on the other side. Tight jeans and a sporty shirt showed off his trim physique.

Honey-colored hair curled around his head in a slightly tousled way.

"My children are on their own now," the woman chatted at him, primping her fluffy hairdo. "They visit my ex-husband but ignore me. And won't they be surprised when I spend all my money and leave them nothing but the cat. Damn thing pisses on my socks and refuses to die even though it was run over five times during a bicycle marathon that went past my house."

The fortune she frittered away one electronic spin at a time might or might not be real. Cassie thought she expected a different kind of jackpot with the friendly young man, so handsome she just might take him home and introduce him to her cat.

"Hello," Cassie said.

He turned to her, an automatic smile curving his lips. "Hi there."

Polished, but not slick. A nature-trail version of yacht-club Jordan.

"I talked to Glenna," Cassie said.

His smile evaporated. "I don't know who that is."

He wasn't very good at this. Jordan would have raised his eyebrows slightly, transitioned to a curious grin, and asked who that strange person, completely unknown to him, might be.

"Then let's say I talked to Rebecca," Cassie said loud enough for the Cougar on the other side of Nate to hear over the noisy machines. "You know, your girlfriend. Who lives with you." The woman stopped feeding the neon monster.

"She believes she's helping you with your"—Cassie made air quotes—"'security job.' She doesn't know you're really targeting winners so you can pick them clean. And snatching debit cards from open purses."

Slot Cougar's gigantic fake designer bag, heavy with bling, rested on the floor between her and Nate. The woman grabbed the pleather strap, protectively pulling it into her lap. She quickly closed every buckle and zipper as if the pockets held her entire divorce settlement.

"I'm Cassie. I'm sure she mentioned me."

Nate gave a worried sideways glance toward his mark. "Rebecca doesn't want anything to do with her old life, and that includes you."

"That sounds more like what you want, not what she wants. She's sixteen, you know." Nate didn't have to believe her. The comment was meant to impact Slot Cougar. "Jailbait. Statutory rape."

"She's twenty-three," Nate said.

"The real Rebecca is twenty-three, but she isn't here anymore. Where is the real Rebecca, exactly? Did something happen to her? Did she become inconvenient and have to go away?"

Slot Cougar gasped, jumped from her chair, and spun Nate around on the swivel stool to face her. "You thought I'd be easy. A quickie in my room, and you'd clear out my bank account."

"Shut up, you cow," he snapped at her. "You think I'd sleep with a witch bitch like you?"

"You fuckin' pile of shit!" Two-fisted as if wielding a bat, the woman swung her heavy bag.

The blow propelled Nate backward. His sideways angle tipped the stool in the opposite direction, clattering it into the aisle between the rows of machines.

Nate crashed against Cassie, knocking her to the floor. He careened into her slot machine, sending colorful flashes across the screen. He planted his hands on the lighted panel to steady himself. The device complained in beeps and strobes. Shuffling his feet under him, he turned and lunged toward the woman.

She propelled her bag into his stomach like a battering ram. He grabbed her wrist with one hand and grasped the metal-encrusted bag with the other, crying out as zippers cut into his palm. They banged against the poor defenseless slot machine. It screeched and dinged with every jolt of the woman's bulk and Nate's wiry frame.

Cassie scrambled across the garish red, blue, green, and gold carpet like a child to get out of their way. Rooting for Team Cougar, she watched the struggle for control of the lethal purse. The woman lacked the muscle power of a twentysomething male, but she made up for it with rage.

Nate let go of the purse and shook his hand in pain. Trying another tactic, he plunged his sore fingers into the woman's puffy hair. She jerked back in horror, tripped and tumbled to the floor screaming. Nate stood over her, eyes wide, jaw hanging open, a voluminous mass of synthetic strands wilting in his fist.

Linebacker and his security pals moved in with Gerald close behind them.

"They attacked me," Nate shouted. "It's their fault."

A first aid team swarmed around Slot Cougar, who sat on the carpet, legs splayed out in front of her, purse in her lap. "My hair! My gorgeous hair!" An EMT checked for injuries while assuring her that the tufts of white sticking up from her scalp looked very chic. The woman probably wished her grown children were as attentive.

Cassie grabbed a stool that was still standing and hoisted herself up. Gerald gave her a questioning look. She nodded that she was okay. His face showed no emotion, but he gave her a wink. "Sir," he said to Nate, "if you'd be so kind, please relinquish the wig and follow these gentlemen."

"They're in it together," Nate insisted. "Seriously. They surrounded me."

"I'm sure we can straighten this out," Gerald said as security ushered away the bad boyfriend.

Cassie found Sutton at the end of the aisle. He tapped the plastic in his ear, letting her know he'd heard the exchange that had been picked up by an overhead microphone. "Not what I was expecting."

"It surprised me too." Cassie had thought Nate would shout and shake a fist, giving security plenty of time to intervene. It hadn't occurred to her that the woman would become violent. "Does that work for you?"

"A loud argument would have been sufficient. But a physical scuffle allows us to take legal action if needed."

"I didn't mean for the woman to get involved. I hope she's okay. I suppose she'll sue."

"Maybe," Sutton said. "The casino's lawyers will gently point out that she landed the first blow, and we're willing to overlook her behavior because we feel she was goaded into violence by Mr. Dalton." He almost smiled. "Plus she's a regular. I think free drinks and VIP tickets to a season of shows will take care of it."

"She's easy. I would have held out for carte blanche at the bakery."

"Is Ms. Lowery really sixteen?"

"I don't know how old she is. Her ID—her real ID, that is, the one she usually uses—shows she's an adult. I thought implying that Nate favored underaged girls would get Slot Cougar to move to another machine."

"Slot Cougar?"

"Bad habit. When I don't know a name, I make up a title."

Sutton listened for a moment to the voice in his earpiece. "Your girl is being shown a replay of what happened. An associate is explaining that her boyfriend does not work for the casino and that he tried to make her an accomplice to illegal activities. Apparently, it's a difficult conversation. Ms. Lowery seems to have her own unique perspective. She was shocked that Dalton lied about his job but more upset that he told you she didn't want to be your friend anymore. She says she can't be with him if he's going to act like that."

"You probably already had Dalton on your radar."

"We were watching him, but he'd been careful not to pull anything on camera. And our guests are often reluctant to report items missing from their private rooms when they've had invited visitors."

"Dalton knew how to pick his victims."

"I'd appreciate it if you'd reinforce with Ms. Lowery that she was involved in a very serious situation. She can't make another mistake, not even a small one. I'll shift her off the casino floor to the dining room. She's been helping out there anyway since we're short-staffed."

Cassie nodded. "Thanks for not firing her."

"Understand, we're handling this internally. No sheriff, no arrest. We can keep Dalton busy with an interview and paperwork for about an hour, but we can't hold him. There's no crime here, unless he wants to press charges against the woman who attacked him, which is unlikely since it would not be to his benefit. Officially, this was a disagreement between two guests. Nothing to do with the casino."

"I need to take Glenna to the apartment so she can get her things."

"You're not going alone. Gerald will go with you."

Cassie didn't like the way he'd already decided. She wanted to stamp her foot and insist she was capable of protecting Glenna. But she didn't, because she knew she wasn't. No black belt in martial arts. No gun in her purse. She was strong—well, strong-ish—and fit—okay, fit-ish—but not trained, not prepared.

But Gerald? She'd be glad to have the impeccable Gerald beside her when negotiating the reduction of nuclear weapons with a hostile government, or in a dispute over a parking space with a stressed-out soccer mom. For a possible confrontation with a pissed-off ex-boyfriend, she would have preferred the linebacker.

Cassie decided against saying so because she had a

bigger favor to ask. "Glenna needs a place to stay that's close by, so she can get to work. Any chance you can help with that?"

She quickly changed her mind. Nate was a small pest. Sutton must deal with bigger threats to the sanctity of the gambling establishment every day. He'd already saved Glenna from incarceration. Cassie couldn't expect one more thing from him. "I'm sorry. That was pushy."

"You went beyond pushy when you held up that sign," Sutton said. "I'm sure I can figure something out. And I need more information. It sounded like you accused Dalton of killing the real Rebecca."

"I don't know what happened to her," Cassie admitted. "She was working at the casino and now she's not. Glenna's interpretation of what Dalton told her is that the previous Rebecca moved to Canada or Mexico."

"That's a lot of territory."

"My guess is the woman is lounging poolside sipping a margarita in *New* Mexico."

"Or she doesn't exist," Sutton said. "Dalton might give a Rebecca license to whatever girl he's conned into living with him at the time."

Cassie guessed none of them stayed very long. There might be enough post-Rebeccas to form a support group.

"We take the well-being of our employees seriously," Sutton said. "I'll look into it."

Cassie knew he would. Personally. Not shuffling it off to his staff then never thinking about it again.

Sutton excused himself. As if on cue, Gerald appeared. "Due to the recent event, it became necessary to terminate activity at the slot machine you were playing. I apologize for the inconvenience."

Event. Cassie thought he made the slugging and shoving sound wholesome, like a picnic or the state fair. "I am done with gambling for a while."

"Here's the voucher for your session. I apologize on behalf of the casino if the payout isn't what you expected."

"You mean because Con Man and Wig Lady did a tango into my slot machine?" Cassie took the slip of paper. It seemed no different than her original ten-dollar bill, only not worth as much. She'd spun the virtual reels on a couple of one-dollar bets, both losers, before she'd grabbed Nate's attention.

Gerald seemed to be fighting off a smirk. "They may have come in contact with the betting panel. If you would, please examine the voucher, then sign here, stating that you accept the amount as accurate." He held a tablet in front of her as if presenting a sacred artifact. A signature box sat below rows of tiny, unreadable print. Cassie raised her index finger to scribble her name on the touchscreen.

Gerald swept away the device. "Please verify the voucher first."

Cassie flourished the paper, snapping it out at arm's length. This was a lot of fuss over a few bucks. She scanned the numbers behind the dollar sign. Then she slowly ran her eyes over them again, from digit to digit to digit to digit to decimal point followed by two zeros.

Gerald was in full grin now. He put the signature screen within easy reach. "Is everything in order?"

Cassie squiggled her name inside the rectangle. "Perfect."

Chapter Forty-One

On the porch of a rustic cabin, a woman in a flowing nightgown leans against a wooden post. A gentle breeze brushes back strands of long amber hair, exposing her generically beautiful face. She gazes into a dusky sky where a distant airplane curves above the last rays of the day. Her slightly parted lips smile wistfully, as if frozen in a sigh.

"Love. Only a flight away."

The caption tells the woman—tells all women—in a calm, sensitive font, that romance is waiting, attainable, simple.

Sure, if you can get time off from work, your credit card can handle the airfare, and you have a magic app that gives you the GPS coordinates of your soulmate.

Cassie's tranquil scene was marred by the blank space needed for the name and logo of the airline that made the absurd promise. The ad was a rush job for Prentice at Fontana Media. The artist it had been assigned to had suddenly taken family leave when his wife went into premature labor. Mom, Dad, baby and two previous kids were doing fine, while Prentice suffered from stress and sleep deprivation. He'd begged her for help, certain he'd be demoted to designing coupon fliers for a big box store if he didn't immediately have a polished graphic to show the client.

Cassie had agreed to the task and two additional projects. She smiled, thinking how the fees would add a cushion to her bank account—her very happy bank account. Usually lean and hungry, it currently swelled with the surprise snack of slot machine winnings, which she had rushed to deposit.

Tap, tap, tap.

Cassie jumped at the noise coming from her office window. A twenty-ish male peered in at her. Long, tawny hair twisted into a man bun, bag hanging from a shoulder, he looked too urban-centric to be local. In jeans and a Rolling Stones t-shirt, he could be from any of a hundred online tabloids.

"Arthur Curwick with the *Falls Press*," he shouted through the barrier. He plastered a business card to the glass as proof.

Cassie scowled. She recognized the name. This must be the grandson of the paper's owner/editor. Now even the town newspaper had zeroed in on her, hoping she'd crack under clever questioning techniques and confess to killing Vicky.

Except Arthur didn't look as if he could crack a peanut.

"I'm not home," Cassie yelled.

"Yes, you are," he shouted back. "I'm a trained journalist. I notice these things."

Cassie snapped the drapes closed. "I just left."

The muffled voice came from behind the fabric folds, "You're on the committee that judged the art show. Can I talk to you about the controversy?"

Cassie stared at the mermaids and conch shells hanging in folds from a thin rod. Neither was present in Lake Beauty. Laurel had picked the fabric when she was eight. Cassie wondered if she dared ask her cousin to replace the nautical curtains.

Tap, tap, tap. "I'm working on an article about Kaitlyn

Hanson. I think I know why she claimed the necklace belonged to her. I'd like you to look at a photograph."

"I know what the necklace looks like."

"This is a picture of Robin Snyder from 1983."

"The one that was in the newspaper?"

"Yes, but larger."

Was it the same one Officer Quigley had? Cassie made a gap between the two panels. "Show me."

Arthur gestured at the window. "This is a little awkward. Can I come in?"

"No. And I warn you, I have a dog."

As if on command, Jupiter jumped into her lap, then up onto the desk. He thrust his furry face through the opening.

"He looks terrifying," Arthur said flatly.

"Hey, in a year he'll be able to knock you flat with a swish of his tail."

Arthur shoved his business card into a shirt pocket. "Then we better get this done now."

"On the deck in ten minutes." No way was she allowing him into the house. This might be a ruse to lure her into talking about Jordan's appeal. She set Jupiter on the floor, angry at herself for abandoning caution in a crazy hope he might supply an important detail that would clear Mariah. Or at least point the investigation toward someone else.

She sent "Wistful Woman with Plane" to Prentice, then went outside through the living room's sliding glass door. Jupiter stared at her as if she were Kevin, whimpering his displeasure at being left in the cabin. The moment she set her phone on the small table beside her chair it buzzed like an angry insect. Jordan's appeal, the new alibi, and his accusation against Cassie continued to shake the hornet's nest.

"Should you answer that?" Arthur asked.

"No." Cassie looked him over. Was he a good candidate for her chocolate thief? "How long have you been at your job?" He'd regret having settled into the Adirondack. The low design was great for relaxing in the sun, but it was like having your butt stuck in a barrel when you tried to stand up.

"I recently moved back here to work at the *Falls Press*."

That felt like deflection. "To join the family business."

"I have a degree in journalism."

Cassie heard the irritation at her implying he'd gotten his job because of blood rather than skill. He was going to be miserable his entire career if he couldn't handle someone shoving a tiny pea under his mattress. Her phone buzzed again.

"Are you famous?" Arthur asked.

It hadn't bothered Cassie when Martin had called her that. But then, he wasn't likely to turn their conversation into a blog. Arthur might.

"No, and I want to stay that way."

"I should ask you a lot of clever, probing questions about that, but I won't."

"Then we'll be fine." So far she hadn't noticed anything even close to clever. "Show me the photograph."

He pawed through his bag. The lounge's V shape forcing him to hunch forward in order to get at the contents. "The Lund girl attacked Kaitlyn because—"

"Not an attack." Sitting in a sensible, upright, faux-rattan chair, Cassie held the psychological advantage of the high ground. "Calling it that misrepresents the situation."

"All right," Arthur said. "The *disagreement* between the two girls is based on ownership of the necklace. But that's not exactly accurate." He paused so Cassie could react.

She didn't. He would explain without any prompting from her. All puffed up with some earthshaking discovery, he couldn't help himself. She expected it to burst from his chest like a baby alien.

"You've seen the new necklace up close. You know what the beads look like."

"It was stolen before the committee met. I only saw a

photo, the same one that was in the *Falls Press*." She didn't add that she'd sketched the lines and curves of the beads from their impressions in the clay on Wolf Haunt. That she knew the pattern by heart.

Arthur pulled out a glossy sheet. "I hope your artistic eye can tell how those beads compare to these."

He handed her the same image Quigley had put in front of her, but the two were not identical. A laser printer had spit out Robo's on flimsy paper. Arthur's eight-by-ten had been commercially inked onto thick, glossy stock, as part of a package sold to Robin's parents. Or perhaps to the girl herself.

Had it been in the newspaper's archives all these years, ready to be used in another tragic story? Or had Kaitlyn pulled it from the family album and given it to the journalist?

The standard blue-gray background of a school photo surrounded Robin. The pink raglan-sleeve sweater contrasted sharply with her ashen complexion. The scooped neckline hung loose from the bony shoulders in '80s style—or because the garment was a size too large.

This teen was not healthy, not cared for.

Cassie remembered drawing the hollowed cheeks and narrow jaw. Her older subject, although also physically weary, was more comfortable with herself than young Robin seemed to be.

Cassie picked up her phone and tapped the screen. "Magnifying app," she explained to Arthur. Zooming the image to the limits of its resolution, she ran her camera across a bronze choker that curved above the knit top, checking each sphere.

A bar interrupted the pattern. Length equivalent to five of the fat beads, the flat metal swirled with ornate curls, framing letters in the identical font that adorned the Gizmo tag. The single word was difficult to read but Cassie knew what it was.

Robin

On silent mode, the phone made no sound as she used "freeze and save" to capture the school picture.

"They're the same as the beads in the Lund girl's necklace, aren't they," Arthur said.

"That's less of a question and more like a statement you want to be true." Cassie closed the app and set the device on the table. It vibrated with another unwanted call.

"I'm just collecting information," Arthur said.

"And motives?"

The reporter seemed uncomfortable on the answering side of a question. "Information can reveal motive."

"Or it can be unconnected."

"You don't think the original necklace is important to identifying Kaitlyn Hanson's killer?"

"You must be following other leads," Cassie said, encouraging him to look away from the obvious suspect.

"If you were in my position, who would you investigate?"

Sure, throw it back at me, Cassie thought. But it was a fair question. Considering what she knew of Kaitlyn's temperament, there must be frenemies and ghosted boyfriends. Males who'd been used and abused. Females who'd been bullied and bad-mouthed.

There was Trevor, who'd lost out on bragging rights when his star student's sure winner was stolen. And Martin, who could be fired over the break-in. Bad publicity meant a loss of donations. And Sutton, who wanted to protect Mariah as much as Cassie did.

And Mrs. Finster because—well, because she spent so much time verbally attacking people.

Cassie kept her list to herself. Let Arthur do his own homework. "I heard she was a member of a model train club. Maybe there was a dispute over HO scale versus N scale. You seem to be a good reporter." Flattery was always a reliable strategy. "I'm sure you have better ideas than I do."

Arthur tried again. "The beads are the same, aren't they?

You know they are because you've been mentoring Mariah all along. You probably gave her the beads."

Cassie returned the photograph to him. "Even if they are the same, there could be thousands just like them out in the world."

Arthur's voice turned harsh. "Of course that's what you'd say. I know you claim you met Robin Snyder years after she disappeared. But that's a lie. It has to be. Kaitlyn knew her aunt was dead, and she was going to prove it."

Cassie took a stab. "When did the two of you start investigating her aunt?"

Arthur twitched. "It's an important story." He tried to stand. The butt-in-the-barrel feature of the Adirondack pulled him back down. He bounced out of the slump to the end of the planks like a toddler, gathered his legs under him and lopsidedly pushed himself to his feet.

"An old disappearance paired with a current murder could really boost a career," Cassie said.

The young man shoved the school photo into his bag and adjusted the shoulder strap as if it were his dignity. "You seem to be smack in the middle of both of them. The sheriff should be investigating you."

Cassie saw his hands curl into fists. Was Arthur going to toss the Adirondack at her or burst into tears? Hard to say which was more likely.

He did neither. Instead, he stomped down the steps to the back yard. Cassie followed as far as the deck railing where she could watch him from high ground. She videoed him stalking across the lawn, his man bun bobbing, and climbing into a late-model beige Camry. She added the journalist's name and license plate number to her contacts. In the notes she typed a comment.

If I end up dead, check this guy for blood spatter.

Danith McPherson

Sunny SunnieChat Day!

I need feedback. The woman in the drawing, what is she thinking?

ASHLEY

Where did I put my car fob?

HOLLY

Should I invest the money in a mutual fund or pay down the mortgage?

KAYLA

The barred owls are noisy tonight.

She's supposed to be thinking about her lover who is flying away in the plane.

ASHLEY

Where did Antonio put the car fob?

HOLLY

Will he notice if I go through his computer history while he's gone?

KAYLA

I can finally catch up on my sleep.

It's for an airline ad.

HOLLY

Did he remember to get travel insurance?

KAYLA

Carbon emissions! When are we going to get solar planes?

ASHLEY

He's finally gone, now I can book that flight to Cancun.

Chapter Forty-Two

After Arthur Curwick left, Cassie searched the *Falls Press* social media feed for articles written by her new least-favorite journalist. One immediately caught her attention.

Art Contest Stained by More Woes
Student claims art altered due to sexual imagery

The student claims a portion of the sculpture representing a specific part of male anatomy was removed without his knowledge or permission. "I was max-ultra slammed," the student said.

Director Martin Brighton contends the sculpture had not been censored by museum personnel. He stated the incident was probably a "misguided prank" by a visitor to the exhibit and denied it had any connection to a recent robbery.

The Granite County Sheriff's Office is investigating the case as vandalism.

The accompanying photo showed a metal framework encompassing a small animal skull. Since the artist was a minor, no name was given. Cassie laughed. Most of the town could guess the student's identity from the quote.

Cassie checked out the Missing Dick media page on her tablet. The banner showed the same art contest photo she'd reviewed. Her eye went to the vacant space below the belt buckle. What had the artist-known-as-Richie clipped there?

Visitors to the site offered substitutes for the absent part. Cassie was disappointed by the lack of imagination. If three people have already posted bananas, you don't need to add another one, even if it has googly eyes. The same applied to real penises.

Hmm. The photograph, taken at the museum before the exhibit opened, showed the symbolic anatomy already absent. That destroyed Martin's story of a prankster snatching it while it was on display.

Had Martin removed the potentially offensive item to keep the museum family friendly? In that case, he should have just said so instead of pointing the finger at an anonymous puritanical hooligan.

She shouldn't be so quick to blame Martin. Trevor might have edited the artwork before it had arrived at the museum, worried he'd be accused of allowing underaged students to produce pornography.

The controversy over depicting body parts—real or abstract, anatomically correct or a banana—was not a new one. Cassie imagined Neanderthal artist Pugg-casso, a stick of charred wood in his hand, having to defend his drawing *Nude Descending a Rock Slope* to the tribe's Cave Art Council.

Cassie's cell blasted out the *Mission: Impossible* theme. She let it go through dum-dum-da-da twice before answering.

"Great job on the crime scene drawing, Special Volunteer Member of the Sheriff's Posse Windom," Adam said over the phone.

"Why, thank you, Deputy Sheriff Berger," Cassie said. "I

just happened to be in the wrong place at the wrong time with a loaded pencil."

"About that, could you confirm a few details in your statement for me?"

"Like what?"

"Whose idea was it to go to the island that morning?"

"Trevor Rothman, as an outing for his art club."

"Did he come up with that himself or did someone else suggest it?"

"He took credit for it." That didn't mean he'd originally proposed the trip. In Cassie's experience, a certain type of man was inclined to claim other people's ideas as his own. She suspected Trevor fit that category.

"Are you a member of the club?" Adam asked.

"No." She wasn't part of any group. Had no social life. Was turning into the Hermit of Beauty Lake. But she didn't say that.

"When did you first meet Rothman?"

"That day." Was Adam asking as an officer of the law or as her maybe boyfriend? "He called and asked if I wanted to go sketching with the group. We didn't actually meet until he picked me up in his boat."

"Based on a phone call, you agreed to go to a secluded island with a man you'd never met."

"And his art club." Okay, she got the point. She'd been a tad reckless and impulsive. She pulled out a semi-logical reason for the sudden invitation. "I was judging the art competition that afternoon. He probably wanted to see if I was worthy of the honor."

"Four members of the art club, including Rothman, plus you" Adam said. "Five people."

"The boat is certified for six, so no watercraft rules were broken." Cassie's irritation at herself for trying to justify her actions dissolved as she recognized an opportunity to do some nudging. "Thinking about it now, it is suspicious that

Rothman"—she didn't want to seem too friendly by using his first name—"suddenly decided to take the club to the island, where he could stomp around, leave footprints, shed some DNA-rich hair, and spit in the dirt."

"You're suggesting he organized the trip so he could contaminate the scene in front of witnesses."

"Wow, you think he did that?" Cassie could almost hear Adam's tolerant sigh.

"I think you want Mariah to be innocent."

"She is."

"We are looking at other suspects."

"Like who?" Cassie asked. Finally the authorities were broadening their investigation.

"It might surprise you, but we came up with the same theory you did, that a person went to the island to compromise the evidence. The investigating team—"

"That would be you, Rhonda, and Sheriff Wells."

"—in coordination with the Minnesota Bureau of Criminal Apprehension, reviewed each of the witnesses' movements that morning. We discovered a very interesting fact."

"Which is?" Cassie thought Adam was having far too much fun dragging this out.

"According to your signed statement, the only person who got close to the body was you."

"Me? That's the best you can do? You are way behind the curve. I'm already on the suspect list." Cassie relayed her experiences with Officer Quigley and Arthur Curwick.

Adam's serve and protect mode kicked in. "I'll check out Curwick. He might be dangerous."

"Don't worry. He won't mess with me. Jordan's case is being appealed again. Google me. I'm trending as killer of the month."

"Keep your doors locked," Adam advised.

"Always."

"I need to explain something."

Cassie braced herself. She hated when men felt the need to explain, especially when they announced they were going to do it.

"The department has to take every murder investigation seriously," Adam said. "I was going to ask if you wanted to go to a movie. Now I can't do that until you're cleared."

Cassie supposed she deserved this detour in their semi-relationship for trying to manipulate him into investigating Trevor. "We need the sheriff's permission to go on a date?"

"I'm sure it'll be straightened out soon. We're both busy on Friday night anyway."

"We are? I am?"

"I'm on duty. And Rhonda told me the Sparks have a job for you."

Chapter Forty-Three

"I suppose it's silly to keep these. Your uncle tossed them out once, but I rescued them." Renee Schroeder lounged in a plush recliner with her feet elevated. She ran a hand across the book in her lap. "He coached these kids when they were in middle grades and was so proud of them. As they moved through high school and graduated, he always bought their yearbooks."

Cassie glanced out the window at people spreading yoga mats in the central courtyard. She thought her aunt had settled in nicely to her apartment at the Bluestem Pond Senior Village.

Two years older than her sister Connie, Cassie's mother, Aunt Renee had the same direct blue eyes and light reddish-brown hair.

"Sorry my timing is bad," Cassie said. "I'm keeping you from your Wednesday hip and knee session."

"I'll catch the one this afternoon."

Cassie took the volume her aunt held out.

The Glacier
Glacier Falls High School
1983

"Thanks. This will help a lot."

"You can get better photos from the internet," Renee said. "What's this really about?"

When Cassie had called to ask if she could borrow one of Uncle Steve's collection, she'd used the excuse that she was working on a marketing campaign with an '80s vibe. Such a weak fib hadn't fooled the well-calibrated bullshit detector of the woman who'd raised Cliff and Rob.

Cassie curled into the matching recliner, the one that had been Uncle Steve's. She pulled out her phone and showed her aunt one of the photos she'd secretly snapped while talking to Arthur. "I'm looking for pictures of Robin Snyder. The 1982-83 school year ended just before she disappeared."

Renee studied the image. "Hmm. I saw this in the paper. She looks so thin. My cribbage club filled me in. Robin's dad Randolph—Kaitlyn's grandfather—worked as a welder, when he could hold down a job. Standard manufacturing stuff. He was good at it from what I heard. Metal art was his side gig. Animal figurines. Jewelry. Robin wore a necklace she and her dad had made together."

Cassie paged through the yearbook, searching for the sophomore section. "That must be the choker she's wearing in the picture. There's a flat bar in the front with her name engraved on it. Could he have made the beads himself?"

"He had the equipment and the skill. My friend Carol has a cardinal she bought from him. He told her it was based on a drawing he'd done, and that he'd made the mold himself."

"Bronze?"

"Definitely." Renee tapped the screen. "Like these beads." She handed the phone back to Cassie.

Cassie needed an assurance that Old Randolph hadn't

flooded the world with his jewelry. "Did he sell his work online?"

"That wasn't a thing back then, and he wasn't the entrepreneur type. He struggled with life. So did his wife. Whether they had mental illnesses or physical ailments or both, no one in my group knew for sure. Whatever it was that wore them down, they didn't have the energy to raise two kids. The churches and just about every organization in town tried to help, but they couldn't make sure that the meals they brought over were warmed up and served to the girls. Or that the clothes they donated were tossed into a washing machine every week. Erica, that would be Kaitlyn's mom, was put in foster care shortly after Robin vanished. When that happened, people stopped posting missing person flyers for Robin. They assumed she'd realized what was coming and ran away rather than end up in foster care."

"I wonder if Erica knew her older sister planned to leave." Cassie would have been furious if her situation had been as grim as the Snyder household and Holly had abandoned the rest of them. Although annoyingly practical, Holly was their foundation during tough times.

"I'm telling you what I was told," Renee said. "I don't know how close it is to the truth. Erica was only eleven. She's always insisted she had no idea what happened to her sister. She wasn't fostered in Glacier. She moved back here when she was an adult and then married Jimmy Hanson. My puzzle club, which has some of the same people in it as my cribbage club, couldn't decide if the Hanson family was happy when Erica married Jim, because of all the Snyder land she would inherit and because it meant their son would stay in Glacier, or if they were unhappy about it because Erica had health problems and dysfunctional parents to deal with and because it meant their son would stay in Glacier."

Cassie flipped pages. "That sounds confusing."

"Parents are always torn. Do they want their kids to live

close by so they can see them all the time, or do they think their kids will have better opportunities and be more successful if they go off somewhere else?"

Cassie knew her mother was on Team Somewhere Else. She'd acted as if her girls would always venture into the great wide world. If they'd hung around too long, she would have shoved them out of the nest herself. In contrast, Cassie's dad would have dug a moat circling the Windom castle and kept the key to the drawbridge on a chain around his neck if his wife had let him.

"What do you think?" Cassie paused at a spread of glossy candids.

"Depends on the kid. Leaving Glacier has been good for the boys. Rob is close enough that he visits every week or so. He was going to stop by the cabin and see you the other day."

Cassie shook her head. "I must have gone into town." A girl in a horsey costume adorned with a long tail posed in a crowded hallway. A spike stuck up from the band around her head.

Cassie used her magnifying app to scan faces in the background. She found Robin, the line of the necklace visible at her throat. Her lips were parted in the middle of a quip that caused the girl with her to smile.

Cassie provided a caption. "I wouldn't be caught dead in a unicorn outfit."

"You would have worn it to school every day for a week if you thought you could embarrass Holly," Renee said.

"Not embarrass, exactly." That had never been Cassie's intent when she'd done crazy things, except maybe once or twice. She'd rather not think about the incident with a spray can of Silly String. "I just wanted her to relax, laugh, enjoy the goofy." Her older sister had been a serious student, breaking out in hives at every test that threatened her perfect GPA. Cassie understood Holly better now that she recognized her own quest for perfection.

She turned the book toward her aunt and pointed. "That's Robin. I think the girl next to her is Tammara Brighton."

"Probably. According to my poker pals, Robin was Tammara's only friend."

Cassie studied the face. This girl looked at ease, happy, so different from the tense adult. A wide strap supported a canvas satchel slung over her shoulder. A large clip heavy with trinkets dangled from a metal buckle. The touch of whimsy softened the austere bag that appeared older than she was.

"Boomer told me she went away to school. That's unusual for around here. Boarding school is where British kids go in movies to tangle with bullies and have unsupervised adventures."

"Your cousins managed to have exciting childhoods, despite your Uncle Steve and me keeping a close eye on them."

Cassie didn't add that she and her sisters had been pulled into a few of those exploits. "I've sort of met Tammara." She couldn't say it had been on the island at a crime scene. Later she'd spill the whole story to her aunt but not now. "And Martin. When I went to judge the art contest."

"I've been thinking about our girls' day at the museum since you called asking about it. I chased Kayla through every room in that place. Her fingerprints are probably still on the display cases. She's lucky she hasn't been accused of the burglary."

Cassie wanted to ask again if her aunt remembered the date, but in person was different from over the phone. At the first hint of an interrogation, she would crumbled like a stale snickerdoodle, revealing the entire Wolf Haunt saga.

How would Cliff and Rob explain to their wives that their mother had grounded them—again?

"Martin tries all sorts of things to keep the place functioning," Renee said. "Kids and parents love the art contest.

And it gives local artists a boost. Mentors of the winning students get highlighted during the Art Fair and the Studio Hop every year. You should get involved in those. Meet some of the artists."

"I've met a few." Cassie didn't feel the need to put a number on it.

"Who?"

"Mel Moreau."

Aunt Renee seemed impressed. "Have you seen her paintings on silk?"

"You mean those beautiful scarves she wears?"

"And other fabric art. All of it colorful and gorgeous. Who else? Any young men?"

Cassie knew her aunt would get around to asking. "I'm past the *young* men stage."

"Age-appropriate men, then," Aunt Renee said. "And available."

"Does Trevor Rothman fit into both categories?"

"He does." Renee crinkled her face in a thoughtful expression. "He's held a few painting classes here. Cassie, with you, we knew your future the moment you smeared creamed peas across the tray of your highchair. Trevor doesn't seem born to art. I have the feeling he's projecting what he thinks an artist should be."

Cassie thought of Trevor's expensive boat. Of course, she didn't know for sure that he owned it. "He appears to be successful."

"He always has things, like that Corvette he drives, but he never seems to have money."

"So if he suggests we go for pizza, I should get clarification on who's paying."

"Has he?"

"No." Cassie didn't say that his jacket hung across the back of a chair in her kitchen.

Her aunt looked out the window to where the yoga class

was ending. "Does the sheriff really think Mariah killed Kaitlyn?"

"He might be following some other leads." Cassie didn't add that, according to her conversation with Adam, she was one of them.

"And you're trying to find some for him?"

"Anything that will point him toward the real killer."

"Who definitely is not Mariah?"

"Yes."

"And you know this because—?"

"Because—" Because she saw her young-artist self reflected in Mariah. Because she needed the killer to be a stranger this time, not someone she knew. Because she couldn't let the wrong person be convicted. "—I can't imagine a young, vibrant girl doing something so ugly."

Renee nodded. "I see."

And Cassie knew that she did. With a feeling of relief, Cassie confessed that she'd made the grisly discovery on the island. "Yes, I had another close personal encounter with a dead body."

"I hope it doesn't become a habit."

"Absolutely do not tell your club or yoga pals, and especially not my parents."

"You're asking me to keep a secret from my sister? As if I haven't done that before. And since we're in that territory, how is Ashley doing?"

"She told you she's pregnant?"

"She hasn't called me in weeks, that's how I know."

"Have you shared that with my mom?"

"We talked last night about her droopy begonia. She's going to bring it over so I can coax it back to health. I suspect it only needs regular watering. Your mom gets busy and forgets the simple things. I held strong and didn't even drop a hint about babies. We have to give Ashley space and let her make the announcement when she's ready."

"That might not be until she starts wearing pants with a roll-over waistband." Cassie hoped Ash would make it to that point, and beyond.

"I knew she'd tell you," Renee said. "Holly worries too much, and Kayla is too far away."

"They figured it out. Now they're mad at me for not immediately breaking my sworn Blood Oath of Silence." Cassie grabbed her phone and pulled up the recent ultrasound. "Here's your new grandniece or nephew. I went with Ashley to a checkup and interrogated the doctor mercilessly. Everything is normal, but Ash is still a nervous wreck."

Cassie didn't add her sister was so tense that if she swallowed a lump of coal, the baby would be born holding a diamond.

Renee smiled at the snow storm. "Send me a copy?"

"On its way."

Chapter Forty-Four

SunnieChat is here for you!

> How big a secret would you keep from a sister?

HOLLY

Asking for a friend?

KAYLA

You mean big like being pregnant?

Bigger

HOLLY

Nothing's bigger than pregnant at eight and a half months.

> More specific. Would you hate your sister if she ran off and left you just as you were going into foster care?

KAYLA

Ok that's big.

Not Her First Murder

ASHLEY

You mean if mom and dad had died when we
were young?

HOLLY

Aunt R and uncle S would have taken us.

KAYLA

They already had three kids. That would have
been asking a lot.

HOLLY

Remember when dad was in the car
accident?

Scared me so bad.

HOLLY

Ash and I had a serious talk with R and S.
They promised we could all live with them if
anything happened.

You never told me that.

KAYLA

Me either.

ASHLEY

You were too little to think about mom and
dad being gone.

No I wasn't. I worried about it.

KAYLA

I didn't worry. I didn't know moms and dads
could die.

I love R and S even more now.

ASHLEY

This hypothetical sister, does she plan to go
off, make a zillion dollars in cryptocurrency
then come roaring back in a limo to get me?

I don't think so.

HOLLY

Then she better just go and not tell me.

ASHLEY

Agreed. Because if she told me, I'd make sure she couldn't leave.

Chapter Forty-Five

Prentice gushed praise for "Wistful Woman with Plane." Cassie was sure he would have been equally enthusiastic if she'd turned in a lasagna stain on an airline ticket. Which didn't fit the advertising campaign but might be effective for a certain demographic.

And could she slap a Santa hat on a turtle by tomorrow? He'd send her the turtle.

Cassie munched a peanut butter sandwich while she scanned her emails. In between deletes, she paged through Uncle Steve's yearbook. Most photos were in gray scale. Only senior portraits sparkled with color, which was expensive in 1983. From the rows of tenth-graders, a monochrome Robin Snyder seemed dull compared to the pink-sweater images Officer Robo and Arthur Curwick possessed.

Cassie suspected Arthur was another one of Kaitlyn's boyfriends, seduced for his investigative usefulness. The journalist's man bun was cinched too tightly if he thought Cassie was connected to the murder.

Except, well, she had gotten arrested with Mariah.

And she had told the police she'd met Robin Snyder.

And Adam had—with far too much personal enjoyment—told her she was a suspect.

Cassie worried the next headline in the *Falls Press* would declare her the Cult Killer of Wolf Haunt.

She stuck a sticky orange square to the top of the portrait page and one to the unicorn page as bookmarks. She liked this girl with the guarded smile and hunted for her through drama club, student council, Snow Daze royalty, choir, sports teams. Best hair (the winner was very Farrah Fawcett), weirdest laugh, class flirt. Most likely to succeed, to play pro hockey, to end up in a Turkish prison.

No Robin.

Can you disappear when you're already invisible?

Cassie turned the page to a school assembly for Talent Day. She remembered those. Crowded bleachers filled the background of the center photo. Classes were forced to sit in assigned areas, making it impossible to hide in the top row.

Shown from behind, a boy in a bedazzled white suit, his hair slicked back and puffed up, froze in a hip twist. Girls in the front row pretended to shriek at the Elvis impersonator as if he were the genuine idol.

Cassie ran her magnifying app across the rows behind the screamers. Robin slouched on the hard bench, Tammara sat next to her. Cassie provided a caption: "Who is this guy supposed to be, and what glue did he use to get his hair like that?"

Robin wore a print blouse with an open collar, showing a bare throat. No necklace. So it wasn't important enough to wear every day. Kaitlyn would have been disappointed. Cassie certainly was.

Tammara's long hair draped loosely around her shoulders. A ruffled V-neck cardigan covered a plain blouse. Top button undone, the open collar exposed the line of a necklace. Robin was not flashing jewelry that day, but her friend was.

Cassie flipped back to the tenth-grade portraits and found

Brighton below the row of Andersons. Tammara sat stiff-backed and impassive, as if she endured a lecture on the proper way for Regency-era ladies to serve tea. The starched, pointed collar of her white blouse, buttoned to the top, wouldn't dare scrunch into a wrinkle. Her hair, brushed flat against her head, swept back from an acne-spotted face into a barrette.

Cassie understood the contrast.

Picture day: a record of your appearance that went home to your parents.

The necklace would be secreted in Tammara's locker along with sweaters she wore in class to hide the crisp blouses that made her look like the president of the Future Accountants of America.

Well, Tammara wasn't the first girl to show off a different persona at school than at home. She must have loved having unrestricted, free-spirited Robin as a friend.

An email from the museum popped up on Cassie's computer, which meant from Martin. Cassie was tempted to look for his class picture. She didn't know what grade he'd been in back then, but he must be somewhere in the yearbook. He probably had a gorgeous head of hair and lifted weights.

She read the email instead.

The formal letter announced the cancelation of the high school level art award for the year. The board had decided that because of the circumstances—that would be the theft and the dead girl, although the message didn't mention either one—the museum "did not want to appear insensitive."

Right. No one wanted to *appear* insensitive to murder. It wasn't that they knew the girl, cared about her, and would miss her. Most of them didn't, didn't, and wouldn't.

Cassie had hated the sympathy-card phrases people had spouted at her after Vicky died. To keep from screaming obscenities at them for their socially appropriate behavior, she'd turned it into a game.

What kind of person was the administrative assistant walking toward her with a somber pout, the one who wore the same dress every Thursday and displayed photos of corgis on her desk? Which standard platitude would she choose?

a) So sorry to hear about your friend

b) My condolences on your loss

c) Sweetie, we're here for you.

Throughout the ordeal, Cassie had ached to hear an echo of her own rage.

> *I want to slice off that guy's balls with a rusty knife*
> *and hang them from the rearview mirror of my car.*

> *I'm applying for a job in hell*
> *so I can watch him burn for all eternity.*

Now *those* would make great sympathy cards for the family and friends of victims.

Cassie had done a mockup of the Rusty Knife card, and mentally put together a gift basket to go with it.

That still wasn't enough. She wanted something that reached beyond the violent event, a gesture that encompassed tragedy as a whole, an acknowledgment that terrible things happened to each of us, and within the great connectedness of the world, they happened to all of us.

She read Martin's email again.

Of course, there were always those people who didn't give a shit about someone else's personal loss or the larger gestalt of human existence.

Some people were just jerks.

Chapter Forty-Six

Cassie waited until school was out, took three deep breaths and called Mariah. "How are you doing?" It was a terrible question. Mariah's life was being whirled through a blender. Cassie knew how that felt. You're rushing through your routine with your feet stomping on firm ground, then suddenly your legs are sucked out from under you by a rip tide.

Jupiter charged into her office, ran in a circle, and sprinted out. Cassie heard a familiar rumble. From her window she watched Dale arrive on the farm's riding lawnmower.

"Wells thinks I killed her," Mariah said. "I'd still be in jail —we don't have money for bail—except Mr. Graywind got me a lawyer, and he got me out. I'm sorry you got arrested too. Please don't be mad at me, but I'm really glad you did. I would've phased into a drama coma in the back of that patrol car if I'd been by myself."

"My pleasure," Cassie said. "But let's not do it again."

"Totally. I don't know how Wells thinks I could ever be the killer. I'd have to drive to Blanchet—in my mom's car which she needs for work all the time—get a boat—as if a bunch of them were just laying around on the shore for anyone to take

—and go to the Haunt *exactly* when that Kaitlyn was there—which was stupid. I mean, it's all crazy, but especially why would she go to the island? My lawyer said she died the night before she was found. There wasn't a party or anything. It's like the killer must have tricked her into going there with him."

Cassie agreed that transportation would have been difficult for the killer—who definitely was not Mariah—but not impossible. Trevor had a speedboat that could be borrowed. The Blazing Star Casino, where Mariah's mom worked, might have a sleek cruiser moored somewhere on the chain of waterways connected to Blanchet. Fishing boats, jet skis and pontoons speckled the shores.

Cassie also thought of a way Mariah could have convinced Kaitlyn to go to Wolf Haunt with her. Did she want to explore that path? No. But she did.

"Mariah, do you know where the beads and Gizmo tag came from?"

"The guy in my class who gave them to me, he never said. I told the sheriff that. Did you see the Satan Rocks post? That girl's sister or mom or something disappeared on the Haunt! Everyone's buzzed about it." She paused a nanosecond. "OMG. That's why she went there. Then some cult guy sacrificed her. And it was a full moon. I'll have to tell my lawyer."

Cassie wanted to correct her. No full moon, and none was needed. In late August sunset wasn't until around eight o'clock. The night of the murder, cultists could have gotten a lot of sacrificing done before they started tripping over tree stumps.

"They haven't found it, my necklace," Mariah said. "That's what they're using against me. That I killed that girl and took it and no one else would do that. So that makes me guilty. And I hadn't even planned on it."

"On what?" Cassie asked. Getting accused of murder?

"On making a necklace. Trevor said to find a theme or inspiration, and I could look around his shop for materials. I don't know if you've seen his studio. He's got piles and bins everywhere. Some of the stuff's left over from his collages. Some of it he's picked up. Like I mean, really picked up. He stops his car—not the Corvette, the other one that breaks down all the time—he stops it practically in the middle of the road and jumps out to pull things out of the ditch."

"It sounds eclectic," Cassie said.

"If that's a way of saying junk, yeah, that's what most of it is. He's my teacher and I've learned a lot from him, but the guy totally has to get past found art, eco-expressionism, and recycling as commentary on fast-fashion. So I was thinking 'raw chic,' but beautiful and elegant. And snap! I knew I was going to make jewelry. And then Richie said I could take some of his stuff and it all fit together."

"I bet Trevor was impressed," Cassie said.

"I was scared to show him, afraid he'd say the usual encouraging teacher things but not mean them. But I finally did, and he looked at it for a long time, all quiet. He was speechless! I couldn't believe it! I swear, his eyes got all misty. I knew he loved it! And he knew I'd win the competition."

"Yes," Cassie said. "I'm sure he did."

Chapter Forty-Seven

Dale dumped his homework in his room. Who gives homework on the second day of school with grief counselors stationed in every hallway?

He'd walked by the poster that promoted taking college courses while still in high school. With all the crying, it seemed like the wrong time to stop in and ask questions.

Next time he would. Just to find out stuff. Not to make a commitment. He already had plenty of those. They piled up around him like stacks of magazines in a hoarder's house. If he didn't keep them balanced, they'd topple over and smother him.

Taking a class at the tech school or state college seemed like going into orbit. He thought about how he might manage it, with transportation and everything, as he drove the riding lawnmower over to Cassie's. He parked in the driveway, took off the bulky ear protectors he always wore when using noisy equipment, and went up to the cabin door. Cassie opened it before he could knock. Jupiter shot past him, raced down the deck stairs and did a loop around the yard with a stop at the partially constructed kennel.

"I'm going to cut the grass, if that's okay," Dale said.

"You'll want to close the windows." He held the door as the puppy scooted back in.

Cassie was in full work mode. He could always tell by the faded red shorts and loose t-shirt promoting a jazz festival he'd never heard of. Her hair was ruffled from her running her hand through the bangs. When in thought, she shoved the tufts off her forehead, then ignored them as they flopped back. He bet she didn't realize she did it again and again when she was up against a deadline. She handed him his pay.

"Sorry to ask for it early," Dale said, "but I've got this thing coming up."

Cassie smiled. "You mean the homecoming dance Richie was telling me about?"

"He exaggerates sometimes."

"You mean, three hot girls didn't beg you to be their date?"

Dale shrugged, caught helpless in a tough situation. "They ambushed me. Bribed me with a Blizzard. And only two of them are hot." He didn't add that the third was a bratty kid.

"I would have held out for a Peanut Buster Parfait," Cassie said.

"Yeah, I need to improve my negotiating skills."

"The dance should be fun."

"Everyone tells me that." Dale leaned against the kitchen counter and wiggled a foot at Jupiter. The puppy sat on his boot and collapsed against his leg. His parents would flip into fire-breathing dragons if they knew he'd asked for an advance on his wages. The stereo lecture they would give him played in his head like an annoying ringtone. Poor planning on his part. He should have saved up for emergencies. And what did he spend all his money on anyway? He had food and a roof over his head. What more did a teenage boy need?

The Petrosky girls assured him they'd take care of all expenses. That should be okay because they'd asked him, and it wasn't a real date anyway. But as a guy, the setup didn't seem right to Dale. Maybe because his parents had raised him as if they were living a hundred years ago. Maybe because money gave you power to make decisions. Maybe because with cash in his pocket, Dale felt less like a worker bee, bought and paid for by the Petrosky Queens.

"Just so you know," Dale said, "Berger talked to Richie about his giving Mariah those beads and the Gizmo plate. Richie made it sound like he got them a long time ago when he and his uncle were hitting garage sales looking for car parts."

Cassie nodded. "If it happens to come up in conversation, I'll swear you never mentioned digging on private property to me."

Dale wished she hadn't expressed her support that way. He tried not to think about the shovel he and Richie had left on the island. And that the description of the murder weapon in the latest *Falls Press* posting sounded exactly like it.

Cassie did that stressed-induced swipe at her bangs. "Did Richie explain about the skull?"

"Berger didn't ask."

"Richie should be prepared, in case Adam does a follow up. Gizmo belonged to Kaitlyn's aunt, the one who disappeared. The dog's tag is another connection between Kaitlyn and Mariah."

Dale tugged at the neck of his sweaty shirt. "A week ago I didn't know Mariah existed. Now the media-verse has convicted her of murdering Kait, Kurt Cobain and one of the Prince Williams."

"As in multiple Prince Williams?"

"There's a whole thread about clones and masks."

"Like *The Man in the Iron Mask?*"

Dale nodded. "There are photos. Cosplayers swear the helmets must be EVA foam. That's what they use for their costumes. But there's a Real Iron page with a few followers."

Cassie laughed. "Alexandre Dumas must be a popular read with teens."

Dale had picked up the book because of the buzz. "More like they saw one of the movies." He'd seen four or five of them, including an animated version.

"I wish the sheriff wasn't so focused on Mariah," Cassie said.

Dale felt he had a chance to spill what he knew to an adult who might take him seriously. "I saw this guy with Kait. And then he was at her memorial. He seemed out of place. People hang together when something really sad happens. This guy was by himself."

"What does he look like? Maybe we can track him down."

"I found out who he is. His name is Mitch Hendrick."

"Mitch who works at the museum in Sunset," Cassie said as if there was only one Mitch and everyone in the entire world had known him for years except Dale.

He should have been upset that she'd hijacked his big reveal. Instead, he felt he'd discovered a co-conspirator. "Yeah. I even saw him there. I was on this school thing for art class. He was circulating through the girls, skimming for digits. You know, phone numbers. He tried to chat up Jennifer."

Dale was sorry he'd let the name slip. Now he had to explain more than he wanted to. "Jennifer Petrosky. She was on the field trip too."

"Tried," Cassie repeated. "Sounds like he failed."

"He gave her a slime-line about her height. She sliced and diced him good."

"So she's not a fan."

"I won't repeat how she described him." He'd memorized it in case he got caught in a situation that needed creative trash talk.

"He was doing this while in a relationship with Kaitlyn," Cassie said thoughtfully.

"I don't know if they were a couple, not for sure. Kait had

a short attention span when it came to guys. No ring, no foul. But, yeah, either that's Mitch's move all the time or he already knew he needed a new girlfriend."

There. He'd said it. He'd meant it to come out as edgy and funny/not funny. Hearing it out loud, he realized how absolutely not funny it was, and that the possibility it was true had been burning a hole in him.

"Shit." Dale pushed away from the counter, sending Jupiter scurrying. "It's just that the field trip was the same day she was found. I can't stop thinking that he's a psycho-cold killer, who trolled for babes that day so he could swear he didn't have a girlfriend, who definitely was not Kait."

Chapter Forty-Eight

Dale drove the rumbling lawnmower across Cassie's yard, trying not to think about predator Mitch hunting for his next victim at the museum and again at the memorial service for his maybe-girlfriend, who he may or may not have murdered.

The turf had gotten thicker under his care, but years of neglect couldn't be corrected in one summer. He took some pride in how well the refurbished garden was doing. Cassie had taken his advice and planted inexpensive marigolds, red and yellow snapdragons, and multicolored coleus.

The tangled roses he'd hacked almost to the ground had sent out healthy canes that were now sprinkled with a few blooms. Next year Cassie could add perennials. If she stayed. Sometimes she seemed settled, but she hadn't exactly bonded with the place. Or was it more that she hadn't bonded with a person. Like Berger. Maybe the guy thought he was playing it casual, but it looked more like he was playing it absent.

Dale ran the machine along the perimeter of the partially assembled kennel, thinking of strategies. Not that he was in a position to give a grown guy advice on his love life, but he might get a chance to drop a hint. Every guy knew it was easy to score "pet points." Jupiter always acted as if a brain-sucking alien hid inside Berger's human costume. The deputy should take Cassie out to dinner and bring the Akita leftover steak. Dale doubted even that would get Jupiter to accept Berger as a cuddle buddy, but it was worth a shot.

A car on the country road slowed, as if the driver checked the address marker beside the mailbox.

But not just any car. The Corvette purred into Cassie's driveway. Dale, chugging along on the oxcart of a mower, wanted to bow down before the sleek Night Race Blue babe-magnet beauty.

His reverence didn't include the driver. Trevor Rothman emerged, as if unfolding from a starship. Dale didn't know him, not really. He'd listened to Richie express low tolerance for the man's brags. Using real expletives, not the ED shorthand they'd adopted, Richie had pointed out that saying you went to places didn't mean you'd ever been there. And claiming you chummed around with celebs didn't mean it had ever happened, and if it had happened, it didn't prove they were actually your friends or were even famous. Which was ultra-perceptive for Richie.

Dale wasn't impressed by what Richie had shown him of Rothman's artwork either. The guy must have a side gig peddling forgeries in order to afford a Vette.

And insurance on a Vette.

And winter storage for a Vette, since you'd never get through a snowdrift with clearance that low, and one season of road salt would eat the thing to pieces.

Rothman sauntered toward the cabin. He flapped a hand at Dale as if to say "I have to wave at you because this is Minnesota and that's what we do, we wave." Dale nodded, a socially acceptable response when you're operating machinery.

What was the guy doing at Cassie's in his ego-penis on wheels?

Okay, he was an artist visiting another artist. Nothing unusual there. Dale still felt uneasy. How long would Rothman stay? Dale slowed the mower to stretch out a task he usually zipped through. His dad would be angry at the delay.

But then, his dad already had a thorn up his butt. Dale had ducked out on his chores at home, cutting off his dad's recital of the long list of jobs his son should be doing on a warm day coming up to harvest. His dad seemed to think it would improve the yield if Dale swept out the barn, cleaned out the back of the truck, and did a dozen other things the corn and soy beans didn't care about.

But that was his dad. Walking the rows, willing the sun to shine. Glaring at the sky to force the rain to fall (or not fall).

Strange. Bad weather was the enemy, yet his dad worshiped it. A dedicated storm-chaser, Irv Steinhaus was happiest sitting in the cab of a truck with a Sparks buddy, gobbling junk food out of foil-lined bags and gulping down pop while scanning the sky for twisters.

Was everyone blind to their own contradictions? Dale wondered what his were that he couldn't see?

Chapter Forty-Nine

Cassie plopped in front of her computer, wishing she had time for deep-breathing exercises.

And a large chunk of chocolate.

And a glass of merlot.

She'd planned on washing Trevor's jacket before returning it. Since he'd barged in unexpectedly, she hadn't felt obligated to do more than give it a shake and shove it at him.

She'd explained that she was swimming in work and had a video call in a few minutes, hating that she even had to state a reason to get rid of him. Not taking the hint, he'd leaned against the kitchen counter, jacket draped over his shoulder, marveling at how she'd managed to capture a contract with a body wash company.

Cassie had sensed a vibe under his casual manner, as if he'd expected more than conversation. Jupiter, seeming to feel it too, had stayed close to her and stared down the stranger. She'd finally bluntly told Trevor that he had to leave.

He'd tried to keep the conversation going by praising her for having so many clients that she couldn't take a few minutes to chat with a friend. His twisting a compliment into a judgy guilt trip had freed her from social niceties, and she'd verbally tossed him out.

Cassie ran a comb through her bob, which still seemed too short even though it had been months since she'd gotten the cut. She logged onto the video call only a minute late, wondering if she looked as rushed as she felt.

The lawyer who'd contacted her was waiting. Cassie recognized the woman's suit, or rather, the style and intent of the suit, because she'd been locked into that look when she'd worked for Fontana Media. Worsted wool blazer, Egyptian cotton blouse, a touch of gold at clavicle and earlobes. Professional without being prim.

In the ladder of assistants to the district attorney prosecuting Jordan's case, this woman was definitely a few rungs up from the intern who'd called Cassie earlier. The white-blond hair, with currently fashionable dark roots, was scraped back into a clip at the nape of her neck. In a flash she could undo the barrette, give her mane a shake and be ready for dinner at a four-star restaurant.

"You walked into the bedroom and saw the body—"

Cassie interrupted her. "I saw Victoria Danner, my best friend, dead."

"You saw Ms. Danner. Mr. McCray's bracelet was in the bed next to her. Is that correct?"

"That's where the police found it. I didn't see it. If you'd prepared for this interview, you'd know that."

The woman remained unruffled. "Since Mr. McCray's appeal is moving forward, I need to verify everyone's statement."

"I'd expect you to focus on the anonymous woman who's suddenly giving him an alibi."

"You'd be surprised what we find when we reexamine a case from all angles."

No. Cassie didn't think she'd be the least bit surprised. "Such as, you realize the defendant is even more of a scumbag than you originally thought, and you're glad he was declared guilty and locked up so he can't kill his next girlfriend?"

"I was not expecting this attitude since you're in a relationship with Mr. McCray."

"His sending me letters through his law firm is not a relationship. The fancy return address doesn't trick me into reading them. They still go into a bin unopened."

The woman leaned forward, as if attempting to forge an intimate connection with Cassie through the barrier of electronics. "I know you've read them, because you've replied to them."

"I haven't so much as glanced at a salutation, and I haven't responded in any way."

The woman almost smirked, as if she interrogated Cassie on the witness stand and had caught her in an incriminating lie. "Mr. McCray's letters to you reference the rather graphic details that you've written to him in your letters."

"About what?"

"About your romantic attachment to Mr. McCray and your jealousy toward Ms. Danner."

"You haven't actually seen these letters, have you?"

"Mr. McCray has not chosen to share them. We're pursuing legal channels to get them released."

"Good luck with that, since they don't exist."

"Mr. McCray's lawyers have provided copies of the correspondence he's sent to you. In them Mr. McCray references your letters. That indicates they are real."

Cassie sat back in her chair and folded her arms. She'd been naive to hope that Jordan wrote to her to confess his guilt and beg for forgiveness. She should have realized the contents of the fat envelopes were part of a long con. A scam, setting up an alternate scenario he could use as the foundation for overturning his conviction.

Cassie could tell the woman on the screen, who was

supposed to be keeping a killer in jail, had been swayed by them toward Team Jordan.

"To clarify," Cassie said, "your evaluation of my feelings for Mr. McCray is completely based on what Mr. McCray has written. Is that correct?"

The woman's lips twitched but she didn't reply.

"Tell me, in this one-sided, penpal world Mr. McCray has created, how often does he drop in provocative compliments to himself? 'Oh, Cassie, you're embarrassing me with your adoration of my wavy sun-kissed hair and mesmerizing eyes. And you really must stop obsessing over my enormous, hot dick.'"

Crimson flooded the woman's face. Far deeper than a blush, her coloring flashed with realization and anger.

"That would be a lot then." Cassie said. "You have sooo been played."

Chapter Fifty

Dale forced the mower to crawl slowly, slowly across the lawn toward Cassie's cabin, hoping she would kick out Rothman soon.

As if she'd received the mental vibes, the door opened. Dale was disappointed that the guy stepped out under his own power instead of being shoved onto the deck.

Rothman strutted past the mower toward his gleaming car, a jacket slung over one shoulder like those models you see on your computer in popup ads for hair plugs. The man's hand seemed to have a renewed arrogance, as it did the wave thing again.

Dale gave a slow nod, hoping that Jupiter had pissed on the guy's shoe. He increased pressure on the gas pedal and spun the mower around the giant oak that dominated the yard.

He pointed the mower at Rothman. The man glanced back in surprise at the roar behind him and danced to the side. Dale adjusted his path to compensate.

The man's lips moved in a pattern Dale recognized. "What the fuck."

Dale tapped his ear protectors. *Can't hear ya.* He veered again, heading toward the dark blue dream-mobile.

Rothman dashed ahead of him. He scrambled onto the driveway, stumbling to catch the jacket before it hit the gravel. He spread himself protectively across the Vette, his shocked expression like a deer in the headlights.

Dale swerved, skimming the lawn's edge. Clippings shot out from the mower, splattering the car's perfect finish. His back to Rothman, he followed the property edge, pretending that had been his planned route all along.

A blue streak shot past on the road. Rothman probably gave him the finger while gunning the high-powered engine. Dale felt too satisfied to care. He'd been tempted to cut in closer, spraying the car with scratchy grit; but that would've been wrong.

Even if a guy with early-onset middle life crisis owns it, ya gotta respect the Vette.

Chapter Fifty-One

It's always Sunny at SunnieChat!

KAYLA

I decided Galapagos is my first choice. I had a real sitdown talk with our team leader, reinforced my skills and experience. Liam is furious. He accused me of undermining him. I think that's what he said. He used a Scottish phrase. Something chib something. I still struggle with the accent. Especially when he shouts and talks fast.

HOLLY

Proud of you. But apply for the New Zealand job too.

KAYLA

I did. So did Liam. More complications.

ASHLEY

Apply for a new boyfriend.

I heard there are multiple Prince Williams. You could find one of those.

HOLLY

Triplets, quads, quints?

As many as you like.

ASHLEY

That's how he can be at a country fete and a lunch at Windsor Castle at the same time.

You can tell them apart by the ears.

ASHLEY

H, bet you can't resist a literary comment.

HOLLY

You mean because their ears are bent from wearing iron masks.

ASHLEY

Glad you got that out before you exploded. Now who wants to make a Paul McCartney reference?

KAYLA

I don't understand any of that.

HOLLY

Read Dumas.

ASHLEY

Ask grandma to explain "I buried Paul."

KAYLA

I'll just google it.

Chapter Fifty-Two

A woman in a Blazing Star polo shirt delivered the package. "With Mr. Graywind's compliments." Cassie wondered if the casino required employees to endure etiquette training.

She hoped the surprisingly large carton held something wonderful. She needed an absolutely safe, not-tampered-with parcel after Trevor's unwanted visit followed by the video interrogation about Vicky's murder.

She opened the elegant box with abandon. Inside she found a book, wider than tall in a landscape-style format. Sealed in a plastic bag, it was surrounded by tissue-paper nests cradling croissants and tiny jars of jam.

The goodies would be Gerald's touch. Cassie loved it when people sent her food! Which reminded her that a two-footed version of Kevin the Squirrel had deprived her of chocolates, and taunted her by returning the last one, which might or might not contain poison.

She stored away the treats. Knowing they waited for her in the kitchen added to the pleasure. Then she opened the plastic bag and settled at her desk with the book. She imagined the generic registry being plucked off the shelf of a discount store by a museum volunteer who then rushed to reach the checkout before the lady with a cart full of black paper plates, cups, and napkins for an Over the Hill party.

The faux leather cover suffered dark stains from sticky fingers. Cassie thought of Kayla and took the blotches as a good sign. Holding her breath, she opened the cover and read the notation.

June 12 to Sept. 25, 2003

She exhaled. "Thank you, Mr. Graywind."

She flipped through the pages, sure her own entry would attract her eye like a magnet. She scanned the penned names, hometowns, and comments.

Swede from Wisconsin
Came all the way from Florida, thought we'd see snow
Love the beaver!

A daisy sketched in the margin made Cassie wish she'd thought to add a leaf or a ladybug by her name. Of course, she hadn't known that years later she'd need a sign.

R. Schroeder, Enjoying an outing with my special girls

Cassie felt a flush of warmth. How very like Aunt Renee to write that! She moved her finger down the names, recognizing the ornate signature Ashley had been practicing in case she became famous. Kayla Windom was printed over two lines as if it were school paper. Holly and Laurel had skipped the formality. They'd been in "too cool for you" mode that day.

Cassandra Windom.

In a self-absorbed phase, Cassie had been signing her art, and everything else, with her full first name, trying out various styles. Someday she'd drop the Windom and just be Cassandra, using a single name as if she were Banksy, the political activist/street artist, only minus the tacky stencils and spray paint.

Cassie felt vindicated. She'd try not to gloat when she contacted Officer Robo. Well, she'd gloat a little. Let his mechanical brain process that!

She still needed the exact month and day. The individual pages weren't dated. She searched for a clue and found—

ANNA Happy Birthday to Me!! 🖤 🖤 🖤 *July 11*

Hmm. This wasn't absolute proof that she and Anna had been there on the same day. Maybe her sisters remembered a girl with frosting on her face, wearing a party dress who'd complained that she'd wanted to celebrate at a water park.

Cassie would do another check with the sibs, just in case, but this was close enough.

She photographed the page. She'd send it to Officer Robo as proof that she'd met Robin Snyder on Wolf Haunt July ninth, two days before Anna's most un-favorite birthday ever.

Sun Sun SunnieChat!

> Have you remembered anything more about our trip to the museum?

HOLLY

> I sat down a lot. My new sandals hurt my feet but they looked great.

ASHLEY

> H, they were so worth the blisters.

Not Her First Murder

KAYLA

Laurel gave me her frosted lip gloss. I put some on the beaver.

ASHLEY

I noticed it had dry lips. Good job.

Did you see a girl who looked like it was her birthday?

KAYLA

What does a girl who's having a birthday look like?

ASHLEY

You mean the princess holding a balloon standing next to the clown?

HOLLY

I think the clown was there by himself.

You guys are no help.

ASHLEY

You're welcome.

Chapter Fifty-Three

The moment Cassie walked into the cavernous room and smelled the varnish, an unsettled familiarity descended on her, as if she'd crossed into a distortion of a memory. Basketball hoops hung from the high ceiling. The dark rectangle of a scoreboard, unlit now, held a position of honor on the far wall. This was every small town's gymnasium.

Adorning the wall above a folded-up bank of bleachers, "Go Icebergs" floated over a jagged white peak supported by squiggly blue waves. With bright paint and an updated font, the logo almost duplicated a monochrome photo in Uncle Steve's 1983 yearbook.

Cassie searched for Rhonda in the bustle of adults setting up tables and hanging glittery stars.

"Think it will come together in time for the dance tomorrow?" Trevor Rothman stood at Cassie's shoulder. "I haven't done this before. Not since high school in Wisconsin. What about you?"

"Same here, except for the Wisconsin part."

"Sorry I had to rush off yesterday," Trevor said. "I had a lot to do for today."

"No problem." Cassie wondered if he believed his own revisionist history.

Martin Brighton and his sister adjusted wire panels suitable for holding a display of historical photographs. *Can't let the kids have a night of fun without injecting a bit of education,* Cassie thought. For siblings who didn't get along, the two seemed to bond over the museum. Cassie wondered if they were locked into it through some family obligation or if they used it as a way to bridge their personality conflicts. If it was the latter, they weren't getting across any rivers today. Tammara vigorously gestured at one location, while her brother emphatically pointed at another.

Cassie wanted to rush over and shriek at Martin for canceling the high school art competition, but she didn't. The man already looked miserable. She felt some satisfaction knowing he wasn't going to win the argument with his sister.

"The art club did the cutouts," Trevor said. "You know, painted characters with holes where the heads are supposed to be. You stick your face through the opening and get your picture taken. I'm told adults love the photo op more than the kids. It wasn't my choice for a project, but sometimes you have to ride the enthusiasm." He hefted a tape measure. "I'm afraid the muse overpowered some of the artists. The sets are on wheels, so they can be moved around until we finalize the arrangement and hook them together, but we still have a footage problem. Either the floor plan has to be revamped, or we have to slice off a pirate and an astronaut."

"Art can be brutal," Cassie said.

"How about you? What are you doing to enhance the homecoming dance experience?"

"I don't know yet," Cassie said.

Trevor frowned and shook his head, causing a fetching curl to sway across his forehead. "Bad answer. That's how you end up assigned to trash can duty. A guy with a clipboard already tried to put me on that list. Tell them you're with the art club. We could use the help."

"Rhonda already has a job for me."

"Deputy Rhonda with the brick-red hair? She knows how to chill a room. I got hypothermia being questioned by her about our trip to the Haunt." Trevor grimaced. "I am sorry how that turned out. I thought we'd spend a sunny morning sketching. Then I was going to take you to lunch at this charming place I know."

Cassie kept her expression neutral in front of the handsome artist, wearing impressively tight jeans and a t-shirt advertising a showing of his own work at a gallery in Madison. She resented his version of the island outing—with three other people just before a storm—as an interrupted date on a perfect day.

Trevor seemed to be waiting for her to ask about the "charming" bistro. Cassie thought through the possibilities. The Municipal Liquor Store's menu was limited to snacks in crinkly bags. The Crow Bar's ambiance consisted of oak tables stained with beer bottle marks, which some clients swore protected the establishment from evil spirits. The Safari Club, a strip joint at the edge of town that a local citizens' group picketed nightly, didn't serve lunch.

That left the Dairy Queen; Pizza Heaven, which had a buffet; and Lorraine's Cafe.

Hmm, Lorraine's did have exceptional pie.

But she was definitely not going to gush "Where is this wonderful restaurant? I'd love to try it. How about tomorrow?" She wouldn't, because he wanted her to. Correction. Because he *expected* her to. And she was sure this wasn't the first time Trevor had used that strategy to trick a woman into initiating a date.

"It rained," Cassie said. "A lot. There was lightning. And a body." She looked to where students placed a large photograph of Kaitlyn on an easel. Paper hearts and tissue flowers surrounded the smiling face that seemed too vibrant to ever fade.

"You're right," Trevor said. "That was a terrible day."

"I should find Rhonda."

Trevor moved a hand as if to touch her arm in a comforting way. Instead he let it drop to his side. His lips twitched into a slim grin. "Watch out for the guy with the clipboard."

Rhonda was nowhere in sight, so Cassie zeroed in on Helen Steinhaus. Dale's mother directed the placement of tables according to a diagram she held at arm's length.

"Thank you for the hot dish," Cassie said. "It was delicious."

"Dale told me you were working against a deadline. I thought you'd appreciate a meal you didn't have to bother fixing yourself."

Cassie didn't remember telling Dale she was under time pressure. He must have picked up on the bad habits she tumbled into when stressed. The chicken and wild rice casserole had been a welcome alternative to a quickly smeared peanut butter sandwich.

Harry Ziegler rushed up to Helen, clutching what must be the dreaded clipboard. "Irv says you have to shift the tables. The art club needs five more feet."

Helen spotted her tall husband. He and Trevor stretched out a tape measure and frowned at one another in a guy moment. She pushed the sleeves of her shirt up to her elbows. "I suppose he expects me to lean against the gym wall and shove it sixty inches into the parking lot." She headed toward the two men.

Harry checked an item off his list. "Probably does." He raised his pen, poised for action. "Cassie, can I put you down for cleanup?"

She was glad to have a defensive move already prepared. "Sorry. Rhonda has a job for me."

"Maybe you could still fit in emptying out a few trash bins? It wouldn't take much time. Volunteers get Berg Bucks. Good at any store showing the Iceberg logo."

"I'll have to get back to you on that."

Rhonda appeared carrying two folding chairs. She pressed one into Cassie's hands. "Follow me."

They set their chairs at the edge of the bustle. Rhonda pulled a paper out of her pocket. Her nails, enameled a deep burgundy, made Cassie think longingly of wine.

"What's that?" Cassie asked.

"A decoy. I need a break. If you look like you have a task, people leave you alone so you won't ask them to help you with it."

Cassie wished that simple solution worked in all situations. "What's the job you have for me? It better be good, because I passed up an opportunity to be Garbage Czar."

Rhonda pretend to read the piece of paper. "Sorry, nothing with a title, although you can wear a crown if you have your own. It's simple stuff for the fire department website. Come to the homecoming dance. Take photos of the members. Scribble a few notes you can turn into a couple of paragraphs for the blog about interacting with the community. That's all."

"What will the Sparks and Sparkles be doing?"

"Directing traffic, staffing the refreshment table and working security. Mostly protecting the nonalcoholic sanctity of the punch bowl, stopping kids from making bad choices, and calming down video-crazy parents."

"Sounds very photogenic. I'm not in the habit of turning down paid employment, but couldn't everyone take turns snapping pictures?"

"We've tried that and ended up with a hundred photos of people's kids and grandkids. Almost none of the firefighters. It works better if it's an official role assigned to one person.

Boomer said he'd do it, then he decided he'd rather be on punch bowl patrol."

Cassie examined Rhonda's decoy, a flyer for the hamburger basket at the Crow Bar. She wondered if Trevor knew about the sizzling patty and crispy fries at a special price.

Rhonda ran her finger under "beverage extra" as if they discussed Coke versus Pepsi. "I might have swayed Boomer toward refreshment table duty with strategic comments about the advantage of having first crack at Helen's pizza rolls. Seriously, he's a good soul, and he's raised a great bunch of kids, but the man has no clue how to frame a photo."

Cassie watched a woman carry a piñata shaped like a flying saucer across a free throw line and set it under a basketball hoop. "I don't remember homecoming being like this, or this early in the school year."

"A few years ago an alumni group took control away from the student council. They did a big push to bring back past graduates who'd moved away. Got the chamber of commerce involved. Turned the dance into a multigenerational event. You know how it goes. Something happens once, suddenly it's a tradition. It's early because a change in the football schedule put the next home game in conflict with the fall choir concert. Trust me, you don't want to mess with the choir director."

Cassie took the 1983 yearbook from her bag. "I've got a better decoy than an ad from the Crow." She smoothed out the Elvis page and pointed to the two girls, heads tilted together. "Robin Snyder had a friend." Cassie resisted glancing at the real-life adult Tammara less than a basketball court away.

Rhonda wasn't as shy. She looked up from the page and stared straight at the woman. "I'm betting if Tammara's parents had known, she would have been shipped off to boarding school a lot sooner."

"I wonder if they did find out, but too late in the school year to get her enrolled somewhere else until the next fall."

"Then Robin dropped off the face of the earth, solving the problem."

"They still sent away their daughter."

Rhonda nodded. "So it wouldn't happen again. Can't have a Brighton mixing with commoners. Mom and dad were controlling as hell from what I've heard. Tammara's marriage to a guy named Meyer was arranged. Money to money. It fell apart pretty fast."

Cassie turned pages to the individual portraits, and tapped Robin's black-and-white. "Arthur Curwick has a large one of these in color. He thinks I gave Mariah the beads. Well, that's what he said. He was probably fishing." She relayed an abbreviated version of her conversation with the journalist. "Arthur seems sure I'm mixed up in Kaitlyn's death. He must have been disappointed that I didn't have the murder weapon laying around on my deck."

The vision of Kaitlyn prone in the mud rushed through her. The gash on the back of the girl's skull glowed vivid in black and red. She clenched her jaw against the threatening darkness. Vicky's hand rested on her shoulder and Rhonda sat beside her. She was with friends.

Cassie hadn't thought about what had made the wound. "Was it a rock? But not the Satan one."

"We found a shovel with blood on it propped against that old shed. Forensics is running tests."

"Good to know. I want to get the details right in case Arthur kidnaps me and tortures me into confessing."

Rhonda nodded. "He could be the type."

"Shouldn't you be reassuring me he's harmless?"

"No one is harmless. And Arthur gets obsessive about the stories he works on. Proprietary. Like he owns them. He grew up at the newspaper. Seriously. His mom and dad had a playpen at the office. They took him to fires and car accidents in a baby carrier strapped to their chests. Early on, he wrote obituaries. He reported on high school events when he should have been participating in them."

"Kaitlyn got him interested in her aunt's disappearance."

"She talked to me about using ground-penetrating radar to search for a body."

"On the Haunt?" That was the first place Cassie would look.

"And at some of the old Snyder land," Rhonda said.

"The family's kept the Glacier Falls property. The Sunset land was sold off, which complicates things."

"Who owns it now?"

"Mel Moreau owns a chunk. Harry Ziegler has a few acres he keeps as a natural prairie. Trevor Rothman bought the original homestead. That's where he has his house and studio."

Cassie watched a taxidermied moose roll past, propelled by two Sparks. Hmm. A flying saucer and now wildlife. "Just what is the theme for the homecoming dance?"

Chapter Fifty-Four

"I had a feeling something was about to happen. I've got a sixth sense for these things."

Cassie surveyed the snack aisle at the Falls Market. She could hear Mrs. Finster, Glacier Falls Gossip Guru, holding court in the produce section.

She'd emailed Officer Robo the photo of the page from the museum log, showing her name with birthday-girl Anna's inscription below it. He'd written back unimpressed, refusing to accept it as support that she'd met Robin Hanson.

She set aside her frustration with Robocop and instead thought about the photography job Rhonda had outlined. It was an easy gig and she'd get to see Dale march with his dates.

Bags of potato chips and pretzels couldn't muffle Mrs. Finster's pretend whisper. "When I heard it on the scanner, a knife went right through me. A body. On the Haunt. Dead." The woman shrieked as if she'd discovered the corpse herself.

"Poor Kaitlyn." Cassie recognized the voice of the man who always wore the North Stars cap. His loyalty to the hockey team hung on decades after the franchise had moved from Minnesota to Texas.

"If her mother hadn't already died of a broken heart, this would have killed her," Mrs. Finster said.

Cassie decided against weaving through the Finsterites just to score some Romain. As long as she had peanut butter and crackers, she had a meal.

Crackers! One aisle over. She took the long route down the row and turned the corner into the next lane. The saltine display sat at the far end, close to the produce section. She made the trek toward the danger zone, ready to grab a box and scurry—in a dignified way—to the cheese display.

"Oh, that family," Mrs. Finster said. "I'm thinking Sheriff Wells will finally have to get serious about looking for Robin Snyder."

Cassie froze, hugging her jacket around her against the store's air conditioning. She was trapped now. A fly caught in the rumormonger's web.

"Robin disappeared years ago," a squeaky-voiced woman said. "It's one of those unsolved cases, like on TV."

"I remember her and that little dog," Mrs. Finster continued. "Not many do. They forgot about her the minute she disappeared. She was pretty in a trashy sort of way. Dressed like she shopped at garage sales. And her hair was always a tangle."

"Her folks weren't much for parenting," Squeaky said. "They could barely take care of themselves. Our Lutheran Christian Ladies' group delivered meals to the house sometimes. And toys for the girls."

"The St. Mary's Christian Ladies' group did too," North Stars said.

"Land rich, cash poor," Mrs. Finster said. "They could have lived like kings and dressed their daughters like royalty if they'd sold off the acreage old Jebeze Snyder snatched up during the Great Depression. But they couldn't even be bothered to farm it proper."

"Their health problems—" Squeaky began.

Mrs. Finster interrupted. "Now that hound was a whole different world. Robin brushed it and pampered it like one of those little lion dogs that Chinese empresses keep stuffed in their big sleeves. I saw that very thing on the History Channel the other night. But those are purebreds, of course. Robin's was a stray for sure. You can always tell if you know what to look for. She probably found it at the side of the road after some reckless driver hit it. Grizzly, she called it. What a terrible name."

"The dog's name was Gizmo," a different woman said.

Cassie recognized the voice. Scarf Lady, Mel Moreau.

"Oh, I'm sure it's Grizzly," Mrs. Finster insisted. "You wouldn't know. You live almost way over in Sunset. And you just moved here."

"It was in the newspaper," Mel said.

Mrs. Finster scoffed. "Daniel's idiot grandson Arty probably wrote that. He gets things wrong all the time. And Daniel—he's the editor, you probably don't know that—he's too lazy to do proper fact checking."

"I know Daniel," Mel said, her words adding to the store's cool atmosphere. "He's very professional."

Pretending to read the nutritional value of a saltine, Cassie shuffled closer to where the aisle mushroomed into the fresh fruit bins. She glanced toward the gathering.

Mel Moreau breached the inner circle. A scarf swirling with orange and turquoise held back her steel-gray hair. She hefted a lethal cantaloupe, as if about to lob it at Mrs. Finster's puckered face.

Mrs. Finster looked down her nose at the artist who dared to challenge her, then she slowly turned toward North Stars, as if Mel no longer existed. "A cult killed Kaitlyn for sure."

"A cult!" Squeaky wobbled as if she might swoon. Cassie thought it funny the woman should be shocked, since she was part of a cult herself. Cassie cringed at the thought of Finsterites swooping around the emoji-speckled rock on Wolf

Haunt naked, chanting in an unintelligible language, preparing to slaughter a goat and start an orgy.

Mrs. Finster continued with confidence. "I saw her with a strange boy—man, really. Much older than her. He probably lured the poor girl to the island saying he was going to buy drugs. That's how they reel in their victims. They groom them with pills and sex. Get them used to meeting in unusual places, then make them pledge themselves to the devil. If they refuse, they become sacrifices. Especially a virgin like Kaitlyn."

Mel plopped the melon into her basket, perhaps to remove temptation. "Was she groomed with sex or was she a virgin? Which is it? It can't be both."

Mrs. Finster spun back to her, flustered. "Well—well, it's obvious. They tried to corrupt her, but she resisted. Yes, that's what happened. When they couldn't trick her into pledging loyalty to their demon-god, they absolutely had to kill her."

"So the man-friend killed Kaitlyn," North Stars said.

"Because he's a drug dealer," Squeaky said.

"Because he's in a cult," another woman corrected. Her hair style was a sagging version of Mrs. Finster's blue-gray clawlike curls. She'd been following the action silently as if it were her favorite daytime drama.

"Not a drug dealer?" Squeaky asked.

"He is," Saggy Curls said, "but he's a murderer because of the cult, not because of the drugs."

The disciples tossed around comments faster than Cassie could follow.

"The cult killed Kaitlyn's dog?"

"No. The dog belonged to Robin."

"And Robin's in the cult."

"Robin's dead. Everyone knows that."

"I can tell you exactly what happened," Mrs. Finster announced, reclaiming attention. Her scratchy voice rang loud and assured. "Robin Snyder is alive. She's the cult's high priestess. She came back to take revenge on her family for casting her out."

Cassie tucked back out of sight and slapped a hand over her mouth. She tried not to collapse in a Rolling On The Floor Laughing moment.

Mel's deep, energetic roar rose into the high ceiling and spread like a cloud of mirth across the entire store. Cassie peeked back at the cantaloupe display to see her guffawing with abandon. Having lost dominance, Mrs. Finster scurried away, her cart screeching as if in pain. Her groupies scattered, suddenly remembering they needed frozen waffles and toilet paper.

Chapter Fifty-Five

Mel Moreau scooted onto the brown vinyl, still catching her breath from her laugh attack. "Let's not talk about The Finster."

Cassie slid into the booth across from her. "Agreed. Thank you for not mentioning our adventure on the island in front of the other judges."

"They would have asked questions. I didn't have any answers. I'm glad I went right back to the boat. It was awful reading about it in the newspaper later."

Lorraine's Cafe bustled, loud and busy. Cousin Laurel had clued Cassie in on the unusual properties of this specific booth. Due to a remodeling job when the place had expanded into the failed antique store next door, the space was an acoustic haven.

The server sloshed coffee from a pot into mismatched mugs. Cassie wrapped her hands around the warmth, still shivering from the perpetually cold grocery store. Farm machinery adorned her squat, wide cup. Red letters advertised a tractor pull event from four years ago.

"Sheriff Wells gave the Sams and me a lecture at the boat," Mel said. "How we were honor bound to keep our mouths shut and respect the girl's family. Then he inducted us into his personal posse."

"Not Trevor? He must have already been a member."

"Probably, but he wasn't there to get sworn in. That was when he went to check on you. I guess he didn't see you though. One of the Sparks sent him back to the boat."

"Unlucky day to have planned a trip to the Haunt."

Mel shook her head. "Not scheduled. I guess Trevor woke up that morning and decided he wanted to sketch the fir trees under rolling clouds. I didn't mind the short notice. I like going to the island, and the Sams don't get out much on their own. I don't know if he called anyone else in the club or not."

"Are you hinting his reason for the sudden outing was more than the scenery?"

Mel smiled. "Do we agree that, based on the photographs, Mariah was sure to win the contest?"

"Absolutely."

"Trevor likes attention and isn't shy about inserting himself into someone else's accomplishments. If his student had gotten the top prize, he would have bragged as if he'd made the necklace himself."

"He must have been crushed when it was stolen."

Mel shrugged. "The sudden excursion might have been a Plan B. While we were sketching the natural beauty, Trevor could have commented to the Sams, who were not judges, that it was a shame about Mariah's piece, but he had another student whose project showed remarkable talent."

Cassie expanded on the thought. "Then he'd drop a detail that made that item recognizable to the two judges who just happened to be close by."

Mel tapped a stubby nail thoughtfully against one of the dancing pancakes circling her mug. "You must have wondered why you were invited. I'm surprised you accepted."

Cassie swerved away from explaining. "I don't know how

my name came up as a candidate for a judge. Martin couldn't remember who recommended me."

Mel patted the orange koi swimming through turquoise on the scarf wrapped around her head. "Most summers the art program turns away students. Martin was in a panic this year when the casino increased its support and we were able to finance multiple classes at every age group. We needed more teachers, which dried up the pool of potential judges."

"Now I understand why the woman who contacted me sounded like she'd jump off a bridge if I turned her down," Cassie said.

"That was Lisa. Getting people willing to pick winners and losers is always hard. You make a few people happy and a whole lot of people upset. Randy Spooner dumped manure on the judges' lawns when his daughter's needlepoint of van Gogh's *Starry Night* didn't get first place. He couldn't understand that copying another artist's work in a different medium doesn't make it original."

Cassie wondered if she'd made a mistake being swayed by Lisa's desperation. With the chocolate thief on the loose, she didn't need more enemies. Although her yard could use the fertilizer. "Sounds like the judge's packet needs a warning label."

The corners of Mel's mouth turned up but didn't really form a smile. "It's all fun and games until you start handing out ribbons."

"Martin's master key is missing. Could Kaitlyn have gotten it, then used it to steal the necklace?" Cassie didn't want to accuse Mitch of anything but hoped Mel would.

"Sven Svenberg probably borrowed it. He's been a volunteer since forever. They practically built that barn around him. I bet he put it in a pocket and forgot about it." Mel took a sip from her mug, then set it down carefully. "Kaitlyn's death probably has nothing to do with the necklace."

Cassie thought that sounded more like a wish than a conviction. "Kaitlyn wore evidence of the robbery out in the open. If someone helped her steal it, he would have been pretty upset at her arguing over it with Mariah on a public street."

"How might a betrayed partner in crime react?" Mel mussed. "Would he verbally berate the girl by the organically grown carrots in the grocery store, like Mrs. Finster? Would he dump dung on her lawn, like Randy Spooner? Or would he attack her on a deserted island, like"—she nudged her dancing pancakes mug to the left then back again—"like someone who's used to being in control of a situation and suddenly isn't?"

Cassie gripped her tractor mug and closed her eyes. Jordan smiled, pleased with himself for some clever comment he'd made. He grabbed her neck and slowly squeeze away her breath.

A voice whispered, "We've all been there."

Cassie jolted back to the café. "Sorry. I have a headache."

Mel nodded. "Migraines are a bitch." A server swept by with a quick double splash of coffee. "You should be talking to a museum board member about the burglary, like that totally rockin' hunk Sutton Graywind, instead of a fat old lady like me."

"The man does look good in a suit," Cassie said.

"And out of one too, I bet. But you're doing all right with Deputy Adam Berger. A man in uniform. Also a hot look."

"Don't believe everything you hear from 'she who rules over the cabbage.'"

Mel gave a mock look of surprise. "You mean you're not eight and a half months pregnant with the deputy's love child that was conceived in the back of his squad car during a shoot-out at a meth lab?"

"Fortunately, no."

"For me, the Falls Market Maven is an intellectual

experiment," Mel said. "I doubt she's ever studied game theory, but she's got a real QAnon-style instinct for rallying her enablers."

"I noticed she's good at ignoring facts that contradict her story."

"I don't think she hears them, not in a way that registers. It's like she can't absorb anything outside the bubble of her own narrative."

"I didn't realize you were researching conspiracy believers."

"Everyone needs a hobby."

Cassie mentally labeled that as semi-true. Mel challenging Mrs. Finster didn't seem like a casual pursuit today. The artist had gotten close to going dodgeball with a cantaloupe.

Mel grabbed the reusable hemp bag holding the items she'd gotten at the grocery store. "Thanks for the coffee and the chat. Stop by my studio sometime. We can talk art."

Cassie studied the International Harvester tractor on her mug. Yes, it would be nice to discuss Georgia O'Keeffe instead of murder.

Chapter Fifty-Six

There's always a friend on SunnieChat!

BRITTANY

Hi Im back to being Glenna. We can text on Britts phone until I get one. She says its ok cause were roomies. Im ok. I miss Nate but hes a liar. Gerald is really sweet and has helped totes. Judy and the kids came to visit. She wants me to move back in and I might do that. 😃 🤍 🤍 🤍

Chapter Fifty-Seven

The flat, charcoal sky, a breath past dusk, showed not a single speck of light.

No star gazing tonight. Cassie poured herself a red blend she'd become fond of that didn't crush her budget.

Hidden by the drab blanket, Jupiter the planet slowly rose above the horizon. The bright disk streaked with reddish bands was one of her favorites, but she was relieved that the weather gave her permission to stay inside with a glass of wine after too many busy days in a row.

Tomorrow she'd be scurrying around taking photos for the Sparks at the homecoming dance. Tonight she'd relax and contemplate life.

Cassie sat in the squishy chair, pulled out her phone and again examined the school photo of young Robin. The original necklace rested above the neckline of the vivid pink sweater. She switched to a closeup she'd taken with her magnifying app. Flanked by the molded beads, the ID bar held the same number of letters as Gizmo's tag but extended about an inch longer.

Cassie would have tightened the scrollwork design and shortened the plate, embedding Robin's name in a cozier nest of swirls and loops. Still, she admired the artistry. Robin's father, whatever his demons, had a flair and a steady hand.

She'd only had a few glances at the ID bracelet Tammara wore, but she was certain the engraving was in the same motif, made by the same hands. She found the woman aloof and abrasive but was glad the girl who couldn't wear her necklace in a school photo was now an adult who wore whatever bling she pleased.

Cassie stared at the screen. Dale and Richie had found the beads from Robin's necklace but not the name plate. What had happened to it?

Let it go for tonight. She sipped her wine, put her feet up on the ottoman, and sent her sisters a text.

Happy SunnieChat Day!

Tomorrow I'm taking photos at the homecoming dance for the fire department's website.

ASHLEY

Are they expecting arson?

They're in charge of the refreshment table.

ASHLEY

More like guard the punch bowl so no one douses it with vodka and drops in a match.

KAYLA

Punch flambé. Thank you autocorrect for the e.

HOLLY

Does that vodka thing work? Wait. Don't tell me and especially don't tell me how you know.

Not Her First Murder

KAYLA

Being chaperoned by the fire department. I bet the kids are thrilled.

Double thrilled. A lot of them are the kids' parents.

HOLLY

Will the cousins be there?

Don't know about Rob and Cliff. Laurel plans to go. Aunt Renee beat both of us at gin rummy the other day. I still have the scars.

HOLLY

Cards are a blood sport in our family.

ASHLEY

Will Deputy Dreamy be there to make sure no one steals the decorations?

Don't know.

ASHLEY

That means you do know and he will be there.

Maybe. In an official law enforcement capacity.

HOLLY

Will your new artist friend be there?

The one who took me on a romantic cruise with three other people to a murder? His art club is painting scenery and stuff. He might be there.

HOLLY

Two guys, one girl at a nostalgic high school dance. I feel the sugar rush of a Hallmark movie coming on.

I'll be working. I won't have time for either of them.

ASHLEY

You'll have to take their photos. As part of
your job.

KAYLA

Send pics.

Chapter Fifty-Eight

Cassie reviewed the outfit she'd selected for her job at the homecoming dance tonight. She swapped out a lacy sweater for a blazer with practical pockets.

"Breaking News" flashed across the feed on her tablet. She almost ignored it. The pretentious banner was slapped on everything from an earthquake swallowing a village to a hamster being rescued from a heating duct.

This time she sucked in a breath and scanned the post.

Appeal denied for convicted killer Jordan McCray
Alibi proved false

Under questioning, the witness, who previously swore McCray was with her at a Los Angeles nightclub during the time of the murder, admitted she was actually in Boise, Idaho, and she could not recall the name of the man she was with.

The anonymous woman corresponded with McCray for almost a year before she came forward with her now discredited story. Although the two have never met, she claims she gave birth to his child.

Cassie's phone went off with a song she used to like. She declined the call and silenced the device. The bloggers would have to invent her responses to the news. They were going to do that anyway. She didn't feel obligated to participate.

Besides, she had a full schedule tonight. She was going to the homecoming dance.

Chapter Fifty-Nine

Dale towered over the freshman class, most of whom longed for a growth spurt that would never happen. He tried not to squirm in the rented suit that seemed too tight across the shoulders and too loose in the waist.

Brianna Petrosky, his date of the moment, grabbed his arm as if he were a prop, which he knew he was. With her other hand, she reached down to poke at the strap on her three-inch heels, while never letting go of her phone. "Mom wouldn't let me get the sequined four-inchers because Heather'd already grabbed them. These are such baby shoes." She rustled the skirt of her skinny plum-colored, floor-length gown. Dale thought it made her look like a purple pencil.

"At least I talked Mom out of the fairy princess, flouncy thing. I don't do pastels. Or ruffles." Brianna straightened, almost reaching Dale's height, and let go of his arm. She adjusted the purple rose pinned to his lapel. A cluster of similar blooms circled her wrist. "You have to smile when we stand in the arch. My mom'll die if she doesn't get a good snap."

She checked her phone again. "Crap."

Dale tried to show concern. "Did Mr. Dahl's toupee fall in the punch bowl?"

"That guy's here."

"Which one?"

"The shit-brain who got slimy with Jen."

"The museum guy?" Mitch Hendrick. What was he doing here? Dale had to tell—uh—who? And how would he explain?

There's this guy who was Kaitlyn's boyfriend and I don't have any proof but I'm pretty sure he killed her because he probably helped her steal that necklace from the museum. And he says creepy things to girls.

Dale couldn't approach Sheriff Wells or Deputy Berger with a story that limp.

He needed a different angle. Mitch wasn't a graduate of Glacier Falls High, so he didn't have a right to be at homecoming.

Except the guy could *technically* be an alumnus. Maybe he'd been locked in an attic and homeschooled by a meth-crazy uncle who got arrested and sent to rehab just in time for Mitch to attend the last day of classes at GFHS and get an Iceberg diploma.

And a bunch of the people filling the bleachers weren't alums. The dance was more a community event, like a play or a band concert. Guards didn't stand at the door demanding to see your school transcript.

Dale decided to tell his dad, who was working security with his Sparks bros. They might not be able to toss the guy out, but they'd keep an eye on him.

And he'd tell his mom. She and the Sparkles would assault Mitch with maternal attention, shoving cookies at him so he wouldn't have time to slither up to any of the girls like the snake he was.

Brianna typed on her phone. Up and down the line of couples, girls studied their screens. Dale figured every ninth-grade female had been alerted to the danger by now. Brianna read the latest text. "He's with your girl."

"What do you mean?"

"Whitney. Sleaze Sneeze is her date."

"She doesn't even know him." But Dale couldn't be sure about that. Had his non-girlfriend searched so desperately for a partner to the dance that she'd actually entered a museum?

"IRL." In real life. "Heather says they're lining up with the sophomores." Brianna showed him a photo. A crowd of mostly tenth graders semi-listened to instructions from Mr. Stokely. She enlarged it, zeroing in on Whitney.

Dale barely recognized the raccoon-masked face surrounded by a shell of black hair. The lavender streak sweeping through Whitney's bangs matched her dress and lipstick.

"She went smoky eye," Brianna said. "You know, like that actress in that series."

"The one who married the guy in a group with his brothers?" the girl behind them asked. "Are they divorced yet?" The girl studied Whitney's makeup. "That is so much work. It takes infinity to get it right."

Dale had no idea what they were talking about. That happened to him a lot with girls. Their cultural framework was in a different zip code than his.

Brianna didn't look like Brianna either. Her long honey-colored strands, usually in a ponytail, which was the Petrosky family hairdo, waved back from her face into a cluster of curls. Her eyelids matched her dress.

"Glad Whit dumped the goth," the girl said. "I like the lilac. Maybe I'll go swatchy in red. And get ink on my shoulder. A rose or a butterfly."

"You should totes do that," Brianna said.

Dale silently told himself not to panic, even though it seemed appropriate. If he asked the Sparks and Sparkles to watch Mitch, it would be like spying on Whitney. He'd seem jealous, which he definitely was not, instead of worried about her, which he definitely was.

He couldn't dump it on an unsupervised Richie in a text.

He'd already told Cassie about the museum guide, so she wouldn't need a long explanation. He pulled out his phone and thumbed her a quick message.

Sounds of a symphony drifted into the hallway from the gym. The classical composition, heavy with strings, provided a soothing background for the march. Running on a loop, the recording by a famous orchestra substituted for the school band, which was unable to provide the music, since all of the members were involved in the march.

Dale moved forward with the line, closer to the colored lights, and the banner glittering with the theme for the dance.

Memories Forever

What did that even mean? The evening already felt like forever, and he was still on the first of three escort missions. He suddenly realizing he'd be in the Petrosky photo album for the rest of eternity. Propped against basketball trophies, pictures of him would adorn the mantel. They'd be pinned to poster boards at the girls' graduation parties.

Shit, in eighty years or so, he'd be smiling from slideshows at the girls' funerals. Not that it would matter to him by then. He'd inherited his dad's genes. The Steinhaus men tended toward blocked arteries and early heart attacks.

Brianna and Dale entered the gym and climbed the stairs to the platform that covered a portion of the basketball court like a small stage. Dale wiped sweaty palms on his rented pants as they waited just outside of the spotlight while the couple before them had their moment. *Think James Bond*, he told himself. *The dark-haired one, or the one before him, not the pouty one.*

Brianna slipped her hand into the crook of his arm. "Don't you dare hunch."

Dale forced a smile as their names were announced. They walked across the squeaky platform built by the shop class and paused for their fifteen seconds of fame in the arch formed by blue-and-white helium-filled balloons. He couldn't see a thing beyond the spotlight glare, but he knew Mrs. Petrosky and his mom stood with the other parents, recording the entire ordeal.

He fought off the impulse to swiped at his damp forehead. Brianna kept him steady as they went down the stairs to the gym floor and followed the path marked in masking tape to the end of the photo-op gauntlet.

Brianna released his arm. "That went okay." She rushed to a swarm of gowned girls who'd marched ahead of them. They shoved cell phones at her, showing her proof that she'd looked gorgeous at every step.

Chapter Sixty

One-third of his obligation behind him, Dale rushed out the double doors into the hallway, calculating how much time he had from freshman Petrosky to sophomore Petrosky. The ninth-grade Stewart cousins, and tenth-grade Jones triplets gave him an edge.

He took the series of sharp turns through the corridors bordering the gym and reached the lineup of pairs waiting for their magic moment. He found Heather in front of Lacey and Ella, an openly queer couple, and behind Lindy and Ross who were not a couple but had decided to march together.

Heather unpinned the purple rose from Dale's lapel and replaced it with a red one that matched the corsage on her wrist, and her red-and-gold gown. Tight in the torso, it did an adequate job of emphasizing her small breasts, then flowed freely from hips to floor. She inspected him as if he were a Ken doll. "Don't slouch."

Dale tried to stand a little taller. She nodded her approval. He peered past her, up the alphabet chain. Under five feet tall, Whitney Lutsen was barely visible through the Nelsons and the Olsons. He wished he could shoot laser beams from his eyes at the male beside her. Slimy Mitch.

Dale tugged at his new boutonniere so the long pin would stop pricking him. He couldn't approach the guy now. He had a job to do first. An obligation.

"Bri says you won the war for the shoes," he said to Heather. The heels boosted the girl's height, putting her taller than he was. It was a strange feeling, having to look up a few inches to meet her eyes. He'd never seen her with her hair loose around her face, false eyelashes and makeup before.

Heather raised her skirt and flashed sparkly gold stilettos. "I always win. I'm the oldest."

"The oldest by what? A whole ten minutes?"

"Seven and a half. Still the oldest."

"Is that why you get to march with your own class under your last name while Jennifer has to be with my class under Steinhaus?"

"I didn't have to pull birth order on her." Heather gave him one of those looks. "She's okay with it."

"Did you just drop girl code on me?" Dale asked.

"You'll figure it out." Heather put her hands on his shoulders as if she were his coach. "You're going to go out there and look like a babe. Like that guy in that movie where he rescues everyone."

Dale didn't have a clue who she was talking about. He raised an eyebrow and gave her a smoldering Doctor Strange scowl.

"Never do that again," she said.

He considered an anime bad boy smirk. Too risky. If he messed up, Heather was likely to slam dunk him into the nearest hoop. Instead he slid into a confident Captain Kirk grin, from the reboot movie, not the original series.

She laughed and gave him a little shove. "Come on, Arm Candy."

"Whitney Lutsen and her guest Mitchell Hendrick" boomed from the PA system.

Dale felt his grin slip.

Chapter Sixty-One

Since Dale's text about the museum guide/alleged thief/person of interest, Cassie had hoped to talk to Rhonda. She saw her chance as the scarlet-haired woman took Reverend Gunther's place protecting the punch bowl.

"Mitch Hendrick is here somewhere," Cassie quietly told her. "His date's name is Whitney."

"I know her." Rhonda tapped the word SECURITY on her oversized t-shirt. "I'll spread the word."

"I thought you'd be in uniform."

"Some officers are. Adam is, and looking very handsome in case you hadn't noticed."

"I might have." She'd seen him across the softly lit gymnasium while recorded violins swelled with promise then collapsed into bassoons.

Rhonda ran a blue-and-white nail under the second line on her shirt.

We're Here to Help

"The sheriff wants things to look more community-monitored."

"Wasn't Boomer on punch duty?"

"The school's sound system died, so he brought in his own equipment. He has to manually restart the recording every time it gets to the end. The rest of us are filling in until the march is over. Don't be surprised if polka music suddenly blares from the speakers."

Laurel, an apron protecting her dressy pants suit, nudged Cassie. "Help me get cookies." Cassie followed her cousin, who looked like a younger version of Aunt Renee, to the Family and Consumer Science room. She'd spoken to Cliff in passing. He currently sat in the bleachers keeping his mom company.

The evening was far more entertaining than she'd expected. The football team had won the game (Go Icebergs), putting students and adults in the mood to celebrate. Girls floated about in a rainbow of dresses, flaunting curly updos and wavy down-dos. In suits and ties, most of the boys looked as if their parents were forcing them to be ushers at their least favorite uncle's third wedding.

She'd taken a great shot of manly Sparks pretending to be horrified by the UFO piñata as if it were a real alien spaceship hanging from the basketball hoop. Her favorite photo so far showed Helen Steinhaus, teased hair adding five inches to her height, reaching across a giant bowl of reddish punch with a paper cup. A girl in a flattering jade-green gown accepted it, smiling as if it were ambrosia served to her on the most wonderful night of her life.

Cassie knew she should capture the display in memory of Kaitlyn. And she would. But not yet. The foam board thick with snapshots of the girl, hand-drawn hearts, and signatures of her classmates expressed a pain that didn't belong to her. She had no right to intrude.

Around her, efficient Sparkles arranged goodies on platters. She kept an ear tuned to the names being announced in the gym so she wouldn't miss Dale and his second date.

Laurel handed her plates of blue circles topped with white frosting that gave the impression of icebergs in the ocean. "Is Rob here?" Cassie asked.

Laurel balanced a mound of brownies in one hand and a bowl of multicolored mints in the other. "Of course. He wouldn't miss a chance to visit the scene of his many crimes." They headed back toward the gym where the sophomore class neared the midpoint of the alphabet.

". . . and her guest Mitchell Hendrick."

Cassie almost dropped her cookies. She'd missed a chance to get Mitch's picture. Thinking the older boy's date must be at least a junior, she hadn't expected him to be marching this soon. She and Laurel delivered the treats to the refreshment table. Cassie readied her Nikon for Dale's next appearance.

A mature woman in a floor-length white gown glided up to the table. A slit revealed her platform heels and a lot of leg. Platinum hair hugged the back of her head in a tight French twist. Her fingers blazed with diamonds. "Elizabeth" hung at her throat from a thin chain as if she'd signed her name in gold.

Helen smiled sweetly and handed her a filled cup. "Careful, we wouldn't want any punch to spill on that beautiful dress."

The woman gave a nod worthy of England's Elizabeth I. She honored Cassie with an especially long gaze and lingered for a moment without taking a sip, as if advertising the biodegradable container. She swayed away, gravitating toward a group of men.

Smile still plastered to her face, Helen said, "I hope that cup leaks and dribbles straight into her cleavage."

"Who is she?" Cassie asked. The woman had been all over the room tonight. It seemed every time Cassie framed a photo, she was in it.

"Elizabeth Anderson," Helen said. "Related to the Turtle Creek Andersons, not Father Anderson. Homecoming queen of 1980-something. You know how men hang on to their high school glory days when they were on the championship football team? She can't let go of the moment that crown was placed on her head. She swoops in every year dressed like she's still teen royalty. Flirts with all the men. Tries to impress everyone with her trips to places no one can spell."

"At least she stopped wearing the tiara," Rhonda said.

"Something about her necklace," Cassie said.

"Too many letters for her skinny neck," Rhonda said. "She should have gone with Liz or Beth."

Cassie couldn't figure out why the signature-style name tugged at her. It was different from Gizmo's tag and Robin's bar engraved with curlicues. Still—

Its significance wouldn't come to her now. It would probably pop into her head at three in the morning, along with revelations about D.B. Cooper, the lost colony of Roanoke, and the chemical composition of Twinkies. Then she'd float back to sleep. Her epiphanies would sink into the part of her brain that held her passwords, never to surface again.

The announcer introduced a Nelson and his date. Helen rushed to get a good spot, leaving Rhonda to handle the snacks.

Cassie moved closer to the platform but didn't crowd the ever-changing wave of parents shoving phones and cameras at their children. Her height and the adjustable lens on her Nikon gave her an advantage.

"He better not screw up," The girl beside her muttered.

Cassie recognized the ninth-grade Petrosky sister. She had to look up at the tall girl in heels. "Dale did great escorting you. Love your dress."

The girl tapped out a text message, barely looking at her phone's screen.

"You're not taking photos?" Cassie asked.

"Between my mom and Dale's mom, we'll have about a

zillion. Mom will want to wallpaper the living room with them."

"I have some too, if she wants to include a hallway."

"She'll totes want copies," Brianna said. "Dad's doing a video." She consulted her cell as if it were the oracle of Delphi. "I hope Dale remembers to change his boutonniere. Heather's probably staggering around in those four-inch heels trying to pin it on him. If they miss this, my mom'll bust an artery."

Cassie had noticed the flower in Dale's lapel had matched the exact shade of Brianna's gown. Of course each girl's dress would be a different color so he'd have to switch flowers. Cassie and her sisters had often negotiated wardrobe palettes. Once they'd almost gone to war over who had first dibs on turquoise because it went perfectly with a pair of expensive earrings they'd purchased together and took turns wearing. But they'd never tried to share the blue teardrops on the same night, as Brianna and her sisters were doing with their single escort.

Something clicked in Cassie's mind that she couldn't quite grab.

"Heather Petrosky and her escort Dale Steinhaus," the announcer said.

Dale stood a little stiffly. Heather smiled as if she'd broken the state record for three-pointers.

Cassie followed them with her camera, firing off shots. *Don't trip,* she mentally sent in their direction. She immediately pulled back the thought, afraid it would become a jinx.

The couple successfully stepped down the treacherous stairs to the flat floor dand moved smoothly along the row of cutouts. Well, half of the cutouts.

Trevor and his group had been forced to divide them up, placing some in front of the stage and the rest bordering the compressed bleachers that would normally accommodate the visiting team. Cassie took a relieved breath when the pair safely passed the faceless Mona Lisa and Blue Boy.

"Dad will have that clip running in our living room twenty-four/seven," Brianna said. "FYI: Jen and Dale are marching with the juniors under Steinhaus." She turned away before Cassie could thank her.

"I'll plan accordingly," Cassie said softly to the skinny strip of purple that receded into the crowd like a grape popsicle.

Chapter Sixty-Two

Heather insisted Dale do the full escort thing. They strolled to a cluster of tables in the back that the girls' basketball team had claimed. "Brianna told you that Mitch guy is here, right?" he said. "He might try to move in on you, thinking you're Jen." Dale suspected the guy wouldn't notice any difference between the twins, and wouldn't care which sister he approached anyway.

"Yeah, he's the kind who'd do that right in front of his date," Heather said.

Dale felt a twinge of worry. Where was Whitney? Richie and Bridget would be lining up with the junior class, so she'd be on her own with Mitch.

Heather tilted her head toward her teammates. "I've got backup. Go make my sister look like a queen."

Dale ducked out into a dark hallway. Someone had turned off the harsh fluorescents in this section so they wouldn't spill into the gym and spoil the illusion of a magical starland or a balloon paradise or whatever was supposed to evoke Memories Forever.

He broke into a speed walk to get back to the lineup area and pulled out his phone, checking for a message from Cassie.

Something like "M arrested for being an asshole" would be good.

Ahead of him a guy reached a lighted area and ran a hand through his brown hair.

Mitch.

Dale almost tripped. He expected the guy to swing into the boys' bathroom, but he kept skulking down the hall.

Dale slowed and pressed close to the wall. Names blasting from the PA vibrated along the locker-lined corridor, alphabetically advancing toward the last of the sophomores.

Mitch stopped where electric candles illuminated a display of animal plushies propped around Kaitlyn's locker. Counselors had sanctioned the display as a healthy expression of grief. Principal Westlund wasn't likely to disturb it until the devastated family was ready to deal with the personal items stashed inside.

Mitch stepped over the candles. He leaned toward the locker and rested his forehead against the surface. Dale's contempt drained away. It was just the two of them in the long tunnel. He felt like a trespasser invading a guy's last moment with his dead girlfriend.

Memories Forever.

Mitch swiveled his head to look back along the corridor. Dale froze, hoping to be invisible in the dark.

Metal scraped against metal. Dale jumped at a familiar clank as a locker latch came free.

Mitch swung open the narrow door, tumbling shadows of dislodged plushies across the electric glow.

Dale's sympathy vanished. He doubted Kaitlyn had given the guy the combination and wasn't impressed that Mitch was able to break in. Dale knew four ways to glitch the flimsy locks. None of them required code numbers or power tools.

A light bloomed inside the locker. Mitch ran the white beam around the cramped space. With his other hand he pawed through Kaitlyn's things. Dale saw the guy's fist emerge and slide something into his jacket pocket.

The light winked out. The door disappeared in sync with a metal clunk.

Dale gripped his own phone as if it were a weapon. The item Mitch had taken was sure to be evidence of the museum theft. Of murder.

Dale moved away from the wall like a white-hat gunslinger, the vinyl under his feet transformed into a dusty street.

Let him see me coming.

The rectangle in his hand vibrated, pulling his attention to the screen. The text from Jennifer shouted at him.

NOW!!!!!!

He heard the recorded music loop once again to the beginning of the classical masterpiece everyone recognized, but no one could name. "Let's welcome the junior class. Alyson Anderson and . . ."

A short distance ahead to Dale's right, a side hall bordering the gym led to Jennifer. She waited for him so they could stroll together under the balloon arch.

Straight on, fake candles spread a radiance behind Mitch, turning him into a looming monster straight out of a bedroom closet at midnight.

Dale sprinted down the corridor.

Chapter Sixty-Three

"A reminder," the announcer said as the first Anderson of the junior class and her date prepared to be introduced, "after the dance, the Alum Chums invite the adults to gather at the VFW. You all know where that is." There were murmurs that confirmed they did. "I hope to see your wrinkled faces there for some conversation and a brew or two."

Cassie wondered how long it would take to get to Steinhaus. Elizabeth was suddenly beside her. Or maybe not so suddenly, since it seemed the former homecoming queen had been orbiting around her most of the evening.

"I heard about the tornado." Elizabeth fluttered a hand, as if she expected Cassie to kiss one of her many rings. "It must have been terrifying."

Cassie didn't know how to respond. There had been two twisters recently. Neither had gone well for her or the town. She tried not to stare at the gold script resting on the woman's artificially tanned skin. The bulky bling seemed more appropriate for a rapper than a glammed-up grandmother.

Elizabeth pointed a manicured nail at Cassie's Nikon. "You must be with the newspaper."

"Arthur Curwick is covering the event for the *Falls Press*." Cassie had crossed his path a few times during the evening. They'd nodded but not spoken. "I'm with the Sparks and Sparkles, taking photos of their community service for the fire department's website."

"Amazing," the woman said.

Cassie wondered which part inspired such awe, that she knew how to operate a camera, or that an organization in Glacier Falls had an online presence.

Elizabeth gazed beyond her to the painted face boards. Was the woman tempted to rush over and shove her perfectly crafted features through one of the openings? Was she the skydiver type, a long scarf trailing as she plunged toward the ground? Or did she have a secret yen to plant a flag on the moon?

Elizabeth snapped her attention back to Cassie. She flashed a smile that must have cost a fortune in orthodonture and whitening treatments. "The Sparks do such a wonderful job, don't they? Volunteering and everything. I went to school with many of them, and we're such good friends. I'm a homecoming queen, so it's wonderful to come back and see them all. You can take my picture if you like. I'm sure they'd love to see it on their welcome page."

"Thanks," Cassie said. "But I'm not doing formal shots, just candids. Mostly showing people talking to one another and being social, that kind of thing. I bet Arthur would love to interview you. I saw him taking photos of the deejay." The journalist wasn't carrying a camera, but Elizabeth didn't know that.

"Lovely," Elizabeth said. "We'll talk later, dear."

Cassie watched her sway away. She felt as if she'd been patted on the head like a good little dog, but she enjoyed the thought of Arty being stalked.

She wandered over to the row of painted characters. Mel held the edge of the African wildlife scene on the end flush against a buccaneer being threatened by a kraken, Jolly Roger unfurled in the background. Trevor worked a screwdriver against a wheel. His hair seemed especially wavy tonight. She marked him as the attraction that had interrupted Queen Liz's self-promotion.

"Okay if I make a record of your contribution to the homecoming experience?" Cassie asked. The overhead lights were dimmed in this area to keep the focus on the couples marching across the brightly illuminated platform, but she thought she could get an acceptable shot. The artists group might want to advertize their community service too. She would appreciate another local customer who, unlike her East Coast/West Coast clients, wasn't obsessed with trends and deadlines.

"Sure," Trevor said. "Just securing this stubborn wheel lock. Can't have the unit sliding around."

Cassie stepped back and adjusted the telephoto lens. Trevor squatted, screwdriver in hand. He angled toward her, giving an "I'm concentrating on my work" frown. Facing away from the camera, a shy Mel gripped the painted plywood, as if the fate of the jungle scene depended on her.

A sparkling yeti swooped into the scene. Elizabeth posed, clearly identifiable in any candid photo Cassie might happen to take at that moment. Here she was being social, chatting with a friend as one does. Definitely not a calculated move. Nothing artificial about it. She touched Mel on the shoulder, causing her to twist toward the camera.

On the Nikon's monitor Cassie watched Mel's surprise turn to irritation. "You're mistaken," her lips said. "I didn't graduate from here."

Unruffled, Elizabeth put a hand to her cheek, not blocking her face yet showing off her rings and bracelets. She tilted her head amicably as if to say, *Of course I remember you. I remember all the little people who added joy to my high school years.*

His work interrupted, Trevor stood. "I didn't graduate from here either," Cassie thought he said.

Elizabeth smiled as if he'd given her a compliment.

How nice of you to say I don't look a day older than when I was crowned homecoming queen, especially since it's so true.

Cassie heard the announcer introduce Somebody Randal and his date.

She'd apologize to Mel and Trevor later for putting them in the cross hairs of Elizabeth's ego. Right now, she had to get into position. She didn't want to miss the finale to Dale's trilogy.

Chapter Sixty-Four

The blaze of electric candles reflected off the metal lockers, as if a hole in the ceiling allowed moonlight to flood the hallway. Dale sprinted toward the dark bulk blocking the glow. He had a plan. He'd slam into Mitch and grab whatever the guy had taken from Kaitlyn's locker.

He was resolute. Determined. Nothing could stop him.

His cell buzzed with another panicked text from Jennifer.

Shit. Damn. ED.

If he bailed on his commitment, the Wrath of the Petrosky Cabal would last a lifetime. And Jennifer was waiting.

Straight on to a killer or the branching corridor to the girl?

One second to decide.

Half a second.

Dale hung a hard right. As he ran, he detached the red boutonniere from the lapel of his rented jacket and shoved it into a pocket. Ahead Mr. Stokely directing the seniors into a line.

Dale shot past them and rounded the last corner. Jennifer stood behind Larry Zane and his date, an azure rose in one hand, looking as if her puppy was being held for ransom by international terrorists.

Dale grabbed her free hand and rushed forward, trying to gain on the moving couples.

"Slow it down, slow it down," his classmates spread to one another along the line ahead of him.

In a slim dress and heels, Jennifer couldn't keep up. She dropped his hand, hiked up her dress and ran.

"Hurry!" Nick Stevenson motioned them into the gap he'd made in front of him.

Dale and Jennifer skidded into place. Jennifer stabbed a pin into Dale's lapel, attaching the rose that matched her sky-blue gown. "Good thing I got the dress with the slit." She smoothed the spaghetti straps and adjusted her long, straight hair across her shoulders. Her face glowed from the sprint and a touch of blush. Sparkly eye shadow emphasized her bright eyes. Dale marveled at how much the identical twins were, well, identical, yet Jennifer was so—Jennifer.

She smiled at him as if they were about to take a relaxing stroll on a tropical beach. "Ready?"

Dale could almost smell the ocean. Okay, that might be her shampoo. "No worries, I've done this before. Twice. Recently." A few strides with their long legs, and they were up the ramp. The enthusiastic narrator read their names. Dale felt an easy grin curve his lips as they posed under the inflated bower. Applause came from Jennifer's teammates. He seemed to float down the stairs and glide to the tables at the back of the room.

Heather motioned toward chairs she'd saved for them.

"Jen, your dress is getting lots of four hearts," Brianna said, consulting her phone. "That's bonk. It's totally five hearts. That's what I'm giving it right now."

Jennifer sat next to her twin and crossed her long legs. Dale was doubly glad she'd chosen the dress with the slit and definitely scored the gown a hundred percent plus on any scale.

"You did good," Jennifer said.

Dale sat, relieved to be off his feet. "Well," he said, automatically correcting her grammar. "I did well."

"Well, you did good," Jennifer said with a smirk. "The Petrosky Dynasty thanks you for your service. You are hereby and forthwith released from your contracted duties. We will of course make sure you get home safely if you decide to stay."

Now that the hard part was over, Dale thought the colorful lights and decorations weren't that limp. "Since I'm here and all dressed up and everything, I guess I'll hang around for the food. My mom made a ton of pizza rolls."

"And dancing? I know it's not part of the agreement, but my mom would really like photos of us girls dancing with a male of the species—not just goofing around to music at home. And in girly dresses instead of sweatpants and t-shirts."

"And you should make the most of the non-ponytail hair."

Jennifer nodded. "We have to get in the shoes too. Heather will want a close-up of her sequined stilettos. Don't expect me to say that fast three times."

Dale again thought of his face pinned up in the Petrosky living room while people ate cake and congratulated the girls on their multimillion-dollar pro-ball contracts, marrying famous guys with multimillion-dollar pro-ball contracts, and/or turning down multimillion-dollar pro-ball contracts to save the sea turtles.

He'd have the same status as Heather's heels.

Much as he wanted to, Dale couldn't forget about Double Slime. He scanned the crowd and found Mitch standing at the astronaut end of a row of cutouts. The guy snuggled against Whitney. A tiny girl encased in a humungous lavender cloud, her low-cut bodice displayed cleavage worthy of a science fiction movie poster from the fifties. The pastel of her dress invaded her dark hair with a shiny streak. Dale thought her eye make was an exaggeration of her usual goth, but Brianna had called it something else.

Mitch held Whitney's hand as if they were a real couple.

Whit seemed more interested in chatting with Bridget, who wore a neon pink dress. Almost as boob-enhancing as Whitney's, the gown cinched in tight at the waist, then flared from the hips with enough netting to protect everyone in the gym from mosquitoes. Beside her Richie, in the dark suit and blue tailored shirt his parents insisted he wear to funerals and weddings, slouched as if he wore his usual jeans and a techno band tee.

Did Richie recognize Mitch as the museum guide? He and Dale had talked about the guy, but Dale might not have actual said the guy's name, and Richie, being Richie, didn't always connect things.

"Sorry," Dale told Jennifer. "There's something I've got to do. Then I'll be back." He didn't want to look over at the foursome, but, as if on automatic, his eyes swung to them.

Jennifer turned her head and followed his gaze, landing on Whitney. "Really, Dale? She's with that creep from the museum."

"That's why I have to talk to Richie."

"You can do whatever you want," Jennifer said. "You're on your own time."

Dale bent close to her. "Seriously. That guy was Kaitlyn's boyfriend."

Jennifer looked at him as if he were totally ignorant when it came to girls, which he was. "Kaitlyn guy-surfed, depending on what she wanted." She waved her hand at the transformed gym. "Like for homecoming, she was working on Todd *and* Shawn because they were both up for king. If she was going out with that guy at the same time, it didn't mean a thing to her."

"Maybe it meant something to him. Guys can get weird about girls."

"I've noticed."

Dale was immediately sorry he'd dumped this on his last date of the evening. There she was, looking glamorous, even sexy, with her velvety eyes. He should sit quietly and play boyfriend, hoping it would turn into the real thing. He drew back, caught off balance by that sudden idea. Which really wasn't that much of a revelation, now that he thought about it. He should do that, let go of the murder stuff, act like a normal guy with an extraordinary girl who could be with someone smarter, better looking, athletic, popular, funny.

Shit. The relationship was doomed. He might as well stick to pursuing a killer.

Jennifer glanced at Mitch, who let go of Whitney's hand and draped an arm around her bare shoulders. "Looks like he set a record for whipping through the five stages of grief."

"I saw him break into Kaitlyn's locker. That's why I was late for the march. He took something from it."

"He had her combination?"

Dale tilted his head and raised his eyebrows at her.

"Okay, stupid question. Maybe he was getting back a ring. Something he'd given her. Something innocent."

"Does he seem innocent to you?"

She watched Mitch lean in close to Whitney, stare down her dress and whisper in her ear. "He looks like a cobra hypnotizing his next meal. You better go play mongoose."

Chapter Sixty-Five

Even with Jennifer's permission, Dale felt like a jerk for leaving her. What could have been the best night of his life was now a pile of bald tires soaked in kerosene, and he was about to strike a match.

He forced himself to put one foot in front of the other.

Eyes on Richie.

Don't look at Mitch.

Don't look at Whitney. Or Bridget.

Really. Don't look at Whitney.

But he could see her in his peripheral vision. She squared her shoulders as if settling in for battle, lowered her head and glared at him, letting him know she was max-ultra mad and he was a shithead. She leaned against her date. *Look what I've got. I don't need you.*

Dale couldn't just ignore her. "Hey." He gave her a nod, without making eye contact. "Richie, a minute, man."

They walked out of earshot from the other three. Dale could feel frost beams shooting from Whitney and Bridget, boring into his back.

Richie gave him a jab in the arm. "Three hot dates, bro. Well, two and a half. Brianna's a brat."

Dale wanted to shut Richie up before he said something crude about condoms and the girls being great ball handlers. "Listen, that guy with Whitney—"

Richie squinted at him. "Whoa, didn't think that would get your boxers in a twist. You're with three girls and Whit's only with one guy, so you don't have the right-of-way at that intersection."

Dale had planned to ease into the murderous-date thing, but he had to break Richie's rant. "Shut up and listen. I think he killed Kaitlyn."

"Who did?"

"Mitch. The guy I told you about who works at the museum, and they probably robbed the place together. The guy glued to Whitney. That's him."

"Mitch, the guy with Whitney, Mitch?"

"Yeah, the one standing right over there looking down Whitney's dress. And Bridget's too, every chance he gets."

Richie shrugged. "Good view, man."

"Focus, Richie. I think Mitch is dangerous. Like violent. You get it?"

"How sure are you? One to ten?"

Dale had to think. When they were kids, they had hooked pinkies, placed their free hands on a copy of a Superman comic book, and sworn to be totally honest with their ratings. Dale had raised his evaluation of *Sharknado 2: The Second One* by a point because Richie liked the movie better than he did. He wondered if Richie had ever adjusted his number so it would be closer to Dale's.

Dale had to be honest. "Seven. But it's a solid seven."

"That's what you gave *War for the Planet of the Apes*."

Dale explained about the locker break-in. "He took something."

"That could raise it to an eight," Richie said. "Let's ask him."

Dale grabbed Richie's sleeve. "Ask him what? If he murdered Kaitlyn?"

"Duh, not right away." Richie walked back toward the astronaut painting.

At the balloon archway Weston and Wheeler exited the spotlight. The last of the seniors, they'd been a couple since alphabetical seating charts in eighth grade. A final applause closed out the march. The spotlights went dark. Mood lighting flooded the gym.

The deejay, who was someone's dad and a member of the Sparks, cued up a song for the first dance.

Dale trailed behind Richie. He'd meant to get the trio to dump Mitch. He hadn't expected a confrontation. He searched the crowd for his dad or another security-vested Spark. Or anyone, really. Boomer moved around plates at one end of the refreshment table. His mom had more muscle and would be better backup than the wiry accordion player, but he didn't want to get her involved. At the other end of the counter Harry Ziegler rescued the neo-hippie artist woman from a conversation with a former homecoming queen who acted as if she'd been crowned this year and not last century.

Cassie photographed two Sparkles at the safari scene, their faces pressed into the heads of a lion and a rhinoceros. She was a possibility. No muscle, but a good talker.

"Hey, Mitch," Richie said. "You swipe any painted rocks shaped like hearts from your ex-girlfriend's locker?"

"Richie, what are you doing?" Whitney demanded.

"You shouldn't smoke weed until after the dance," Mitch said flatly.

"I saw you at Kaitlyn's locker," Dale said.

"I was paying my respects," Mitch said. "It's nice to see she had so many friends."

"You stole something," Dale said.

"I didn't take anything that belonged to her," Mitch said.

Whitney shoved his arm off of her shoulders. "You

quizzed me about Kait as if you'd never met her. Is that why you asked me to the dance? So you could come into the school and paw through her things for a souvenir?"

"Shit," Richie said, "you didn't have to get all dressed up just to do that. Easy in through industrial tech, easy out through any window."

Dale shoved an elbow into his side. "Hey!" Richie protested.

Mitch turned his focus to his date. "It's your school. You asked me to the dance."

Whitney's quick fingers dipped into Mitch's jacket pocket and came out holding a carabiner hung with figurines. She rattled the collection at him. "I don't think this is yours, unless you're a fan of Hello Kitty."

"My dick!" Richie shouted.

"What?" Dale, Bridget and Whitney shouted in unison.

"From my man sculpture," Richie said. "You know, the part that got sensed."

"Censored." Dale said.

"Yeah, that," Richie said.

Dale noticed something new swaying amid the discolored jumble that had been buried with poor dead Gizmo's bones. A shiny key.

His attention flipped to Brianna weaving through the crowd toward him, ready to claim him for a dance.

Shit. Not now.

Mitch grabbed for Whitney's wrist. Dale stepped between them and held out his hand to Whitney. "I better take that."

She plopped it into his palm. "Here. It's totally gross."

The cloth square in Dale's breast pocket was only a fake handkerchief. He offered it to her. "Sorry, this is all I've got." She seemed on the verge of bursting into tears. How waterproof was all that charcoal stuff around her eyes?

From behind, Mitch grabbed Dale's arm. Dale jerked an elbow to shake him off, slamming him in the chest.

Mitch stumbled backward into the faceless astronaut, rippling the plywood.

Dale turned toward Brianna. He'd tell her ten minutes. *Just give me ten minutes.*

A blow to his back pitched him forward. He stumbled. The stolen bundle soaring from his grasp like a missile. Brianna snatched it one-handed.

Mitch charged past Dale, aimed at the basketball star. Dale lunged at him, missed, and flopped to the floor. He heard a crash and a shout. But it wasn't his crash, not his shout. He had his own crisis to deal with.

Brianna pivoted. In a basketball uniform wearing high-performance kicks, she moved like a gazelle. Hampered by a skinny dress and heels, she swerved haltingly around knots of startled dancers.

Someone screamed.

Dale scrambled to his feet. In horror he watched Mitch reach to grab Brianna.

A vision in red and gold appeared on the court.

Brianna launched the trinkets at Heather, who neatly plucked them from midair. Classmates and alums, realizing they were in the wrong place, scattered.

Mitch changed trajectory and rushed at Heather.

Heather lobed the jangly cluster toward a dream girl in sky blue. Jennifer stretched up a long arm. Hello Kitty and company smacked into her palm as if she'd called them to her.

Heather pointed out positions. Her sisters adjusted to form a triangle.

Jennifer smirked, dangling the clip at Mitch. He lurched at the younger twin. She pitched the cluster to Brianna.

Mitch darted toward the girl in purple. Just as he reached her, she sent his target soaring to Heather.

A slow learner, Mitch spun from girl to girl, not getting that he was the pickle in the middle against adversaries who towered over him, shared a hive mind and were on familiar turf.

"That's so cool it's hot," Richie said at Dale's elbow. Dale entered the triangle and put a hand on Mitch's arm. "Enough."

Richie backed him up. "Yeah, you're screwed, dude. Accept it."

Sheriff Wells, flanked by Sparks in security shirts, strolled into the cleared area. His gaze slid across the three boys, then took in the three girls. "It appears we've got a situation to straighten out. I'm going to need you gentlemen and you ladies to come with me."

Chapter Sixty-Six

Two Sparkles stuck their heads through the holes in the safari scene. Cassie framed the shot so it didn't catch the flattened bleachers on one side and the painted ocean on the other. Lion gave a snarly grin. Rhino lowered her eyebrows and puckered her lips in an angry pose.

Cassie had gotten enough official photographs to fill the fire department's website—plus brochures, t-shirts, billboards, park benches, and the sides of buses should the small town ever get public transportation. Now she enjoyed helping others have a good time.

With the march over, the soothing recorded symphony abruptly ended. A deejay took possession of the platform, spinning a fast tune. Cassie recognized the song but didn't know the artist. Or the title. Or the words.

I'm not that *old,* she thought. But she felt ancient, removed from the students who seemed to move as a group rather than a collection of couples or individuals. She remembered doing that. Just dancing with her friends. No partner needed. Life should be like that. Yet, there was always social pressure to be attached.

Cassie *did* want to form a connection with another human

being. Male. Intelligent. Someone who adored her. Movie-star handsome in an unassuming way. Able to speak in complete sentences. Understands the power of a bar of soap. Knows a Monet from a Mondrian.

Maybe that last one was asking too much.

Okay. She'd settle for a man who could pick out van Gogh's *Sunflowers* from a collection of third-graders' crayon portraits of Abraham Lincoln.

Sutton Graywind had an eye for art. She glanced toward the museum display where he talked/argued with Martin. Tammara stood to the side, scowling as if she wanted to jump in and defend her big brother but she didn't. Maybe she was reluctant to go up against another board member. Maybe she was hoping Martin would defend himself.

Cassie had taken a few photos of Sutton during the evening. Had he graduated from Glacier Falls or was he at homecoming to support it as a cultural event? He wasn't a Spark and didn't have anything to do with the fire department as far as she knew. He definitely got her vote for Best Suit. And Best-Looking Man in a Suit. And Most Likely to Be on the Cover of GQ Minnesota, if such a publication ever sprang up. The magazine was unlikely to survive past the first issue, unless plaid flannel shirts and jeans suddenly became a thing at New York Fashion Week. Which they might. Stranger things had happened.

Loving the telephoto lens on her Nikon, she'd captured Adam and Dale's dad in serious conversation. They probably discussed nuances of the homecoming football game.

She'd experienced a warm, pleasant thrill seeing Adam, but she'd resisted letting that bud bloom into a rose, or that spark to burst into a flame, afraid it would be more like encouraging a snowball to roll down the mountain, growing larger and larger until it crushed the hamlet in the valley, killing unsuspecting villagers while they sipped hot chocolate.

Whatever the metaphor, there'd be no blooming or

flaming tonight. Adam had said a few words to her in passing as he'd patrolled the perimeter, giving her slightly more attention than Arthur had but considerably less than she'd gotten from Elizabeth.

Well, he was working. And when he was working, she was just another private citizen.

She'd been hoping for a chance to talk to Dale now that his date duties were officially over. He was definitely more at ease with the last girl. Jennifer. Was that from practice with the previous two? Or because of the girl herself?

She glanced down the row of cutouts to where he stood at the end by the space scene. His discussion with Richie, two girls and a boy who had his back to Cassie seemed pretty important, so she didn't want to bother him right now.

Mitch Hendrick's presence continued to worry her. She wished she'd at least seen the color of his suit so she'd have a better chance at spotting him in the crowd.

The lion Sparkle and rhino Sparkle switched places. They grinned as Cassie clicked the camera. "Fabulous!"

A wooden clatter jolted her attention back toward Dale. A young man thrashed against the astronaut and big-eyed alien. Cassie recognized Mitch Hendrick. She'd been scanning faces in the bleachers and at the tables when he'd only been a few cartoonish characters away.

Mitch pushed against the moon. The unit tilted. The astronaut and his sidekick wobbled in a valiant attempt to stay upright. They lost the struggle and crashed into the bleachers.

As if in slow motion, the collapse rippled toward Cassie along the row of loosely tacked together paintings, toppling a firefighter dousing a flame, downing skydivers holding hands, defeating the kraken that flailed its tentacles at the pirate as if reaching for help.

The Lion and the Rhino shrieked as the quake reached the jungle. Horrified, Cassie jumped onto the beam supporting the scene. She grabbed the top of the acacia tree to keep the unit from crushing her photo subjects.

The shocked Sparkles shoved at the unstable structure that swayed with Cassie's weight. The patch of cattails anchoring the savanna to the pirate ship popped free. A wheel lock snapped, defying Trevor's repair job.

The scene careened across the floor on rattling casters, aimed directly at the refreshment station. Unable to change the trajectory, unable to let go, Cassie wondered if any of the screams were hers.

She braced herself for impact. The runaway painting slammed broadside against the end of the long table. Metal legs scraped across the varnished floor, screeching like a banshee. The counter flew into Boomer, smacking him sideways. It lifted Helen off her feet, tossing her onto her famous pizza rolls and the National Honor Society's contribution of cherry-star cookies.

The forceful attack by the wild animals swung the other end of the rectangle toward Harry, Mel, and Elizabeth. A red wave sloshed from the punch bowl onto the flowered cloth under it.

Harry dove into the museum's display, ramming Sutton Graywind against stoic fur traders. Mesh panels supporting the framed historical figures toppled, crumpling under the two men.

Elizabeth scrambled out of the plank's path on slippery shoes.

Mel pushed out her hands as if she could stop the catastrophe. She shuffled backward, barely cleared the spinning arc.

The punch bowl slid along the plank on the loose cloth filled with grape vines. As it reached the artist, it shot off the table's edge.

The crystal basin plopped into Mel's outstretched arms. She staggered under the sudden weight of cranberry juice, lemonade, ginger ale, and an ice ring speckled with pineapple chunks and raspberries.

Gallons of rolling liquid lurched at her, paused at the bowl's rim, then sloshed in the opposite direction.

A fruity tsunami surged from the cut glass vessel onto the former homecoming queen, a coral wave drenching her white gown.

Elizabeth shrieked and fell on her ass. Her French twist sprung loose. The fake hairpiece hung from her head like a desperate Pekingese, its little claws digging into her scalp as if it were too scared to jump free.

Aghast, Cassie leapt from the rolling savanna a second before it smashed into the platform where the deejay spun tunes under the blue and white balloon arch. She rushed to the punch bowl disaster. Shamelessly, she grabbed the camera hanging from her neck, and snapped the best photos of the evening.

Chapter Sixty-Seven

"On a normal day," Sheriff Justin "Justice" Wells said, "not that there is such a thing, I'd haul you all down to the jail and sort this out. But the homecoming committee put a lot of time and effort into decorating the VFW banquet hall and getting karaoke set up for the Alum Chums after party. We don't want to spoil that for them, now do we."

Cassie shifted uncomfortably in the folding chair on the third tier of the layered band room. She glanced around, wondering what all these people had to do with her wildlife ride.

To Cassie's right, Helen dabbed a paper towel at tomato sauce splotches on her Sparkles shirt. Farther down, Tammara and Martin sat sullenly. Cassie wondered how much damage had been done to the precious historical photographs.

Mitch slumped at the end of the tier, ostracized by his date, who sat on the second tier with Richie's date. Either the girls had both dumped their escorts for the evening, or they were reluctant to climb stairs in their voluminous gowns.

Elizabeth grabbed a seat in the middle on the main floor, as if beating out the competition for it, which she hadn't. Everyone else climbed up at least one of the semicircular levels to be farther away from Wells, as if he were the pastor of the church.

Adam escorted in Trevor, and gestured for him to sit on the first tier beside Mel and Harry. The artist was probably here to help defend his group from liability for the collapsed cutouts. He spotted Cassie and strode up between the chairs to drop into the empty seat on her left, ignoring the officer's seating recommendation.

Adam noticed but kept an unreadable expression. Cassie suppressed a frown. She would not allow herself to be upset by her almost-boyfriend not reacting to a handsome man purposely sitting close to her.

"I'm a witness too. I get to stay," Arthur said, although no one had questioned his presence. He climbed to tier four and sat behind Cassie.

Wells continued, "We're going to sort out this disorderly conduct and property damage situation in an orderly fashion. Looks to me like it's associated with a serious crime my officers have been working on. I don't like serious crimes in my county. They make me binge foods I'm supposed to stay away from. According to my doctor, the stress is bad for me and the sugar is worse. Officers Olson and Berger here are giving each of you a piece of paper and a pen, although you might have to share pens because we couldn't find many. You will write down your name, address and contact information. Then you will describe the event that happened in the gym from your perspective. Be sure to include all pertinent details."

"How do I know if a detail's pert?" Richie shouted from tier four. Dale sat next to him. The Petrosky girls claimed a length of that row as well, undeterred by the climb. Their shorter mother had scaled the heights to sit beside them.

"Just put down what you remember." Wells held up a clear bag holding a cluster of animal figurines and cartoon characters clipped together. "The disturbance seems to be centered on this. Someone want to tell me what it is?"

"It's a KOK," Richie said, pronouncing it cock. "The dick from my sculpture."

Helen gave him a stern look. "Language, Richard."

"Sorry, Mrs. S. I mean it's a K-O-K, Keychain of Keychains. That's meta. You know, like thinking about thinking, or thinking about skydiving while you're really skydiving. I used it for the, ah, the private parts of my metal guy. All that's pert, right? Then someone at the museum castrated my sculpture and took it."

Dale looked at his friend in amazement. "You always screw up censored, but you remember castrated."

Richie shrugged. "I know the important stuff."

Martin raised his hand as if he were a student asking for permission to speak. "As a representative of the museum, I would like to remind everyone that the art contest is for school-aged children. The item was removed due to consideration for the younger participants."

Cassie wondered if the director realized he'd just confessed to taking the item.

"That wasn't your decision to make," Trevor said. "Creativity must be encouraged, not smothered."

"The issue isn't creativity," Martin countered. "It's age-appropriateness."

"The board should have been consulted." Sutton Graywind sat a space away from Martin. Both he and his suit had survived being flattened by Harry without suffering a single wrinkle. "It is not your role to alter artwork."

"You gentlemen can hash that out later," Wells said. "Mr. Hendrick, make sure your statement includes your relationship to this here. Let's call it evidence." He jangled the bag.

Cassie couldn't think of a term that described the contents. Richie's "keychain of keychains," fit fairly well. But amid the trinkets, she could only see one key.

Mitch looked at the paper and pen Adam handed him as

if they were useless. "It's not my fault. The museum is spooky. That stuff is haunted. Really, it is. Especially the room that's fixed up to look like the old sawmill. Guys got killed by those blades. You can feel it. And babes like to cling when they get creeped out."

"It sounds like you've taken a lot of girls to the sawmill room." Cassie accepted a stubby pencil from Rhonda, and a stark white sheet that must have been commandeered from the tray of a convenient printer. She didn't know how to manage the assigned task. Her chair was just a chair with no writing surface.

"Never after closing before," Mitch said. "But Kaitlyn thought it would be fun, like in that movie. What's the name? You know, where the dummies and the animals come to life in the museum at night."

Dale, Richie, Heather, Jennifer, Whitney and Bridget chorused, "*Night at the Museum.*"

"Honest," Mitch said, "we were just going to sneak in and have an adventure. Kaitlyn planned it. She said we should dress in black and carry flashlights. We'd switch around a few photographs. Take that knitted shawl off the pioneer woman sitting in the rocking chair and drape it on the trading post guy. Put a coonskin cap on that stupid beaver."

"Sort of meta," Richie commented.

"She was really into it," Mitch said. "We'd make it look like the sawmill ghost did it. People would mob the place if they thought it was haunted. They love that stuff."

Martin scoffed. "So you've tried to impress upon me many times. But I will never allow a place of historical education to be promoted as if it were a tourist trap."

Mitch seemed unable to stop unburdening himself. "Kaitlyn wanted to mess around on the fox pelts because they're so soft." He paused. "You know, do it." He paused again. "Have sex."

Dale, Richie, Heather, Jennifer, Brianna, Whitney and Bridget voiced variations of "Yeah, we get it."

Martin scrunched up his face in horror, probably thinking about the similar animal skins at the wrecked museum display in a pile on the gymnasium floor, unprotected from lusty teens.

Cassie bristled at Mitch blaming the dead girl while still managing to slip in a sex brag. She wanted to throttle him in a reality check, but she also wanted him to spill his guts, so she kept her tone calm. "You borrowed the master key to get into the museum."

Mitch acted as if he'd found a friend. "Yeah, borrowed it. That's all. Just for one night. I was going to put it back. Kaitlyn met me at the museum. She was excited and said we were like spies. And she was all touchy feely. I mean, she was all over me."

"As if," Brianna said.

"Not pert," Richie added.

Mitch seemed to take it as encouragement. "She wanted to open the door herself, so I gave her the key. Bam! She went all alternate persona. Ran off through the halls like she knew exactly what she was after. I saw her flashlight beam go into Lake Superior. By the time I got there she'd wrecked the place. She was wearing the necklace, said it was hers. I thought she was pulling a cosplay, but she was deadass about it."

"Sounds like you're the innocent victim here," Wells said.

Cassie could tell the sheriff didn't think the young man was innocent or a victim, but Mitch latched on to the classification as if wrestling his grandmother for the last parachute on the plane.

He shook his head, seeming to expect sympathy for his own stupidity. "Yeah, Kaitlyn used me. She tossed this 'Loved the tour' shit at me and ditched. Left me standing in the dark thinking 'what the hell?' She ghosted me. Wouldn't return my calls or texts. And then I found out—" He lowered his head as if overcome by emotion. Cassie was sure his eyes were desert dry.

Wells held up the bag containing Hello Kitty, a dolphin and assorted companions. "You skipped over the doodad."

Mitch looked at the trinkets and stiffened. Cassie could almost see the synapses in his brain scurrying around like ants, trying to find an explanation that didn't muddy his virtuous image. "Kaitlyn took it."

"Where did she take it from?" Cassie asked. It had been removed from Richie's sculpture before the official photographs were taken, so it wasn't on the display in the Lake Superior Room.

"This is not a group participation interview," Wells said. "I'll do the questioning." He poked at the doodad through the clear evidence bag, separating out the key. Then he showed it to Martin. "Can you confirm the identity of this item?"

Martin's face crinkled as if he really might cry. Beside him, Tammara sat stiff, her cheeks flushed as if they burned. Cassie wondered which one would lapse into cardiac arrest first.

"That's the master key to the museum." Martin didn't seem happy it had been found.

The sheriff set the bag on a music stand tilted flat. Cassie wondered how long it would take him to get around to asking *her* question, probably repeating it as if it were his own. The hell with that shit. "Martin, when you confiscated the doodad from Richie's sculpture, you must have put it someplace safe."

Martin shifted uncomfortably. "I secured it of course."

"In your office, which was locked but could be opened with the master key?" Cassie probed.

"Yes. In my office, in my desk."

"I didn't do anything," Mitch protested. "Kaitlyn wanted to raid the donation box by the beaver. I told her Martin takes the money out every day when he closes up and we're lucky if we get twenty bucks, but she headed straight for his office."

Mitch blinked wide-eyed to show his virtue and purity. "I didn't go in. Honest. I didn't see her take any cash."

Maybe, maybe not, Cassie thought. He still carried the guilt, no matter how much he tried to pull off a "plausible deniability" plea.

"Did you know she took my dick?" Richie asked.

"She jangled it in my face so I could see she'd put the key on it," Mitch said. "She wouldn't give it back. Told me it was a souvenir and would look all retro hanging in her locker. She acted like it was nothing serious. But I could lose my job."

Mitch seemed to think his story washed him squeaky clean. Cassie saw it as motive for revenge. He'd expected a quick hookup involving sexy fox fur. Instead he'd been lured into committing several crimes then gotten dumped.

Had it made him angry enough to prank Kaitlyn in return? He could have coaxed her to the Haunt with *No worries, let's do a photo op with your necklace and post on the Satan Stone sites.* Then he could have threatened to leave her stranded on the island unless she returned the money, key, KOK and necklace.

A gambit like that could easily accelerate into violence. By accident. Not planned. Not premeditated.

Except for the murder weapon. It hadn't been a rock or a fallen tree branch that could be picked up in a moment of fury. It had been a shovel.

No implements would be stored in the decaying shed. A Brighton or an estate worker wouldn't straighten a No Trespassing sign then leave behind a tool that would encourage drunken teens to enlarge the fire pit.

Cassie imagined Kaitlyn noticing it in the boat and quizzing Mitch about it as he revved the outboard.

Oh, don't mind that, babe. It's just in case we get attacked by jumping walleye.

Cassie envisioned dusk settling on the island that August

evening. No witnesses. Wait until Kaitlyn turns her back. Swing shovel. Smash skull.

Drop weapon in the lake on your way home.

Or plop it into the freshly poured concrete of your new patio.

Maybe toss it into the dumpster behind Pizza Heaven.

But do *not* leave the tool that you got for Christmas, your initials and "Love from Mom and Dad" burned into the handle thick with your DNA and fingerprints, at the crime scene.

Well, the DNA and fingerprints part anyway.

Yet there it was. Not abandoned in haste beside the body, as in *oh, shit, what have I done?* But neatly leaning against the shed, as in *murder weapon right here, just hanging out waiting to be discovered by clever investigators.*

Rhonda should have updated forensics information by now. Cassie would ask her about it later.

"You have a lot of explaining to do to the board of directors," Sutton said to Martin. "You didn't report that the thieves had been in your office and stolen cash and an item confiscated from a student's artwork."

"So all this chasing across the gym and tossing around the doodad was about the robbery." Wells wagged a finger at his assembled witnesses. "But don't you let any of this influence what you write down. You just say what you did and what you saw firsthand. Turn in your papers to my officers when you're done. We'll contact you if we need more information."

Cassie looked at her blank page, wondering where to start. Rode a plywood rhino. Was that pert?

"What about me?" Elizabeth waved a bejeweled hand at Mel. "She threw punch at me."

"Ms. Moreau hit you?" Wells asked.

"She didn't 'throw a punch' at me. She threw *punch* at me." Elizabeth stood and modeled her stained dress. She'd removed the dislodged French roll and teased her unnaturally platinum hair into a puff ball.

"The bowl flew at me and just fell into my arms," Mel said. "It was an accident."

"She ruined my dress because she wants me to leave," Elizabeth said, "so I won't tell who she really is. I don't remember her name, but it isn't *Moreau*." Elizabeth fluttered bracelets at the adults in the room. "How long has she been living here, calling herself that, fooling all of you?"

"I don't live here," Mel said calmly. "I live in Sunset." She pointed to a Florida-shaped stain on her peasant blouse. "And the punch sloshed onto me too."

Suddenly light-headed, Cassie looked carefully at the woman. She lowered the unused paper and pen to the floor, pulled out her phone and scrolled through photos.

Look with your artist's eye, Vicky said.

The screen stuck on the deteriorating shed. This wasn't the image she searched for, but she paused. A shiver seized her as if arctic air blasted through the room. Trevor cupped his palm under her trembling hand.

Cassie absorbed the flaking shingles and weathered wood. She followed the roof line where it sagged into the foreground corner, bowing to the wild rye that bordered the worn siding like a feathery wreath.

Reset your compass, girl, Vicky told her. *Center your chi.*

Is that a real thing? Cassie silently asked.

She was surprised that Trevor held her hand that held her phone. She reclaimed both and gave him a smile. "I'm fine. It's just adrenaline. What a crazy night."

She flicked the screen until she found the gaunt face looking into the distance. Mentally, Cassie padded the sharp cheekbone and filled the hollow that ran above to the jaw. She imagined the sallow skin turned rosy with nutrition, the lips plump with health.

Cassie quickly blanked the screen so Trevor and no one

around her would see. The secret was about to go nuclear, but she would not contribute to the explosion.

Wells hooked his thumbs into his belt and looked from the Earth Mother artist to the beauty queen. "Who do *you* think she is?"

Mel interrupted. "My driver's license says Melissa Moreau. I can show it to you."

Elizabeth ignored her. "She's that girl who went to school here. The one who caused the big commotion when she ran away."

"That can't be," Martin mumbled.

Tammara's complexion drained to ash. She was sure to beat her brother to the first heart attack, but he'd come in a close second. Maybe they'd get a family discount on the ambulance ride to the hospital.

Mel stood and faced Elizabeth. "My name is Melissa Robin Snyder Moreau, you bubble-brained, Valley Girl poser. I've been living here for four years. The people I grew up with —Tam, Marty—the people who saw me every day when I was a kid never recognized me. You and I had two classes together, American Lit. and World History. You never noticed me then, except to say something cruel. Now you prance in, wearing that ridiculous dress, like you're still head mean girl. *You're* the one who recognizes me, but you still can't remember my name."

Elizabeth fumed. "This gown is a Vera Wang."

"An online knockoff of a Vera Wang," Mel said.

"Even with the punch you dumped on it, it's got more style than your country-hick floral." Elizabeth snatched the scarf holding back Mel's long silver hair.

Tammara shrieked. Cassie jumped up in shock.

The former queen strutted like a diva, flapping the colorful fabric through the air. "I just got done with the milking, and now I'm ready for the square dance. Hope you don't mind cow pies stuck to my boots." She pivoting back toward Mel, prepared to curtsy to an adoring audience. She stopped, letting the scarf droop. "What the hell happened to you?"

Mel put a shaky hand to a bald crescent above the temple on the right side of her head. Thick ridges twisted through her scalp like exposed tree roots.

Cassie rushed down and grabbed the painted scarf from Elizabeth. "Bitch." If questioned later, she'd swear she'd said "witch," technically less offensive and maybe even complimentary, depending on your perspective.

She undid the knot. Rich with black-capped chickadees, tiger swallowtail butterflies, and dots of purple asters, the silk draped softly through her fingers. Many times she'd brushed back squirmy Emma's locks and wrapped a ribbon around the girl's head. Holly's oldest preferred Aunt Cassie's patience to her mother's doing and redoing.

Cassie felt the same comfortable connection as with her niece. She folded the fabric to highlight the robin and placed it on Mel's forehead. "You hold it in place. I'll tie it in the back."

The painted fabric was so much prettier than the woven hat that had covered the woman's scar on the island. She'd bragged to Officer Robo about her skill remembering faces, yet she'd missed what was obvious to her now. She should have recognized the girl in the school photo, should have instinctively known Mel was her ghost.

How many spirits do you need? Vicky sassed at her.

Cassie secured the band, rippling the colorful tails down Mel's back. "I have something I've wanted to show you for a long time," she whispered.

Chapter Sixty-Eight

"This is all very interesting, in a serialized documentary sort of way," Wells said, "but let's get the gym situation sorted out before we move on to a missing person. I don't see anything intentional or malicious, but we've got property damage."

Harry Ziegler spoke from his position on the first tier. "As an attorney, I'd like to offer my services to anyone Sheriff Wells attempts to arrest for the unfortunate accidents in the gym."

"You're a retired real estate lawyer," Wells said.

"Still a lawyer," Harry said.

Helen spoke up. "The Sparkles have probably already cleaned up the mess. And I'm sure the Sparks will take care of repairs."

"The casino will make a donation to cover any costs," Sutton said.

Brianna waved her phone. "I finished my statement centuries ago. Who do I send it to?"

Wells pretended he hadn't heard. Rhonda gave the girl her email address. Cassie wished she'd thought to do her explanation electronically. Except she hadn't done it at all and she didn't intend to.

"Those of you involved in and with knowledge of the museum robbery and gymnasium incident, hand in your statements to the officers," Wells said. "You are free to leave, except for you, Mr. Hendrick. I believe you are a legal adult?"

"I'm nineteen."

"In that case, Officer Quigley will escort you to our finest, deluxe jail cell, and we'll have a little chat later on."

Cassie expected Harry to offer his legal services, but he seemed uninterested in the guide.

Wells shifted his weight from foot to foot, as if they ached from supporting his bulk for too long. "Those of you with knowledge of Ms. Moreau's disappearance and reappearance are advised to stay. That includes you, Ms. Windom, since you claim to have seen Ms. Moreau a few years back. But I won't be needing Ms. Anderson at the moment. I do thank you for the revelation, and we'll be in touch in a day or two."

Cassie thought Elizabeth should stay to explain how she'd seen scrawny Robin hidden within robust Mel. Maybe the sheriff wasn't as curious. More likely he just wanted the woman gone. Cassie was okay with that.

Elizabeth seemed insulted by the dismissal. She hastily scribbled on her paper and slammed it into Rhonda's hand. "Someone is going to pay for this dress to be cleaned."

"That would be you, honey," Rhonda said.

"I've been investigating this story," Arthur said sharply. "As a member of the press, I demand to stay,"

"Not this time, Arty," Wells said. "I'll send your dad a press release later."

Helen and Mrs. Petrosky herded out the students. Elizabeth maneuvered Trevor into holding the door open for her while she latched on to Arthur. Sutton spoke quietly to Wells then left. Cassie wondered why Harry stayed.

Tammara stood, avoiding eye contact with Mel. "Come on, Martin."

"Tam," Martin protested.

"I'd appreciate it if the two of you would stay," the sheriff said. "It has come to my attention that you and Robin Snyder attended school together. Recent allegations suggest Ms. Snyder is buried on your property."

Martin spoke to his sister. "Please."

"This has nothing to do with us," she replied, "and we have nothing to say."

"I'm staying," Martin said.

Tammara plopped back into the chair, clasping her ID bracelet to her wrist.

Cassie made a final adjustment to Mel's scarf. "You were ill when we met on the island."

Mel shrugged, showing little interest in the disease she'd beaten. "Cancer. Nasty stuff. I felt like a walking corpse most of the time. I never expected to find an amazing team of doctors with a treatment that worked."

The sheriff ran a hand across the top of his head, through the hair that mostly was no longer there. "I need solid proof that you're Robin Snyder."

Mel nodded to Harry. "I can verify her identity." He moved to center front, as if he spoke in a courtroom. "When Mrs. Snyder passed away, I handled the family properties for Robin and her sister."

Wells folded his arms across his ample chest. "You didn't inform the authorities that a missing girl wasn't missing?"

"I'd been an adult for a long time by then," Mel said. "No one had the right to take away my privacy."

"Especially not me," Harry said. "She's my client. I'm obligated professionally and as a friend to respect her wishes."

Cassie suddenly saw a younger Harry, hat and sunglasses shading him from the summer sun. He reclined into vinyl cushions, sipping a cold beer while waiting for his client/friend to return to the shiny speedboat snuggled up to Wolf Haunt.

"In my occupation," Harry said, "we say 'follow the land.' Title transfers are public record. If the sheriff's office had been working Mel's disappearance as an open case, you would have found her then."

A laugh bubbled out of Martin. "It is her. It really is."

Tammara turned to her brother as if in physical pain. "Quiet."

"You saw blood on the legs of my jeans that night when I took the shovel from the garage," Martin said. "I yelled at you to stay in the house. You knew what I was telling you. You understood what I'd done. What I thought I'd done. But now we both know I didn't kill her."

"Shut up, Martin," Tammara ordered.

Martin jumped up. "I knew the two of you were planning something. All those whispered conversations at school. Then, Tam, you borrowing money from me. You'd never done that before. That terrible night you snuck out of the house with your old satchel. It was so heavy you had to carry it in both arms. I followed you to our picnic spot on the peninsula." He pointed to the evidence bag on the music stand. "That childish junk clanked with every step you took.

"You dropped the satchel by the big stone and ran back to the house. I was crouching in the sumac. You rushed right past me. I heard Robin paddling up to the dock and knew I had to convince her to leave before you returned."

Tammara clenched her fists. "You don't know what you're saying. It was a dream. A nightmare."

"You had a few hundred dollars that would be gone in a week. You'd end up living in a cardboard box under a freeway, selling yourself for a hot meal. And I'd have to deal with Mother and Father alone. You were the only thing that kept me from exploding in that prison of a house. I couldn't let her take you away."

Tammara spoke to the sheriff with shaky authority. "Please forgive Martin's imagination. He read a lot of comic books at that age. I simply left some food for Robin, as I often did. My brother misunderstood."

"What happened when Ms. Snyder arrived?" the sheriff asked.

Martin's elation evaporated in the heat of his sister's rebuke, and with the realization that he was surrounded by law enforcement. He continued carefully. "I demanded she go away. By herself. And she did."

Cassie reminded him, "You skipped over the part with the bloody—"

Sheriff Wells interrupted. "You mentioned bloodstains on your clothes, Mr. Brighton. That needs explaining."

Martin straightened his cardigan sweater. "Robin had that yappy little beast of a dog with her. It attacked me. I still have a mark on my ankle."

"Gizmo was defending me," Mel said. "And you kicked him to death."

"Yes," Martin said stiffly. "Sheriff Wells, I am a criminal. I confess to killing a dog when I was a minor-aged child." He held out his fists as if expecting to be handcuffed.

"Dial down the theatrics," Harry said. "You're long past the statute of limitations."

"When Martin hurt Gizmo, is that when you got your injury?" Cassie asked Mel.

Mel put a hand to the scarred patch hidden by the painted robin. "I knelt down to help Gizzy. Martin grabbed the satchel and slammed it into my head so hard I blacked out. When I came to, he was gone and poor Gizmo was lifeless.

"Chunks of my scalp and hair were ripped off by the buckle and Tam's mini-pals. That's what she called the figures she'd collected. She showed them off at school but kept them hidden at home so her parents wouldn't see them. Frivolous, cheap things weren't allowed in the Brighton mansion."

Cassie could almost hear Mel's unspoken completion of that thought.

Frivolous, cheap things weren't allowed in the Brighton mansion, including me.

"I was bleeding and stunned," Mel said. "My only thought was to get away from Martin, and from my life. I rummaged through the pack, grabbing things more by instinct than reason. I don't know how I managed to stagger to the water and paddle away."

Mel let her hand fall from the old wound. "The infection was severe by the time I found a free clinic that didn't ask questions. The scars will never go away, but I used up all my anger long ago fighting a worse monster.

"Tam, when I saw your bag waiting for me, I was so hurt. You chose a comfortable cage over freedom and me. We'd planned to start new lives together. Instead I was on my own."

Martin moved away from his sister, closer to Mel. "You lay in the grass so still. You had to be dead. I thought Erica must know what you'd planned. She'd tell everyone you ran away. When I came back and you were gone, I convinced myself you were fine." He spoke to Wells. "I buried the dog and the pack. For a while I was proud of myself for saving my sister from making a huge mistake. Then I researched head wounds. In our family that's how we deal with issues, we research. I was hoping to reassure myself that the human skull was more durable than a dog's."

"Head injuries are tricky," Cassie said.

"So I discovered," Martin agreed. "You can walk away from a light blow and die hours later. Night after night, I wondered if tomorrow Robin's body would wash up on the shore of Lake Blanchet."

"This is a cruel hoax," Tammara said. "Martin, stop acting like any of it is true, because it isn't. Harry, you don't know who this woman is. Anyone could have shown up to sign real estate papers. Erica probably found this woman at some organic commune and set up the charade in order to get the estate settled."

"That's what DNA tests are for," Wells said.

Cassie was too impatient to wait for lab results. Besides, she already knew. "I can prove who she is right now." All eyes turned to her.

"Enlighten us, Ms. Windom," Wells said. "And don't say it's because you drew a picture of her."

Cassie spoke to Mel. "You were wearing the necklace, the original one, that night on Wolf Haunt. When Martin hit you, it broke and the pieces scattered."

"When I realized it was gone, I was crushed," Mel said. "My best friend abandoned me, and I lost a special reminder of her."

Cassie remembered the yearbook photos. Unicorn: Robin in a necklace but not Tammara. Elvis: Tammara in a necklace but not Robin.

She remembered thinking Robin's ID bar was excessively long for the short name containing a skinny i. Almost as long as Elizabeth's scripted bling.

"Tammara," Cassie said, "please show us your ID bracelet."

Tammara thrust out a fist. "I wear it all the time. Everyone's seen it." Her ornately etched name fit comfortably within the swirls and loops bordering the bronze bar held close to her wrist on a short chain.

"Mel, tell us what's inscribed on the other side of the tag," Cassie said.

Mel smiled. "My name. My old name. Robin. That plate came from the necklace my dad and I made. It was on a swivel. Everyone thought there were two necklaces but there was only one that we shared. It was our special secret."

"Is that correct?" Wells asked Tammara.

Tammara pulled back her arm and covered the bar with her other hand, saying nothing.

Cassie imagined Martin's panic to bury Gizmo, the bloody satchel and the broken necklace. It would have been easy to miss the ID plate. The bar could have been hidden under pine needles and leaf mold for a day or a thousand days before Tammara discovered it. She would have accepted it as further proof that her brother had murdered her best friend. The narrow bronze rectangle might have stayed tucked into a box of mementos for a long time before the woman finally felt in control of her own life, and her own past, enough to transform it into the bracelet she wore every day.

"For now," Sheriff Wells said to Mel, "I acknowledge that you are the person formerly known as Robin Snyder. I'll have an officer arrange the scientific verification."

Mel went over to the music stand and nudged the evidence bag so Hello Kitty became visible through the plastic. "I was at the museum when Trevor hauled in his students' art. I laughed so hard when I saw the mini-pals hanging from that sculpture. If you need a sample of Robin Snyder's DNA, I bet you'll find my blood all over these."

"That would be most useful," Wells said. "Should you want to pursue legal action concerning the alleged attack on your person by Mr. Brighton, we can discuss it. But I should point out what I'm sure Mr. Ziegler is itching to say, that the statute of limitations has passed and Mr. Brighton was a minor at the time."

"A civil suit for long-term damages is still possible," Harry couldn't help adding. "But since the evidence is connected to a current crime, I'd advise a wait-and-see approach."

Chapter Sixty-Nine

The destroyed decorations and an impromptu game of pickle in the middle hadn't halted the dance. A K-pop tune assaulted Cassie the moment she exited the band room. Sheriff Wells had released her and the others after a stern warning not to leave the state.

Cassie imagined them renting an RV together and fleeing to Canada. The thought was tempting. Definitely not the together part. Just the Canada part. She suddenly craved french fries drizzled with gravy.

The coral-red puddle marring the gym floor had disappeared. It seemed the Sparkles knew where the mops and buckets were kept. This probably wasn't their first disaster at a school event. Helen supervised the relocation of the refreshment table, squeezing it among the café-style area by the doors to the main hallway. Black-and-yellow-striped caution tape blocked off the damaged cutouts. Trevor stood, trusty screwdriver in hand, observing the wreckage as if he didn't know where to begin.

More tape looped around the twisted museum display. The animal pelts appeared unmolested by hormone-driven teens.

Cassie felt a crunch under her shoe. She picked up one of the sparkly stars that had been arranged around the cookie trays, then wished she hadn't. Gold flecks jumped onto her hand like swarming bees.

Mel walked beside her. The woman stepped back as if Cassie had broken out in plague boils. "The alumni group made those. I don't allow glitter in my studio, not even for little kids' projects. You think you've swept up every grain, then months later the light catches on a pink speck, and you realize it's still all around you."

Glitter, a metaphor for the past, Cassie thought. She tossed the bent star into a trash bin on top of crumbled cookies that hadn't survived the swinging table.

Tammara and Martin brushed by without a word. The siblings ducked under the caution tape to inspect the toppled wire stands and fallen artifacts.

"Tam won't talk to me," Mel said. "She won't even look at me. I suppose I deserve that."

Cassie tried to be comforting. "Give her time. When something happens that changes what you thought you knew about your world, it's hard to process." She didn't add that it might be a century before Tammara showed up on Mel's doorstep with a basket of cupcakes.

"I was never going to come back," Mel said. "When our parents' estate needed settling, I told my sister she could have everything. But she insisted we divide up the land. When my husband died, the Sunset property became my quiet place to grieve. I'd planned to stay a few months then sell. I didn't see any reason to rebuild old bonds when I was just going to break them again. Funny how a year drifts into two, then four."

Cassie had her own deadline circled on the calendar. She didn't want to think beyond the day her lease was up on the cabin. Not yet. Would she turn into Mel and stay here forever? That was a scary thought no matter how she looked at it.

Mel shrugged. "I guess my plan was more of a guideline. I

should have sorted things out with Tam right away. I didn't want to tell Sheriff Wells this, but Jim, Kaitlyn's dad, knows I'm alive, although I don't think he knows I'm living here. I asked to see Kaitlyn. He refused to allow it and swore he'd deny I was Robin. Erica forgave me for leaving her alone to take care of our parents, but Jim is never going to let it go."

Cassie immediately thought of her own nieces and nephew. If something happened to Holly, Evan would have to get a restraining order to keep her away from the kids.

"The hell with Jim," Mel said. "I called Kaitlyn anyway. I told her I'd known her mother in elementary school."

"How did that go?"

"Not as I'd hoped. She asked if I'd known her aunt Robin. She wanted to interview me for a podcast on my own disappearance."

"That must have been uncomfortable."

"I know I shouldn't have dropped it over the phone, but I confessed I was Robin. She called me a liar and a few other imaginatively phrased, unflattering names. She said I wasn't the first one to try to steal her idea so I could grab the fame for myself."

Cassie wondered if one of those media hogs was Arthur.

Mel brushed at punch stains that would never wash out of her peasant blouse. "Every kid with a cell phone thinks the world gives a flying fuck about their favorite protein bar. It doesn't." She patted the scarf where it covered her scar. "I better go help Trevor. He gets wrapped up in details and loses perspective."

That happens to us all, Cassie thought, wishing for some fresh perspective of her own. She considered following Mel to where Trevor tried to separate a flame from a skydiver.

Bad idea, babe, Vicky sang in Cassie's head. *Listen to me, girlfriend, your brain needs to deal with some shit before you go chasing a Monet/Mondrian guy in a pair of tight jeans. With all that wavy hair. And, oooh, those soft eyes.*

You're not helping, Cassie thought.

Then get with what's really on your mind, Vicky shot back.

Cassie thought about Kaitlyn's planning a podcast series. The girl must have been collecting fragments of information for some time. Mostly rumors and speculation until the beads and Gizmo's tag appeared. Finally, tangible links to her aunt.

She had a story.

She had visuals, suitable for upgrading from audio to video.

And she had an attention-grabbing location.

Wolf Haunt.

Cassie needed to visit the island again when she wasn't in a memory fugue tripping over a crime scene like last time. She could sneak onto the property like everyone else, but it would be wise to get permission from the owners.

Tammara handed her brother a monochrome photo of a pre-safety-helmet football team. With what had happened tonight, Cassie probably wasn't the Brightons' favorite person. *Hey, mind if I paddle over to your scene-of-the-crime island and do some sleuthing?* was likely to get her punched in the face. By Tammara.

She needed an excuse that sounded reasonable. Well, nothing fit that category. How about something the siblings would accept as weird but not surprising from an annoying, eccentric artist who lacked sensitivity and basic social skills?

This wouldn't be the first time Cassie had played that card.

Chapter Seventy

The museum's crumpled booth had turned into a mini convention center, complicating Martin and Tammara's efforts to clean up the mess. Arthur, phone held toward Sutton to record the man's response to some question, seemed only vaguely interested in the reply. Harry, in his role as event coordinator, examined the damage and made notes on his clipboard.

Cassie approached with caution but thought the numbers worked in her favor. She was less likely to be thumped on the head with an antique ladle if there were witnesses.

"Sorry to interrupt," Cassie said. "I hope this doesn't seem insensitive." She now appreciated the convenience and usefulness of the word. By invoking it in an apology, she automatically absolved herself of any responsibility for actually being insensitive. "But I've been wanting to ask you something."

Tammara pried a grainy scene of a sod house from a bent mesh display panel with more force than necessary.

"I'm sure it can wait," Martin said. "We're both rather exhausted."

He seemed the opposite of exhausted. Cassie thought of

the text-versation she'd had with her sisters about *The Rime of the Ancient Mariner*. Unburdened by the weight of his personal albatross, the curator appeared ready to row his own rescue boat to shore.

Tammara slapped bubble wrap around the prairie scene, shoulders hunched, as if the bird who'd been slain by the old sailor now hung from her neck.

"I'd like to sketch the shed on Wolf Haunt," Cassie said.

Martin wrinkled up his nose. "The shed?"

Cassie pulled her phone out of her blazer pocket. The photo she'd been looking at in the music room popped onto the screen. Along with it came the memory of Trevor supporting her hand. She showed Martin the weathered structure. She definitely was not going to explain that she'd originally drawn the building when she'd trespassed on the family's property at age thirteen. "I'm intrigued by the roof's slant and the texture of the wood." She hoped that came out more "eccentric artist" and less "obsessive ghoul."

Martin studied the photo as if it showed dirty socks. "You took this when?"

"When I was on the island with Trevor's art club. Just before I discovered, uhm. You know, that day." Cassie tried to make it sound as if her need to visit the island was completely unconnected to the murder.

Harry looked over Martin's shoulder and scrunched up his face. "I know a guy who can build you a new one."

Arthur gave it a glance. "Can I get a copy to go in the paper? We'd give you a photo credit."

Cassie forced herself to smile at the reporter as if she didn't have a baseball bat by the front door just for him. "Sure." *When hell freezes over and the Icebergs win a state championship,* she thought.

Sutton studied the image more carefully. "You have a good eye. I'd like to see more of your work."

Was he hinting she should invite him to the cabin with a

bottle of wine to look at her etchings? More likely she'd been right to speculate that photography was his medium of choice.

Martin gestured to his sister. "Ask her. She lives there. I don't."

"It's just a deteriorating old shack." Tammara shoved the artifact encased in lumpy plastic at her brother.

The rift between the siblings seemed wider than ever. Cassie thought it was destined to stay that way until Tammara accepted Mel's identity. Even then, old wounds don't magically heal in an instant.

Cassie wasn't going to let their family trauma deter her. She shoved the photo at Tammara. "That's what makes it interesting. The weathered woodgrain, the sagging corner."

Tammara sucked in a breath and scowled at Cassie's phone. Then she did that thing she'd done outside the museum the day the body was found. The woman who'd built two successful companies gave her head a little shake, as if canceling her current emotional state and rebooting herself. "It would be inconvenient right now. Perhaps at a later time." Tammara turned her back to Cassie, and wrenched a placard from a bent grid.

Inconvenient. That was another one of those useful words.

"Of course. Another time." Which would never arrive. Cassie wasn't likely to get access through the family. She wondered if her Sheriff Department's Posse status could get her on the island.

Since she'd already pissed off Tammara, she might as well put her other foot in her mouth. She knew from experience there was plenty of room for both at the same time. She hesitated for a moment as Martin picked the potentially lethal ladle from the rubble. "I'm going to suggest to Mariah that she enter her necklace in the art contest next year."

The museum director gave her a sour look. "It's my understanding that the item has not been found."

"I'm sure it will be when the killer is caught."

"What do you mean?" Sutton asked.

"Kaitlyn was wearing the necklace on the island, but it's missing, so the killer took it."

"How do you know?" Arthur challenged, the phone in his hand on "record" pointed at her now.

Cassie couldn't let it slip that she had a drawing to prove it. "I'm just guessing."

"No, you're not," Arthur said. "You have inside information."

"No, Arty. I do not." She didn't feel at all guilty invoking his childish nickname. "Martin, my point is either Mariah will get her necklace back when the person who has it is arrested, or she can make a new one. She'd take the summer class again of course. I didn't find anything in the rules to prevent it." That wasn't a lie. She hadn't found any provision against such a situation, because she hadn't actually read the rules all the way through.

"I understand your wanting to support a fledgling artist," Martin said, "but because she participated this year, she is unlikely to be accepted into the program next year. Besides, her talent is questionable. She might make a living selling earrings on the internet or at pop-up markets. Perhaps, like yourself, she might do commercial work. But the girl is unlikely to produce serious art of any consequence."

Cassie registered the personal slam that he stuck in the middle of his low evaluation of Mariah. She suspected he intended to rattle her so she'd stalk away to put a cold compress on her bruised ego. He didn't know much about a career in "commercial work." She'd had her creations smacked around like an extra in a Jackie Chan movie. A client who couldn't draw a black cat in an alley on a moonless night with a Sharpie had labeled her image of a noble elk sniffing the air on a jutting cliff at sunset amateurish.

She swallowed down the sharp words dancing on the tip of her tongue and gave Martin a sincere gaze. "That's disappointing." She put a hand on his shoulder and ran it down the sleeve of his navy-blue cardigan. "I'm sure Mariah will understand when you explain it to her." She saw the flicker of terror in his eyes at the thought of telling a teenager her dreams had been smashed against the hard rock of adult inflexibility.

Thinking pleasant thoughts about the trail of shiny specks that had transferred from the bent star to her hand to Martin's wool sleeve, Cassie ducked under the yellow tape, exiting the smashed booth. The glitter she left behind would be with him for eternity.

Harry chased after her. He pointed to a brown plastic bin. "Would you please take it to the loading dock and bring back an empty one? It will only take a minute." He gave her quick left and right directions. "It's a school, lots of straight lines and signage, you can't miss it."

Cassie accepted trash duty as karma for the glitter. She removed the camera strap and set the Nikon on the container's lid, glad to no longer have the weight on her neck. She steered the contraption on its rumbling wheels down the hallway, thinking about the girl who wasn't here. Would Kaitlyn have worn a dress in a pastel shade or in a vivid hue?

Definitely an intense color, Cassie decided. Something bold to match her personality.

She'd tricked Mitch into helping her steal from the museum. She'd kept the key linking him to the theft. If they got caught, she'd blame him. Considering the girl's "use them then lose them" attitude, she was sure to have pissed off all sorts of grudge-holding types with access to weapons.

The crime lab confirmed that Kaitlyn's blood and tissue were on the shovel found at the scene. Rhonda had been vague about the rest of the report, referring to the results as confusing and unhelpful.

In her mind, Cassie propped the tool against the shed, where it had been discovered. She would find it uncomfortable to use a shovel with such a short handle but it would fit in a small watercraft. Mentally she beached a rowboat beside the structure. She changed it to a canoe, the transformation so much easier in her imagination than on paper.

No boat or canoe was found.

Cassie decided she'd doodle the pertinent items tonight after she got home and settled into the comfy chair with a glass of wine. She remembered Richie's question.

How *do* you know what's pert?

A heavy drum and strong melody vibrated through the building as the deejay spun a new tune. Cassie bounced to the beat. She would have sung along if she'd known the words, which she didn't.

She twirled the trash bin as if it were a dancer. "Well done, Fred," she told it as she reached the easy-to-spot signage.

Cassie pushed open one of the double doors to the loading dock. She gave the heavy panel an extra shove, clicking the latch into the magnetic holder. No need to pat the walls, searching for a switch to the overheads. Light from the hallway formed a pathway leading directly to a cluster of bins.

Her shadow bulged before her like a Godzilla parade balloon. "Your friends are waiting for you," she told her dance partner. "You can tell them that you had punch. Well, paper towels soaked in punch. And you gobbled up cardboard stars covered with glitter. I bet that was your favorite part." In response to the catchy rock beat, she did some quick steps to the left and then to the right. "And you shook your booty. Don't forget to tell them that."

Cassie parked the bin beside its mates. "Thanks for the dance, Fred." Now to find an empty container to take back to the gym. She gave one a jiggle. From the weight, she knew it was full. She rattled another, heard clanking and felt the heaviness.

It was easy to figure out something was there, harder to recognize when it wasn't.

Cassie stood still in the bright swatch from the corridor. As if the light flooded her with revelation, she suddenly realized what was missing.

A shadow darted over Cassie and vanished. A metallic clank echoed through the cavernous room. The white ribbon narrowed and disappeared with a bang, leaving her in darkness.

The remnant of her reptile brain urged her to rub two sticks together to start a blaze. Her modern mind reasoned that the shadow had been someone speed walking in the hall, getting in their daily steps. The drumbeat pulsing through the building must have dislodged the door from its magnetic cuff, allowing the barrier to swing shut.

She was used to being out in the dark with her telescope. Her eyes would adjust soon. Multiple flashlight apps cluttered her phone. Nothing to worry about. Nothing at all.

Except for the footsteps pounding toward her.

Run for the cave, her reptile brain shouted. *Run!*

Chapter Seventy-One

Footsteps pounded across the loading dock's concrete floor toward Cassie, adding a menacing beat to the vibrating rock song. Miles away it seemed, the exit sign glowed over the door that had betrayed her by taking away the light.

Run for the cave, the primitive part of her brain shouted.

Where exactly is this stone shelter, she thought *and how am I supposed to find it in the dark?*

She grasped the plastic handles of her former dance partner and swiveled the bin between her and the approaching slaps. She pulled the can on her right close to her, building a barrier around herself. She flipped open the lid, hoping it held cinched bags and not loose trash.

She reached in. Her hands hit crinkly plastic. She wrenched the bulk free of the container and chucked it in the direction of the footsteps. The bundle smacked onto the hard floor, sounding too close to have hit the target.

Cassie hid her disappointment with a yell. "The dark doesn't scare me." That was mostly true. She wasn't afraid when she was out in her own yard with her telescope.

And holding a flashlight, the beam tinted red so it wouldn't ruin her night vision.

And with Jupiter at her side, even though he was less a guard dog and more a comfort puppy.

Thump. Crunch. Slosh. She heard stumbling steps and mumbled swearing as the booming treads encountered the bag she'd tossed. Refuse clattered. A whiff of industrial cleanser invaded the air.

"You better go back," Cassie shouted. "That stuff will eat right through your shoes." She hoped the echo in the cavernous room masked her location. She considered retrieving her cell from the small bag she wore like a prom sash. A call might bring help but the glow would give away her location.

"Ahh!" she yelled. "Help, help, help!" Her cries bounced back at her, repelled by the thick walls and the thunderous love song that owned the building.

"Quiet!" a gruff, disguised voice shouted. "I won't hurt you if—"

"You won't hurt me at all, shithead. Help, help! Reward offered! Dairy Queen treats for a month!" She was sure that would get Sheriff Wells's attention even over the roar of a Black Hawk helicopter landing on the roof.

"Ahhh—ahhh—ahhh," Cassie screamed, modulating between a horror movie cry and a yodeling contest entry. The attempt to top the deejay's cranked up sound system ripped her throat. A few more like that and she'd be unable to utter a sound.

Her eyes were adapting to the reduced light. A utility door to the outside shone dull gray under its own exit sign, but it was farther away than the double doors to the hall. The loading dock gates to the outside were down. Somewhere a button raised them. She scanned for an LED light with a Press Here To Escape sign. There didn't appear to be one.

Her best way out was the same way she'd entered. Creeping shuffles squished closer, directly between her and her goal. A maneuvered to the side would give her a better shot at the door. How to do that while maintaining her Fortress of Dumpsters?

She nudged a rectangular bin protecting her left flank. The lidless cart slung lower and longer than the others. The metal handle formed part of a frame that cradled a sturdy tub-o-trash. Heavier and not as nimble as Fred and her other plastic pal, steering it would be like wrestling grandpa and his walker across a busy parking lot. Cassie needed to lighten the load.

Cringing, she reached in. Her fingers sunk into a plastic membrane that crumpled in her grasp, releasing a pungent puff. Not wanting to waste ammunition, she jerked out the mass and propelled it toward the Creeper. Lacking aerodynamics but carrying a lethal load, the sack smashed against the hard floor, added another choking odor to the room.

Creeper gagged. "Did you *have* to do that?"

"Yes," Cassie said, trying to wave away the foul air. "I absolutely did." She rattled Fred. "There's more where that came from."

"Give me your phone."

Cassie shouldn't be surprised but she was. She'd flashed around the image of the old shed, too wrapped up in the memory of her first visit to Wolf Haunt to realize what it showed, or rather what it didn't show. The Creeper must have immediately understood that the photo led straight to Kaitlyn's killer.

Her phone unlocked with a four-digit code, which was embarrassingly easy to guess. The crucial evidence that would save Mariah could be erased from the device and from synched storage in the cloud (wherever/whatever that was) in an instant.

Stall. Stall.

"I have a terrible data plan," Cassie yelled. "You'll have to use someone else's to scam senior citizens out of their life savings."

Insecure steps slurped closer through what she hoped was discarded broccoli and Jell-O from the school lunch program. She edged backward, shifting to the side, losing distance but gaining a better angle to the exit sign. If she could keep moving so that her dance partner and the others stayed between her and the blob, she had a chance.

"I'd hate to lose the pics of my dad in a grass skirt doing the hula at his birthday party."

"Give me your phone and I'll go away," the low, distorted voice said.

The lie hit Cassie like a January blizzard. Creeper planned to do more than hack her account. She had to be deleted too, the person most likely to figure out what the photo meant, the artist who could describe the scene in detail. She'd be a body sprawled in a bed of garbage. Mariah would be convicted of murder and the real killer would go free.

Cassie grabbed a bag from the low cart and hurled it, not even trying to aim. She heard her weapon split open with a splash. Unseen items rolled with an oozy wetness.

Try navigating through that in the dark!

She listened, not sure she'd be able to hear movement over and the constant music and the rapid pounding of her own heart. Strangely, the noise seemed to recede. A stillness settled over the room. This was bad, so very bad.

An ultra-white blaze flared in her face. She jerked away from the brilliance, barely avoiding a blow from the hand that lashed out at her across Fred's lid.

She squeezed the round plastic handle of the bin, tilted her trusty protector onto its back wheels, and shoved.

"Oof." The impact whooshed the breath out of her attacker and popped Creeper's phone-turned-flashlight skyward. The beam spun, strobing across the walls and high ceiling. Gravity yanked it down. Cassie winced as the device cracked against industrial flooring.

Still spilling out light, the beacon turned her attacker into a crazed shadow. Cassie again slammed Fred into the figure.

"Shit!" he spat out, no longer bothering to disguise his voice.

Cassie aligned the bin for another charge. The figure dodged and yanked at the low frame protecting her left side. She released the upright bin and latched onto the cart's handle opposite Creeper. The wheels squealed as he tried to twist it to his advantage. Heavier than the tall containers, the vehicle resisted.

His silhouetted shape loomed like a sumo wrestler. She grappled with the wagon, fighting his efforts to wrench it from her grasp. *He's not as big as he looks,* she told herself, hoping it was true. Even with the help of the stubborn cart, she couldn't keep up the tug-of-war for long.

Cassie gritted her teeth. First her left hand and then her right, she switched her grip on the cold bar. She heaved the wagon upward, lifting it onto the locked wheels at the other end.

The far side plunged under Creeper's weight. Off balance, he tumbled forward.

Cassie shoved with all her might and let go. The cart flipped, pinning her assailant beneath it.

"Damn! Shit! Damn!" Explosions of popped bubble wrap punctuated Creeper's muffled cries.

"What, no f-bombs?" Cassie shouted. A shiny thread trickled across the floor, reflecting sparse light from the Creeper's fractured phone. She tried very hard not to imagine what liquids formed the slurry oozing from under the edges of the improvised prison.

She hadn't thought the air could get more pungent, but it reeked like a swamp swirling with toxic waste. Her churning stomach told her to rush toward anything less putrid than fermented Friday leftovers garnished with kid-strength disinfectant. The red exit sign glowed softly, inviting her to escape. Even without the smell, she should bolt for the door. She really should.

The inverted cart shook, as if a monster turtle attempted to rise from radioactive waste. She flashed back to watching *Gamera* with her sisters.

The exit sign or the turtle.

In another environment, Cassie would have taken a deep breath before making her decision. In the school's odorous loading dock, she took a shallow sniff and scrambled onto the metal frame. The thick plastic of the overturned container it cradled indented slightly under her.

"Let me out!"

"Quiet." Cassie twisted into an uncomfortable sitting position. "That's what you told me."

"I'm suffocating!"

The shell bulged under her. She imagined feet pushing against the surface. She suddenly wished she'd given in more to her chocolate addiction and been less concerned about her weight.

"Careful or you'll use up all the oxygen. I hope fermenting peas aren't lethal." Considering the rancid air quality under the dome, this might end badly if she couldn't get assistance soon. "Oh, did I mention that you're under arrest? I'm a member of the Sheriff's Posse. I can do that. Arrest people. I'll let you out when the cavalry gets here."

She looped an arm around the frame for security and slipped her phone out of her bag. She squinted at the screen.

No service.

Cursing at the cinderblock and concrete room, she held the device high, slowly sweeping it in an arc.

No service. One bar. No service.

She couldn't hold a signal long enough to make a call, but

a text would sprint out into the world in a nanosecond if she hit the right spot.

Who to message? Wells barely acknowledged that electricity existed, so he was out. Adam? Rhonda? Officer Robo? "Shit."

"It smells worse than that under here. Get me out before I retch!"

"Pop some bubble wrap. It'll calm you down. I have to send a text."

"Sure. Check your email, too. Scroll through your social media of choice. You don't want to miss the video of the cat riding a skateboard."

"Oh, I love cat videos. Where do I find that one?" Cassie held her thumbs over the screen, pondering how to communicate her current situation.

Help I have an attempted killer trapped in the garage in garbage. He might die of asphyxiation from toxic fumes if you don't get here right away.

Okay, probably something shorter and more informative, without concern for what autocorrect would do with garage and garbage. And asphyxiation might be a challenge for both her and the texting app.

Come quick before I commit murder by garbage. In self-defense of course.

Better, but not it.

Beneath the shell, her prisoner rustled restlessly. She quickly punched in her message.

Attacked need help loading dock

She pressed the send icon, then waved her cell overhead as if she flourished a candle app at a concert. A tone assured her the pithy message had successfully sprinted on its way and been delivered.

Delivered didn't mean read.

She and her arrestee might be stuck here until school

started on Monday morning. She stowed away her phone, needing both hands to stay stable on the uncomfortable perch.

"I found that cat video," Cassie said. "It's adorable. Have you seen the one with the penguins?"

No reaction.

Was he sobbing? Cassie slammed a fist into the tub. "Martin, this is your fault. Your silence screwed up lives, including your own. If you'd told Tammara that you hadn't killed Robin, that you hadn't buried her on Wolf Haunt, this wouldn't have happened." Shadows swallowed the already dark room. Her legs straddling the tub, Cassie sagged forward and rested her head against the slick cradle.

The muffled voice below her vibrated through her skull. "It seemed impossible she could survive. Blood. So much blood."

Cassie knew about blood.

The familiar red-drenched scene flooded her. She scanned for signs that Jordan had done this horrific deed. She found none, yet she knew in the core of her being that he'd slaughtered her best friend.

She watched herself go to the living room and retrieve the gold chain Vicky had bought him. She saw herself return to the bedroom and slide the expensive trinket under the drenched sheet beside her friends's lifeless hand.

Was it really that wrong, arranging the scene to absolutely, without a doubt link a killer to his crime?

Cassie sharply inhaled, shocked at her own thought. Was that how she viewed it now? Arranging? As if she'd casually moved a chair or stuffed flowers in a vase? As if it were—

She heard Martin say, "After a while what I'd done still sickened me, but felt strangely—"

"—normal," Cassie whispered.

"—normal," Martin said.

Cassie sat up and coughed out foul, burning air. Was she

still as convinced of Jordan's guilt as she'd been the night she'd found Vicky's body?

Well, am I?

The loading dock came back into focus. Fred and his cohorts formed a cluster of dark mesas. Cassie swiped at her damp bangs. "When your sister came back, you were both adults. You could have talked it through."

"We reconciled in a way," Martin said. "But if I'd told her what happened that night, she would have spent years expecting a call or a postcard. She was better off thinking Robin was gone forever."

Cassie felt Vicky's hand on her shoulder. She would give anything to know that her best friend was alive and out in the world, even if she would never see her again. "It wasn't better for Kaitlyn."

Silence. The cart seemed to rise and fall with Martin's sigh. "I did it," he said. "I killed that girl. Let me out. I'll tell the sheriff everything."

"Explain it to me first. Did you swim to the island?"

"I waded across on what's left of the old road. When the water level is low, like it's been this summer, it's easy."

Easy if you know where it is, Cassie thought, *because you walked it, or pedaled your bike over it every day when you were a kid.* "And?"

"I found her trespassing. I told her to leave. She refused. She got belligerent, so I hit her."

"Belligerent how? Did she use bad words? Make fun of your bald head? Threaten to name you as a suspect in her true crime podcast about Robin's disappearance?"

"There's nothing wrong with being bald."

"What did you hit her with?"

Martin was silent.

Cassie tapped on the plastic under her. "It's not a trick question." But in a way it was.

"A shovel. I hit her with the shovel that's been tested and has her blood on it."

"Oh," Cassie said, "you mean the shovel found leaning against the shed *after* the island was swarming with officers, the one that is *not* in the photo I took when I stood beside the body? The reason you want to destroy my phone." *And me,* she didn't add.

Silence.

Cassie needed to keep him talking so she knew he hadn't passed out from the fumes under the cart. Although that might not be so bad. "You better give your version some thought before you pitch it to Wells. We can work on it together."

She twisted on the slippery plastic, stiff from holding her precarious position. Had a moment passed or an eternity since she'd sent her cry for help? Ding. Ding. Ding. The phone chimed with her movement. Sure, *now* there was a one-bar sweet spot where her cell hung next to her rib cage.

Don't message, Cassie silently told the senders, *show up on white horses waving swords.*

The cart's shell quaked. It rose from the garbage, like a nuked turtle emerging from the ocean. She tumbled from her perch, rolling through damp paper towels. Bam! Flipped back over, the metal frame barely missing her head.

A monster eclipsed the skewed beam seeping from the cracked screen a distance away. Cassie grabbed at surrounding refuse, hoping a student had recently disposed of a knife-building project.

Her hands closed on soft tissues, clouds of them, as if she'd landed in litter from an early wave of the flu. She tossed fistfuls like snowballs at the huge shadow, hoping that in a week or so Martin would succumb to respiratory failure.

An immense mass swooped down, crushing her arms against her chest. She strained to push it away. A heavy film encased her face, molding over her nose and mouth. She turned her head to the side, managing a gym-sock-tainted gulp.

Cassie vowed not to let her obituary read "suffocated by garbage." She gauged where Martin's jaw was on the other side of the bag and punched against the pressure pinning her arms.

She sucked in another shallow gulp of *eau de* locker room and held her breath. Again and again she pounded toward the imagined target. With each blow the bulk holding her down crunched and shifted, changing shape.

Double fisted, she jabbed, jabbed, jabbed. Jagged edges pierced the smothering plastic, scraped her knuckles, shredded her arms. She gritted her teeth against stinging shards that nicked her cheeks.

A jolt pulsed through her clenched hands as she connected with the beast. Chest suddenly free, she sucked in a great fetid breath. She batted aside the tattered bag and pushed up onto her elbows, hoping to reach a tender part of Martin's anatomy with a swift kick.

Chapter Seventy-Two

The loading dock lights snapped on. Through the fluorescent blaze, shredded paper fluttered around Cassie like confetti. Adam and Rhonda headed a mob that gaped at the scattered garbage, looking less like the cavalry and more like villagers who'd forgotten their torches and pitchforks.

Dale, Richie, Mel, Tammara, Helen, Harry and a number of people Cassie didn't know who were definitely not on her contact list crowded in.

Adam sprinted to Cassie. "You're bleeding. Do you need an ambulance?"

"No," Cassie said, "but I better check that my tetanus shot is up to date."

"*I* need an ambulance," Martin shouted nasally from where he slumped over Cassie's former dance partner, a knit cuff pressed against his bleeding nose.

Rhonda examined his injury. "Looks like you lost the brawl."

Mel brought paper towels from a dispenser by a utility sink on the side wall. "Tip your head back, Marty, and don't be a baby."

Someone flipped a switch. Fans softly hummed, clearing the stinky air. Adam led Cassie to a stack of cardboard boxes and eased her onto a carton. He ripped off her tattered sleeves, and dabbed at her wounds, smearing crimson onto the soft camel fabric. "Sorry this isn't sterile."

Cassie watched the demise of her favorite wool blazer, one of the few things from her corporate wardrobe she still loved. "The dry-cleaning chemicals will do me in before any germs."

Helen, Dale and Richie stood behind Adam. Helen frowned at her phone. "No service. Dale, go get Janice. She's on first aid duty."

"Cassie held me captive," Martin whimpered. "That's kidnapping. Imprisonment. She trapped me and tortured me."

"Self-defense," Cassie told Adam. "Even the torture part. He tried to smother me with a trash bag."

"Harsh," Richie said.

Tammara frowned at the docking bay floor adorned with the carcass of the disemboweled UFO piñata and crumpled cups dripping punch. "I'm sure Martin can explain this as a simple misunderstanding to which Ms. Windom overreacted as is her nature."

Having just been physically attacked, Cassie bristled at the assault on her character. "He told me he killed Kaitlyn."

Tammara stiffened. "That's absurd. You're the one who turned finding the body into a circus. I bet you love the attention." She stalked to her brother like an angry parent. "Martin, I'll handle this. Don't complicate the situation just when—" She couldn't finish.

"Just when you found out you'd spent decades hating your brother for no reason," Cassie said.

"Martin, I've never hated you," Tammara said. "I hated what I thought you'd done. But we've resolved that. We'll move on and everything will be fine."

To Cassie, that sounded less like reassurance and more like a command. Well, good luck with that approach. In Cassie's experience, moving on meant dragging the past with you like roadkill stuck to the muffler of your car.

"I was under duress," Martin said. "I take it back."

"You injured Cassie." Adam said.

"Not intentionally," Martin said weakly.

Cassie took out her cell and showed Adam the image of the old shed. "I took it just before I discovered Kaitlyn's body." She zoomed in. "You've studied the photos that were taken when the scene was processed. What's in them that you *don't* see here?"

"The shovel," Adam said.

Cassie poked a finger at the screen. "Someone propped it against the shed after I took this, but before the area was searched."

She looked to the brother and sister. She'd shown both of them the image of the shed when she'd asked for permission to go back to the Haunt. "Tammara, did you realize the importance of the photo and tell Martin? Or did he figure it out on his own?"

Tammara lifted her chin defiantly. "You're implying we had something to do with that tragic situation. How absurd! That Lund person must have tricked the girl into going to the island, probably by promising an invented revelation for her ridiculous podcast. Then she killed her."

Cassie had wanted to give Tammara a chance to explain, but the woman had quickly blamed Mariah and didn't deserve sympathy. "You have better access to the Haunt than anyone. I'd place you at the top of the suspect list."

"You think I just float over on an inner tube whenever I feel like it?" Tammara said sarcastically.

"No inflatable necessary," Cassie said. "I'm sure a number of people noticed the absence of a watercraft on shore when you showed up at the crime scene. You waded across the channel that morning in your sturdy hiking boots. Martin told me it's easy to go back and forth to the manor house this summer."

Tammara scowled at her brother.

"We should continue this discussion at the sheriff's office," Rhonda said.

"Am I under arrest?" Tammara asked.

"I would like to review your previous interview in an official setting," Rhonda said.

"No arrest then," Tammara said. "In that case I will say whatever I please, to whomever I please." She zeroed in on Cassie. "Ms. Windom, I suppose you assert that Kaitlyn came searching for her aunt's body. That I fell into a rage because she dug up my favorite poison ivy, so I killed her with her own shovel while the Lund girl applauded."

"You're the only one who could have placed the murder weapon against the shed after I found the body but before the officers arrived," Cassie said. "That's what Martin realized when he saw my photo. He concluded you'd murdered Kaitlyn. To protect you and destroy the proof, he was going to kill me."

"I'm sorry," Martin said. "I never would have gone through with it."

Cassie was pretty sure he would have. Mel took a step away from Martin and put a hand to the twisted flesh hidden by her scarf. She seemed to be thinking the same thing. A weariness engulfed Cassie. She hated where this was going, hated where she had to take it. "Please, I really, really need to know. Tammara, where did you find the shovel?"

"I must caution you," Rhonda said.

Tammara shrugged. "Speaking speculatively, as Ms. Windom is fond of doing, *perhaps* one morning I noticed the arrival of a boat on the island. Thinking it was another annoying visit from Ms. Hanson, I went to explain that I planned to take legal action against her. *Possibly* I was surprised to notice a figure on the ground that may or may not have been Ms. Hanson, and further surprised to see Ms. Windom approaching on the path from the shore. If I were ever in such a situation, it would seem convenient to allow Ms. Windom to deal with the scene. *Hypothetically*, I might have returned to the manor to discover I'd previously strolled past a bloody shovel, propped beside the kitchen door by a killer determined to incriminate me or a family member." She glanced toward Martin. "The appropriate place for a murder weapon is, of course, beside the victim. When that site is not accessible due to excessive activity, a nearby location, such as a shed, might be acceptable."

Cassie understood the tragic implications buried in the woman's detached account. Suddenly lightheaded, she braced a hand on the box next to her. The scene was as clear to her as if she'd drawn it herself. "You're right that Kaitlyn didn't go to the Haunt alone. Her killer was with her, but it wasn't Mariah Lund. This would be a good time for that person to confess."

"No one confess, please," Rhonda shouted to the group. "Not right now. Plenty of time for that later." She motioned Adam over to her. Together they spoke quietly to Tammara and Martin. Cassie recognized Adam's "supportive but in charge officer of the law" stance. She supposed he explained to the Brighton siblings—in a quiet, non-handcuff way—that they would be escorted to the sheriff's office for questioning. It would probably be the first time either one had set foot in the VFW building.

"Ms. Windom might want to press charges against Mr. Brighton," Cassie heard Adam say. "That's a hard yes," she yelled at him.

"We want a lawyer," Martin shouted, crinkled paper still pressed to his nose even though it no longer bled. Cassie bit her lip to stifle a laugh. The glitter she'd swiped onto his sweater now sparkled gold on his chin. All eyes shifted to Harry. At the center of a group near the door, he tapped a pen on his clipboard. "Not me."

"I have one of the top firms in the country on retainer," Tammara said. "They're corporate attorneys; they have experience with criminal law."

Mel eased down next to Cassie. "Is it wrong for me to take pleasure in seeing those two squirm?"

Cassie thought it was justified, in a way. "You ignored your brother-in-law's wishes and contacted Kaitlyn again. How did you convince her to go to the Haunt with you?"

"Sentimental fool that I am, I occasionally borrow Harry's boat and go to the island. A few months ago, under unusual circumstances, I happened to discover where the satchel and Gizmo were buried. I still miss that dog. He should have been with me on my adventure. Not all the beads from my necklace were recovered and used in the new one. I thought Kaitlyn would be interested in finding more of them. And there was something else. I'd given Tam a bronze figurine of a robin that my dad made. She carried it in a special pocket of that terrible bag her parents made her use. I knew we'd find it in Gizmo's grave."

"You thought Kaitlyn would accept it as proof that you are Aunt Robin."

"I thought I could resolve my disappearance for both of us. And made amends for leaving my sister to deal with our parents. This time Kaitlyn said she wanted to believe me. She seemed kind and understanding. When we got to the island, she suddenly turned tough and cruel. She pulled out her phone and started recording. I had a shovel that someone had left behind. She grabbed it and brandished it at me, demanding I confess that I was a fraud. When I insisted I was her aunt, she swung it at me and knocked me down. Suddenly I was sixteen with Martin slamming me into the dirt and screaming that my best friend never wanted to see me again. This time I didn't black out. Kaitlyn laughed, mean and sharp. She dropped the shovel and turned her back on me."

As if you were powerless, Cassie thought.

"I've forced myself to get back up. Every single time," Mel said. "No matter how big or how small the battle. No matter what or who I faced. I picked up the shovel. The crack of the blade smashing her skull was deafening."

"A self-defense plea might have worked if you'd called for medical help," Cassie said. "And if you hadn't taken the necklace off Kailyn's body."

"I didn't care about my dad's beads. I just wanted Gizmo's dog tag to remember him by."

"You really shouldn't have tried to blame the Brightons by putting the murder weapon on their doorstep." Cassie felt Vicky's presence close behind her. *I'm not being a hypocrite,* she silently told her friend. *Jordan murdered you. Tammara and Martin haven't killed anyone.* She thought about the slick bag of garbage smothering her. *Not successfully, anyway.*

Mel brushed a hand across her scarf. "Wounds can form scars and still not heal."

"I didn't want it to be you." Cassie reexamined the art club outing to Wolf Haunt through a different lens. Mel needed Kaitlyn's body found before the old, battered shovel got merged into the estate's tool collection, or more likely tossed out as useless. The woman had initiated the trip, knowing Trevor would claim the idea as his own. She'd reinforced that lie with a story about Trevor wanting to influence judges. She'd borrowed the boat from Harry knowing Trevor would insist on driving. Had inviting Cassie along been her idea too? On the island had Mel hung back on purpose so Cassie would be the one to discover the crime scene?

Mel gave a deep sigh. "Years ago, I rejected anger, and I defeated my illness. Unfortunately, the cancer is back, and the white-hot rage came with it. I find myself facing those twin demons all over again. I'm afraid this time they're both going to consume me."

Cassie couldn't look at Mel. She watched a stern

Tammara and an animated Martin in discussion with Adam and Rhonda.

"Thanks for the therapy session," Mel said. "Please excuse me. I need to speak to the officers. I hope prison provides chemo treatments."

Cassie wanted to embrace Mel, to hold her back, to plead with her to stay silent. Instead she watched her speak to Adam. The two moved away from the others for a private conversation.

Richie sauntered over to Cassie. "Don't forget about the college thing. Dale needs to do that."

Janice appeared with first aid gear. Ignoring Martin's whines for assistance, Helen directed her to Cassie. The young woman wrapped Cassie's arms in enough gauze to cover a mummy. "Promise you'll go straight to the hospital to get checked out. But someone should drive you."

Cassie winced at the sting from antiseptic being dabbed on her cheek. "Richie will take me."

"Sure, I can do that," Richie said.

Janice declared the patient would live and went to tend Martin's nose. Cassie took out her phone and sent the shed photo to Adam and Rhonda. "I'm not going to the hospital."

"Yeah, I knew that," Richie said. "That's why I said I'd be your ride. I gotta go find my date before she takes off with another guy."

He sauntered away as Dale came toward her. The two boys stopped for a shoulder smash, fist bump, and double elbow tap, then continued on.

"Did you have to text my mom for help?" Dale asked Cassie.

"I sent it to everyone in my contact list. I expect my dental hygienist to show up any minute now."

"You okay?"

"Fine." She wanted to curl up under a quilt that smelled

of cedar and sleep for a week. She watched Adam and Rhonda escort Mel out the double doors.

Adam halting and spoke to the crowd. "Please give Harry your name and number so we can interview you later." He gave Cassie a nod before disappearing under the glowing exit sign. Her scholarly sister Holly would see it as a metaphor. "How's your evening going?" she asked Dale.

"Oh, you know, three dates, fight at the dance, almost got arrested. Usual stuff."

"No date for me."

Dale twisted his face. "Well—"

Cassie examined her arms, sticking out like giant pipe cleaners from her stained blazer that was now more of a vest. "Yeah, I know. Not exactly dressed for the ball."

"You'll want to be careful combing your hair."

Cassie raised a hand to pat her head, then decided that was risky without more information and a mirror. "What's in it? Do I need an exterminator?"

"Lots of colors."

"Please don't say glitter."

"The UFO piñata was full of it. Along with poorly wrapped taffy."

"What psycho who hates all of human kind made that decoration?"

"Mrs. Petrosky, my dates' mom."

Cassie shook her head in disbelief. "And she has such nice daughters."

"Five out of six anyway. There's Brianna." He sat on the stacked boxes next to her. "About the shovel."

"I suddenly feel that I should put my fingers in my ears and hum the score from *Hamilton*."

"Is it really the murder weapon?"

"Asking for a friend?"

"A friend who would be crazy happy to know it hadn't killed anyone."

"Sorry," Cassie said. "Although the crime lab is having a tough time sorting out the evidence on it. I'm guessing Tammara rubbed it down with some pretty strong solvent before sneaking it back to the island."

Dale stood up. "Good to know."

"Richie thinks you should take college courses."

Dale plopped back down. "Wow, you really went for the jugular at a vulnerable moment."

"Not apologizing."

"Richie offered to let me use the Bomb," Dale said.

"Muffin will love higher education."

The villagers who had come to save the day stood in a line in front of Harry. He scribbled their information on the sacred clipboard. Helen probably could write out the list herself from memory.

Adam reappeared in the doorway. *Where's an entrance sign when you need one?* Cassie thought. The officer consulted with Harry and Helen then walked toward Cassie.

"Can I have your attention," Harry shouted. "I know you'll all be disappointed, but we have been ordered to leave everything as it is. No clean up. I'll finish getting your information for the sheriff's department and then . . ."

Cassie didn't hear the rest. Adam leaned down and kissed her, firm and decisive. "I'll call you tomorrow."

She watched him walk away. Was that a swagger in his step? It was! Officer Berger was certainly pleased with himself.

"PDA," Dale said quietly. "Public display of affection. Serious stuff."

Cassie hoped she wasn't blushing like a Victorian maiden. "No one else saw that, right?"

"Everyone's going to claim they did. But if there's no pic, it didn't happen."

"The Nikon!" Cassie remembered removing the strap from around her neck and placing it on Fred's closed cover. Now lidless, her dance partner leaned against one of its pals, a long way from where she thought she'd left the brown upright.

She stood and surveyed the concrete expanse strewn with tangled streamers and crushed orange peels, wondering how she was going to find the expensive camera holding her entire evening's work without disturbing the crime scene.

And she shouldn't disturb the crime scene. She really shouldn't.

Cassie waded into the mess.

Well, it was *her* crime scene. And not even her first one.

Chapter Seventy-Three

Make your day bright with SunnieChat!

ASHLEY

Death by garbage. That's one way to become a legend. Although not my fame maker of choice.

KAYLA

You'd be talked about at every family gathering for generations.

Yeah laughed at.

HOLLY

Here lies Cassie, smothered by trash. We wore crushed pop can corsages to the funeral.

ASHLEY

Your honor, I submit Exhibit A, the murder weapon, a Hefty bag and the catalog of its contents.

HOLLY

The prosecution would have to keep it as evidence forever.

Danith McPherson

Considering the smell, the judicial system is lucky I survived.

Chapter Seventy-Four

SunnieChat Loves You!

ROB

Good seeing you at homecoming. Sorry I missed the fun and games. Mom was tired and wanted to go home right after the march. Glad youre ok.

ROB

You should have come to the bar for karaoke. Cliff channeled Beyonce. Someone named Elizabeth asked about you. Sutton said you were a good art comp judge. Glad I gave him your name.

ROB

Forgot to say stopped by cabin after visiting mom a couple times but you werent home. Best chocolate covered strawberries ever. Brought you back the last one. Youre welcome.

Meet the Author

Meet the Author

Like her character Cassie Windom, DANITH McPHERSON spends many nights under the stars with her telescope. In keeping with her Scottish heritage, she is a kiltmaker and proudly wears McPherson tartan. Her writing includes science fiction, fantasy and mysteries. Her short story "Roar at the Heart of the World" was selected for *The Year's Best Fantasy and Horror, Seventh Annual Collection.*

Find out more at https://danithmcpherson.com/

Check out her posts on facebook at Danith McPherson

amazon.com/author/danith

goodreads.com/danith

Leave a Review

If you enjoyed *Not Her First Murder*, please leave a review on Amazon and Goodreads through the links below. Like most authors, I depend on reviews to help readers find my stories. Thank you for reading!

Amazon

Goodreads

AVERTED VISION
A Cassie Windom Mystery

Sometimes you have to look away to see murder clearly.

After a frightening tornado, a figure floats on the surface of Beauty Lake. Cassie swims out, desperately hoping the person is still alive.

If not, well, this isn't her first dead body.

Haunted by the vicious murder of her best friend by an abusive lover, Cassie Windom abandons her career in Los Angeles and flees back home to Minnesota.

She hopes to leave behind the guilt of a gruesome secret and to reshape her life. But escape is not as easy as changing geography, and a quirky small town is not the quiet retreat she expected.

Buy from Barnes and Noble

Buy from Amazon